THE JOHN HARVARD LIBRARY

Howard Mumford Jones
Editor-in-Chief

THE DAMNATION OF
THERON WARE

By

HAROLD FREDERIC

Edited by Everett Carter

THE BELKNAP PRESS OF
HARVARD UNIVERSITY PRESS
Cambridge, Massachusetts, and
London, England

CONTENTS

THE DAMNATION OF THERON WARE

PART I

PART II

CONTENTS

PART III

PART IV

INTRODUCTION

The American decade of the eighteen-nineties was an end
and a beginning. It was the end of Mark Twain's "infinitely
greatest and worthiest of all the centuries the world has seen" [1]
and the beginning of an age whose catchwords would be anxiety and despair. It was the end of an era whose literary idol
was William Dean Howells, and the beginning of one whose
representative figure would be T. S. Eliot. It was the end of
a time which literary historians would say was dominated by
something called "realism," and the beginning of a school
of letters which the observer, searching for suitable terms,
would label "naturalism." It was the end of American lais-
sez faire (the anti-trust laws had just been enacted, and the
Roosevelt reforms were soon to follow); it was the end of an
age when "liberalism" meant "less government," and the
start of an era when it would mean "more government." It
was the end of certain sustaining beliefs (they would soon be
called by the ambiguous name of "myths"). E. W. Howe, in
The Story of a Country Town, had undermined faith in the
conviction about the necessary virtue of the rural life; in
Main-Travelled Roads Hamlin Garland had shaken certainty
about the emotional commitment of Americans to the frontier. It was a time, in short, of major change in American culture; Henry Steele Commager has termed it the great "watershed" [2] in American intellectual history. And for these cur-
rents and countercurrents, these swirls and eddies of thought
and action, where old faiths were meeting new doubts and
artists were struggling to find the forms to contain this turbu-
lence, Harold Frederic's *The Damnation of Theron Ware* is

[1] Mark Twain, *Life on the Mississippi* (New York, 1917), p. 334.
[2] Henry Steele Commager, *The American Mind* (New Haven, 1950), p. 41.
"The decade of the nineties is the watershed of American history."

an illuminating literary document, and one of the most satis-
fying aesthetic forms.

This is a large claim for a work which has yet to be generally recognized as a major effort of the American imagination.
Yet, while it has not received general acceptance into the
canon of the classics, it has had a devoted band of followers
from the time of its publication in America, and England
(under the title of *Illumination*), in 1896. It caused Stephen
Crane, for example, to seek out Frederic when he visited
England in 1897 as one of the two writers he wished to meet.
A year later, Crane gave public testimony that Frederic was
"one . . . of the better American novelists" and that his
work displayed "perfect evenness of craft" with "excellence
. . . always sustained. . . ." [3] At the appearance of *The
Damnation of Theron Ware*, he said, audiences at last gave
him justice, and declared, "Here is a Writer!" [4] This is the
testimony of the major new talent to arise in those years, and
it has been occasionally echoed by other writers (Gertrude
Atherton, Scott Fitzgerald) and by commentators and critics.

One of the difficulties the book has had in finding more
general and continuing acceptance is its uniqueness among
the works of its author. There is little else that Frederic wrote
(despite Crane's admiration for almost all that he did up to
his "English" novels) that would indicate that he was the po-
tential author of even a minor masterpiece. Indeed, Joseph
Conrad's description of him as a "notable journalist," a
description he amplified with the telling parenthesis " (who
had written some novels)," [5] is accurate. Were it not for *The
Damnation of Theron Ware*, Frederic's small fame would
rest upon his achievement as a newspaperman.

His career in journalism began in Utica, in the Mohawk
Valley of Central New York, where he had been born in 1856,

---

[3] Stephen Crane, "Harold Frederic," *The Chap-Book*, March 15, 1898,
p. 359.
[4] *Ibid.*
[5] Joseph Conrad, Introduction to *Stephen Crane*, by Thomas Beer (New
York, 1923), p. 2.

INTRODUCTION

the son of moderately poor parents. His father had been killed
in a railway accident when Harold was eighteen months old.
His mother later married a decent hard-working dairyman,
so that the young boy's life appears to have been a not abnormal one. He had left school at fourteen (Howells and
Twain had ended their formal education even earlier), and
the various odd jobs he had worked at until 1875 were not
excessively trying. In brief, there is no foundation for a
legend of early tragedy or hardship upon which to construct
a romanticized biography. His becoming proofreader for the
Utica Morning Herald was the first step in a career that led
him to the news desk, then to the full direction of the *Utica
Observer*, the evening paper, and then to the editorship of
the *Albany Evening Journal*. Finally, after a change in
ownership caused his dismissal, he became, in 1884, London
correspondent for *The New York Times* and a minor international celebrity. He was a fixture first of the Savage Club,
and then of the Liberal Club; his dispatches to America
were featured in America's greatest newspaper for fifteen
years; his daring and courage (he covered the cholera epidemic in Southern France and Italy in 1884, and reassured
his readers that "no intelligent community of . . . well-
managed sewer pipes need have an alarming fear") [6] made
him the forerunner of the next generation of romantic foreign correspondents.[7]

He had made a tentative gesture in the direction of fiction
as early as 1877, with a tale whose heroine was patterned
after his bride-to-be; and after his removal to England he
began a productive double literary life, composing, in addi-
tion to his regular dispatches, a collection of short stories and
nine novels before his death in 1898. Of the latter, three
deal with the English scene, and they are scarcely worth men-

[6] Harold Frederic, "Down Among the Dead Men," *The New York Times*,
July 27, 1884, p. 1.
[7] Paul Haines, "Harold Frederic," unpublished doctoral thesis, New York
University, 1945. The biographical information is largely derived from this,
the only full length attempt at a life of Frederic.

tioning. The reappearance of Celia Madden in *The Market Place*, providing as it does the support for our reading of her role in *The Damnation* as an evil one, is practically the only interest of this last group. Stephen Crane was right in looking upon them with a "sense of desertion." [8] In a word, Frederic, writing in England, wrote well only when he wrote of America, and of that small section of America — upper New York State and the Mohawk Valley — which he knew well.

While he was reporting, writing, and taking his place in the literary world of London, his personal life was complicated by an irregular domestic arrangement. He had brought his wife, Grace Williams Frederic, and their two daughters to London; but in 1890 he had left his family, and had established a second household with Kate Lyon, by whom he had three more children. During his fatal illness in 1898, Kate, a devout Christian Scientist, persuaded him to seek spiritual rather than physical medication, and, upon his death, both she and a Reader were tried for manslaughter, but acquitted. All this was a matter of public scandal, and called for the comment by Louise Imogen Guiney:

By an attitude and conduct which can have no defenders among those who knew the facts, Harold Frederic put in abeyance the love and allegiance of half his friends.[9]

Such "erratic course and defiance of the law" defines one of the elements of any assessment of Frederic's place in the literary history of his era. Like Stephen Crane, his very life seems a break with the tradition of which he was avowedly a part. That tradition was embodied in many of its aspects by two most exemplary family men, Mark Twain and William Dean Howells, both of whom represented a careful attention to domestic regularity in their lives and equally careful abstention from involvement with overt sexual passion in

---

[8] Crane, "Harold Frederic," p. 359.
[9] Louise Imogen Guiney, "Harold Frederic: A Half-Length Sketch from the Life," *Book Buyer*, January 1899, p. 602.

their literature. Just as Frederic's life is a departure from this norm, so is his major work, *The Damnation of Theron Ware.*

But first we must acknowledge and define the tradition, and Frederic's conscious acceptance of the tradition as his mode. By the middle of the eighteen eighties, it had been established as "realism": a method which accented observation and reporting; a choice of materials which emphasized the commonplace and the world of things, facts, and social arrangements; a tone which sounded the muted comic note of the meaning and value of the world of middle-class American life, and of the belief that empirical common sense and pragmatic reasoning could result in a happy ending. Frederic, of course, had excellent training for a career as a realist; the newspaper life seems often to have been a school for writers of realistic fiction: witness the long line of journalist-novelists from Defoe down through Howells and Mark Twain. After an early effort in historical romance had been rejected by an editor, he "determined to proceed with [a] contemporary story . . . to learn what it was really like to cover a whole canvas." [10] The kind of canvas he had in mind was of the Dutch school of sixteenth-century realism, for he preferred "the contribution of plodding, nature-loving Holland to idealistic Italy." [11] We remember that Edward Eggleston, at the beginning of the movement in American fiction, had derived his inspiration from the *Philosophy of Art in the Netherlands.*[12]

The art of Holland was, of course, a representational art, a result of acute observation and of painstaking depiction of factual detail; it was an art devoted to the commonplace of its day, to the contours of the usual, to the colors and lights of the lowlands, and not to the light that never was on sea or land. The American writer and critic devoted to the plodding and the ordinary was William Dean Howells, and Harold

[10] Harold Frederic, *In The Sixties* (New York, 1897), pp. vii–viii.
[11] Quoted in Haines, p. 40.
[12] George Cary Eggleston, *The First of The Hoosiers* (Philadelphia, 1903), p. 297.

Frederic considered himself a disciple of this acknowledged dean of American realism. In 1885 he sat among his friends at the Savage Club and listened with delight while English artists and critics agreed that "in shading of character . . . and in the quality of life in dialogue . . ." Howells' work "marked a distinct step in fiction. . . ." [13] Frederic continued to regard Howells as the "chief of American novelists," and paid his personal respects to him on revisiting America in 1888. He carried away from this journey to his homeland ". . . no other recollection . . . equal in value to the memory" [14] of this call. He continued in his devotion to the older man, and to what he represented: "With you," he wrote to him, "I will belong to any hose-company or target-shoot that takes your fancy. . . ." [15] A year before this unqualified testimonial, he had begged Hamlin Garland to give Howells "messages of admiration, gratitude and fealty." [16]

But Frederic was uneasy about his mentor's reception of *The Damnation*. "You never told me whether you hated 'Illumination' as much as I feared," [17] he hesitantly wrote to him. To Hamlin Garland he declared: "I wanted always to know how Theron Ware struck him, but he would never tell me." [18] He obviously sensed that there was in the book not only materials and methods which Howells used and practiced well, but something more, something disturbing and different. In an examination of the ways in which *The Damnation* was a work in the realistic tradition of Howells, and yet something more, we may come close to a description of its meaning and value for American literary history.

The novel is based on the realistic method. This called,

[13] Harold Frederic to William Dean Howells, May 5, 1885 (MS), Houghton Library. Citations from the Frederic-Howells Correspondence are to MSS in Houghton Library.

[14] Frederic to Howells, December 11, 1890.

[15] Frederic to Howells, June 16, 1898.

[16] Harold Frederic to Hamlin Garland, May 12, 1897, MS pasted in copy of *Seth's Brother's Wife*, University of Southern California Library.

[17] Frederic to Howells, June 16, 1898.

[18] Frederic to Garland, May 12, 1897.

first of all, for a fidelity to the life one knew, and all the better
if this life were the life of a provincial area of American society, with its unique customs, and its local dialect and folk-
ways. *The Damnation* is a rich example of an almost pains-
takingly documentary summary of life in a little-chronicled
corner of America. A friend and biographer of Frederic's
described how "all sorts of jottings . . . went into his exquisitely neat notebooks," [19] to provide the factual base upon
which he could erect his fictional structures. He did an
enormous amount of research into Methodism and its insti-
tutions, and added this knowledge to his personal experiences
as reporter and editor, husband and friend. Grace Williams
provided many of the lineaments of Alice Ware; the scene
of her betrothal to Theron at the beside of her dying mother
is a replica of Frederic's own circumstances of engagement.
Father Forbes was patterned closely after a modernist priest,
Father Edward Terry, whom Frederic had known, and whose
activities he had reported, in Utica.[20] The technique in
short, follows closely the precept of Howells that one should
write of the life one knows. Its dialogue is a faithful transcrip-
tion of the dialect of the region, and its conversational tone
stays as close to the natural as possible. We hear the authen-
ticity in Brother Pierce's words:

. . . our folks don't take no stock in all that pack o' nonsense
about science, such as tellin' the age of the earth by crackin' up
stones . . . It'd be a good idee to pitch into Catholics in general
whenever you can . . . I've got Eyctalians in the quarries now.
They're sensible fellows. . . .[21]

The novel, too, maintains the general sense of pragmatic
attitude and morality that had dominated the realistic movement. Before Charles Sanders Peirce had invented the term,
and long before William James popularized it, America's

[19] Guiney, p. 602.
[20] Haines, pp. 28f.
[21] Harold Frederic, *The Damnation of Theron Ware*, pp. 30, 31. All page
references to *The Damnation* are to pagination in the John Harvard Library
edition.

novelists instinctively were making pragmatism the philosophy of their fiction. The pragmatic Dr. Ravenel, of *Miss Ravenel's Conversion from Secession to Loyalty* (1867), is the first in a line of realistic protagonists which stretches down through Twain's intelligent Pauper, his Huckleberry Finn, his Connecticut Yankee, and his Puddn'head Wilson, and to all of Howells' sensible men of practical wisdom. As it came to be formulated by William James, pragmatism turned away from false absolutes, from "abstraction . . . from bad *a priori* reasons, from fixed principles and closed systems. . . ." [22] After rejecting the absolute, pragmatism went on to affirm experience as the test of truth and, indeed, as truth itself; it looked away from first causes to "fruits, consequences, facts"; [23] it acknowledged that "truth independent . . . truth no longer malleable to human need, truth incorrigible. . . ." [24] is simply nowhere to be found. And of all these pragmatic attitudes, Brother Soulsby, and most of all, his marvellous wife, Sister Candace Soulsby, are complete and exuberant embodiments. They could have been illustrations for James's text that truth is how we *act*; they are professional actors, mountebanks, performers. Their "act," their assuming of an outward demeanor, their making the appearance become a reality, seem almost a parable of James's insistence that an emotion literally is identical with its physical manifestation. To serve the pragmatic purposes of conversion, she writes hymns to the songs of Chopin:

We take these tunes, written by a devil-may-care Pole who was living with George Sand openly at the time, and pass 'em off on the brethren for hymns. It's a fraud, yes; but it's a good fraud. So they are all good frauds. I say frankly that I'm glad that the change and the chance came to help Soulsby and me to be good frauds. [25]

Sister Soulsby can heal Theron with the firm, sane assertion

[22] William James, *Pragmatism* (New York, 1907), p. 51.
[23] *Ibid.*, pp. 54–55.
[24] *Ibid.*, pp. 64–65.
[25] Frederic, *The Damnation of Theron Ware*, pp. 185–186.

that ". . . as long as human life lasts, good, bad, and indifferent are all braided up together in every man's nature. . . ." [26]

This hard-headed acceptance of the world of fact, operating through practical modes of behavior, is the central reality of the tale. For Sister Soulsby is described not as a "sister" but as a "mother," a healing and restoring madonna, a madonna in bangles and tights, to whom Theron instinctively turns after his other "mothers" prove inadequate or misleading. The stages of his journey to awareness are marked by his religious-sexual devotion, first to Alice, then to Celia, and finally to Sister Soulsby. Alice is described as the embodiment of golden innocence with which he enriched his youth; his association with her is described as a "daily communion" [27] with this "most worshipful of womankind." [28] Dissatisfied with his state of innocence, he turns to Celia, the representation of the absolute of beauty: the religion of art. He sees her pictured in the stained glass window of a cathedral, a halo about her head; her apartment is decorated with "variations of a single theme — the Virgin Mary and the Child." [29] After his betrayal by Celia, he rises from the gutter to find himself at the entrance to a theater, under a poster featuring "a woman in tights"; [30] at that moment he remembers Sister Soulsby and knows she is a friend, and the only one he has on earth. He comes straight to her, and, like a child, casts himself "on his knees at her feet," [31] and abases his head "to bury it among the folds of the skirts at her ankles." [32] She soothes him, "a motherly intonation in her voice," [33] a "soft, maternal touch" [34] in her hand. And then she gives him the

[26] *Ibid.*, p. 346.
[27] *Ibid.*, p. 201.
[28] *Ibid.*
[29] *Ibid.*, p. 197.
[30] *Ibid.*, p. 343.
[31] *Ibid.*, p. 340.
[32] *Ibid.*
[33] *Ibid.*
[34] *Ibid.*, p. 341.

basis in self-recognition of the new religion of modern pragmatic humanism: "You weren't altogether good a year ago, any more than you're altogether bad now." [35] Theron Ware, in her maternal embrace, discovers his shabby humanity; as she tells Alice: "He isn't going to be an angel of light, or a saint, or anything of that sort . . . he'll be just an average kind of a man. . . ." [36] Theron Ware turns his eyes to the future and to the West, and towards a new century, no hero, no "angel of light," [37] but a man who has been told the homely, unpretty truth of the realistic, the pragmatic attitude towards life.

This attitude had been involved, in nineteenth-century American realism, with a sense of the comic rather than a vision of the tragic; in this, American realism had aligned itself with the tradition that stretched from Cervantes through Defoe, Fielding, Jane Austen, and Anthony Trollope. Erich Auerbach has pointed out that the European realistic tradition has been generally associated with a tragic sense, but that in Cervantes there was a "gaiety in the portrayal of everyday reality that has not been attempted again in European letters." [38] But Fielding specifically tried once more, and in a work modelled on Don Quixote attempted his "comic epic in prose." Howells admired the Spanish picaresque and the English realistic novel, and Don Quixote was Twain's lifelong favorite. In the works of both American writers down to 1890, there had been a dominance of the comic: the happy ending of Huckleberry Finn; the rise of Silas Lapham. And in *The Damnation*, Frederic partakes of this sense of the comic, rather than the tragic perception of everyday reality. The hard, ugly Methodists of his congregation, Sister Soulsby reminds Theron, are no villains, but people with the usual admixture of good and evil. Theron does not end in physical and social disaster but is, after all, saved and soothed by

[35] *Ibid.*, p. 346.
[36] *Ibid.*, p. 352.
[37] *Ibid.*
[38] Erich Auerbach, *Mimesis* (Princeton, 1953), p. 358.

Sister Soulsby, and reunited with his long-suffering wife.

But despite these hallmarks of the preceding age, the novel is, after all, the story of a damnation; its ending is uncertain and ambiguous; the healing of Theron seems no final salve to his soul, but a temporary repair to a shattered psyche prepared to face the twentieth century with only a sense of its own inadequacies. The subtitle of the American edition, and the title of the English, was *Illumination*; the term is bitter irony, of course. "I can use no word for my new state short of illumination," [39] Theron tells Dr. Ledsmar, when he is well on the road to the dark hell of knowledge. The torment of Theron struck a new note: the note of a modern tragic irony which regards man and his society as mere delusive appearances, and the cosmos as hostile and malignant. For Theron, the world becomes all black, "plunged in the Egyptian night," [40] and he finds himself "alone among awful, planetary solitudes. . . ." [41] The universe holds him "at arm's length as a nuisance." [42] His question at the end: "Was it a sham . . . or isn't there any God at all, — but only men who live and die like animals?" [43] introduces a terrible cosmic doubt — the same doubt that Stephen Crane had expressed the year before in *The Black Rider,* where "the world was a ship . . . for ever rudderless . . . Going ridiculous voyages." [44] Two years later Mark Twain would sink into his years of despair, and begin the first sketches of *The Mysterious Stranger.* Henry Adams would soon contemplate the jackals creeping down the desert ruins and would see in the picture the essence of man's plight in a waterless wasteland of an age of unbelief.[45] And this was the new tone which began to insinuate itself into Frederic's depiction of the fall of intellectual America from innocence into knowledge.

[39] Frederic, *The Damnation of Theron Ware,* p. 224.
[40] *Ibid.,* p. 333.
[41] *Ibid.*
[42] *Ibid.*
[43] *Ibid.,* p. 345.
[44] Stephen Crane, *Collected Poems* (New York, 1930), p. 8.
[45] Henry Adams, *The Education of Henry Adams* (Boston, 1918), p. 360.

The fall, as we shall see, is specifically a sexual one; the story is, after all, the account of an errant husband. The strength of the work, however, lies in its merging of the sexual fall with the fall from innocence to experience in other kinds of knowledge as well: religious, scientific, and aesthetic. Frederic tried to make Theron's innocence typical: his features are described as "moulded into that regularity of strength which characterized the American Senatorial type in those far-away days . . . before the War." [46] At the beginning he knows, as did Whitman, "that we never *feel* quite so sure of God's goodness . . . as we do in these wonderful new mornings of spring." [47] He can affirm with the hymns and with Emerson that " '. . . we know that all things work together for good.' " [48] Alice, the embodiment of this simplicity, is his love, and she is sunlit and golden. He is, in her words, "just a good, earnest, simple young servant of the Lord." [49]

The first part of his fall is into the subleties of theological truth. The overwhelming impact of the new biblical criticism, the entire conception of the symbolic rather than the literal truth of revealed religion is brilliantly presented by Father Forbes. Religious skepticism and the new criticism of the Bible was far from novel, of course; but the large popular awareness of the crumbling of fundamental faith in the solution of scientific skepticism was still to come. When *Robert Elsmere*, a novel which deals with this theme, was reviewed in America, the editor of *Harper's* was dismayed by Howells' intention to review it favorably, insisting that if the magazine appeared to approve the book, its circulation would suffer, and it would incur "the imputation of immorality." [50] When Theron is introduced to the theory of the autochtho-

---

[46] Frederic, *The Damnation of Theron Ware*, p. 8.
[47] *Ibid.*, p. 15.
[48] *Ibid.*, p. 12.
[49] *Ibid.*, p. 212.
[50] Henry M. Alden to William Dean Howells, August 31, 1888, MS in Houghton Library.

nous character of Abraham, he sees that "he was an extremely ignorant and rudely untrained young man." [51] Before, he had been blind. "Now all at once his eyes were open." They are opened, of course, to intellectual illumination and to emotional darkness. "Heretofore," we are told, Theron had seen the Biblical heroes with "a poetic light . . . about them, where indeed they had not glowed in a halo of sanctification." [52] But with his new understanding "this light was gone, and he saw them instead as untutored . . . barbarians." [53] The mind of man, Forbes tells him, in an amalgam of Feuerbach, Renan, and a prevision of Jung, is "alive with . . . thoughts and beliefs, the wraiths of dead races' faiths and imaginings," in which we should find "whole receding series of types of this Christ-myth of ours." [54]

Theron's pitiful defense against this onslaught is his own naïveté and the contumacious fundamentalism of Brother Pierce: "What we want here, sir, is straight-out, flat-footed hell. . . ." [55] It is scarcely sufficient armament. And when the attack is combined in the closest possible terms with the general impact of nineteenth-century science upon a mind of simple faith, the effect is overwhelming. Forbes's closest friend — so close that he feels the jealousy of a lover — is Dr. Ledsmar, and Ledsmar is the essence of experimental science. Such is his devotion to its cold ideal that he has given up a career as doctor of medicine, for to him healing was not truly scientific. Celia Madden is not far off when she bitterly denounces him and "his heartless, bloodless science." [56] We see Ledsmar in his laboratory, experimenting upon animals, plants, and a man: a sleeping Chinese deep in an opium trance. The doctor explains that he is "increasing his dose monthly by regular stages, and the results promise to be

[51] Frederic, *The Damnation of Theron Ware*, p. 61.
[52] *Ibid.*, p. 62.
[53] *Ibid.*
[54] *Ibid.*, p. 74.
[55] *Ibid.*, p. 29.
[56] *Ibid.*, p. 102.

rather remarkable." Heretofore, he goes on, to emphasize his abandonment of human sympathy, "observations have been made . . . on diseased . . . subjects . . . This fellow of mine is strong as an ox. . . ." [57]

With this description of Ledsmar, we have come to a turning point in the treatment of men of science by major literary sensibilities in America. We have broken with the dedication of Howells and Twain to the scientist, and are back with Hawthorne and his denunciation of the unpardonable sin of the cold intellect. We are once more on the *Neversink* with Melville, watching Dr. Cuticle as he amputates a leg and considers the operation perfectly successful despite the death throes of the patient; we are back in the ruined garden of Dr. Rappaccini. The realistic movement, involved as it was with the twin idols of science and democracy, had quickly rescued the man of science, and had helped to elevate him to the status of a culture hero. A doctor was the sanest man of DeForest's pioneering novel, and he was described as one whose only plotting had been "for the benefit of the human race." [58] Four years after *Miss Ravenel's Conversion,* Mark Twain collaborated with Charles Dudley Warner on *The Gilded Age,* a novel aimed at exposing the emptiness of the sentimental and speculative spirit and the value of applying reason to human affairs. He made his heroine a doctor of medicine, and his hero an engineer. Howells frequently used characters of scientific profession or leaning to resolve the moral chaos threatened by false absolutisms; just three years before *The Damnation,* he had introduced Dr. Edward Olney, in *An Imperative Duty,* who brought reason to bear on the incipient tragedy of a racial tangle. The appearance of Ledsmar at this point in the tradition indicates a sharp break and a new temper; we are back in a climate of doubt about the advances of man through empirical reason, and looking forward to an amplification of those doubts in much of the

[57] *Ibid.,* p. 229.
[58] John DeForest, *Miss Ravenel's Conversion from Secession to Loyalty* (New York, 1939), p. 217.

fiction of the next century. Just as the Titan of Innovation, of the fire-bringing enlightenment, was, for Hawthorne, double in nature, both fiend and angel, so the illumination of Theron Ware is also a greater darkness and a moral disaster.

This double fall into religious and scientific knowledge is controlled by a third descent, embodied in the most alluring of the trio of seducers of innocence. It is, of course, Celia Madden. Much of the power of the novel derives from Frederic's projection, through her, of sex as a primary energy. Sex, he knew, was ". . . man's power to deal his only counter-blow against the enemy, death." It is, he stated with a bluntness and a perception rare in his age, "the mainspring of human activity." [59] This bringing of the power of sex from the background to the foreground of realistic fiction was the most striking aspect of Frederic's break with his tradition. Perhaps it was this that made Frederic fear Howells' reaction to his work. Howells would, in the next decade, feel that sexual relations constituted an important ground through which the pioneer should break his way; and he would even add: "it is time the way were broken." [60] But the eighteen nineties were still reticent. *Maggie* had difficulty in finding a publisher. *Sister Carrie,* printed in 1900, would be withdrawn from sale. It was not only in America that this was true. Frederic, in *Mrs. Albert Grundy,* described how the title character, an English Lady, would permit her daughters only hastily to skim a recent novel because "the morals were rocky," [61] and absolutely prohibited them from reading one in which the shaky morals were combined with low characters. The differences between the English and the American edition of *The Damnation* are twice in the direction of substituting less suggestive words in the English! In face of this temper, Frederic not only dealt with sex, but made it the mainspring of his action.

[59] Quoted in Haines, p. 138.
[60] William Dean Howells, "The Novels of Robert Herrick," *North American Review*, June 1909, p. 815.
[61] Harold Frederic, *Mrs. Albert Grundy* (London, 1896), pp. 14–16.

We have already indicated, in some sense, the daring fusion
Frederic made between sex and religion when he described
the progression of Theron through three kinds of Madonna-
worship. Ledsmar underscores the point when he sneers that
a woman intuitively feels, in the presence of a young priest,
"a sort of backwash of the old pagan sensuality and lascivious
mysticism. . . ." [62] At the opening of the book, Theron is
portrayed as a sensual innocent, devoted to Alice in whom
there is all of the golden purity of a golden state of unfallen
nature; she is described, as she stands on her new kitchen
stoop, with the "bright flood of May-morning sunshine" [63]
completely enveloping "her girlish form, clad in a simple,
fresh-starched calico gown." He rightly associates her with
"the placid radiance of the landscape. . . ." [64] Like the pro-
tagonist in *Seth's Brother's Wife,* Theron is drawn from her
innocence to the dark knowledge of the flesh. Celia Madden,
when he meets her, has already been whispered about; her relation with Father Forbes "touched close upon a delicately
sore spot" [65] in the hearts of the Catholics of Tecumseh. She
frankly dissociates herself from the sacrament of marriage,
and proclaims her freedom to know love without it; and then
she gives Theron her lips, in a gesture which the age understood as a symbol of complete possession. The memory of the
kiss abides with him; like Aaron's rod "it swallowed up one
by one all competing thoughts and recollections, and made
his brain its slave." [66] The kiss becomes the embodiment of all
pagan and illicit sensation. The Fall from sexual purity into
sexual knowledge is the part of the fable that collects into
itself all the other aspects of the tale, and makes the story
a personalized unity.

Just as the novel pioneers in subject, so does it give evidence
of shifts in technique away from the realistic and towards the

[62] Frederic, *The Damnation of Theron Ware,* p. 226.
[63] *Ibid.,* p. 13.
[64] *Ibid.,* p. 39.
[65] *Ibid.,* p. 97.
[66] *Ibid.,* p. 269.

symbolic and the mythical; away from the social and towards the individual. Frederic, like Crane and Norris, found himself interested in primitive passions, unconscious stirrings, racial memories in a collective mind; and like these other writers of his generation, and like Henry James who would soon forge a new style to carry the load of his last fiction, Frederic began to experiment with techniques for revealing his fleeting insights into new dimensions of mind and character. The very title, in which the theme of the Faust legend advances from the dim recesses of allusion to complete overtness, signals these changes; and it is reinforced by the English title, whose paradox is reminiscent of Hawthorne's light-giving but darkness-bringing "Earth's Holocaust" of the Enlightenment. The passage we have quoted earlier demonstrates that Spencer's admonition to write as simply and clearly as possible, an admonition heeded by Twain and Howells and William James, is no longer operating. The play upon the function of seeing, and upon the word "light" has ambiguities enough to please the metaphysical poet: when Theron's eyes had been closed to knowledge, the Biblical heroes had glowed with a poetic light; when his eyes were opened, "this light was gone. . . ." [67] As well as this paradox, there is an insistence upon the magic of numbers: "three" begins to be the pattern of experience much as it was in *Moby Dick* or *The Scarlet Letter*. Theron is involved with three women; the temptations presented to him are three. Nature and the seasons begin to play their part in this poeticizing of realistic prose fiction. Alice's garden is indeed a garden of the modern world; and when the serpent of knowledge comes into her life, "the gayety and color of the garden were gone, and in their place was shabby and dishevelled ruin." [68] The presence of the diabolical is as clearly indicated as it had been in the romance: after Ledsmar witnesses the fall of Theron, he holds a lizard with a "pointed, evil head,"

[67] *Ibid.*, p. 62.
[68] *Ibid.*, p. 292.

and murmurs to it: "Your name isn't Johnny any more, It's the Rev. Theron Ware." [69]

The technique of Frederic, then, was one of the landmarks in the change from a method which unobtrusively used symbols and allusions to reinforce the logical, natural surface of the narrative, to a "symbolism" which insists upon itself as the embodiment of a fable's otherwise obscure significance. With its attention to detail, its local color, its faithfulness to the life Frederic knew, *The Damnation of Theron Ware* points backwards to Howells; with its conscious use of heightened imagery it points forward to Norris, Henry James, and the "symbolic realism" that has become a major mode of the twentieth century. A critic at the time of its publication was perceptive enough to see this change; the characters, an anonymous reviewer wrote,

while they are perfectly life-like at the time of reading, by some curious mental process present themselves when we come to look back upon the book as whole . . . in the light of mysterious, impersonal, Titanic forces." [70]

As a transition between the methods of verisimilitude and symbolism, between the world view of Howells and Twain and that of Adams and Eliot, and as a depiction of America's necessary fall into sophistication, *The Damnation of Theron Ware* recommends itself as a continually interesting contribution to American sensibility.

Davis, 1959   Everett Carter

[60] *Ibid.*, p. 233.
[70] *The Critic*, May 2, 1892, p. 310.

The edition followed is the first American (Chicago: Stone and Kimball, 1896), as noted in Jacob Blank, *Merle Johnson's American First Editions* (New York, 1942). It has been collated with the fifth English edition, which appeared under the title *Illumination* (London: William Heinemann, 1896). Frederic was in London during the year, and it is therefore reasonable to assume that he was responsible for some of the changes. None of them are major, or seriously significant. There are many variations of spelling and punctuation, all of them accountable to differences in usage; these have not been noted. There are some interesting changes, however. The least significant of these obviously have the purpose of making the text more suitable for an English audience: "débris" (p. 42, line 4) becomes "rubbish"; "cotton-batting" (p. 45, line 8) becomes "cotton-wool." Two of the changes in this category are in the direction of prudery: "lewdness" (p. 230, line 33) becomes "immodesty," and the possible suggestiveness of a passage on p. 204 is modified by the omission of the word "creamy" (line 5). Some of the changes and additions, slight as they are, remedy some awkwardnesses, and, at one point, clarify the narrative. The speech of Father Forbes to Theron (p. 291, line 2) for example reads, in the American edition: "I am leaving town tomorrow for some days. . . ." The English edition reads: "I am going to New York tomorrow evening." This change at once makes Theron's suspicions more understandable, and makes Forbes's trip less surreptitious.

THE DAMNATION OF
THERON WARE

By

HAROLD FREDERIC

PART I

—•—

CHAPTER I

No such throng had ever before been seen in the building during all its eight years of existence. People were wedged together most uncomfortably upon the seats; they stood packed in the aisles and overflowed the galleries; at the back, in the shadows underneath these galleries, they formed broad, dense masses about the doors, through which it would be hopeless to attempt a passage.

The light, given out from numerous tin-lined circles of flaring gas-jets arranged on the ceiling, fell full upon a thousand uplifted faces, — some framed in bonnets or juvenile curls, others bearded or crowned with shining baldness, — but all alike under the spell of a dominant emotion which held features in abstracted suspense and focussed every eye upon a common objective point.

The excitement of expectancy reigned upon each row of countenances, was visible in every attitude, — nay, seemed a part of the close, overheated atmosphere itself.

An observer, looking over these compact lines of faces and noting the uniform concentration of eagerness they exhibited, might have guessed that they were watching for either the jury's verdict in some peculiarly absorbing criminal trial, or the announcement of the lucky numbers in a great lottery. These two expressions seemed to alternate, and even to mingle vaguely, upon the upturned lineaments of the waiting throng, — the hope of some unnamed stroke of fortune and the dread of some adverse decree.

But a glance forward at the object of this universal gaze would have sufficed to shatter both hypotheses. Here was neither a court of justice nor a tombola. It was instead the closing session of the annual Nedahma Conference of the

Methodist Episcopal Church, and the Bishop was about to read out the list of ministerial appointments for the coming year. This list was evidently written in a hand strange to him, and the slow, nearsighted old gentleman, having at last sufficiently rubbed the glasses of his spectacles, and then adjusted them over his nose with annoying deliberation, was now silently rehearsing his task to himself, — the while the clergymen round about ground their teeth and restlessly shuffled their feet in impatience.

Upon a closer inspection of the assemblage, there were a great many of these clergymen. A dozen or more dignified, and for the most part elderly, brethren sat grouped about the Bishop in the pulpit. As many others, not quite so staid in mien, and indeed with here and there almost a suggestion of frivolity in their postures, were seated on the steps leading down from this platform. A score of their fellows sat facing the audience, on chairs tightly wedged into the space railed off round the pulpit; and then came five or six rows of pews, stretching across the whole breadth of the church, and almost solidly filled with preachers of the Word.

There were very old men among these, — bent and decrepit veterans who had known Lorenzo Dow, and had been ordained by elders who remembered Francis Asbury and even Whitefield. They sat now in front places, leaning forward with trembling and misshapen hands behind their hairy ears, waiting to hear their names read out on the superannuated list, it might be for the last time.

The sight of these venerable Fathers in Israel was good to the eyes, conjuring up, as it did, pictures of a time when a plain and homely people had been served by a fervent and devoted clergy, — by preachers who lacked in learning and polish, no doubt, but who gave their lives without dream of earthly reward to poverty and to the danger and wearing toil of itinerant missions through the rude frontier settlements. These pictures had for their primitive accessories log-huts, rough household implements, coarse clothes, and patched old saddles which told of weary years of journeying; but to even the least sympathetic vision there shone upon them the glorified light of the Cross and Crown. Reverend survivors of the heroic times, their very presence there — sitting meekly at the altar-rail to hear again the published record of their uselessness and of their dependence upon church charity — was in the nature of a benediction.

The large majority of those surrounding these patriarchs were middle-aged men, generally of a robust type, with burly shoulders, and bushing [1] beards framing shaven upper lips, and who looked for the most part like honest and prosperous farmers attired in their Sunday clothes. As exceptions to this rule, there were scattered stray specimens of a more urban class, worthies with neatly trimmed whiskers, white neckcloths, and even indications of hair-oil, — all eloquent of citified charges; and now and again the eye singled out a striking and scholarly face, at once strong and simple, and instinctively referred it to the faculty of one of the several theological seminaries belonging to the Conference.

The effect of these faces as a whole was toward goodness, candor, and imperturbable self-complacency rather than learning or mental astuteness and curiously enough it wore its pleasantest aspect on the countenances of the older men. The impress of zeal and moral worth seemed to diminish by regular gradations as one passed to younger faces; and among the very beginners, who had been ordained only within the past day or two, this decline was peculiarly marked. It was almost a relief to note the relative smallness of their number, so plainly was it to be seen that they were not the men their forbears had been.

And if those aged, worn-out preachers facing the pulpit had gazed instead backward over the congregation, it may be that here too their old eyes would have detected a difference, — what at least they would have deemed a decline.

But nothing was further from the minds of the members

[1] English ed. (London, 1896, fifth edition) reads "bushy" for "bushing."

of the First M. E. church of Tecumseh than the suggestion
that they were not an improvement on those who had gone
before them. They were undoubtedly the smartest and most
important congregation within the limits of the Nedahma
Conference, and this new church edifice of theirs represented
alike a scale of outlay and a standard of progressive taste in
devotional architecture unique in the Methodism of that
whole section of the State. They had a right to be proud of
themselves, too. They belonged to the substantial order of
the community, with perhaps not so many very rich men as
the Presbyterians had, but on the other hand with far fewer
extremely poor folk than the Baptists were encumbered with.
The pews in the first four rows of their church rented for
one hundred dollars apiece, — quite up to the Presbyterian
highwater mark, — and they now had almost abolished free
pews altogether. The oyster suppers given by their Ladies'
Aid Society in the basement of the church during the winter
had [2] established rank among the fashionable events in
Tecumseh's social calendar.

A comprehensive and satisfied perception of these advantages was uppermost in the minds of this local audience, as
they waited for the Bishop to begin his reading. They had
entertained this Bishop and his Presiding Elders, and the
rank and file of common preachers, in a style which could
not have been remotely approached by any other congregation in the Conference. Where else, one would like to know,
could the Bishop have been domiciled in a Methodist house
where he might have a sitting-room all to himself, with his
bedroom leading out of it? Every clergyman present had
been provided for in a private residence, — even down to
the Licensed Exhorters, who were not really ministers at
all when you came to think of it, and who might well thank
their stars that the Conference had assembled among such
open-handed people. There existed a dim feeling that these
Licensed Exhorters — an uncouth crew, with country store-

[2] English ed. reads "took" for "had."

keepers and lumbermen and even a horse-doctor among their number — had taken rather too much for granted, and were not exhibiting quite the proper degree of gratitude over their reception.

But a more important issue hung now imminent in the balance, — was Tecumseh to be fairly and honorably rewarded for her hospitality by being given the pastor of her choice?

All were agreed — at least among those who paid pew-rents — upon the great importance of a change in the pulpit of the First M. E. Church. A change in persons must of course take place, for their present pastor had exhausted the three-year maximum of the itinerant system, but there was needed much more than that. For a handsome and expensive church building like this, and with such a modern and go-ahead congregation, it was simply a vital necessity to secure an attractive and fashionable preacher. They had held their own against the Presbyterians these past few years only by the most strenuous efforts, and under the depressing disadvantage of a minister who preached dreary out-of-date sermons, and who lacked even the most rudimentary sense of social distinctions. The Presbyterians had captured the new cashier of the Adams County Bank, who had always gone to the Methodist Church in the town he came from, but now was lost solely because of this tiresome old fossil of theirs; and there were numerous other instances of the same sort, scarcely less grievous. That this state of things must be altered was clear.

The unusually large local attendance upon the sessions of the Conference had given some of the more guileless of visiting brethren a high notion of Tecumseh's piety; and perhaps even the most sophisticated stranger never quite realized how strictly it was to be explained by the anxiety to pick out a suitable champion for the fierce Presbyterian competition. Big gatherings assembled evening after evening to hear the sermons of those selected to preach, and the church had been

almost impossibly crowded at each of the three Sunday services. Opinions had naturally differed a good deal during the
earlier stages of this scrutiny, but after last night's sermon
there could be but one feeling. The man for Tecumseh was
the Reverend Theron Ware.

The choice was an admirable one, from points of view
much more exalted than those of the local congregation.

You could see Mr. Ware sitting there at the end of the
row inside the altar-rail, — the tall, slender young man with
the broad white brow, thoughtful eyes, and features moulded
into that regularity of strength which used to characterize
the American Senatorial type in those far-away days of clean-
shaven faces and moderate incomes before the War. The
bright-faced, comely, and vivacious young woman in the
second side pew was his wife — and Tecumseh noted with approbation that she knew how to dress. There were really no
two better or worthier people in the building than this young
couple, who sat waiting along with the rest to hear their fate.
But unhappily they had come to know of the effort being
made to bring them to Tecumseh; and their simple pride in
the triumph of the husband's fine sermon had become swallowed up in a terribly anxious conflict of hope and fear.
Neither of them could maintain a satisfactory show of composure as the decisive moment approached. The vision of
translation from poverty and obscurity to such a splendid
post as this, — truly it was too dazzling for tranquil nerves.

The tedious Bishop had at last begun to call his roll of
names, and the good people of Tecumseh mentally ticked
them off, one by one, as the list expanded. They felt that it
was like this Bishop — an unimportant and commonplace
figure in Methodism, not to be mentioned in the same breath
with Simpson and Janes and Kingsley — that he should begin
with the backwoods counties, and thrust all these remote
and pitifully rustic stations ahead of their own metropolitan
charge. To these they listened [3] but listlessly, — indifferent

---

[3] English ed. reads "attended" for "listened."

alike to the joy and to the dismay which he was scattering among the divines before him.

The announcements were being doled out with stumbling hesitation. After each one a little half-rustling movement through the crowded rows of clergymen passed mute judgment upon the cruel blow this brother had received, the reward justly given to this other, the favoritism by which a third had profited. The Presiding Elders, whose work all this was, stared with gloomy and impersonal abstraction down upon the rows of blackcoated humanity spread before them. The ministers returned this fixed and perfunctory gaze with pale, set faces, only feebly masking the emotions which each new name stirred somewhere among them. The Bishop droned on laboriously, mispronouncing words and repeating himself as if he were reading a catalogue of unfamiliar seeds.

"First church of Tecumseh — Brother Abram C. Tisdale!"

There was no doubt about it! These were actually the words that had been uttered. After all this outlay, all this lavish hospitality, all this sacrifice of time and patience in sitting through those sermons, to draw from the grab-bag nothing better than — a Tisdale!

A hum of outraged astonishment — half groan, half wrathful snort — bounded along from pew to pew throughout the body of the church. An echo of it reached the Bishop, and so confused him that he haltingly repeated the obnoxious line. Every local eye turned as by intuition to where the calamitous Tisdale sat, and fastened malignantly upon him.

Could anything be worse? This Brother Tisdale was past fifty, — a spindling, rickety, gaunt old man, with a long horse-like head and vacantly solemn face, who kept one or the other of his hands continually fumbling his bony jaw. He had been withdrawn from routine service for a number of years, doing a little insurance canvassing on his own account, and also travelling for the Book Concern. Now that he wished to return to parochial work, the richest prize in the whole list, Tecumseh, was given to him, — to him who had never been asked to preach at a conference, and whose archaic nasal singing of "Greenland's Icy Mountains" had made even the Licensed Exhorters grin! It was too intolerably dreadful to think of!

An embittered whisper to the effect that Tisdale was the Bishop's cousin ran round from pew to pew. This did not happen to be true, but indignant Tecumseh gave it entire credit.[4] The throngs about the doors dwindled as by magic, and the aisles cleared. Local interest was dead; and even some of the pewholders rose and made their way out. One of these murmured audibly to his neighbors as he departed that *his* pew could be had now for sixty dollars.

So it happened that when, a little later on, the appointment of Theron Ware to Octavius was read out, none of the people of Tecumseh either noted or cared. They had been deeply interested in him so long as it seemed likely that he was to come to them, — before their clearly expressed desire for him had been so monstrously ignored. But now what became of him was no earthly concern of theirs.

After the Doxology had been sung and the Conference formally declared ended, the Wares would fain have escaped from the flood of handshakings and boisterous farewells which spread over the front part of the church. But the clergymen were unusually insistent upon demonstrations of cordiality among themselves, — the more, perhaps, because it was evident that the friendliness of their local hosts had suddenly evaporated; and, of all men in the world, the priest incumbent of the Octavius pulpit now bore down upon them with noisy effusiveness, and defied evasion.

"Brother Ware — we have never been interduced — but let me clasp your hand! And — Sister Ware, I presume — yours too!"

He was a portly man, who held his head back so that his face seemed all jowl and mouth and sandy chin-whisker. He

[4] English ed. reads "credence" for "credit."

smiled broadly upon them with half-closed eyes, and shook hands again.

"I said to 'em," he went on with loud pretence of heartiness, "the minute I heerd your name called out for our dear Octavius, 'I must go over an' interduce myself.' It will be a heavy cross to part with those dear people, Brother Ware, but if anything could wean me to the notion, so to speak, it would be the knowledge that you are to take up my labors in their midst. Perhaps — ah — perhaps they *are* jest a trifle close in money matters, but they come out strong on revivals. They'll need a good deal o' stirrin' up about parsonage expenses, but, oh! such seasons of grace as we've experienced there together!" He shook his head, and closed his eyes altogether, as if transported by his memories.

Brother Ware smiled faintly in decorous response, and bowed in silence; but his wife resented the unctuous beaming of content on the other's wide countenance, and could not restrain her tongue.

"You seem to bear up tolerably well under this heavy cross, as you call it," she said sharply.

"The will o' the Lord, Sister Ware, — the will o' the Lord!" he responded, disposed for the instant to put on his pompous manner with her, and then deciding to smile again as he moved off. The circumstance that he was to get an additional three hundred dollars yearly in his new place was not mentioned between them.

By a mutual impulse the young couple, when they had at last gained the cool open air, crossed the street to the side where over-hanging trees shaded the infrequent lamps, and they might be comparatively alone. The wife had taken her husband's arm, and pressed closely upon it as they walked. For a time no word passed, but finally he said, in a grave voice, —

"It is hard upon you, poor girl."

Then she stopped short, buried her face against his shoulder, and fell to sobbing.

He strove with gentle, whispered remonstrance to win her from this mood, and after a few moments she lifted her head and they resumed their walk, she wiping her eyes as they went.

"I couldn't keep it in a minute longer!" she said, catching her breath between phrases. "Oh, *why* do they behave so badly to us, Theron?"

He smiled down momentarily upon her as they moved along, and patted her hand.

"Somebody must have the poor places, Alice," he said consolingly. "I am a young man yet, remember. We must take our turn, and be patient. For 'we know that all things work together for good.' "

"And your sermon was so head-and-shoulders above all the others!" she went on breathlessly. "Everybody said so! And Mrs. Parshall heard it so *direct* that you were to be sent here, and I know she told everybody how much I was lotting on it — I wish we could go right off to-night without going to her house — I shall be ashamed to look her in the face — and of course she knows we're poked off to that miserable Octavius. — Why, Theron, they tell me it's a worse place even than we've got now!"

"Oh, not at all," he put in reassuringly. "It has grown to be a large town — oh, quite twice the size of Tyre. It's a great Irish place, I've heard. Our own church seems to be a good deal run down there. We must build it up again; and the salary *is* better — a little."

But he too was depressed, and they walked on toward their temporary lodging in a silence full of mutual grief. It was not until they had come within sight of this goal that he prefaced by a little sigh of resignation these further words, —

"Come, let us make the best of it, my girl! After all, we are in the hands of the Lord."

"Oh, don't, Theron!" she said hastily. "Don't talk to me about the Lord to-night; I can't bear it!"

CHAPTER II

"THERON! Come out here! This is the funniest thing we have heard yet!"

Mrs. Ware stood on the platform of her new kitchen stoop. The bright flood of May-morning sunshine completely enveloped her girlish form, clad in a simple, fresh-starched calico gown, and shone in golden patches upon her light-brown hair. She had a smile on her face, as she looked down at the milk boy standing on the bottom step, — a smile of a doubtful sort, stormily mirthful.

"Come out a minute, Theron!" she called again; and in obedience to the summons the tall lank figure of her husband appeared in the open doorway behind her. A long loose, open dressing-gown dangled to his knees, and his sallow, clean-shaven, thoughtful face wore a morning undress expression of youthful good-nature. He leaned against the door-sill, crossed his large carpet slippers, and looked up into the sky, drawing a long satisfied breath.

"What a beautiful morning!" he exclaimed. "The elms over there are full of robins. We must get up earlier these mornings, and walk."

His wife indicated the boy with the milk-pail on his arm, by a wave of her hand.

"Guess what he tells me!" she said. "It wasn't a mistake at all, our getting no milk yesterday or the Sunday before. It seems that that's the custom here, at least so far as the parsonage is concerned."

"What's the matter, boy?" asked the young minister, drawling his words a little, and putting a sense of placid irony into them. "Don't the cows give milk on Sunday, then?"

The boy was not going to be chaffed. "Oh, I'll bring you milk fast enough on Sundays, if you give me the word," he said with nonchalance. "Only it won't last long."

"How do you mean, — 'won't last long'?" asked Mrs. Ware, briskly.

The boy liked her, — both for herself, and for the doughnuts fried with her own hands, which she gave him on his morning round. He dropped his half-defiant tone.

"The thing of it's this," he explained. "Every new minister starts in saying we can deliver to this house on Sundays, an' then gives us notice to stop before the month's out. It's the trustees that does it."

The Rev. Theron Ware uncrossed his feet and moved out on to the stoop beside his wife. "What's that you say?" he interjected. "Don't *they* take milk on Sundays?"

"Nope!" answered the boy.

The young couple looked each other in the face for a puzzled moment, then broke into a laugh.

"Well, we'll try it, anyway," said the preacher. "You can go on bringing it Sundays till — till —"

"Till you cave in an' tell me to stop," put in the boy. "All right!" and he was off on the instant, the dipper jangling loud incredulity in his pail as he went.

The Wares exchanged another glance as he disappeared round the corner of the house, and another mutual laugh seemed imminent. Then the wife's face clouded over, and she thrust her under-lip a trifle forward out of its place in the straight and gently firm profile.

"It's just what Wendell Phillips said," she declared. " 'The Puritan's idea of hell is a place where everybody has to mind his own business.' "

The young minister stroked his chin thoughtfully, and let his gaze wander over the backyard in silence. The garden parts had not been spaded up, but lay, a useless stretch of muddy earth, broken only by last year's cabbage-stumps and the general litter of dead roots and vegetation. The door of the tenantless chicken-coop hung wide open. Before it was a great heap of ashes and cinders, soaked into grimy hardness by the recent spring rains, and nearer still an ancient chopping-block, round which were scattered old weather-beaten hardwood knots which had defied the axe, parts of broken barrels and packing-boxes, and a nameless débris of tin cans, clam-shells, and general rubbish. It was pleasanter to lift the eyes, and look across the neighbors' fences to the green, waving tops of the elms on the street beyond. How lofty and beautiful they were in the morning sunlight, and with what matchless charm came the song of the robins, freshly installed in their haunts among the new pale-green leaves! Above them, in the fresh, scented air, glowed the great blue dome, radiant with light and the purification of spring.

Theron lifted his thin, long-fingered hand, and passed it in a slow arch of movement to comprehend this glorious upper picture.

"What matter any one's ideas of hell," he said, in soft, grave tones, "when we have that to look at, and listen to, and fill our lungs with? It seems to me that we never *feel* quite so sure of God's goodness at other times as we do in these wonderful new mornings of spring."

The wife followed his gesture, and her eyes rested for a brief moment, with pleased interest, upon the trees and the sky. Then they reverted, with a harsher scrutiny, to the immediate foreground.

"Those Van Sizers ought to be downright ashamed of themselves," she said, "to leave everything in such a muss as this. You *must* see about getting a man to clean up the yard, Theron. It's no use your thinking of doing it yourself. In the first place, it wouldn't look quite the thing, and, second, you'd never get at it in all your born days. Or if a man would cost too much, we might get a boy. I daresay Harvey would come around, after he'd finished with his milk-route in the forenoon. We could give him his dinner, you know, and I'd bake him some cookies. He's got the greatest sweet-tooth you ever heard of. And then perhaps if we gave him a quarter, or say half a dollar, he'd be quite satisfied. I'll speak to him in the morning. We can save a dollar or so that way."

"I suppose every little does help," commented Mr. Ware, with a doleful lack of conviction. Then his face brightened. "I tell you what let's do!" he exclaimed. "Get on your street dress, and we'll take a long walk, way out into the country. You've never seen the basin, where they float the log-rafts in, or the big saw-mills. The hills beyond give you almost mountain effects, they are so steep; and they say there's a sulphur spring among the slate on the hill-side, somewhere, with trees all about it; and we could take some sandwiches with us —"

"You forget," put in Mrs. Ware, — "those trustees are coming at eleven."

"So they are!" assented the young minister, with something like a sigh. He cast another reluctant, lingering glance at the sunlit elm boughs, and, turning, went indoors.

He loitered for an aimless minute in the kitchen, where his wife, her sleeves rolled to the elbow, now resumed the interrupted washing of the breakfast dishes, — perhaps with vague visions of that ever-receding time to come when they might have a hired girl to do such work. Then he wandered off into the room beyond, which served them alike as living-room and study, and let his eye run along the two rows of books that constituted his library. He saw nothing which he wanted to read. Finally he did take down "Paley's Evidences," and seated himself in the big armchair, — that costly and oversized anomaly among his humble household gods; but the book lay unopened on his knee, and his eyelids half closed themselves in sign of revery.

This was his third charge, — this Octavius which they both knew they were going to dislike so much.

The first had been in the pleasant dairy and hop country many miles to the south, on another watershed and among a different kind of people. Perhaps, in truth, the grinding labor, the poverty of ideas, the systematic selfishness of later rural experience, had not been lacking there; but they played no part in the memories which now he passed in tender review. He recalled instead the warm sunshine on the fertile expanse of fields; the sleek, well-fed herds of "milkers" coming lowing down the road under the maples; the prosperous and hospitable farmhouses, with their orchards in blossom and their spacious red barns; the bountiful boiled dinners which cheery housewives served up with their own skilled hands. Of course, he admitted to himself, it would not be the same if he were to go back there again. He was conscious of having moved along — was it, after all, an advance? — to a point where it was unpleasant to sit at table with the unfragrant hired man, and still worse to encounter the bucolic confusion between the functions of knives and forks. But in those happy days — young, zealous, himself farm bred — these trifles had been invisible to him, and life there among those kindly husbandmen had seemed, by contrast with the gaunt surroundings and gloomy rule of the theological seminary, luxuriously abundant and free.

It was there too that the crowning blessedness of his youth — nay, should he not say of all his days? — had come to him. There he had first seen Alice Hastings, — the bright-eyed, frank-faced, serenely self-reliant girl, who now, less than four years thereafter, could be heard washing the dishes out in the parsonage kitchen.

How wonderful she had seemed to him then! How beautiful and all-beneficent the miracle still appeared! Though herself the daughter of a farmer, her presence on a visit within the borders of his remote country charge had seemed to make everything there a hundred times more countrified than it had ever been before. She was fresh from the refinements of a town seminary: she read books; it was known that she could play upon the piano. Her clothes, her manners, her way of speaking, the readiness of her thoughts and sprightly tongue, — not least, perhaps, the imposing current understanding as to her father's wealth, — placed her on a glorified pinnacle far away from the girls of the neighborhood. These honest and good-hearted creatures indeed called ceaseless attention to her superiority by their deference and open-mouthed admiration, and treated it as the most natural thing in the world that their young minister should be visibly "taken" with her.

Theron Ware, in truth, left this first pastorate of his the following spring, in a transfiguring halo of romance. His new appointment was to Tyre, — a somewhat distant village of traditional local pride and substance, — and he was to be married only a day or so before entering upon his pastoral duties there. The good people among whom he had begun his ministry took kindly credit to themselves that he had met his bride while she was "visiting round" their country-side. In part by jocose inquiries addressed to the expectant groom; in part by the confidences of the postmaster at the corners concerning the bulk and frequency of the correspondence passing between Theron and the now remote Alice, — they had followed the progress of the courtship through the autumn and winter with friendly zest. When he returned from the conference, to say good-bye and confess the happiness that awaited him, they gave him a "donation," — quite as if he were a married pastor with a home of his own, instead of a shy young bachelor, who received his guests and their contributions in the house where he boarded.

He went away with tears of mingled regret and proud joy in his eyes, thinking a good deal upon their predictions of a distinguished career before him, feeling infinitely strengthened and upborne by the hearty fevor of their God-speed, and taking with him nearly two wagon-loads of vegetables, apples, canned preserves, assorted furniture, glass dishes, cheeses, pieced bedquilts, honey, feathers, and kitchen utensils.

Of the three years' term in Tyre, it was pleasantest to dwell upon the beginning.

The young couple — after being married out at Alice's home in an adjoining county, under the depressing conditions of a hopelessly bedridden mother, and a father and brothers whose perceptions were obviously closed to the advantages of a matrimonial connection with Methodism — came straight to the house which their new congregation rented as a parsonage. The impulse of reaction from the rather grim cheerlessness of their wedding lent fresh gayety to their light-hearted, whimsical start at housekeeping. They had never laughed so much in all their lives as they did now in these first months, — over their weird ignorance of domestic details; with its mishaps, mistakes, and entertaining discoveries; over the comical superabundances and shortcomings of their "donation" outfit; over the thousand and one quaint experiences of their novel relation to each other, to the congregation, and to the world of Tyre at large.

Theron, indeed, might be said never to have laughed before. Up to that time no friendly student of his character, cataloguing his admirable qualities, would have thought of including among them a sense of humor, much less a bent toward levity. Neither his early strenuous battle to get away from the farm and achieve such education as should serve to open to him the gates of professional life, nor the later wave of religious enthusiasm which caught him up as he stood on the border-land of manhood, and swept him off into a veritable new world of views and aspirations, had been a likely school of merriment. People had prized him for his innocent candor and guileless mind, for his good heart, his pious zeal, his modesty about gifts notably above the average, but it had occurred to none to suspect in him a latent funny side.

But who could be solemn where Alice was? — Alice in a quandary over the complications of her cooking stove; Alice boiling her potatoes all day, and her eggs for half an hour; Alice ordering twenty pounds of steak and half a pound of sugar, and striving to extract a breakfast beverage from the unground coffee-bean? Clearly not so tenderly fond and sympathetic a husband as Theron. He began by laughing because she laughed, and grew by swift stages to comprehend, then

frankly to share, her amusement. From this it seemed only
a step to the development of a humor of his own, doubling,
as it were, their sportive resources. He found himself discovering a new droll aspect in men and things; his phraseology
took on a dryly playful form, fittingly to present [1] conceits
which danced up, unabashed, quite into the presence of lofty
and majestic truths. He got from this nothing but satisfaction;
it obviously involved increased claims to popularity among
his parishioners, and consequently magnified powers of use-
fulness, and it made life so much more a joy and a thing to
be thankful for. Often, in the midst of the exchange of merry
quip and whimsical suggestion, bright blossoms on that tree
of strength and knowledge which he felt expanding now with
a mighty outward pushing in all directions, he would lapse
into deep gravity, and ponder with a swelling heart the vast
unspeakable marvel of his blessedness, in being thus enriched
and humanized by daily communion with the most worshipful of womankind.

This happy and good young couple took the affections of
Tyre by storm. The Methodist Church there had at no time
held its head very high among the denominations, and for
some years back had been in a deplorably sinking state, owing
first to the secession of the Free Methodists and then to the
incumbency of a pastor who scandalized the community by
marrying a black man to a white woman. But the Wares
changed all this. Within a month the report of Theron's
charm and force in the pulpit was crowding the church building to its utmost capacity, — and that, too, with some of Tyre's
best people. Equally winning was the atmosphere of jollity
and juvenile high spirits which pervaded the parsonage under
these new conditions, and which Theron and Alice seemed
to diffuse wherever they went.

Thus swimmingly their first year sped, amid universal
acclaim. Mrs. Ware had a recognized social place, quite outside the restricted limits of Methodism, and shone in it with
an unflagging brilliancy altogether beyond the traditions of

[1] English ed. reads "to fittingly present" for "fittingly to present."

Tyre. Delightful as she was in other people's houses, she was still more naïvely fascinating in her own quaint and somewhat harum-scarum domicile; and the drab, two-storied, tin-roofed little parsonage might well have rattled its clapboards to see if it was not in dreamland, — so gay was the company, so light were the hearts, which it sheltered in these new days. As for Theron, the period was one of incredible fructification and output. He scarcely recognized for his own the mind which now was reaching out on all sides with the arms of an octopus, exploring unsuspected mines of thought, bringing in rich treasures of deduction, assimilating, building, propounding as if by some force quite independent of him. He could not look without blinking timidity at the radiance of the path stretched out before him, leading upward to dazzling heights of greatness.

At the end of this first year the Wares suddenly discovered that they were eight hundred dollars in debt.

The second year was spent in arriving, by slow stages and with a cruel wealth of pathetic detail, at a realization of what being eight hundred dollars in debt meant.

It was not in their elastic and buoyant natures to grasp the full significance of the thing at once, or easily. Their position in the social structure, too, was all against clear-sightedness in material matters. A general, for example, uniformed and in the saddle, advancing through the streets with his staff in the proud wake of his division's massed walls of bayonets, cannot be imagined as quailing at the glance thrown at him by his tailor on the sidewalk. Similarly, a man invested with sacerdotal authority, who baptizes, marries, and buries, who delivers judgments from the pulpit which may not be questioned in his hearing, and who receives from all his fellow-men a special deference of manner and speech, is in the nature of things prone to see the grocer's book and the butcher's bill through the little end of the telescope.

The Wares at the outset had thought it right to trade as exclusively as possible with members of their own church society. This loyalty became a principal element of martyrdom. Theron had his creditors seated in serried rows before him, Sunday after Sunday. Alice had her critics consolidated among those whom it was her chief duty to visit and profess friendship for. These situations now began, by regular grada- tions, to unfold their terrors. At the first intimation of dis- content, the Wares made what seemed to them a sweeping reduction in expenditure. When they heard that Brother Potter had spoken of them as "poor pay," they dismissed their hired girl. A little later, Theron brought himself to drop a laboriously casual suggestion as to a possible increase of salary, and saw with sinking spirits the faces of the stewards freeze with dumb disapprobation. Then Alice paid a visit to her parents, only to find her brothers doggedly hostile to the no- tion of her being helped, and her father so much under their influence that the paltry sum he dared offer barely covered the expenses of her journey. With another turn of the screw, they sold the piano she had brought with her from home, and cut themselves down to the bare necessities of life, neither receiving company nor going out. They never laughed now, and even smiles grew rare.

By this time Theron's sermons, preached under that stony glare of people to whom he owed money, had degenerated to a pitiful level of commonplace. As a consequence, the at- tendance became once more confined to the insufficient mem- bership of the church, and the trustees complained of griev- ously diminished receipts. When the Wares, grown desperate, ventured upon the experiment of trading outside the bounds of the congregation, the trustees complained again, this time peremptorily.

Thus the second year dragged itself miserably to an end. Nor was relief possible, because the Presiding Elder knew something of the circumstances, and felt it his duty to send Theron back for a third year, to pay his debts, and drain the cup of disciplinary medicine to its dregs.

The worst has been told. Beginning in utter blackness, this third year, in the second month, brought a change as welcome as it was unlooked for. An elderly and important citizen of Tyre, by name Abram Beekman, whom Theron knew slightly, and had on occasions seen sitting in one of the back pews near the door, called one morning at the parsonage, and electrified its inhabitants by expressing a desire to wipe off all their old scores for them, and give them a fresh start in life. As he put the suggestion, they could find no excuse for rejecting it. He had watched them, and heard a good deal about them, and took a fatherly sort of interest in them. He did not deprecate their regarding the aid he proffered them in the nature of a loan, but they were to make themselves perfectly easy about it, and never return it at all unless they could spare it sometime with entire convenience, and felt that they wanted to do so. As this amazing windfall finally took shape, it enabled the Wares to live respectably through the year, and to leave Tyre with something over one hundred dollars in hand.

It enabled them, too, to revive in a chastened form their old dream of ultimate success and distinction for Theron. He had demonstrated clearly enough to himself, during that brief season of unrestrained effulgence, that he had within him the making of a great pulpit orator. He set to work now, with resolute purpose, to puzzle out and master all the principles which underlie this art, and all the tricks that adorn its superstructure. He studied it, fastened his thoughts upon it, talked daily with Alice about it. In the pulpit, addressing those people who had so darkened his life and crushed the first happiness out of his home, he withheld himself from any oratorical display which could afford them gratification. He put aside, as well, the thought of attracting once more the non-Methodists of Tyre, whose early enthusiasm had spread such pitfalls for his unwary feet. He practised effects now by piecemeal, with an alert ear, and calculation in every tone. An ambition, at once embittered and tearfully solicitous, possessed him.

He reflected now, this morning, with a certain incredulous

interest, upon that unworthy epoch in his life history, which seemed so far behind him, and yet had come to a close only a few weeks ago. The opportunity had been given him, there at the Tecumseh Conference, to reveal his quality. He had risen to its full limit of possibilities, and preached a great sermon in a manner which he at least knew was unapproachable. He had made his most powerful bid for the prize place, had trebly deserved success — and had been banished instead to Octavius!

The curious thing was that he did not resent his failure. Alice had taken it hard, but he himself was conscious of a sense of spiritual gain. The influence of the Conference, with its songs and seasons of prayer and high pressure of emotional excitement, was still strong upon him. It seemed years and years since the religious side of him had been so stirred into motion. He felt, as he lay back in the chair, and folded his hands over the book on his knee, that he had indeed come forth from the fire purified and strengthened. The ministry to souls diseased beckoned him with a new and urgent significance. He smiled to remember that Mr. Beekman, speaking in his shrewd and pointed way, had asked him whether, looking it all over, he didn't think it would be better for him to study law, with a view to sliding out of the ministry when a good chance offered. It amazed him now to recall that he had taken this hint seriously, and even gone to the length of finding out what books law-students began upon.

Thank God! all that was past and gone now. The Call sounded, resonant and imperative, in his ears, and there was no impulse of his heart, no fibre of his being, which did not stir in devout response. He closed his eyes, to be the more wholly alone with the Spirit, that moved him.

The jangling of a bell in the hallway broke sharply upon his meditations, and on the instant his wife thrust in her head from the kitchen.

"You'll have to go to the door, Theron!" she warned him, in a loud, swift whisper. "I'm not fit to be seen. It's the trustees."

"All right," he said, and rose slowly from sprawling recumbency to his feet. "I'll go."

"And don't forget," she added strenuously; "I believe in Levi Gorringe! I've seen him go past here with his rod and fish-basket twice in eight days, and that's a good sign. He's got a soft side somewhere. And just keep a stiff upper lip about the gas, and don't you let them jew you down a solitary cent on that sidewalk."

"All right," said Theron, again, and moved reluctantly toward the hall-door.

CHAPTER III

WHEN the three trustees had been shown in by the Rev. Mr. Ware, and had taken seats, an awkward little pause ensued. The young minister looked doubtingly from one face to another, the while they glanced with inquiring interest about the room, noting the pictures and appraising the furniture in their minds.

The obvious leader of the party, Loren Pierce, a rich quarryman, was an old man of medium size and mean attire, with a square, beardless face as hard and impassive in expression as one of his blocks of limestone. The irregular, thin-lipped mouth, slightly sunken, and shut with vice-like firmness, the short snub nose, and the little eyes squinting from half-closed lids beneath slightly marked brows, seemed scarcely to attain to the dignity of features, but evaded attention instead, as if feeling that they were only there at all from plain necessity, and ought not to be taken into account. Mr. Pierce's face did not know how to smile, — what was the use of smiles? — but its whole surface radiated secretiveness. Portrayed on canvas by a master brush, with a ruff or a red robe for masquerade, generations of imaginative amateurs would have seen in it vast-reaching plots, the skeletons of a dozen dynastic cupboards, the guarded mysteries of half a century's international diplomacy. The amateurs would have been wrong again. There was nothing behind Mr. Pierce's juiceless countenance more weighty than a general determination to exact seven per cent for his money, and some specific notions about capturing certain brickyards which were interfering with his quarry-sales. But Octavius watched him shamble along its sidewalks quite as the Vienna of dead and forgotten yesterday might have watched Metternich.

Erastus Winch was of a breezier sort, — a florid, stout, and sandy man, who spent most of his life driving over evil country roads in a buggy, securing orders for dairy furniture and certain allied lines of farm utensils. This practice had given him a loud voice and a deceptively hearty manner, to which the other avocation of cheese-buyer, which he pursued at the Board of Trade meetings every Monday afternoon, had added a considerable command of persuasive yet noncommittal language. To look at him, still more to hear him, one would have sworn he was a good fellow, a trifle rough and noisy, perhaps, but all right at bottom. But the County Clerk of Dearborn County could have told you of agriculturists who knew Erastus from long and unhappy experience, and who held him to be even a tighter man than Loren Pierce in the matter of a mortgage.

The third trustee, Levi Gorringe, set one wondering at the very first glance what on earth he was doing in that company. Those who had known him longest had the least notion; but it may be added that no one knew him well. He was a lawyer, and had lived in Octavius for upwards of ten years; that is to say, since early manhood. He had an office on the main street, just under the principal photograph gallery. Doubtless he was sometimes in this office; but his fellow-townsmen saw him more often in the street doorway, with the stairs behind him, and the flaring show-cases of the photographer on either side, standing with his hands in his pockets and an unlighted cigar in his mouth, looking at nothing in particular. About every other day he went off after breakfast into the country roundabout, sometimes with a rod, sometimes with a gun, but always alone. He was a bachelor, and slept in a room at the back of his office, cooking some of his meals himself, getting others at a restaurant close by. Though he had little visible practice, he was understood to be well-to-do and even more, and people tacitly inferred that he "shaved notes." The Methodists of Octavius looked upon him as a queer fish, and through nearly a dozen years had never quite outgrown their hebdomadal tendency to surprise at seeing him enter their church. He had never, it is true, professed religion, but they had elected him as a trustee now for a number of terms, all the same, — partly because he was their only lawyer, partly because he, like both his colleagues, held a mortgage on the church edifice and lot. In person, Mr. Gorringe was a slender man, with a skin of a clear, uniform citron tint, black waving hair, and dark gray eyes, and a thin, high-featured face. He wore a mustache and pointed chin-tuft; and, though he was of New England parentage and had never been further south than Ocean Grove, he presented a general effect of old Mississippian traditions and tastes startlingly at variance with the standards of Dearborn County Methodism. Nothing could convince some of the elder sisters that he was not a drinking man.

The three visitors had completed their survey of the room now; and Loren Pierce emitted a dry, harsh little cough, as a signal that business was about to begin. At this sound, Winch drew up his feet, and Gorringe untied a parcel of account-books and papers that he held on his knee. Theron felt that his countenance must be exhibiting to the assembled brethren an unfortunate sense of helplessness in their hands. He tried to look more resolute, and forced his lips into a smile.

"Brother Gorringe allus acts as Seckertary," said Erastus Winch, beaming broadly upon the minister, as if the mere mention of the fact promoted jollity. "That's it, Brother Gorringe, — take your seat at Brother Ware's desk. Mind the Dominie's pen don't play tricks on you, an' start off writin' out sermons instid of figgers." The humorist turned to Theron as the lawyer walked over to the desk at the window. "I allus have to caution him about that," he remarked with great joviality. "An' do *you* look out afterwards, Brother Ware, or else you'll catch that pen o' yours scribblin' lawyer's lingo in place o' the Word."

Theron felt bound to exhibit a grin in acknowledgment of this pleasantry. The lawyer's change of position had involved some shifting of the others' chairs, and the young minister found himself directly confronted by Brother

Pierce's hard and colorless old visage. Its little eyes were watching him, as through a mask, and under their influence the smile of politeness fled from his lips. The lawyer on his right, the cheese-buyer to the left, seemed to recede into distance as he for the moment returned the gaze of the quarryman. He waited now for him to speak, as if the others were of no importance.

"We are a plain sort o' folks up in these parts," said Brother Pierce, after a slight further pause. His voice was as dry and rasping as his cough, and its intonations were those of authority. "We walk here," he went on, eying the minister with a sour regard, "in a meek an' humble spirit, in the straight an' narrow way which leadeth unto life. We ain't gone traipsin' after strange gods, like some people that call themselves Methodists in other places. We stick by the Discipline an' the ways of our fathers in Israel. No new-fangled notions can go down here. Your wife'd better take them flowers out of her bunnit afore next Sunday."

Silence possessed the room for a few moments, the while Theron, pale-faced and with brows knit, studied the pattern of the ingrain carpet. Then he lifted his head, and nodded it in assent. "Yes," he said; "we will do nothing by which our 'brother stumbleth, or is offended, or is made weak.' "

Brother Pierce's parchment face showed no sign of surprise or pleasure at this easy submission. "Another thing: We don't want no book-learnin' or dictionary words in our pulpit," he went on coldly. "Some folks may stomach 'em; we won't. Them two sermons o' yours, p'r'aps they'd do down in some city place; but they're like your wife's bunnit here, they're too flowery to suit us. What we want to hear is the plain, old-fashioned Word of God, without any palaver or 'hems and ha's.' They tell me there's some parts where hell's treated as played-out, — where our ministers don't like to talk much about it because people don't want to hear about it. Such preachers ought to be put out. They ain't Methodists at all. What we want here, sir, is straight-out, flat-footed hell,

— the burnin' lake o' fire an' brimstone. Pour it into 'em, hot an' strong. We can't have too much of it. Work in them awful deathbeds of Voltaire an' Tom Paine, with the Devil right there in the room, reachin' for 'em, an' they yellin' for fright; that's what fills the anxious seat an' brings in souls hand over fist."

Theron's tongue dallied for an instant with the temptation to comment upon these old-wife fables, which were so dear to the rural religious heart when he and I were boys. But it seemed wiser to only nod again, and let his mentor go on.

"We ain't had no trouble with the Free Methodists here," continued Brother Pierce, "jest because we kept to the old paths, an' seek for salvation in the good old way. Everybody can shout 'Amen!' as loud and as long as the Spirit moves him, with us. Some one was sayin' you thought we ought to have a choir and an organ. No, sirree! No such tom-foolery for us! You'll only stir up feelin' agin yourself by hintin' at such things. And then, too, our folks don't take no stock in all that pack o' nonsense about science, such as tellin' the age of the earth by crackin' up stones. I've b'en in the quarry line all my life, an' *I* know it's all humbug! Why, they say some folks are goin' round now preachin' that our grand-fathers were all monkeys. That comes from departin' from the ways of our forefathers, an' puttin' in organs an' choirs, an' deckin' our women-folks out with gewgaws, an' apin' the fashions of the worldly. I shouldn't wonder if them kind did have some monkey blood in 'em. You'll find we're a different sort here."

The young minister preserved silence for a little, until it became apparent that the old trustee had had his say out. Even then he raised his head slowly, and at last made answer in a hesitating and irresolute way.

"You have been very frank," he said. "I am obliged to you. A clergyman coming to a new charge cannot be better served than by having laid before him a clear statement of the views and — and spiritual tendencies — of his new flock, quite at the outset. I feel it to be of especial value in this case, because I am young in years and in my ministry, and am conscious of a great weakness of the flesh. I can see how daily contact with a people so attached to the old, simple, primitive Methodism of Wesley and Asbury may be a source of much strength to me. I may take it," he added upon second thought, with an inquiring glance at Mr. Winch, "that Brother Pierce's description of our charge, and its tastes and needs, meets with your approval?"

Erastus Winch nodded his head and smiled expansively. "Whatever Brother Pierce says, goes!" he declared. The lawyer, sitting behind at the desk by the window, said nothing.

"The place is jest overrun with Irish," Brother Pierce began again. "They've got two Catholic churches here now to our one, and they do jest as they blamed please at the charter elections. It'd be a good idee to pitch into Catholics in general whenever you can. You could make a hit that way. I say the State ought to make 'em pay taxes on their church property. They've no right to be exempted, because they ain't Christians at all. They're idolaters, that's what they are! I know 'em! I've had 'em in my quarries for years, an' they ain't got no idee of decency or fair dealin'. Every time the price of stone went up, every man of 'em would jine to screw more wages out o' me. Why, they used to keep account o' the amount o' business I done, an' figger up my profits, an' have the face to come an' talk to me about 'em, as if that had anything to do with wages. It's my belief their priests put 'em up to it. People don't begin to reelize, — that church of idolatry'll be the ruin o' this country, if it ain't checked in time. Jest you go at 'em hammer'n' tongs! I've got Eyetalians in the quarries now. They're sensible fellows: they know when they're well off; a dollar a day, an' they're satisfield, an' everything goes smooth."

"But they're Catholics, the same as the Irish," suddenly interjected the lawyer, from his place by the window. Theron pricked up his ears at the sound of his voice. There was an anti-Pierce note in it, so to speak, which it did him good to hear. The consciousness of sympathy began on the instant to inspire him with courage.

"I know some people *say* they are," Brother Pierce guardedly retorted; "but I've summered an' wintered both kinds, an' *I* hold to it they're different. I grant ye, the Eyetalians *are* some given to jabbin' knives into each other, but they never git up strikes, an' they don't grumble about wages. Why, look at the way they live, — jest some weeds an' yarbs dug up on the roadside, an' stewed in a kettle with a piece o' fat the size o' your finger, an' a loaf o' bread, an' they're happy as a king. There's some sense in *that;* but the Irish, they've got to have meat an' potatoes an' butter jest as if — as if —"

"As if they'd b'en used to 'em at home," put in Mr. Winch, to help his colleague out.

The lawyer ostentatiously drew up his chair to the desk, and began turning over the leaves of his biggest book. "It's getting on toward noon, gentlemen," he said, in an impatient voice.

The business meeting which followed was for a considerable time confined to hearing extracts from the books and papers read in a swift and formal fashion by Mr. Gorringe. If this was intended to inform the new pastor of the exact financial situation in Octavius, it lamentably failed of its purpose. Theron had little knowledge of figures; and though he tried hard to listen, and to assume an air of comprehension, he did not understand much of what he heard. In a general way he gathered that the church property was put down at $12,000, on which there was a debt of $4,800. The annual expenses were $2,250, of which the principal items were $800 for his salary, $170 for the rent of the parsonage, and $319 for interest on the debt. It seemed that last year the receipts had fallen just under $2,000, and they now confronted the necessity of making good this deficit during the coming year, as well as increasing the regular revenues. Without much discussion, it was agreed that they should endeavor to secure the services of a celebrated "debt-raiser," early in the autumn, and utilize him in the closing days of a revival.

Theron knew this "debt-raiser," and had seen him at work, — a burly, bustling, vulgar man who took possession of the pulpit as if it were an auctioneer's block, and pursued the task of exciting liberality in the bosoms of the congregation by alternating prayer, anecdote, song, and cheap buffoonery in a manner truly sickening. Would it not be preferable, he feebly suggested, to raise the money by a festival, or fair, or some other form of entertainment which the ladies could manage?

Brother Pierce shook his head with contemptuous emphasis. "Our women-folks ain't that kind," he said. "They did try to hold a sociable once, but nobody came, and we didn't raise more'n three or four dollars. It ain't their line. They lack the worldly arts. As the Discipline commands, they avoid the evil of putting on gold and costly apparel, and taking such diversions as cannot be used in the name of the Lord Jesus."

"Well — of course — if you prefer the debt-raiser' — " Theron began, and took the itemized account from Gorringe's knee as an excuse for not finishing the hateful sentence.

He looked down the foolscap sheet, line by line, with no special sense of what it signified, until his eye caught upon this little section of the report, bracketed by itself in the Secretary's neat hand:

INTEREST CHARGE

First mortgage (1873) .. $1,000 .. (E. Winch) . @ 7 . $ 70
Second mortgage (1876) . 1,700 .. (L. Gorringe) . @ 6 . 102
Third mortgage (1878) . 2,100 .. (L. Pierce) .. @ 7 . 147
$4,800 $319

It was no news to him that the three mortgages on the church property were held by the three trustees. But as he looked once more, another feature of the thing struck him as curious.

"I notice that the rates of interest vary," he remarked without thinking, and then wished the words unsaid, for the two trustees in view moved uneasily on their seats.

"Oh, that's nothing," exclaimed Erastus Winch, with a boisterous display of jollity. "It's only Brother Gorringe's pleasant little way of making a contribution to our funds. You will notice that, at the date of all these mortgages, the State rate of interest was seven per cent. Since then it's b'en lowered to six. Well, when that happened, you see, Brother Gorringe, not being a professin' member, and so not bound by our rules, he could just as well as not let his interest down a cent. But Brother Pierce an' me, we talked it over, an' we made up our minds we were tied hand an' foot by our contract. You know how strong the Discipline lays it down that we must be bound to the letter of our agreements. That bein' so, we seen it in the light of duty not to change what we'd set our hands to. That's how it is, Brother Ware."

"I understand," said Theron, with an effort at polite calmness of tone. "And — is there anything else?"

"There's this," broke in Brother Pierce: "We're commanded to be law-abiding people, an' seven per cent *was* the law — an' would be now if them ragamuffins in the Legislation —"

"Surely we needn't go further into that," interrupted the minister, conscious of a growing stiffness in his moral spine. "Have we any other business before us?"

Brother Pierce's little eyes snapped, and the wrinkles in his forehead deepened angrily. "Business?" he demanded. "Yes, plenty of it. We've got to reduce expenses. We're nigh onto $300 behind-hand this minute. Besides your house-rent, you get $800 free an' clear, — that is $15.38 every week, an' only you an' your wife to keep out of it. Why, when I was your age, young man, and after that too, I was glad to get $6 [1] a week."

[1] English ed. reads "$4" for "$6."

"I don't think my salary is under discussion, Mr. Pierce —"

"*Brother* Pierce!" suggested Winch, in a half-chuckling undertone.

"Brother Pierce, then!" echoed Theron, impatiently. "The Quarterly Conference and the Estimating Committee deal with that. The trustees have no more to do with it than the man in the moon."

"Come, come, Brother Ware," put in Erastus Winch, "we mustn't have no hard feelin's. Brother love is what we're all lookin' after. Brother Pierce's meanin' wasn't agin your drawin' your full salary, every cent of it, only — only there are certain little things connected with the parsonage here that we feel you ought to bear. F'r instance, there's the new sidewalk we had to lay in front of the house here only a month ago. Of course, if the treasury was flush we wouldn't say a word about it. An' then there's the gas bill here. Seein' as you get your rent for nothin', it don't seem much to ask that you should see to lightin' the place yourself."

"No, I don't think that either is a proper charge upon me," interposed Theron. "I decline to pay them."

"We can have the gas shut off," remarked Brother Pierce, coldly.

"As soon as you like," responded the minister, sitting erect and tapping the carpet nervously with his foot. "Only you must understand that I will take the whole matter to the Quarterly Conference in July. I already see a good many other interesting questions about the financial management of this church which might be appropriately discussed there."

"Oh, come, Brother Ware!" broke in Trustee Winch, with a somewhat agitated assumption of good-feeling. "Surely these are matters we ought to settle amongst ourselves. We never yet asked outsiders to meddle with our business here. It's our motto, Brother Ware. I say, if you've got a motto, stand by it."

"Well, my motto," said Theron, "is to be behaved decently to by those with whom I have to deal; and I also propose to stand by it."

Brother Pierce rose gingerly to his feet, with the hesitation of an old man not sure about his knees. When he had straightened himself, he put on his hat, and eyed the minister sternly from beneath its brim.

"The Lord gives us crosses grievous to our natur'," he said, "an we're told to bear 'em cheerfully as long as they're on our backs; but there ain't nothin' said agin our unloadin' 'em in the ditch the minute we git the chance. I guess you won't last here more'n a twelve-month."

He pulled his soft and discolored old hat down over his brows with a significantly hostile nod, and, turning, stumped toward the hall-door without offering to shake hands.

The other trustees had risen likewise, in tacit recognition that the meeting was over. Winch clasped the minister's hand in his own broad, hard palm, and squeezed it in an exuberant grip. "Don't mind his little ways, Brother Ware," he urged in a loud, unctuous whisper, with a grinning backward nod: "he's a trifle skittish sometimes when you don't give him free rein; but he's all wool an' a yard wide when it comes to right-down hard-pan religion. My love to Sister Ware;" and he followed the senior trustee into the hall.

Mr. Gorringe had been tying up his books and papers. He came now with the bulky parcel under his arm, and his hat and stick in the other hand. He could give little but his thumb to Theron to shake. His face wore a grave expression, and not a line relaxed as, catching the minister's look, he slowly covered his left eye in a deliberate wink.

.   .   .   .   .

"Well? — and how did it go off?" asked Alice, from where she knelt by the oven door, a few minutes later.

For answer, Theron threw himself wearily into the big old farm rocking-chair on the other side of the stove, and shook his head with a lengthened sigh.

"If it wasn't for that man Gorringe of yours," he said dejectedly, "I think *I* should feel like going off — and learning a trade."

CHAPTER IV

On the following Sunday, young Mrs. Ware sat alone in the preacher's pew through the morning service, and everybody noted that the roses had been taken from her bonnet. In the evening she was absent, and after the doxology and benediction several people, under the pretence of solicitude for her health, tried to pump her husband as to the reason. He answered their inquiries civilly enough, but with brevity: she had stayed at home because she did not feel like coming out, — this and nothing more.

The congregation dispersed under a gossip-laden cloud of consciousness that there must be something queer about Sister Ware. There was a tolerably general agreement, however, that the two sermons of the day had been excellent. Not even Loren Pierce's railing commentary on the pastor's introduction of an outlandish word like epitome — clearly forbidden by the Discipline's injunction to plain language understood of the people — availed to sap the satisfaction of the majority.

Theron himself comprehended that he had pleased the bulk of his auditors; the knowledge left him curiously hot and cold. On the one hand, there was joy in the apparent prospect that the congregation would back him up in a stand against the trustees, if worst came to worst. But, on the other, the bonnet episode entered his soul. It had been a source of bitter humiliation to him to see his wife sitting there beneath the pulpit, shorn by despotic order of the adornments natural to her pretty head. But he had even greater pain in contemplating the effect it had produced upon Alice herself. She had said not a word on the subject, but her every glance and gesture seemed to him eloquent of deep feeling about it. He made sure that she blamed him for having defended his own gas and sidewalk rights with successful vigor, but permitted the sacrifice of her poor little inoffensive roses without a protest. In this view of the matter, indeed, he blamed himself. Was it too late to make the error good? He ventured a hint on this Sunday evening, when he returned to the parsonage and found her reading an old weekly news- paper by the light of the kitchen lamp, to the effect that he fancied there would be no great danger in putting those roses back into her bonnet. Without lifting her eyes from the paper, she answered that she had no earthly desire to wear roses in her bonnet, and went on with her reading.

At breakfast next morning Theron found himself in com- mand of an unusual fund of humorous good spirits, and was at pains to make the most of it, passing whimsical comments on subjects which the opening day suggested, recalling quaint and comical memories of the past, and striving his best to force Alice into a laugh. Formerly her merry temper had al- ways ignited at the merest spark of gayety. Now she gave his jokes only a dutiful half-smile, and uttered scarcely a word in response to his running fire of talk. When the meal was fin- ished, she went silently to work to clear away the dishes.

Theron turned over in his mind the project of offering to help her, as he had done so often in those dear old days when they laughingly began life together. Something decided this project in the negative for him, and after a few lingering moments he put on his hat and went out for a walk.

Not even the most doleful and trying hour of his bitter experience in Tyre had depressed him like this. Looking back upon those past troubles, he persuaded himself that he had borne them all with a light and cheerful heart, simply because Alice had been one with him in every thought and emotion. How perfect, how ideally complete, their sympathy had always been! With what absolute unity of mind and soul they had walked that difficult path together! And now — henceforth — was it to be different? The mere suggestion of such a thing chilled his veins. He said aloud to himself as he walked that life would be an intolerable curse if Alice were to cease sharing it with him in every conceivable phase.

He had made his way out of the town, and tramped along

ever since that memorable discovery of indebtedness in Tyre, and had long ago recognized the hopelessness of endeavor in every channel save that of literature. Latterly his fancy had been stimulated by reading an account of the profits which Canon Farrar had derived from his "Life of Christ." If such a book could command such a bewildering multitude of readers, Theron felt that there ought to be a chance for him. So clear did constant rumination render this assumption that the young pastor in time had come to regard this prospective book of his as a substantial asset, which could be realized without trouble whenever he got around to it.

He had not, it is true, gone to the length of seriously considering what should be the subject of his book. That had not seemed to him to matter much, so long as it was scriptural. Familiarity with the process of extracting a fixed amount of spiritual and intellectual meat from any casual text, week after week, had given him an idea that any one of many subjects would do, when the time came for him to make a choice. He realized now that the time for a selection had arrived, and almost simultaneously found himself with a ready-made decision in his mind. The book should be about Abraham!

Theron Ware was extremely interested in the mechanism of his own brain, and followed its workings with a lively curiosity. Nothing could be more remarkable, he thought, than to thus discover that, on the instant of his formulating a desire to know what he should write upon, lo, and behold! there his mind, quite on its own initiative, had the answer waiting for him! When he had gone a little further, and the powerful range of possibilities in the son's revolt against the idolatry of his father, the image-maker, in the exodus from the unholy city of Ur, and in the influence of the new nomadic life upon the little deistic family group, had begun to unfold itself before him, he felt that the hand of Providence was plainly discernible in the matter. The book was to be blessed from its very inception.

Walking homeward briskly now, with his eyes on the side-

the country hill-road for a considerable distance, before a
merciful light began to lessen the shadows in the picture of
gloom with which his mind tortured itself. All at once he
stopped short, lifted his head, and looked about him. The
broad valley lay warm and tranquil in the May sunshine at
his feet. In the thicket up the side-hill above him a gray
squirrel was chattering shrilly, and the birds sang in tireless
choral confusion. Theron smiled, and drew a long breath.
The gay clamor of the woodland songsters, the placid radiance
of the landscape, were suddenly taken in and made a part of
his new mood. He listened, smiled once more, and then
started in a leisurely way back toward Octavius.

How could he have been so ridiculous as to fancy that
Alice — his Alice — had been changed into some one else? He
marvelled now at his own perverse folly. She was overworked,
tired out, — that was all. The task of moving in, of setting
the new household to rights, had been too much for her. She
must have a rest. They must get in a hired girl.

Once this decision about a servant fixed itself in the young
minister's mind, it drove out the last vestige of discomfort.
He strode along now in great content, revolving idly a dozen
different plans for gilding and beautifying this new life of
leisure into which his sanguine thoughts projected Alice. One
of these particularly pleased him, and waxed in definiteness as
he turned it over and over. He would get another piano for
her, in place of that which had been sacrificed in Tyre. That
beneficent modern invention, the instalment plan, made
this quite feasible, — so easy, in fact, that it almost seemed
as if he should find his wife playing on the new instrument
when he got home. He would stop [1] in at the music store and
see about it that very day.

Of course, now that these important resolutions had been
taken, it would be a good thing if he could do something to
bring in some extra money. This was by no means a new
notion. He had mused over the possibility in a formless way

[1] English ed. reads "step" for "stop."

walk and his mind all aglow with crowding suggestions for the new work, and impatience to be at it, he came abruptly upon a group of men and boys who occupied the whole path, and were moving forward so noiselessly that he had not heard them coming. He almost ran into the leader of this little procession, and began a stammering apology, the final words of which were left unspoken, so solemnly heedless of him and his talk were all the faces he saw.

In the centre of the group were four workingmen, bearing between them an extemporized litter of two poles and a blanket hastily secured across them with spikes. Most of what this litter held was covered by another blanket, rounded in coarse folds over a shapeless bulk. From beneath its farther end protruded a big broom-like black beard, thrown upward at such an angle as to hide everything beyond to those in front. The tall young minister, stepping aside and standing tip-toe, could see sloping downward behind this hedge of beard a pinched and chalk-like face, with wide-open, staring eyes. Its lips, of a dull lilac hue, were moving ceaselessly, and made a dry, clicking sound.

Theron instinctively joined himself to those who followed the litter, — a motley dozen of street idlers, chiefly boys. One of these in whispers explained to him that the man was one of Jerry Madden's workmen in the wagon-shops, who had been deployed to trim an elm-tree in front of his employer's house, and, being unused to such work, had fallen from the top and broken all his bones. They would have cared for him at Madden's house, but he had insisted upon being taken home. His name was MacEvoy, and he was Joey MacEvoy's father, and likewise Jim's and Hughey's and Martin's. After a pause the lad, a bright-eyed, freckled, barefooted wee Irishman, volunteered the further information that his big brother had run to bring "Father Forbess," on the chance that he might be in time to administer "extry munction."

The way of the silent little procession led through back streets — where women hanging up clothes in the yards hurried to the gates, their aprons full of clothes-pins, to stare open-mouthed at the passers-by — and came to a halt at last in an irregular and muddy lane, before one of a half dozen shanties reared among the ash-heaps and débris [2] of the town's most bedraggled outskirts.

A stout, middle-aged, red-armed woman, already warned by some messenger of calamity, stood waiting on the roadside bank. There were whimpering children clinging to her skirts, and a surrounding cluster of women of the neighborhood, some of the more elderly of whom, shrivelled little crones in tidy caps, and with their aprons to their eyes, were beginning in a low-murmured minor the wail which presently should rise into the keen of death. Mrs. MacEvoy herself made no moan, and her broad ruddy face was stern in expression rather than sorrowful. When the litter stopped beside her, she laid a hand for an instant on her husband's wet brow, and looked — one could have sworn impassively — into his staring eyes. Then, still without a word, she waved the bearers toward the door, and led the way herself.

Theron, somewhat wonderingly, found himself, a minute later, inside a dark and ill-smelling room, the air of which was humid with the steam from a boiler of clothes on the stove, and not in other ways improved by the presence of a jostling score of women, all straining their gaze upon the open door of the only other apartment, — the bed-chamber. Through this they could see the workmen laying MacEvoy on the bed, and standing awkwardly about thereafter, getting in the way of the wife and old Maggie Quirk as they strove to remove the garments from his crushed limbs. As the neighbors watched what could be seen of these proceedings, they whispered among themselves eulogies of the injured man's industry and good temper, his habit of bringing his money home to his wife, and the way he kept his Father Mathew pledge and attended to his religious duties. They admitted freely that, by the light of his example, their own

[2] English ed. reads "rubbish" for "débris."

husbands and sons left much to be desired, and from this wandered easily off into domestic digressions of their own. But all the while their eyes were bent upon the bedroom door; and Theron made out, after he had grown accustomed to the gloom and the smell, that many of them were telling their beads even while they kept the muttered conversation alive. None of them paid any attention to him, or seemed to regard his presence there as unusual.

Presently he saw enter through the sunlit street doorway a person of a different class. The bright light shone for a passing instant upon a fashionable, flowered hat, and upon some remarkably brilliant shade of red hair beneath it. In another moment there had edged along through the throng, to almost within touch of him, a tall young woman, the owner of this hat and wonderful hair. She was clad in light and pleasing spring attire, and carried a parasol with a long oxidized silver handle of a quaint pattern. She looked at him, and he saw that her face was of a lengthened oval, with a luminous rose-tinted skin, full red lips, and big brown, frank eyes with heavy auburn lashes. She made a grave little inclination of her head toward him, and he bowed in response. Since her arrival, he noted, the chattering of the others had entirely ceased.

"I followed the others in, in the hope that I might be of some assistance," he ventured to explain to her in a low murmur, feeling that at last here was some one to whom an explanation of his presence in this Romish house was due. "I hope they won't feel that I have intruded."

She nodded her head as if she quite understood. "They'll take the will for the deed," she whispered back. "Father Forbes will be here in a minute. Do you know is it too late?"

Even as she spoke, the outer doorway was darkened by the commanding bulk of a new-comer's figure. The flash of a silk hat, and the deferential way [3] in which the assembled neighbors fell back to clear a passage, made his identity

---

[3] English ed. reads "haste" for "way."

clear. Theron felt his blood tingle in an unaccustomed way as this priest of a strange church advanced across the room, — a broad-shouldered, portly man of more than middle height, with a shapely, strong-lined face of almost waxen pallor, and a firm, commanding tread. He carried in his hands, besides his hat, a small leather-bound case. To this and to him the women courtesied and bowed their heads as he passed.

"Come with me," whispered the tall girl with the parasol to Theron; and he found himself pushing along in her wake until they intercepted the priest just outside the bedroom door. She touched Father Forbes on the arm.

"Just to tell you that I am here," she said. The priest nodded with a grave face, and passed into the other room. In a minute or two the workmen, Mrs. MacEvoy, and her helper came out, and the door was shut behind them.

"He is making his confession," explained the young lady. "Stay here for a minute."

She moved over to where the woman of the house stood, glum-faced and tearless, and whispered something to her. A confused movement among the crowd followed, and out of it presently resulted a small table, covered with a white cloth, and bearing on it two unlighted candles, a basin of water, and a spoon, which was brought forward and placed in readiness before the closed door. Some of those nearest this cleared space were kneeling now, and murmuring a low buzz of prayer to the click of beads on their rosaries.

The door opened, and Theron saw the priest standing in the doorway with an uplifted hand. He wore now a surplice, with a purple band over his shoulders, and on his pale face there shone a tranquil and tender light.

One of the workmen fetched from the stove a brand, lighted the two candles, and bore the table with its contents into the bedroom. The young woman plucked Theron's sleeve, and he dumbly followed her into the chamber of death, making one of the group of a dozen, headed by Mrs. MacEvoy and her children, which filled the little room, and

overflowed now outward to the street door.[4] He found himself bowing with the others to receive the sprinkled holy
water from the priest's white fingers; kneeling with the others
for the prayers; following in impressed silence with the others
the strange ceremonial by which the priest traced crosses of
holy oil with his thumb upon the eyes, ears, nostrils, lips,
hands, and feet of the dying man, wiping off the oil with a
piece of cotton-batting [5] each time after he had repeated the
invocation to forgiveness for that particular sense. But most
of all he was moved by the rich, novel sound of the Latin as
the priest rolled it forth in the *Asperges me, Domine,* and
Misereatur vestri omnipotens Deus, with its soft Continental
vowels and liquid *r*'s. It seemed to him that he had never
really heard Latin before. Then the astonishing young
woman with the red hair declaimed the *Confiteor,* vigorously
and with a resonant distinctness of enunciation. It was a different Latin, harsher and more sonorous; and while it still
dominated the murmured undertone of the other's prayers,
the last moment came.

Theron had stood face to face with death at many other
bedsides; no other final scene had stirred him like this. It
must have been the girl's Latin chant, with its clanging reitera-
tion of the great names, — *beatum Michaelem Archangelum,
beatum Joannem Baptistam, sanctos Apostolos Petrum et
Paulum,* — invoked with such proud confidence in this squalid
little shanty, which so strangely affected him.

He came out with the others at last, — the candles and
the folded hands over the crucifix left behind, — and walked
as one in a dream. Even by the time that he had gained the
outer doorway, and stood blinking at the bright light and
filling his lungs with honest air once more, it had begun
to seem incredible to him that he had seen and done all this.

[4] English ed. reads: "and with difficulty held back the pushing throng
outside" for "and overflowed now outward to the street door."
[5] English ed. reads "cotton-wool" for "cotton-batting."

CHAPTER V

WHILE Mr. Ware stood thus on the doorstep, through a minute of formless musing, the priest and the girl came out, and, somewhat to his confusion, made him one of their party. He felt himself flushing under the idea that they would think he had waited for them — was thrusting himself upon them. The notion prompted him to bow frigidly in response to Father Forbes' pleasant "I am glad to meet you, sir," and his outstretched hand.

"I dropped in by the — the merest accident," Theron said. "I met them bringing the poor man home, and — and quite without thinking, I obeyed the impulse to follow them in, and didn't realize —"

He stopped short, annoyed by the reflection that this was his second apology. The girl smiled placidly at him, the while she put up her parasol.

"It did me good to see you there," she said, quite as if she had known him all her life. "And so it did the rest of us."

Father Forbes permitted himself a soft little chuckle, approving rather than mirthful, and patted her on the shoulder with the air of being fifty years her senior instead of fifteen. To the minister's relief, he changed the subject as the three started together toward the road.

"Then, again, no doctor was sent for!" he exclaimed, as if resuming a familiar subject with the girl. Then he turned to Theron. "I dare-say you have no such trouble; but with our poorer people it is very vexing. They will *not* call in a physician, but hurry off first for the clergyman. I don't know that it is altogether to avoid doctor's bills, but it amounts to that in effect. Of course in this case it made no difference; but I have had to make it a rule not to go out at night unless they bring me a physician's card with his assurance that it is a genuine affair. Why, only last winter, I was routed up after midnight, and brought off in the mud and pelting rain up one of the new streets on the hillside there, simply because a factory girl who was laced too tight had fainted at a dance. I slipped and fell into a puddle in the darkness, ruined a new overcoat, and got drenched to the skin; and when I arrived the girl had recovered and was dancing away again, thirteen to the dozen. It was then that I made the rule. I hope, Mr. Ware, that Octavius is producing a pleasant impression upon you so far?"

"I scarcely know yet," answered Theron. The genial talk of the priest, with its whimsical anecdote, had in truth passed over his head. His mind still had room for nothing but that novel death-bed scene, with the winged captain of the angelic host, the Baptist, the glorified Fisherman, and the Preacher, all being summoned down in the pomp of liturgical Latin to help MacEvoy to die. "If you don't mind my saying so," he added hesitatingly, "what I have just seen in there *did* make a very powerful impression upon me."

"It is a very ancient ceremony," said the priest; "probably Persian, like the baptismal form, although, for that matter, we can never dig deep enough for the roots of these things. They all turn up Turanian if we probe far enough. Our ways separate here, I'm afraid. I am delighted to have made your acquaintance, Mr. Ware. Pray look in upon me, if you can as well as not. We are near neighbors, you know."

Father Forbes had shaken hands, and moved off up another street some distance, before the voice of the girl recalled Theron to himself.

"Of course you knew *him* by name," she was saying, "and he knew *you* by sight, and had talked of you; but *my* poor inferior sex has to be introduced. I am Celia Madden. My father has the wagon-shops, and I — I play the organ at the church."

"I — I am delighted to make your acquaintance," said Theron, conscious as he spoke that he had slavishly echoed the formula of the priest. He could think of nothing better to add than, "Unfortunately, we have no organ in our church."

The girl laughed, as they resumed their walk down the

street. "I'm afraid I couldn't undertake two," she said, and laughed again. Then she spoke more seriously. "That ceremony must have interested you a good deal, never having seen it before. I saw that it was all new to you, and so I made bold to take you under my wing, so to speak."

"You were very kind," said the young minister. "It was really a great experience for me. May — may I ask, is it a part of your functions, in the church, I mean, to attend these last rites?"

"Mercy, no!" replied the girl, spinning the parasol on her shoulder and smiling at the thought. "No; it was only because MacEvoy was one of our workmen, and really came by his death through father sending him up to trim a tree. Ann MacEvoy will never forgive us that, the longest day she lives. Did you notice her? She wouldn't speak to me. After you came out, I tried to tell her that we would look out for her and the children; but all she would say to me was: 'An' fwat would a wheelwright, an' him the father of a family, be doin' up a tree?' "

They had come now upon the main street of the village, with its flagstone sidewalk overhung by a lofty canopy of elm-boughs. Here, for the space of a block, was concentrated such fashionable elegance of mansions and ornamental lawns as Octavius had to offer; and it was presented with the irregularity so characteristic of our restless civilization. Two or three of the houses survived untouched from the earlier days, — prim, decorous structures, each with its gabled centre and lower wings, each with its row of fluted columns supporting the classical roof of a piazza across its whole front, each vying with the others in the whiteness of those wooden walls enveloping its bright green blinds. One had to look over picket fences to see these houses, and in doing so caught the notion that they thus railed themselves off in pride at being able to remember before the railroad came to the village, or the wagon-works were thought of.

Before the neighboring properties the fences had been

swept away, so that one might stroll from the sidewalk straight across the well-trimmed sward to any one of a dozen elaborately modern doorways. Some of the residences, thus frankly proffering friendship to the passer-by, were of wood painted in drabs and dusky reds, with bulging windows which marked the native yearning for the mediæval, and shingles that strove to be accounted tiles. Others — a prouder, less pretentious sort — were of brick or stone, with terra-cotta mouldings set into the walls, and with real slates covering the riot of turrets and peaks and dormer peepholes overhead.

Celia Madden stopped in front of the largest and most important-looking of these new edifices, and said, holding out her hand: "Here I am, once more. Good-morning, Mr. Ware."

Theron hoped that his manner did not betray the flash of surprise he felt in discovering that his new acquaintance lived in the biggest house in Octavius. He remembered now that some one had pointed it out as the abode of the owner of the wagon factories; but it had not occurred to him before to associate this girl with that village magnate. It was stupid of him, of course, because she had herself mentioned her father. He looked at her again with an awkward smile, as he formally shook the gloved hand she gave him, and lifted his soft hat. The strong noon sunlight, forcing its way down between the elms, and beating upon her parasol of lace-edged, creamy silk, made a halo about her hair and face at once brilliant and tender. He had not seen before how beautiful she was. She nodded in recognition of his salute, and moved up the lawn walk, spinning the sunshade on her shoulder.

Though the parsonage was only three blocks away, the young minister had time to think about a good many things before he reached home.

First of all, he had to revise in part the arrangement of his notions about the Irish. Save for an occasional isolated and taciturn figure among the nomadic portion of the hired help in the farm country, Theron had scarcely ever spoken to a

person of this curiously alien race before. He remembered
now that there had been some dozen or more Irish families
in Tyre, quartered in the outskirts among the brickyards,
but he had never come in contact with any of them, or given
to their existence even a passing thought. So far as personal
acquaintance went, the Irish had been to him only a name.

But what a sinister and repellent name! His views on this
general subject were merely those common to his communion
and his environment. He took it for granted, for example,
that in the large cities most of the poverty and all the drunk-
enness, crime, and political corruption were due to the perverse qualities of this foreign people, — qualities accentuated
and emphasized in every evil direction by the baleful influence of a false and idolatrous religion. It is hardly too
much to say that he had never encountered a dissenting
opinion on this point. His boyhood had been spent in those
bitter days when social, political, and blood prejudices were
fused at white heat in the public crucible together.[1] When
he went to the Church Seminary, it was a matter of course
that every member of the faculty was a Republican, and that
every one of his classmates had come from a Republican
household. When, later on, he entered the ministry, the rule
was still incredulous of exceptions. One might as well have
looked in the Nedahma Conference for a divergence of opinion on the Trinity as for a difference in political conviction.
Indeed, even among the laity, Theron could not feel sure
that he had ever known a Democrat; that is, at all closely.
He understood very little about politics, it is true. If he had
been driven into a corner, and forced to attempt an explanation of this tremendous partisan unanimity in which he had
a share, he would probably have first mentioned the War, —
the last shots of which were fired while he was still in petti-
coats. Certainly his second reason, however, would have been
that the Irish were on the other side.

[1] English ed. reads "crucible of War together" for "public crucible together."

He had never before had occasion to formulate, even in his own thoughts, this tacit race and religious aversion in which he had been bred. It rose now suddenly in front of him, as he sauntered from patch to patch of sunlight under the elms, like some huge, shadowy, and symbolical monument. He looked at it with wondering curiosity, as at something he had heard of all his life, but never seen before, — an abhorrent spectacle, truly! The foundations upon which its dark bulk reared itself were ignorance, squalor, brutality, and vice. Pigs wallowed in the mire before its base, and burrowing into this base were a myriad of narrow doors, each bearing the hateful sign of a saloon, and giving forth from its recesses of night the sounds of screams and curses. Above were sculptured rows of lowering, ape-like faces from Nast's and Keppler's cartoons, and out of these sprang into the vague upper gloom, on the one side, lamp-posts from which negroes hung by the neck, and on the other gibbets for dynamiters and Molly Maguires; and between the two glowed a spectral picture of some black-robed, tonsured men, with leering satanic masks, making a bonfire of the Bible in the public schools.

Theron stared this phantasm hard in the face, and recognized it for a very tolerable embodiment of what he had heretofore supposed he thought about the Irish. For an instant, the sight of it made him shiver, as if the sunny May had of a sudden lapsed into bleak December. Then he smiled, and the bad vision went off into space. He saw instead Father Forbes, in the white and purple vestments, standing by poor MacEvoy's bedside, with his pale, chiselled, luminous, uplifted face, and he heard only the proud, confident clanging of the girl's recital, — *beatum Michaelem Archangelum, beatum Joannem Baptistam, Petrum et Paulum — em! am! um!* — like strokes on a great resonant alarm-bell, attuned for the hearing of heaven. He caught himself on the very verge of feeling that heaven must have heard.

Then he smiled again, and laid the matter aside, with a

parting admission that it had been undoubtedly picturesque
and impressive, and that it had been a valuable experience
to him to see it. At least the Irish, with all their faults, must
have a poetic strain, or they would not have clung so tena-
ciously to those curious and ancient forms. He recalled having heard somewhere, or read, it might be, that they were a
people much given to songs and music. And the young lady,
that very handsome and friendly Miss Madden, had told
him that she was a musician! He had a new pleasure in turning this over in his mind. Of all the closed doors which his
choice of a career had left along his pathway, no other had
for him such a magical fascination as that on which was
graven the lute of Orpheus. He knew not even the alphabet
of music, and his conceptions of its possibilities ran but little
beyond the best of the hymn-singing he had heard at Con-
ferences, yet none the less the longing for it raised on occasion such mutiny in his soul that more than once he had
specifically prayed against it as a temptation.

Dangerous though some of its tendencies might be, there
was no gainsaying the fact that a love for music was in the
main an uplifting influence, — an attribute of cultivation.
The world was the sweeter and more gentle for it. And this
brought him to musing upon the odd chance that the two
people of Octavius who had given him the first notion of
polish and intellectual culture in the town should be Irish.
The Romish priest must have been vastly surprised at his
intrusion, yet had been at the greatest pains to act as if it
were quite the usual thing to have Methodist ministers assist
at Extreme Unction. And the young woman, — how gracefully, with what delicacy, had she comprehended his position
and robbed it of all its possible embarrassments! It occurred
to him that they must have passed, there in front of her
home, the very tree from which the luckless wheelwright had
fallen some hours before; and the fact that she had forborne
to point it out to him took form in his mind as an added
proof of her refinement of nature.

The midday dinner was a little more than ready when Theron reached home, and let himself in by the front door. On Mondays, owing to the moisture and "clutter" of the weekly washing in the kitchen, the table was laid in the sitting-room, and as he entered from the hall the partner of his joys bustled in by the other door, bearing the steaming platter of corned beef, dumplings, cabbages, and carrots, with arms bared to the elbows, and a red face. It gave him great comfort, however, to note that there were no signs of the morning's displeasure remaining on this face; and he immediately remembered again those interrupted projects of his about the piano and the hired girl.

"Well! I'd just about begun to reckon that I was a widow," said Alice, putting down her fragrant burden. There was such an obvious suggestion of propitiation in her tone that Theron went around and kissed her. He thought of saying something about keeping out of the way because it was "Blue Monday," but held it back lest it should sound like a reproach.

"Well, what kind of a washerwoman does *this* one turn out to be?" he asked, after they were seated, and he had invoked a blessing and was cutting vigorously into the meat.

"Oh, so-so," replied Alice; "she seems to be particular, but she's mortal slow. If I hadn't stood right over her, we shouldn't have had the clothes out till goodness knows when. And of course she's Irish!"

"Well, what of *that*?" asked the minister, with a fine unconcern.

Alice looked up from her plate, with knife and fork suspended in air. "Why, you know we were talking only the other day of what a pity it was that none of our own people went out washing," she said. "That Welsh woman we heard of couldn't come, after all; and they say, too, that she presumes dreadfully upon the acquaintance, being a church member, you know. So we simply *had* to fall back on the Irish. And even if they do go and tell their priest everything they see and hear, why, there's one comfort, they can tell about *us* and welcome. Of course I see to it she doesn't snoop around in here."

Theron smiled. "That's all nonsense about their telling such things to their priests," he said with easy confidence.

"Why, you told me so yourself," replied Alice, briskly. "And I've always understood so, too; they're bound to tell *everything* in confession. That's what gives the Catholic Church such a tremendous hold. You've spoken of it often."

"It must have been by way of a figure of speech," remarked Theron, not with entire directness. "Women are great hands to separate one's observations from their context, and so give them meanings quite unintended. They are also great hands," he added genially, "or at least one of them is, at making the most delicious dumplings in the world. I believe these are the best even you ever made."

Alice was not unmindful of the compliment, but her thoughts were on other things. "I shouldn't like that woman's priest, for example," she said, "to know that we had no piano."

"But if he comes and stands outside our house every night and listens, — as of course he will," said Theron, with mock gravity, "it is only a question of time when he must reach that conclusion for himself. Our only chance, however, is that there are some sixteen hundred other houses for him to watch, so that he may not get around to us for quite a spell. Why, seriously, Alice, what on earth do you suppose Father Forbes knows or cares about our poor little affairs, or those of any other Protestant household in this whole village? He has his work to do, just as I have mine, — only his is ten times as exacting in everything except sermons, — and you may be sure he is only too glad when it is over each day, without bothering about things that are none of his business."

"All the same, I'm afraid of them," said Alice, as if argument were exhausted.

CHAPTER VI

On the following morning young Mr. Ware anticipated events by inscribing in his diary for the day, immediately after breakfast, these remarks: "Arranged about piano. Began work upon book."

The date indeed deserved to be distinguished from its fellows. Theron was so conscious of its importance that he not only prophesied in the little morocco-bound diary which Alice had given him for Christmas, but returned after he had got out upon the front steps of the parsonage to have his hat brushed afresh by her.

"Wonders will never cease," she said jocosely. "With you getting particular about your clothes, there isn't anything in this wide world that can't happen now!"

"One doesn't go out to bring home a piano every day," he made answer. "Besides, I want to make such an impression upon the man that he will deal gently with that first cash payment down. Do you know," he added, watching her turn the felt brim under the wisp-broom's strokes, "I'm thinking some of getting me a regular silk stove-pipe hat."

"Why don't you, then?" she rejoined, but without any ring of glad acquiescence in her tone. He fancied that her face lengthened a little, and he instantly ascribed it to recollections of the way in which the roses had been bullied out of her own headgear.

"You are quite sure, now, pet," he made haste to change the subject, "that the hired girl can wait just as well as not until fall?"

"Oh, *my,* yes!" Alice replied, putting the hat on his head, and smoothing back his hair behind her ears. "She'd only be in the way now. You see, with hot weather coming on, there won't be much cooking. We'll take all our meals out here,[1]

---

[1] English ed. reads "We'll just pick a bite here and there" for "We'll take all our meals out here."

and that saves so much work that really what remains is hardly more than taking care of a bird-cage. And, besides, not having her will almost half pay for the piano."

"But when cold weather comes, you're sure you'll consent? he urged.

"Like a shot!" she assured him, and, after a happy little caress, he started out again on his momentous mission.

"Thurston's" was a place concerning which opinions differed in Octavius. That it typified progress, and helped more than any other feature of the village to bring it up to date, no one indeed disputed. One might move about a great deal, in truth, and hear no other view expressed. But then again one might stumble into conversation with one small store-keeper after another, and learn that they united in resenting the existence of "Thurston's," as rival farmers might join to curse a protracted drought. Each had his special flaming grievance. The little dry-goods dealers asked mournfully how they could be expected to compete with an establishment which could buy bankrupt stocks at a hundred different points, and make a profit if only one-third of the articles were sold for more than they would cost from the jobber? The little boot and shoe dealers, clothiers, hatters, and furriers, the small merchants in carpets, crockery, and furniture, the venders of hardware and household utensils, of leathern goods and picture-frames, of wall-paper, musical instruments, and even toys, — all had the same pathetically unanswerable question to propound. But mostly they put it to themselves, because the others were at "Thurston's."

The Rev. Theron Ware had entertained rather strong views on this subject, and that only a week or two ago. One of his first acquaintances in Octavius had been the owner of the principal book-store in the place, — a gentle and bald old man who produced the complete impression of a biblio-phile upon what the slightest investigation showed to be only a meagre acquaintance with publishers' circulars. But at least he had the air of loving his business, and the young

minister had enjoyed a long talk with, or rather, at him. Out
of this talk had come the information that the store was losing money. Not even the stationery department now showed
a profit worth mentioning. When Octavius had contained
only five thousand inhabitants, it boasted four book-stores,
two of them good ones. Now, with a population more than
doubled, only these latter two survived, and they must soon
go to the wall. The reason? It was in a nutshell. A book which
sold at retail for one dollar and a half cost the bookseller
ninety cents. If it was at all a popular book, "Thurston's"
advertised it at eighty-nine cents, — and in any case at a profit
of only two or three cents. Of course it was done to widen the
establishment's patronage, — to bring people into the store.
Equally of course, it was destroying the book business and
debauching the reading tastes of the community. Without
the profits from the light and ephemeral popular literature
of the season, the book-store proper could not keep up its
stock of more solid works, and indeed could not long keep
open at all. On the other hand, "Thurston's" dealt with
nothing save the demand of the moment, and offered only
the books which were the talk of the week. Thus, in plain
words, the book trade was going to the dogs, and it was the
same with pretty nearly every other trade.

Theron was indignant at this, and on his return home told
Alice that he desired her to make no purchases whatever at
"Thurston's." He even resolved to preach a sermon on the
subject of the modern idea of admiring the great for crushing the small, and sketched out some notes for it which he
thought solved the problem of flaying the local abuse without mentioning it by name. They had lain on his desk now
for ten days or more, and on only the previous Friday he
had speculated upon using them that coming Sunday.

On this bright and cheerful Tuesday morning he walked
with a blithe step unhesitatingly down the main street to
"Thurston's," and entered without any show of repugnance
the door next to the window wherein, flanked by dangling

banjos and key-bugles built in pyramids, was displayed the sign, "Pianos on the Instalment Plan."

He was recognized by some responsible persons, and treated with distinguished deference. They were charmed with the intelligence that he desired a piano, and fascinated by his wish to pay for it only a little at a time. They had special terms for clergymen, and made him feel as if these were being extended to him on a silver charger by kneeling admirers.[2]

It was so easy to buy things here that he was a trifle disturbed to find his flowing course interrupted by his own entire ignorance as to what kind of piano he wanted. He looked at all they had in stock, and heard them played upon. They differed greatly in price, and, so he fancied, almost as much in tone. It discouraged him to note, however, that several of those he thought the finest in tone were among the very cheapest in the lot. Pondering this, and staring in hopeless puzzlement from one to another of the big black shiny monsters, he suddenly thought of something.

"I would rather not decide for myself," he said, "I know so little about it. If you don't mind, I will have a friend of mine, a skilled musician, step in and make a selection. I have so much confidence in — in *her* judgment." He added hurriedly, "It will involve only a day or two's delay."

The next moment he was sorry he had spoken. What would they think when they saw the organist of the Catholic church come to pick out a piano for the Methodist parsonage? And how could he decorously prefer the request to her to undertake this task? He might not meet her again for ages, and to his provincial notions writing would have seemed out of the question. And would it not be disagreeable to have her know that he was buying a piano by part payments? Poor Alice's dread of the washerwoman's gossip occurred to him, at this, and he smiled in spite of himself. Then all at once the difficulty vanished. Of course it would come all right somehow. Everything did.

---

[2] English ed. reads "by kneeling admirers on a silver charger" for "on a silver charger by kneeling admirers."

He was on firmer ground, buying the materials for the new book, over on the stationery side. His original intention had been to bestow this patronage upon the old bookseller, but these suavely smart people in "Thurston's" had had the effect of putting him on his honor when they asked, "Would there be anything else?" and he had followed them unresistingly.

He indulged to the full his whim that everything entering into the construction of "Abraham" should be spick-and-span. He watched with his own eyes a whole ream of broad glazed white paper being sliced down by the cutter into single sheets, and thrilled with a novel ecstasy as he laid his hand upon the spotless bulk, so wooingly did it invite him to begin. He tried a score of pens before the right one came to hand. When a box of these had been laid aside, with ink and pen-holders and a little bronze inkstand, he made a sign that the outfit was complete. Or no — there must be some blotting-paper. He had always used those blotting-pads given away by insurance companies, — his congregations never failed to contain one or more agents, who had these to bestow by the armful, — but the book deserved a virgin blotter.

Theron stood by while all these things were being tied up together in a parcel. The suggestion that they should be sent almost hurt him. Oh, no, he would carry them home himself. So strongly did they appeal to his sanguine imagination that he could not forbear hinting to the man who had shown him the pianos and was now accompanying him to the door that this package under his arm represented potentially the price of the piano he was going to have. He did it in a roundabout way, with one of his droll, hesitating smiles. The man did not understand at all, and Theron had not the temerity to repeat the remark. He strode home with the precious bundle as fast as he could.

"I thought it best, after all, not to commit myself to a selection," he explained about the piano at dinner-time. "In such a matter as this, the opinion of an expert is everything. I am going to have one of the principal musicians of the town go and try them all, and tell me which we ought to have."

"And while he's about it," said Alice, "you might ask him to make a little list of some of the new music. I've got way behind the times, being without a piano so long. Tell him not any *very* difficult pieces, you know."

"Yes, I know," put in Theron, almost hastily, and began talking of other things. His conversation was of the most rambling and desultory sort, because all the while the two lobes of his brain, as it were, kept up a dispute as to whether Alice ought to have been told that this "principal musician" was of her own sex. It would certainly have been better, at the outset, he decided; but to mention it now would be to invest the fact with undue importance. Yes, that was quite clear; only the clearer it became, from one point of view, the shadier it waxed from the other. The problem really disturbed the young minister's mind throughout the meal, and his abstraction became so marked at last that his wife commented upon it.

"A penny for your thoughts!" she said, with cheerful briskness. This ancient formula of the farm-land had always rather jarred on Theron. It presented itself now to his mind as a peculiarly aggravating banality.

"I am going to begin my book this afternoon," he remarked impressively. "There is a great deal to think about."

It turned out that there was even more to think about than he had imagined. After hours of solitary musing at his desk, or of pacing up and down before his open book-shelves, Theron found the first shadows of a May-day twilight beginning to fall upon that beautiful pile of white paper, still unstained by ink. He saw the book he wanted to write before him, in his mental vision, much more distinctly than ever, but the idea of beginning it impetuously, and hurling it off hot and glowing week by week, had faded away like a dream.

This long afternoon, spent face to face with a project born of his own brain but yesterday, yet already so much bigger than himself, was really a most fruitful time for the young clergyman. The lessons which cut most deeply into our consciousness are those we learn from our children. Theron, in this first day's contact with the offspring of his fancy, found revealed to him an unsuspected and staggering truth. It was that he was an extremely ignorant and rudely untrained young man, whose pretensions to intellectual authority among any educated people would be laughed at with deserved contempt.

Strangely enough, after he had weathered the first shock, this discovery did not dismay Theron Ware. The very completeness of the conviction it carried with it, saturated his mind with a feeling as if the fact had really been known to him all along. And there came, too, after a little, an almost pleasurable sense of the importance of the revelation. He had been merely drifting in fatuous and conceited blindness. Now all at once his eyes were open; he knew what he had to do. Ignorance was a thing to be remedied, and he would forthwith bend all his energies to cultivating his mind till it should blossom like a garden. In this mood, Theron mentally measured himself against the more conspicuous of his colleagues in the Conference. They also were ignorant, clownishly ignorant: the difference was that they were doomed by native incapacity to go on all their lives without ever finding it out. It was obvious to him that his case was better. There was bright promise in the very fact that he had discovered his shortcomings.

He had begun the afternoon by taking down from their places the various works in his meagre library which bore more or less relation to the task in hand. The threescore books which constituted his printed possessions were almost wholly from the press of the Book Concern; the few exceptions were volumes which, though published elsewhere, had come to him through that giant circulating agency of the General Conference, and wore the stamp of its approval. Perhaps it was the sight of these half-filled shelves which started this day's great revolution in Theron's opinions of himself. He had never thought much before about owning books. He had been too poor to buy many, and the conditions of canvassing about among one's parishioners which the thrifty Book Concern imposes upon those who would have without buying, had always repelled him. Now, suddenly, as he moved along the two shelves, he felt ashamed at their beggarly showing.

"The Land and the Book," in three portly volumes, was the most pretentious of the aids which he finally culled from his collection. Beside it he laid out "Bible Lands," "Rivers and Lakes of Scripture," "Bible Manners and Customs," the "Genesis and Exodus" volume of Whedon's Commentary, some old numbers of the "Methodist Quarterly Review," and a copy of "Josephus" which had belonged to his grandmother, and had seen him through many a weary Sunday afternoon in boyhood. He glanced casually through these, one by one, as he took them down, and began to fear that they were not going to be of so much use as he had thought. Then, seating himself, he read carefully through the thirteen chapters of Genesis which chronicle the story of the founder of Israel.

Of course he had known this story from his earliest years. In almost every chapter he came now upon a phrase or an incident which had served him as the basis for a sermon. He had preached about Hagar in the wilderness, about Lot's wife, about the visit of the angels, about the intended sacrifice of Isaac, about a dozen other things suggested by the ancient narrative. Somehow this time it all seemed different to him. The people he read about were altered to his vision. Heretofore a poetic light had shone about them, where indeed they had not glowed in a halo of sanctification. Now, by some chance, this light was gone, and he saw them instead as untutored and unwashed barbarians, filled with animal lusts and ferocities, struggling by violence and foul chicanery to secure a foothold in a country which did not belong to them, — all rude tramps and robbers of the uncivilized plain.

The apparent fact that Abram was a Chaldean struck him with peculiar force. How was it, he wondered, that this had never occurred to him before? Examining himself, he found that he had supposed vaguely that there had been Jews from the beginning, or at least, say, from the flood. But, no, Abram was introduced simply as a citizen of the Chaldean town of Ur, and there was no hint of any difference in race between him and his neighbors. It was specially mentioned that his brother, Lot's father, died in Ur, the city of his nativity. Evidently the family belonged there, and were Chaldeans like the rest.

I do not cite this as at all a striking discovery, but it did have a curious effect upon Theron Ware. Up to that very afternoon, his notion of the kind of book he wanted to write had been founded upon a popular book called "Ruth the Moabitess," written by a clergyman he knew very well, the Rev. E. Ray Mifflin. This model performance troubled itself not at all with difficult points, but went swimmingly along through scented summer seas of pretty rhetoric, teaching nothing, it is true, but pleasing a good deal and selling like hot cakes. Now, all at once Theron felt that he hated that sort of book. *His* work should be of a vastly different order. He might fairly assume, he thought, that if the fact that Abram was a Chaldean was new to him, it would fall upon the world in general as a novelty. Very well, then, there was his chance. He would write a learned book, showing who the Chaldeans were, and how their manners and beliefs differed from, and influenced —

It was at this psychological instant that the wave of self-condemnation suddenly burst upon and submerged the young clergyman. It passed again, leaving him staring fixedly at the pile of books he had taken down from the shelves, and gasping a little, as if for breath. Then the humorous side of the thing, perversely enough, appealed to him, and he grinned feebly to himself at the joke of his having imagined that he could write learnedly about the Chaldeans, or anything else. But, no, it shouldn't remain a joke! His long mobile face grew serious under the new resolve. He would

learn what there was to be learned about the Chaldeans. He
rose and walked up and down the room, gathering fresh
strength of purpose as this inviting field of research spread
out its vistas before him. Perhaps — yes, he would incidentally
explore the mysteries of the Moabitic past as well, and thus
put the Rev. E. Ray Mifflin to confusion on his own subject.
That would in itself be a useful thing, because Mifflin wore
kid gloves at the Conference, and affected an intolerable
superiority of dress and demeanor, and there would be
general satisfaction among the plainer and worthier brethren
at seeing him taken down a peg.

Now for the first time there rose distinctly in Theron's
mind that casual allusion which Father Forbes had made to
the Turanians. He recalled, too, his momentary feeling of
mortification at not knowing who the Turanians were, at the
time. Possibly, if he had probed this matter more deeply,
now as he walked and pondered in the little living-room, he
might have traced the whole of the afternoon's mental experiences to that chance remark of the Romish priest. But
this speculation did not detain him. He mused instead upon
the splendid library Father Forbes must have.

"Well, how does the book come on? Have you got to 'my
lady Keturah' yet?"

It was Alice who spoke, opening the door from the kitchen,
and putting in her head with a pretence of great and solemn
caution, but with a correcting twinkle in her eyes.

"I haven't got to anybody yet," answered Theron, absently. "These big things must be approached slowly."

"Come out to supper, then, while the beans are hot," said
Alice.

The young minister sat through this other meal, again in
deep abstraction. His wife pursued her little pleasantry about
Keturah, the second wife, urging him with mock gravity to
scold her roundly for daring to usurp Sarah's place, but
Theron scarcely heard her, and said next to nothing. He ate
sparingly, and fidgeted in his seat, waiting with obvious im-

patience for the finish of the meal. At last he rose abruptly.

"I've got a call to make, — something with reference to the book," he said. "I'll run out now, I think, before it gets dark."

He put on his hat, and strode out of the house as if his errand was of the utmost urgency. Once upon the street, however, his pace slackened. There was still a good deal of daylight outside, and he loitered aimlessly about, walking with bowed head and hands clasped behind him, until dusk fell. Then he squared his shoulders, and started straight as the crow flies toward the residence of Father Forbes.

CHAPTER VII

THE new Catholic church was the largest and most imposing public building in Octavius. Even in its unfinished condition, with a bald roofing of weather-beaten boards marking
on the stunted tower the place where a spire was to begin
later on, it dwarfed every other edifice of the sort in the
town, just as it put them all to shame in the matter of the
throngs it drew, rain or shine, to its services.

These facts had not heretofore been a source of satisfaction
to the Rev. Theron Ware. He had even alluded to the subject
in terms which gave his wife the impression that he actively
deplored the strength and size of the Catholic denomination
in this new home of theirs, and was troubled in his mind
about Rome generally. But this evening he walked along the
extended side of the big structure, which occupied nearly
half the block, and then, turning the corner, passed in review its wide-doored, looming front, without any hostile
emotions whatever. In the gathering dusk it seemed more
massive than ever before, but he found himself only pas-
sively considering the odd statement he had heard that all
Catholic Church property was deeded absolutely in the name
of the Bishop of the diocese.

Only a narrow passage-way separated the church from the
pastorate, a fine new brick residence standing flush upon the
street. Theron mounted the steps and looked about for a
bell-pull. Search revealed instead a little ivory button set in
a ring of metal work. He picked at this for a time with his
finger-nail, before he made out the injunction, printed across
it, to push. Of course! how stupid of him! This was one of
those electric bells he had heard so much of, but which had
not as yet made their way to the class of homes he knew. For
custodians of a mediæval superstition and fanaticism, the
Catholic clergy seemed very much up to date. This bell made
him feel rather more a countryman than ever.

The door was opened by a tall gaunt woman, who stood in black relief against the radiance of the hall-way while Theron, choosing his words with some diffidence, asked if the Rev. Mr. Forbes was in.

"He is," came the hush-voiced answer. "He's at dinner, though."

It took the young minister a second or two to bring into association in his mind this evening hour and this midday meal. Then he began to say that he would call again, — it was nothing special, — but the woman suddenly cut him short by throwing the door wide open.

"It's Mr. Ware, is it not?" she asked, in a greatly altered tone. "Sure, he'd not have you go away. Come inside — do, sir! — I'll tell him."

Theron, with a dumb show of reluctance, crossed the threshold. He noted now that the woman, who had bustled down the hall on her errand, was gray-haired and incredibly ugly, with a dark sour face, glowering black eyes, and a twisted mouth. Then he saw that he was not alone in the hall-way. Three men and two women, all poorly clad and obviously working people, were seated in meek silence on a bench beyond the hat-rack. They glanced up at him for an instant, then resumed their patient study of the linoleum pattern on the floor at their feet.

"And will you kindly step in, sir?" the elderly Gorgon had returned to ask. She led Mr. Ware along the hall-way to a door near the end, and opened it for him to pass before her.

He entered a room in which for the moment he could see nothing but a central glare of dazzling light beating down from a great shaded lamp upon a circular patch of white table linen. Inside this ring of illumination points of fire sparkled from silver and porcelain, and two bars of burning crimson tracked across the cloth in reflection from tall glasses filled with wine. The rest of the room was vague darkness, but the gloom seemed saturated with novel aromatic odors, the appetizing scent of which bore clear relation to what Theron's blinking eyes rested upon.

He was able now to discern two figures at the table, outside the glowing circle of the lamp. They had both risen, and one came toward him with cordial celerity, holding out a white plump hand in greeting. He took this proffered hand rather limply, not wholly sure in the half-light that this really was Father Forbes, and began once more that everlasting apology to which he seemed doomed in the presence of the priest. It was broken abruptly off by the other's protesting laughter.

"My dear Mr. Ware, I beg of you," the priest urged, chuckling with hospitable mirth, "don't, don't apologize! I give you my word, nothing in the world could have pleased us better than your joining us here to-night. It was quite dramatic, your coming in as you did. We were speaking of you at that very moment. Oh, I forgot — let me make you acquainted with my friend — my very particular friend, Dr. Ledsmar. Let me take your hat; pray draw up a chair. Maggie will have a place laid for you in a minute."

"Oh, I assure you — I couldn't think of it — I've just eaten my — my — dinner," expostulated Theron. He murmured more inarticulate remonstrances a moment later, when the grim old domestic appeared with plates, serviette, and tableware for his use, but she went on spreading them before him as if she heard nothing. Thus committed against a decent show of resistance, the young minister did eat a little here and there of what was set before him, and was human enough to regret frankly that he could not eat more. It seemed to him very remarkable cookery, transfiguring so simple a thing as a steak, for example, quite out of recognition, and investing the humble potato with a charm he had never dreamed of. He wondered from time to time if it would be polite to ask how the potatoes were cooked, so that he might tell Alice.

The conversation at the table was not continuous, or even enlivened. After the lapses into silence became marked, Theron began to suspect that his refusal to drink wine had annoyed them, — the more so as he had drenched a large section of table-cloth in his efforts to manipulate a siphon instead. He was greatly relieved, therefore, when Father Forbes explained in an incidental way that Dr. Ledsmar and he customarily ate their meals almost without a word.

"It's a philosophic fad of his," the priest went on smilingly, "and I have fallen in with it for the sake of a quiet life; so that when we do have company, — that is to say, once in a blue moon, — we display no manners to speak of."

"I had always supposed — that is, I've always heard — that it was more healthful to talk at meals," said Theron. "Of course — what I mean is — I took it for granted all physicians thought so."

Dr. Ledsmar laughed. "That depends so much upon the quality of the meals!" he remarked, holding his glass up to the light.

He seemed a man of middle age and an equable disposition. Theron, stealing stray glances at him around the lampshade, saw most distinctly of all a broad, impressive dome of skull, which, though obviously the result of baldness, gave the effect of quite belonging to the face. There were gold-rimmed spectacles, through which shone now and again the vivid sparkle of sharp, alert eyes, and there was a nose of some sort not easy to classify, at once long and thick. The rest was thin hair and short round [1] beard, mouse-colored where the light caught them, but losing their outlines in the shadows of the background. Theron had not heard of him among the physicians of Octavius. He wondered if he might not be a doctor of something else than medicine, and decided upon venturing the question.

"Oh, yes, it is medicine," replied Ledsmar. "I am a doctor three or four times over, so far as parchments can make one. In some other respects, though, I should think I am probably less of a doctor than anybody else now living. I haven't practised — that is, regularly — for many years, and I take no interest whatever in keeping abreast of what the profession regards as its progress. I know nothing beyond what was

---

[1] English ed. reads "full" for "round."

being taught in the sixties, and that I am glad to say I have mostly forgotten."

"Dear me!" said Theron. "I had always supposed that Science was the most engrossing of pursuits, — that once a man took it up he never left it."

"But that would imply a connection between Science and Medicine!" commented the doctor. "My dear sir, they are not even on speaking terms."

"Shall we go upstairs?" put in the priest, rising from his chair. "It will be more comfortable to have our coffee there, — unless indeed, Mr. Ware, tobacco is unpleasant to you?

"Oh, my, no!" the young minister exclaimed, eager to free himself from the suggestion of being a kill-joy. "I don't smoke myself; but I am very fond of the odor, I assure you."

Father Forbes led the way out. It could be seen now that he wore a long house-gown of black silk, skilfully moulded to his erect, shapely, and rounded form. Though he carried this with the natural grace of a proud and beautiful belle, there was no hint of the feminine in his bearing, or in the contour of his pale, firm-set, handsome face. As he moved through the hall-way, the five people whom Theron had seen waiting rose from their bench, and two of the women began in humble murmurs, "If you please, Father," and "Good-evening to your Riverence;" but the priest merely nodded and passed on up the staircase, followed by his guests. The people sat down on their bench again.

A few minutes later, reclining at his ease in a huge low chair, and feeling himself unaccountably at home in the most luxuriously appointed and delightful little room he had ever seen, the Rev. Theron Ware sipped his unaccustomed coffee and embarked upon an explanation of his errand. Somehow the very profusion of scholarly symbols about him — the great dark rows of encased and crowded book-shelves rising to the ceiling, the classical engravings upon the wall, the revolving book-case, the reading-stand, the mass of littered magazines, reviews, and papers at either end of the costly and elaborate writing-desk — seemed to make it the easier for him to explain without reproach that he needed information about Abram. He told them quite in detail the story of his book.

The two others sat watching him through a faint haze of scented smoke, with polite encouragement on their faces. Father Forbes took the added trouble to nod understandingly at the various points of the narrative, and when it was finished gave one of his little approving chuckles.

"This skirts very closely upon sorcery," he said smilingly. "Do you know, there is perhaps not another man in the country who knows Assyriology so thoroughly as our friend here, Dr. Ledsmar."

"That's putting it too strong," remarked the doctor. "I only follow at a distance, — a year or two behind. But I daresay I can help you. You are quite welcome to anything I have; my books cover the ground pretty well up to last year. Delitzsch is very interesting; but Baudissin's 'Studien zur Semitischen Religionsgeschichte' would come closer to what you need. There are several other important Germans, — Schrader, Bunsen, Duncker, Hommel, and so on."

"Unluckily I — I don't read German readily," Theron explained with diffidence.

"That's a pity," said the doctor, "because they do the best work, — not only in this field, but in most others. And they do so much that the mass defies translation. Well, the best thing outside of German of course is Sayce. I daresay you know him, though."

The Rev. Mr. Ware shook his head mournfully. "I don't seem to know any one," he murmured.

The others exchanged glances.

"But if I may ask, Mr. Ware," pursued the doctor, regarding their guest with interest through his spectacles, "why do you specially hit upon Abraham? He is full of difficulties, — enough, just now, at any rate, to warn off the bravest scholar. Why not take something easier?"

Theron had recovered something of his confidence. "Oh, no," he said, "that is just what attracts me to Abraham. I like the complexities and contradictions in his character. Take for instance all that strange and picturesque episode of Hagar: see the splendid contrast between the craft and commercial guile of his dealings in Egypt and with Abimelech, and the simple, straightforward godliness of his later years. No, all those difficulties only attract me. Do you happen to know — of course you would know — do those German books, or the others, give anywhere any additional details of the man himself and his sayings and doings, — little things which help, you know, to round out one's conception of the individual?"

Again the priest and the doctor stole a furtive glance across the young minister's head. It was Father Forbes who replied.

"I fear that you are taking our friend Abraham too literally, Mr. Ware," he said, in that gentle semblance of paternal tones which seemed to go so well with his gown. "Modern research, you know, quite wipes him out of existence as an individual. The word 'Abram' is merely an eponym, — it means 'exalted father.' Practically all the names in the Genesis chronologies are what we call eponymous. Abram is not a person at all: he is a tribe, a sept, a clan. In the same way, Shem is not intended for a man; it is the name of a great division of the human race. Heber is simply the throwing back into allegorical substance, so to speak, of the Hebrews; Heth of the Hittites; Asshur of Assyria."

"But this is something very new, this theory, isn't it?" queried Theron.

The priest smiled and shook his head. "Bless you, no! My dear sir, there is nothing new. Epicurus and Lucretius outlined the whole Darwinian theory more than two thousand years ago. As for this eponym thing, why Saint Augustine called attention to it fifteen hundred years ago. In his 'De Civitate Dei,' he expressly says of these genealogical names, '*gentes non homines*;' that is, 'peoples, not persons.' It was as obvious to him — as much a commonplace of knowledge — as it was to Ezekiel eight hundred years before him."

"It seems passing strange that we should not know it now, then," commented Theron; "I mean, that everybody shouldn't know it."

Father Forbes gave a little purring chuckle. "Ah, there we get upon contentious ground," he remarked. "Why should 'everybody' be supposed to know anything at all? What business is it of 'everybody's' to know things? The earth was just as round in the days when people supposed it to be flat, as it is now. So the truth remains always the truth, even though you give a charter to ten hundred thousand separate numskulls to examine it by the light of their private judgment, and report that it is as many different varieties of something else. But of course that whole question of private judgment versus authority is No-Man's-Land for us. We were speaking of eponyms."

"Yes," said Theron; "it is very interesting."

"There is a curious phase of the subject which hasn't been worked out much," continued the priest. "Probably the Germans will get at that too, sometime. They are doing the best Irish work in other fields, as it is. I spoke of Heber and Heth, in Genesis, as meaning the Hebrews and the Hittites. Now my own people, the Irish, have far more ancient legends and traditions than any other nation west of Athens; and you find in their myth of the Milesian invasion and conquest two principal leaders called Heber and Ith, or Heth. That is supposed to be comparatively modern, — about the time of Solomon's Temple. But these independent Irish myths go back to the fall of the Tower of Babel, and they have there an ancestor, grandson of Japhet, named Fenius Farsa, and they ascribe to him the invention of the alphabet. They took their ancient name of Feine, the modern Fenian, from him. Oddly enough, that is the name which the Romans knew the Phœnicians by, and to them also is ascribed the invention of the alphabet. The Irish have a holy salmon of knowledge, just like the Chaldean man-fish. The Druids' tree-worship is identical with that of the Chaldeans, — those pagan groves, you know, which the Jews were always being punished for building. You see, there is nothing new. Everything is built on the ruins of something else. Just as the material earth is made up of countless billions of dead men's bones, so the mental world is all alive with the ghosts of dead men's thoughts and beliefs, the wraiths of dead races' faiths and imaginings."

Father Forbes paused, then added with a twinkle in his eye: "That peroration is from an old sermon of mine, in the days when I used to preach. I remember rather liking it, at the time."

"But you still preach?" asked the Rev. Mr. Ware, with lifted brows.

"No! no more! I only talk now and again," answered the priest, with what seemed a suggestion of curtness. He made haste to take the conversation back again. "The names of these dead-and-gone things are singularly pertinacious, though. They survive indefinitely. Take the modern name Marmaduke, for example. It strikes one as peculiarly modern, up-to-date, doesn't it? Well, it is the oldest name on earth, — thousands of years older than Adam. It is the ancient Chaldean Meridug, or Merodach. He was the young god who interceded continually between the angry, omnipotent Ea, his father, and the humble and unhappy Damkina, or Earth, who was his mother. This is interesting from another point of view, because this Merodach or Marmaduke is, so far as we can see now, the original prototype of our 'divine intermediary' idea. I daresay, though, that if we could go back still other scores of centuries, we should find whole receding series of types of this Christ-myth of ours."

Theron Ware sat upright at the fall of these words, and flung a swift, startled look about the room, — the instinctive glance of a man unexpectedly confronted with peril, and cast-

ing desperately about for means of defence and escape. For
the instant his mind was aflame with this vivid impression, —
that he was among sinister enemies, at the mercy of criminals.
He half rose under the impelling stress of this feeling, with
the sweat standing on his brow, and his jaw dropped in a
scared and bewildered stare.

Then, quite as suddenly, the sense of shock was gone; and
it was as if nothing at all had happened. He drew a long
breath, took another sip of his coffee, and found himself all
at once reflecting almost pleasurably upon the charm of contact with really educated people. He leaned back in the big
chair again, and smiled to show these men of the world how
much at his ease he was. It required an effort, he discovered,
but he made it bravely, and hoped he was succeeding.

"It hasn't been in my power to at all lay hold of what the
world keeps on learning nowadays about its babyhood," he
said. "All I have done is to try to preserve an open mind,
and to maintain my faith that the more we know, the nearer
we shall approach the Throne."

Dr. Ledsmar abruptly scuffled his feet on the floor, and
took out his watch. "I'm afraid — " he began.

"No, no! There's plenty of time," remarked the priest,
with his soft half-smile and purring tones. "You finish your
cigar here with Mr. Ware, and excuse me while I run down
and get rid of the people in the hall."

Father Forbes tossed his cigar-end into the fender. Then
he took from the mantel a strange three-cornered black-velvet
cap, with a dangling silk tassel at the side, put it on his head,
and went out.

Theron, being left alone with the doctor, hardly knew
what to do or say. He took up a paper from the floor beside
him, but realized that it would be impolite to go farther,[2]
and laid it on his knee. Some trace of that earlier momentary
feeling that he was in hostile hands came back, and worried
him. He lifted himself upright in the chair, and then became

[2] English ed. reads "further" for "farther."

conscious that what really disturbed him was the fact that Dr. Ledsmar had turned in his seat, crossed his legs, and was contemplating him with a gravely concentrated scrutiny through his spectacles.

This uncomfortable gaze kept itself up a long way beyond the point of good manners; but the doctor seemed not to mind that at all.

CHAPTER VIII

When Dr. Ledsmar finally spoke, it was in a kindlier tone than the young minister had looked for. "I had half a notion of going to hear you preach the other evening," he said; "but at the last minute I backed out. I daresay I shall pluck up the courage, sooner or later, and really go. It must be fully twenty years since I last heard a sermon, and I had supposed that that would suffice for the rest of my life. But they tell me that you are worth while; and, for some reason or other, I find myself curious on the subject."

Involved and dubious though the compliment might be, Theron felt himself flushing with satisfaction. He nodded his acknowledgement, and changed the topic.

"I was surprised to hear Father Forbes say that he did not preach," he remarked.

"Why should he?" asked the doctor, indifferently. "I suppose he hasn't more than fifteen parishioners in a thousand who would understand him if he did, and of these probably twelve would join in a complaint to his Bishop about the heterodox tone of his sermon. There is no point in his going to all that pains, merely to incur that risk. Nobody wants him to preach, and he has reached an age where personal vanity no longer tempts him to do so. What *is* wanted of him is that he should be the paternal, ceremonial, authoritative head and centre of his flock, adviser, monitor, overseer, elder brother, friend, patron, seigneur, — whatever you like, — everything except a bore. They draw the line at that. You see how diametrically opposed this Catholic point of view is to the Protestant."

"The difference does seem extremely curious to me," said Theron. "Now, those people in the hall —"

"Go on," put in the doctor, as the other faltered hesitatingly. "I know what you were going to say. It struck you as odd that he should let them wait on the bench there, while he came up here to smoke."

Theron smiled faintly. "I *was* thinking that my — my parishioners wouldn't have taken it so quietly. But of course — it is all so different!"

"As chalk from cheese!" said Dr. Ledsmar, lighting a fresh cigar. "I daresay every one you saw there had come either to take the pledge, or see to it that one of the others took it. That is the chief industry in the hall, so far as I have observed. Now discipline is an important element in the machinery here. Coming to take the pledge implies that you have been drunk and are now ashamed. Both states have their values, but they are opposed. Sitting on that bench tends to develop penitence to the prejudice of alcoholism, But at no stage would it ever occur to the occupant of the bench that he was the best judge of how long he was to sit there, or that his priest should interrupt his dinner or general personal routine, in order to administer that pledge. Now, I daresay you have no people at all coming to 'swear off.' "

The Rev. Mr. Ware shook his head. "No; if a man with us got as bad as all that, he wouldn't come near the church at all. He'd simply drop out, and there would be an end to it."

"Quite so," interjected the doctor. "That is the voluntary system. But these fellows *can't* drop out. There's no bottom to the Catholic Church. Everything that's in, stays in. If you don't mind my saying so — of course I view you all impartially from the outside — but it seems logical to me that a church should exist for those who need its help, and not for those who by their own profession are so good already that it is they who help the church. Now, you turn a man out of your church who behaves badly: that must be on the theory that his remaining in would injure the church, and that in turn involves the idea that it is the excellent character of the parishioners which imparts virtue to the church. The Catholics' conception, you see, is quite the converse. Such virtue as they keep in stock is on tap, so to speak, here in the church itself, and the parishioners come and get some for themselves according to their need for it. Some come every day, some only once a year, some perhaps never between their baptism and their funeral. But they all have a right here, the professional burglar every whit as much as the speckless saint. The only stipulation is that they oughtn't to come under false pretences: the burglar is in honor bound not to pass himself off to his priest as the saint. But that is merely a moral obligation, established in the burglar's own interest. It does him no good to come unless he feels that he is playing the rules of the game, and one of these is confession. If he cheats there, he knows that he is cheating nobody but himself, and might much better have stopped away altogether."

Theron nodded his head comprehendingly. He had a great many views about the Romanish rite of confession which did not at all square with this statement of the case, but this did not seem a specially fit time for bringing them forth. There was indeed a sense of languid repletion in his mind, as if it had been overfed and wanted to lie down for awhile. He contented himself with nodding again, and murmuring reflectively, "Yes, it is all strangely different."

His tone was an invitation to silence; and the doctor turned his attention to the cigar, studying its ash for a minute with an air of deep meditation, and then solemnly blowing out a slow series of smoke-rings. Theron watched him with an indolent, placid eye, wondering lazily if it was, after all, so very pleasant to smoke.

There fell upon this silence — with a softness so delicate that it came almost like a progression in the hush — the sound of sweet music. For a little, strain and source were alike indefinite, — an impalpable setting to harmony of the mellowed light, the perfumed opalescence of the air, the luxury and charm of the room. Then it rose as by a sweeping curve of beauty, into a firm, calm, severe melody, delicious to the ear, but as cold in the mind's vision as moonlit sculpture. It went on upward with stately collectedness of power, till the atmosphere seemed all alive with the trembling consciousness of the presence of lofty souls, sternly pure and pitilessly great.

Theron found himself moved as he had never been before. He almost resented the discovery, when it was presented to him by the prosaic, mechanical side of his brain, that he was listening to organ-music, and that it came through the open window from the church close by. He would fain have reclined in his chair and closed his eyes, and saturated himself with the uttermost fulness of the sensation. Yet, in absurd despite of himself, he rose and moved over to the window.

Only a narrow alley separated the pastorate from the church; Mr. Ware could have touched with a walking-stick the opposite wall. Directly facing him was the arched and mullioned top of a great window. A dim light from within shone through the more translucent portions of the glass below, throwing out faint little bars of party-colored radiance upon the blackness of the deep passage-way. He could vaguely trace by these the outlines of some sort of picture on the window. There were human figures in it, and — yes — up here in the centre, nearest him, was a woman's head. There was a halo about it, engirdling rich, flowing waves of reddish hair, the lights in which glowed like flame. The face itself was barely distinguishable, but its half-suggested form raised a curious sense of resemblance to some other face. He looked at it closely, blankly, the noble music throbbing through his brain meanwhile.

"It's that Madden girl!" he suddenly heard a voice say by his side. Dr. Ledsmar had followed him to the window, and was close at his shoulder.

Theron's thoughts were upon the puzzling shadowed lineaments on the stained glass. He saw now in a flash the resemblance which had baffled him. "It *is* like her, of course," he said.

"Yes, unfortunately, it is just like her," replied the doctor, with a hostile note in his voice. "Whenever I am dining here, she always goes in [1] and kicks up that racket. She knows I hate it."

"Oh, you mean that it is she who is playing," remarked Theron. "I thought you referred to — at least — I was thinking of —"

His sentence died off in inconsequence. He had a feeling that he did not want to talk with the doctor about the stained-glass likeness. The music had sunk away now into fragmentary and unconnected passages, broken here and there by abrupt stops. Dr. Ledsmar stretched an arm out past him and shut the window. "Let's hear as little of the row as we can," he said, and the two went back to their chairs.

"Pardon me for the question," the Rev. Mr. Ware said, after a pause which began to affect him as constrained, "but something you said about dining — you don't live here, then? In the house, I mean?"

The doctor laughed, — a characteristically abrupt,[2] dry little laugh, which struck Theron at once as bearing a sort of black-sheep relationship to the priest's habitual chuckle. "That must have been puzzling you no end," he said, — "that notion that the pastorate kept a devil's advocate on the premises. No, Mr. Ware, I don't live here. I inhabit a house of my own, — you may have seen it, — an old-fashioned place up beyond the race-course, with a sort of tower at the back, and a big garden. But I dine here three or four times a week. It is an old arrangement of ours. Vincent and I have been friends for many years now. We are quite alone in the world, we two, — much to our mutual satisfaction. You must come up and see me some time; come up and have a look over the books we were speaking of."

"I am much obliged," said Theron, without enthusiasm. The thought of the doctor by himself did not attract him greatly.

[1] English ed. reads "goes in next door" for "goes in."
[2] English ed. omits "abrupt."

The reservation in his tone seemed to interest the doctor. "I suppose you are the first man I have asked in a dozen years," he remarked, frankly willing that the young minister should appreciate the favor extended him. "It must be fully that since anybody but Vincent Forbes has been under my roof; that is, of my own species, I mean."

"You live there quite alone," commented Theron.

"Quite — with my dogs and cats and lizards — and my Chinaman. I mustn't forget him." The doctor noted the inquiry in the other's lifted brows, and smilingly explained. "He is my solitary servant. Possibly he might not appeal to you much; but I can assure you he used to interest Octavius a great deal when I first brought him here, ten years ago or so. He afforded occupation for all the idle boys in the village for a twelve-month at least. They used to lie in wait for him all day long, with stones or horse-chestnuts or snowballs, according to the season. The Irishmen from the wagonworks nearly killed him once or twice, but he patiently lived it all down. The Chinaman has the patience to live everything down, — the Caucasian races included. He will see us all to bed, will that gentleman with the pigtail!"

The music over in the church has lifted itself again into form and sequence, and defied the closed window. If anything, it was louder than before, and the sonorous roar of the bass-pedals seemed to be shaking the very walls. It was something with a big-lunged, exultant, triumphing swing in it, — something which ought to have been sung on the battlefield at the close of day by the whole jubilant army of victors. It was impossible to pretend not to be listening to it; but the doctor submitted with an obvious scowl, and bit off the tip of his third cigar with an annoyed air.

"You don't seem to care much for music," suggested Mr. Ware, when a lull came.

Dr. Ledsmar looked up, lighted match in hand. "Say musicians!" he growled. "Has it ever occurred to you," he went on, between puffs at the flame, "that the only animals who make the noises we call music are of the bird family, — a debased offshoot of the reptilian creation, — the very lowest types of the vertebrata now in existence? I insist upon the parallel among humans. I have in my time, sir, had considerable opportunities for studying close at hand the various orders of mammalia who devote themselves to what they describe as the arts. It may sound a harsh judgment, but I am convinced that musicians stand on the very bottom rung of the ladder in the sub-cellar of human intelligence, — even lower than painters and actors."

This seemed such unqualified nonsense to the Rev. Mr. Ware that he offered no comment whatever upon it. He tried instead to divert his thoughts to the stormy strains which rolled in through the vibrating brickwork, and to picture to himself the large, capable figure of Miss Madden seated in the half-light at the organ-board, swaying to and fro in a splendid ecstasy of power as she evoked at will this superb and ordered uproar. But the doctor broke insistently in upon his musings.

"All art, so-called, is decay," he said, raising his voice. "When a race begins to brood on the beautiful, — so-called, — it is a sign of rot, of getting ready to fall from the tree. Take the Jews, — those marvellous old fellows, — who were never more than a handful, yet have imposed the rule of their ideas and their gods upon us for fifteen hundred years. Why? They were forbidden by their most fundamental law to make sculptures or pictures. That was at a time when the Egyptians, when the Assyrians, and other Semites, were running to artistic riot. Every great museum in the world now has whole floors devoted to statues from the Nile, and marvellous carvings from the palaces of Sargon and Assurbanipal. You can get the artistic remains of the Jews during that whole period into a child's wheelbarrow. They had the sense and strength to penalize art; they alone survived. They saw the Egyptians go, the Assyrians go, the Greeks go, the late Romans go, the Moors in Spain go, — all the artistic peoples perish. They remained triumphing over all. Now at last their long-belated apogee is here; their decline is at hand. I am told that in this present generation in Europe the Jews are producing a great lot of young painters and sculptors and actors, just as for a century they have been producing famous composers and musicians. That means the end of the Jews!"

"What! have you only got as far as that?" came the welcome interruption of a cheery voice. Father Forbes had entered the room, and stood looking down with a whimsical twinkle in his eye from one to the other of his guests.

"You must have been taken over the ground at a very slow pace, Mr. Ware," he continued, chuckling softly, "to have arrived merely at the collapse of the New Jerusalem. I fancied I had given him time enough to bring you straight up to the end of all of us, with that Chinaman of his gently slapping our graves with his pigtail. That's where the doctor always winds up, if he's allowed to run his course."

"It has all been very interesting, extremely so, I assure you," faltered Theron. It had become suddenly apparent to him that he desired nothing so much as to make his escape, — that he had indeed only been waiting for the host's return to do so.

He rose at this, and explained that he must be going. No special effort being put forth to restrain him, he presently made his way out, Father Forbes hospitably following him down to the door, and putting a very gracious cordiality into his adieux.

The night was warm and black. Theron stood still in it the moment the pastorate door had closed; the sudden darkness was so thick that it was as if he had closed his eyes. His dominant sensation was of a deep relief and rest after some undue fatigue. It crossed his mind that drunken men probably felt like that as they leaned against things on their way home. He was affected himself, he saw, by the weariness and half-nausea following a mental intoxication. The conceit pleased him, and he smiled to himself as he turned and took the first homeward steps. It must be growing late, he thought. Alice would be wondering as she waited.

There was a street lamp at the corner, and as he walked toward it he noted all at once that his feet were keeping step to the movement of the music proceeding from the organ within the church, — a vaguely processional air, marked enough in measure, but still with a dreamy effect. It became a pleasure to identify his progress with the quaint rhythm of sound as he sauntered along. He discovered, as he neared the light, that he was instinctively stepping over the seams in the flagstone sidewalk as he had done as a boy. He smiled again at this. There *was* something exceptionally juvenile and buoyant about his mood, now that he examined it. He set it down as a reaction from that doctor's extravagant and incendiary talk. One thing was certain, — he would never be caught up at that house beyond the race-course, with its reptiles and its Chinaman. Should he ever even go to the pastorate again? He decided not to quite definitely answer *that* in the negative, but as he felt now, the chances were all against it.

Turning the corner, and walking off into the shadows along the side of the huge church building, Theron noted, almost at the end of the edifice, a small door, — the entrance to a porch coming out to the sidewalk, — which stood wide open. A thin, pale, verticle line of light showed that the inner door, too, was ajar.

Through this wee aperture the organ-music, reduced and mellowed by distance, came to him again with that same curious, intimate, personal relation which had so moved him at the start, before the doctor closed the window. It was as if it was being played for him alone.

He paused for a doubting minute or two, with bowed head, listening to the exquisite harmony which floated out to caress and soothe and enfold him. There was no spiritual, or at least pious, effect in it now. He fancied that it must be secular music, or, if not, then something adapted to marriage ceremonies, — rich, vivid, passionate, a celebration of beauty and the glory of possession, with its ruling note of joy only heightened by soft, wooing interludes, and here and there the tremor of a fond, timid little sob.

Theron turned away irresolutely, half frightened at the undreamt-of impression this music was making upon him. Then, all at once, he wheeled and stepped boldly into the porch, pushing the inner door open and hearing it rustle against its leathern frame as it swung to behind him.

He had never been inside a Catholic church before.

CHAPTER IX

JEREMIAH MADDEN was supposed to be probably the richest man in Octavius. There was no doubt at all about his being its least pretentious citizen.

The huge and ornate modern mansion which he had built, putting to shame every other house in the place, gave an effect of ostentation to the Maddens as a family; it seemed only to accentuate the air of humility which enveloped Jeremiah as with a garment. Everybody knew some version of the many tales afloat which, in a kindly spirit, illustrated the incongruity between him and his splendid habitation. Some had it that he slept in the shed. Others told whimsical stories of his sitting alone in the kitchen evenings, smoking his old clay pipe, and sorrowing because the second Mrs. Madden would not suffer the pigs and chickens to come in and bear him company. But no matter how comic the exaggeration, these legends were invariably amiable. It lay in no man's mouth to speak harshly of Jeremiah Madden.

He had been born a Connemara peasant, and he would die one. When he was ten years old he had seen some of his own family, and most [1] of his neighbors, starve to death. He could remember looking at the stiffened figure of a woman stretched on the stones by the roadside, with the green stain of nettles on her white lips. A girl five years or so older than himself, also a Madden and distantly related, had started in despair off across the mountains to the town where it was said the poor-law officers were dealing out food. He could recall her coming back next day, wild-eyed with hunger and the fever; the officers had refused her relief because her bare legs were not wholly shrunken to the bone. "While there's a calf on the shank, there's no starvation," they had explained to her. The girl died without profiting by this official

---

[1] English ed. reads "many" for "most."

apothegm. The boy found it burned ineffaceably upon his brain. Now, after a lapse of more than forty years, it seemed the thing that he remembered best about Ireland.

He had drifted westward as an unconsidered, unresisting item in that vast flight of the famine years. Others whom he rubbed against in that melancholy exodus, and deemed of much greater promise than himself, had done badly. Somehow he did well. He learned the wheelwright's trade, and really that seemed all there was to tell. The rest had been calm and sequent progression, — steady employment as a journeyman first; then marriage and a house and lot; the modest start as a master; the move to Octavius and cheap lumber; the growth of his business, always marked, of late years stupendous, — all following naturally, easily, one thing out of another. Jeremiah encountered the idea among his fellows, now and again, that he was entitled to feel proud of all this. He smiled to himself at the thought, and then sent a sigh after the smile. What was it all but empty and transient vanity? The score of other Connemara boys he had known — none very fortunate, several broken tragically in prison or the gutter, nearly all now gone the way of flesh — were as good as he. He could not have it in his heart to take credit for his success; it would have been like sneering over their poor graves.

Jeremiah Madden was now fifty-three,[2] — a little man of a reddened, weather-worn skin and a meditative, almost saddened, aspect. He had blue eyes, but his scanty iron-gray hair showed raven black in its shadows. The width and prominence of his cheek-bones dominated all one's recollections of his face. The long vertical upper-lip and irregular teeth made, in repose, an unshapely mouth; its smile, though, sweetened the whole countenance. He wore a fringe of stiff, steel-colored beard, passing from ear to ear under his chin. His week-day clothes were as simple as his workaday manners, fitting his short black pipe and his steadfast devotion to

[2] English ed. reads "fifty" for "fifty-three."

his business. On Sundays he dressed with a certain rigor of respectability, all in black, and laid aside tobacco, at least to the public view. He never missed going to the early Low Mass, quite alone. His family always came later, at the ten o'clock High Mass.

There had been, at one time or another, a good many members of this family. Two wives had borne Jeremiah Madden a total of over a dozen children. Of these there survived now only two of the first Mrs. Madden's offspring — Michael and Celia — and a son of the present wife, who had been baptized Terence, but called himself Theodore. This minority of the family inhabited the great new house on Main Street. Jeremiah went every Sunday afternoon by himself to kneel in the presence of the majority, there where they lay in Saint Agnes' consecrated ground. If the weather was good, he generally extended his walk through the fields to an old deserted Catholic burial-field, which had been used only in the first years after the famine invasion, and now was clean forgotten. The old wagon-maker liked to look over the primitive, neglected stones which marked the graves of these earlier exiles. Fully half of the inscriptions mentioned his County Galway, — there were two naming the very parish adjoining his. The latest date on any stone was of the remoter fifties. They had all been stricken down, here in this strange land with its bitter winters, while the memory of their own soft, humid, gentle west-coast air was fresh within them. Musing upon the clumsy sculpture, with its "R. I. P.," or "Pray for the Soul of," half to be guessed under the stain and moss of a generation, there would seem to him but a step from this present to that heart-rending, awful past. What had happened between was a meaningless vision, — as impersonal as the passing of the planets overhead. He rarely had an impulse to tears in the new cemetery, where his ten children were. He never left this weed-grown, forsaken old God's-acre dry eyed.

One must not construct from all this the image of a melancholy man, as his fellows met and knew him. Mr. Madden kept his griefs, racial and individual, for his own use. To the men about him in the offices and the shops he presented day after day, year after year, an imperturbable cheeriness of demeanor. He had been always fortunate in the selection of lieutenants and chief helpers. Two of these had grown now into partners, and were almost as much a part of the big enterprise as Jeremiah himself. They spoke often of their inability to remember any unjust or petulant word of his, — much less any unworthy deed. Once they had seen him in a great rage, all the more impressive because he said next to nothing. A thoughtless fellow told a dirty story in the presence of some apprentices; and Madden, listening to this, drove the offender implacably from his employ. It was years now since any one who knew him had ventured upon lewd pleasantries in his hearing. Jokes of the sort which women might hear he was very fond of, though he had not much humor of his own. Of books he knew nothing whatever, and he made only the most perfunctory pretence now and again of reading the newspapers.

The elder son Michael was very like his father, — diligent, unassuming, kindly, and simple, — a plain, tall, thin red man of nearly thirty, who toiled in paper cap and rolled-up shirt-sleeves as the superintendent in the saw-mill, and put on no airs whatever as the son of the master. If there was surprise felt at his not being taken into the firm as a partner, he gave no hint of sharing it. He attended to his religious duties with great zeal, and was President of the Sodality as a matter of course. This was regarded as his blind side; and young employees who cultivated it, and made broad their phylacteries under his notice, certainly had an added chance of getting on well in the works. To some few whom he knew specially well, Michael would confess that if he had had the brains for it, he should have wished to be a priest. He displayed no inclination to marry.

The other son, Terence, was some eight years younger,

and seemed the product of a wholly different race. The contrast between Michael's sandy skin and long gaunt visage and this dark boy's handsome, rounded face, with its prettily curling black hair, large, heavily fringed brown eyes, and delicately modelled features, was not more obvious than their temperamental separation. This second lad had been away for years at school, — indeed, at a good many schools, for no one seemed to manage to keep him long. He had been with the Jesuits at Georgetown, with the Christian Brothers at Manhattan; the sectarian Mt. St. Mary's and the severely secular Annapolis had both been tried, and proved misfits. The young man was home again now, and save that his name had become Theodore, he appeared in no wise changed from the beautiful, wilful, bold, and showy boy who had gone away in his teens. He was still rather small for his years, but so gracefully moulded in form, and so perfectly tailored, that the fact seemed rather an advantage than otherwise. He never dreamed of going near the wagon-works, but he did go a good deal — in fact, most of the time — to the Nedahma Club. His mother spoke often to her friends about her fears for his health. He never spoke to his friends about his mother at all.

The second Mrs. Madden did not, indeed, appeal strongly to the family pride. She had been a Miss Foley, a dress-maker, and an old maid. Jeremiah had married her after a brief widowerhood, principally because she was the sister of his parish priest, and had a considerable reputation for piety. It was at a time when the expansion of his business was promising certain wealth, and suggesting the removal to Octavius. He was conscious of a notion that his obligations to social respectability were increasing; it was certain that the embarrassments of a motherless family were. Miss Foley had shown a good deal of attention to his little children. She was not ill-looking; she bore herself with modesty; she was the priest's sister, — the niece once removed of a vicar-general. And so it came about.

Although those most concerned did not say so, everybody could see from the outset the pity of its ever having come about at all. The pious and stiffly respectable priest's sister had been harmless enough as a spinster. It made the heart ache to contemplate her as a wife. Incredibly narrow-minded, ignorant, suspicious, vain, and sour-tempered, she must have driven a less equable and well-rooted man than Jeremiah Madden to drink or flight. He may have had his temptations, but they made no mark on the even record of his life. He only worked the harder, concentrating upon his business those extra hours which another sort of home-life would have claimed instead. The end of twenty years found him a rich man, but still toiling pertinaciously day by day, as if he had his wage to earn. In the great house which had been built to please, or rather placate, his wife, he kept to himself as much as possible. The popular story of his smoking alone in the kitchen was more or less true; only Michael as a rule sat with him, too weak-lunged for tobacco himself, but reading stray scraps from the papers to the lonely old man, and talking with him about the works, the while Jeremiah meditatively sucked his clay pipe. One or two evenings in the week the twain spent up in Celia's part of the house, listening with the awe of simple, honest mechanics to the music she played for them.

Celia was to them something indefinably less, indescribably more, than a daughter and sister. They could not think there had ever been anything like her before in the world; the notion of criticising any deed or word of hers would have appeared to them monstrous and unnatural.

She seemed to have come up to this radiant and wise and marvellously talented womanhood of hers, to their minds, quite spontaneously. There had been a little Celia, — a red-headed, sulky, mutinous slip of a girl, always at war with her step-mother, and affording no special comfort or hope to the rest of the family Then there was a long gap, during which the father, four times a year, handed Michael a letter he had received from the superioress of a distant convent, referring with cold formality to the studies and discipline by which Miss Madden might profit more if she had been better brought up, and enclosing a large bill. Then all at once they beheld a big Celia, whom they spoke of as being home again, but who really seemed never to have been there before, — a tall, handsome, confident young woman, swift of tongue and apprehension, appearing to know everything there was to be known by the most learned, able to paint pictures, carve wood, speak in divers languages, and make music for the gods, yet with it all a very proud lady, one might say a queen.

The miracle of such a Celia as this impressed itself even upon the step-mother. Mrs. Madden had looked forward with a certain grim tightening of her combative jaws to the home-coming of the "red-head." She felt herself much more the fine lady now [3] than she had been when the girl went away. She had her carriage now, and the magnificent new house was nearly finished, and she had a greater number of ailments, and spent far more money on doctor's bills, than any other lady in the whole section. The flush of pride in her greatest achievement up to date — having the most celebrated of New York physicians brought up to Octavius by special train — still prickled in her blood. It was in all the papers, and the admiration of the flatterers and "soft-sawd-herers" — wives of Irish merchants and smaller professional men who formed her social circle — was raising visions in her poor head of going next year with Theodore to Saratoga, and fastening the attention of the whole fashionable republic upon the variety and resources of her invalidism. Mrs. Madden's fancy did not run to the length of seeing her step-daughter also at Saratoga; it pictured her still as the sullen and hated "red-head," moping defiantly in corners, or courting by her insolence the punishments which leaped against their leash in the step-mother's mind to get at her.

[3] English ed. omits "now."

The real Celia, when she came, fairly took Mrs. Madden's breath away. The peevish little plans for annoyance and tyranny, the resolutions born of ignorant and jealous egotism, found themselves swept out of sight by the very first swirl of Celia's dress-train, when she came down from her room robed in peacock blue. The step-mother could only stare.

Now, after two years of it, Mrs. Madden still viewed her step-daughter with round-eyed uncertainty, not unmixed with wrathful fear. She still drove about behind two magnificent horses; the new house had become almost tiresome by familiarity; her pre-eminence in the interested minds of the Dearborn County Medical Society was as towering as ever, but somehow it was all different. There was a note of unreality nowadays in Mrs. Donnelly's professions of wonder at her bearing up under her multiplied maladies; there was almost a leer of mockery in the sympathetic smirk with which the Misses Mangan listened to her symptoms. Even the doctors, though they kept their faces turned toward her, obviously did not pay much attention; the people in the street seemed no longer to look at her and her equipage at all. Worst of all, something of the meaning of this managed to penetrate her own mind. She caught now and again a dim glimpse of herself as others must have been seeing her for years, — as a stupid, ugly, boastful, and bad-tempered old nuisance. And it was always as if she saw this in a mirror held up by Celia.

Of open discord there had been next to none. Celia would not permit it, and showed this so clearly from the start that there was scarcely need for her saying it. It seemed hardly necessary for her to put into words any of her desires, for that matter. All existing arrangements in the Madden household seemed to shrink automatically and make room for her, whichever way she walked. A whole quarter of the unfinished house set itself apart for her. Partitions altered themselves; doorways moved across to opposite sides; a recess opened itself, tall and deep, for it knew not what statue, — simply because, it seemed, the Lady Celia willed it so.

When the family moved into this mansion, it was with a consciousness that the only one who really belonged there was Celia. She alone could behave like one perfectly at home. It seemed entirely natural to the others that she should do just what she liked, shut them off from her portion of the house, take her meals there if she felt disposed, and keep such hours as pleased her instant whim. If she awakened them at midnight by her piano, or deferred her breakfast to the late afternoon, they felt that it must be all right, since Celia did it. She had one room furnished with only divans and huge, soft cushions, its walls covered with large copies of statuary not too strictly clothed,[4] which she would suffer no one, not even the servants, to enter. Michael fancied sometimes, when he passed the draped entrance to this sacred chamber, that the portière smelt of tobacco, but he would not have spoken of it, even had he been sure. Old Jeremiah, whose established habit it was to audit minutely the expenses of his household, covered over round sums to Celia's separate banking account, upon the mere playful hint of her holding her check-book up, without a dream of questioning her.

That the step-mother had joy, or indeed anything but gall and wormwood, out of all this is not to be pretended. There lingered along in the recollection of the family some vague memories of her having tried to assert an authority over Celia's comings and goings at the outset, but they grouped themselves as only parts [5] of the general disorder of moving and settling, which a fortnight or so quite righted. Mrs. Madden still permitted herself a certain license of

[4] English ed. reads "containing they knew large casts of statuary not too strictly clothed" for "its walls covered with large copies of statuary not too strictly clothed."

[5] English ed. reads "as features" for "as only parts."

hostile comment when her step-daughter was not present, and listened with gratification to what the women of her acquaintance ventured upon saying in the same spirit; but actual interference or remonstrance she never offered nowadays. The two rarely met, for that matter, and exchanged only the baldest and curtest forms of speech.

Celia Madden interested all Octavius deeply. This she must have done in any case, if only because she was the only daughter of its richest citizen. But the bold, luxuriant quality of her beauty, the original and piquant freedom of her manners, the stories told in gossip about her lawlessness at home, her intellectual attainments, and artistic vagaries, — these were even more exciting. The unlikelihood of her marrying any one — at least any Octavian — was felt to add a certain romantic zest to the image she made on the local perceptions. There was no visible young Irishman at all approaching the social and financial standard of the Maddens; it was taken for granted that a mixed marriage was quite out of the question in this case. She seemed to have more business about the church than even the priest. She was always playing the organ, or drilling the choir, or decorating the altars with flowers, or looking over the robes of the acolytes for rents and stains, or going in or out of the pastorate. Clearly this was not the sort of girl to take a Protestant husband.

The gossip of the town concerning her was, however, exclusively Protestant. The Irish spoke of her, even among themselves, but seldom. There was no occasion for them to pretend to like her: they did not know her, except in the most distant and formal fashion. Even the members of the choir, of both sexes, had the sense of being held away from her at haughty arm's length. No single parishioner dreamed of calling her friend. But when they referred to her, it was always with a cautious and respectful reticence. For one thing, she was the daughter of their chief man, the man they most esteemed and loved. For another, reservations they may have had in their souls about her touched close upon a delicately sore spot. It could not escape their notice that their Protestant neighbors were watching her with vigilant curiosity, and with a certain tendency to wink when her name came into conversation along with that of Father Forbes. It had never yet got beyond a tendency, — the barest fluttering suggestion of a tempted eyelid, — but the whole Irish population of the place felt themselves to be waiting, with clenched fists but sinking hearts, for the wink itself.

The Rev. Theron Ware had not caught even the faintest hint of these overtures to suspicion.

When he had entered the huge, dark, cool vault of the church, he could see nothing at first but a faint light up over the gallery, far at the other end. Then, little by little, his surroundings shaped themselves out of the gloom. To his right was a rail and some broad steps rising toward a softly confused mass of little gray vertical bars and the pale twinkle of tiny spots of gilded reflection, which he made out in the dusk to be the candles and trappings of the altar. Overhead the great arches faded away from foundations of dimly discernible capitals into utter blackness. There was a strange medicinal odor — as of cubeb [6] cigarettes — in the air.

After a little pause, he tiptoed noiselessly up the side aisle toward the end of the church, — toward the light above the gallery. This radiance from a single gas-jet expanded as he advanced, and spread itself upward over a burnished row of monster metal pipes, which went towering into the darkness like giants. They were roaring at him now, — sonorous, deafening, angry bellow, which made everything about him vibrate. The gallery balustrade hid the keyboard and the organist from view. There were only these jostling brazen tubes, as big round as trees and as tall, trembling with their own furious thunder. It was for all the world as if he had wandered into some vast tragical, enchanted cave, and was

[6] English ed. reads "asthma" for "cubeb."

being drawn against his will — like fascinated bird and [7] python — toward fate at the savage hands of these swollen and enraged genii.

He stumbled in the obscure light over a kneeling-stool,[8] making a considerable racket. On the instant the noise from the organ ceased, and he saw the black figure of a woman rise above the gallery-rail and look down.

"Who is it?" the indubitable voice of Miss Madden demanded sharply.

Theron had a sudden sheepish notion of turning and running. With the best grace he could summon, he called out an explanation instead.

"Wait a minute. I'm through now. I'm coming down," she returned. He thought there was a note of amusement in her tone.

She came to him a moment later, accompanied by a thin, tall man, whom Theron could barely see in the dark, now that the organ-light too was gone. This man lighted a match or two to enable them to make their way out.

When they were on the sidewalk, Celia spoke: "Walk on ahead, Michael!" she said. "I have some matters to speak of with Mr. Ware."

[7] English ed. reads "to" for "and."
[8] English ed. reads "kneeling-bench" for "kneeling-stool."

CHAPTER X

"WELL, what did you think of Dr. Ledsmar?"

The girl's abrupt question came as a relief to Theron. They were walking along in a darkness so nearly complete that he could see next to nothing of his companion. For some reason, this seemed to suggest a sort of impropriety. He had listened to the footsteps of the man ahead, — whom he guessed to be a servant, — and pictured him as intent upon getting up early next morning to tell everybody that the Methodist minister had stolen into the Catholic church at night to walk home with Miss Madden. That was going to be very awkward, — yes, worse than awkward! It might mean ruin itself. She had mentioned aloud that she had matters to talk over with him: that of course implied confidences, and the man might put heaven only knew what construction on that. It was notorious that servants did ascribe the very worst motives to those they worked for. The bare thought of the delight an Irish servant would have in also dragging a Protestant clergyman into the thing was sickening. And what could she want to talk to him about, anyway? The minute of silence stretched itself out upon his nerves into an interminable period of anxious unhappiness. Her mention of the doctor at last somehow seemed to lighten the situation.

"Oh, I thought he was very smart," he made haste to answer. "Wouldn't it be better — to — keep close to your man? He — may — think we've gone some other way."

"It wouldn't matter if he did," remarked Celia. She appeared to comprehend his nervousness and take pity on it, for she added, "It is my brother Michael, as good a soul as ever lived. He is quite used to my ways."

The Rev. Mr. Ware drew a long comforting breath. "Oh, I see! He went with you to — bring you home."

"To blow the organ," said the girl in the dark, correctingly. "But about that doctor; did you like him?"

"Well," Theron began, " 'like' is rather a strong word for

so short an acquaintance. He talked very well; that is, fluently. But he is so different from any other man I have come into contact with that — "

"What I wanted you to say was that you hated him," put in Celia, firmly.

"I don't make a practice of saying that of anybody," returned Theron, so much at his ease again that he put an effect of gentle, smiling reproof into the words. "And why specially should I make an exception for him?"

"Because he's a beast!"

Theron fancied that he understood. "I noticed that he seemed not to have much of an ear for music," he commented, with a little laugh. "He shut down the window when you began to play. His doing so annoyed me, because I — I wanted very much to hear it all. I never heard such music before. I — I came into the church to hear more of it; but then you stopped!"

"I will play for you some other time," Celia said, answering the reproach [1] in his tone. "But to-night I wanted to talk with you instead."

She kept silent, in spite of this, so long now that Theron was on the point of jestingly asking when the talk was to begin. Then she put a question abruptly, —

"It is a conventional way of putting it, but are you fond of poetry, Mr. Ware?"

"Well, yes, I suppose I am," replied Theron, much mystified. "I can't say that I am any great judge; but I like the things that I like — and — "

"Meredith," interposed Celia, "makes one of his women, Emilia in England, say that poetry is like talking on tiptoe; like animals in cages, always going to one end and back again. Does it impress you that way?"

"I don't know that it does," said he, dubiously. It seemed, however, to be her whim to talk literature, and he went on: "I've hardly read Meredith at all. I once borrowed his 'Lucile,'

[1] English ed. reads "regret" for "reproach."

but somehow I never got interested in it. I heard a recitation of his once, though, — a piece about a dead wife, and the husband and another man quarrelling as to whose portrait was in the locket on her neck, and of their going up to settle the dispute, and finding that it was the likeness of a third man, a young priest, — and though it was very striking, it didn't give me a thirst to know his other poems. I fancied I shouldn't like them. But I daresay I was wrong. As I get older, I find that I take less narrow views of literature, — that is, of course, of light literature, — and that — that — "

Celia mercifully stopped him. "The reason I asked you was — " she began, and then herself paused. "Or no, — never mind that, — tell me something else. Are you fond of pictures, statuary, the beautiful things of the world? Do great works of art, the big achievements of the big artists, appeal to you, stir you up?"

"Alas! that is something I can only guess at myself," answered Theron, humbly. "I have always lived in little places. I suppose, from your point of view, I have never seen a good painting in my life. I can only say this, though, — that it has always weighed on my mind as a great and sore deprivation, this being shut out from knowing what others mean when they talk and write about art. Perhaps that may help you to get at what you are after. If I ever went to New York, I feel that one of the first things I should do would be to see all the picture galleries; is that what you meant? And — would you mind telling me — why you — ?"

"Why I asked you?" Celia supplied his halting question. "No, I *don't* mind. I have a reason for wanting to know — to satisfy myself whether I had guessed rightly or not — about the kind of man you are. I mean in the matter of temperament and bent of mind and tastes."

The girl seemed to be speaking seriously, and without intent to offend. Theron did not find any comment ready, but walked along by her side, wondering much what it was all about.

"I daresay you think me 'too familiar on short acquaintance,' " she continued, after a little.

"My dear Miss Madden!" he protested perfunctorily.

"No; it is a matter of a good deal of importance," she went on. "I can see that you are going to be thrown into friendship, close contact, with Father Forbes. He likes you, and you can't help liking him. There is nobody else in this raw, overgrown, empty-headed place for you and him *to* like, — nobody except that man, that Dr. Ledsmar. And if you like *him*, I shall hate you! He has done mischief enough already. I am counting on you to help undo it, and to choke him off from doing more. It would be different if you were an ordinary Orthodox minister, all encased like a terrapin in prejudices and nonsense. Of course, if you had been *that* kind, we should never have got to know you at all. But when I saw you in McEvoy's cottage there, it was plain that you were one of *us*, — I mean a *man*, and not a marionette or a mummy. I am talking very frankly to you, you see. I want you on my side, against that doctor and his heartless, bloodless science."

"I feel myself very heartily on your side," replied Theron. She had set their progress at a slower pace, now that the lights of the main street were drawing near, as if to prolong their talk. All his earlier reservations had fled. It was almost as if she were a parishioner of his own. "I need hardly tell you that the doctor's whole attitude toward — toward revelation — was deeply repugnant to me. It doesn't make it any the less hateful to call it science. I am afraid, though," he went on hesitatingly, "that there are difficulties in the way of my helping, as you call it. You see, the very fact of my being a Methodist minister, and his being a Catholic priest, rather puts my interference out of the question."

"No; that doesn't matter a button," said Celia, lightly. "None of us think of that at all."

"There is the other embarrassment, then," pursued Theron, diffidently, "that Father Forbes is a vastly broader and deeper scholar — in all these matters — than I am. How could I possibly hope to influence him by my poor arguments? I don't know even the alphabet of the language he thinks in, — on these subjects, I mean."

"Of course you don't!" interposed the girl, with a confidence which the other, for all his meekness, rather winced under. "That wasn't what I meant at all. We don't want arguments from our friends: we want sympathies, sensibilities, emotional bonds. The right person's silence is worth more for companionship than the wisest talk in the world from anybody else. It isn't your mind that is needed here, or what you know; it is your heart, and what you feel. You are full of poetry, of ideals, of generous, unselfish impulses. You see the human, the warm-blooded side of things. *That* is what is really valuable. *That* is how you can help!"

"You overestimate me sadly," protested Theron, though with considerable tolerance for her error in his tone. "But you ought to tell me something about this Dr. Ledsmar. He spoke of being an old friend of the pr — of Father Forbes."

"Oh, yes, they've always known each other; that is, for many years. They were professors together in a college once, heaven only knows how long ago. Then they separated, — I fancy they quarrelled, too, before they parted. The doctor came here, where some relative had left him the place he lives in. Then in time the Bishop chanced to send Father Forbes here, — that was about three years ago, — and the two men after a while renewed their old relations. They dine together; that is the doctor's stronghold. He knows more about eating than any other man alive, I believe. He studies it as you would study a language. He has taught old Maggie, at the pastorate there, to cook like the mother of all the Delmonicos. And while they sit and stuff themselves, or loll about afterward like gorged snakes, they think it is smart to laugh at all the sweet and beautiful things in life, and to sneer at people who believe in ideals, and to talk about mankind being merely a fortuitous product of fermentation, and twaddle of that sort. It makes me sick!"

"I can readily see," said Theron, with sympathy, "how

such a cold, material, and infidel influence as that must shock and revolt an essentially religious temperament like yours."

Miss Madden looked up at him. They had turned into the main street,[2] and there was light enough for him to detect something startlingly like a grin on her beautiful face.

"But I'm not religious at all, you know," he heard her say. "I'm as Pagan as — anything! Of course there are forms to be observed, and so on; I rather like them than otherwise. I can make them serve very well for my own system; for I am myself, you know, an out-an-out Greek."

"Why, I had supposed that you were full-blooded Irish," the Rev. Mr. Ware found himself remarking, and then on the instant was overwhelmed by the consciousness that he had said a foolish thing. Precisely where the folly lay he did not know, but it was impossible to mistake the gesture of annoyance which his companion had instinctively made at his words. She had widened the distance between them now, and quickened her step. They went on in silence till they were within a block of her house. Several people had passed them who Theron felt sure must have recognized them both.

"What I meant was," the girl all at once began, drawing nearer again, and speaking with patient slowness, "that I find myself much more in sympathy with the Greek thought, the Greek theology of the beautiful and the strong, the Greek philosophy of life, and all that, than what is taught nowadays. Personally, I take much more stock in Plato than I do in Peter. But of course it is a wholly personal affair; I had no business to bother you with it. And for that matter, I oughtn't to have troubled you with any of our — "

"I assure you, Miss Madden!" the young minister began, with fervor.

"No," she broke in, in a resigned and even downcast tone; "let it all be as if I hadn't spoken. Don't mind anything I have said. If it is to be, it will be. You can't say more than that, can you?"

[2] English ed. reads "Main Street" for "the main street."

She looked into his face again, and her large eyes produced an impression of deep melancholy, which Theron found himself somehow impelled to share. Things seemed all at once to have become very sad indeed.

"It is one of my unhappy nights," she explained, in gloomy confidence. "I get them every once in a while, — as if some vicious planet or other was crossing in front of my good star, — and then I'm a caution to snakes. I shut myself up — that's the only thing to do — and have it out with myself. I didn't know but the organ-music would calm me down, but it hasn't. I sha'n't sleep a wink to-night, but just rage around from one room to another, piling all the cushions from the divans on to the floor, and then kicking them away again. Do *you* ever have fits like that?"

Theron was able to reply with a good conscience in the negative. It occurred to him to add, with jocose intent: "I am curious to know, do these fits, as you call them, occupy a prominent part in Grecian philosophy as a general rule?"

Celia gave a little snort, which might have signified amusement, but did not speak until they were upon her own sidewalk. "There is my brother, waiting at the gate," she said then, briefly.

"Well, then, I will bid you good-night here, I think," Theron remarked, coming to a halt, and offering his hand. "It must be getting very late, and my — that is — I have to be up particularly early to-morrow. So good-night; I hope you will be feeling ever so much better in spirits in the morning."

"Oh, that doesn't matter," replied the girl, listlessly. "It's a very paltry little affair, this life of ours, at the best of it. Luckily it's soon done with, — like a bad dream."

"Tut! tut! I won't have you talk like that!" interrupted Theron, with a swift and smart assumption of authority. "Such talk isn't sensible, and it isn't good. I have no patience with it!"

"Well, try and have a little patience with *me*, anyway, just for to-night," said Celia, taking the reproof with gentlest humility, rather to her censor's surprise. "I really am unhappy to-night, Mr. Ware, very unhappy. It seems as if all at once the world had swelled out in size a thousandfold, and that poor me had dwindled down to the merest wee little red-headed atom, — the most helpless and forlorn and lonesome of atoms at that." She seemed to force a sorrowful smile on her face as she added: "But all the same it has done me good to be with you, — I am sure it has, — and I daresay that by to-morrow I shall be quite out of the blues. Good-night, Mr. Ware. Forgive my making such an exhibition of myself. I *was* going to be such a fine early Greek, you know, and I have turned out only a late Milesian, — quite of the decadence. I shall do better next time. And good-night again, — and ever so many thanks."

She was walking briskly away toward the gate now, where the shadowy Michael still patiently stood. Theron strode off in the opposite direction, taking long, deliberate steps, and bowing his head in thought. He had his hands behind his back, as was his wont, and the sense of their recent contact with her firm, ungloved hands was, curiously enough, the thing which pushed itself uppermost in his mind. There had been a frank, almost manly vigor in her grasp; he said to himself that of course that came from her playing so much on the keyboard; the exercise naturally would give her large, robust hands.

Suddenly he remembered about the piano; he had quite forgotten to solicit her aid in selecting it. He turned, upon the impulse, to go back. She had not entered the gate as yet, but stood, shiningly visible under the street lamp, on the sidewalk, and she was looking in his direction. He turned again like a shot, and started homeward.

The front door of the parsonage was unlocked, and he made his way on tiptoe through the unlighted hall to the living-room. The stuffy air here was almost suffocating with the evil smell of a kerosene lamp turned down too low. Alice sat asleep in her old farmhouse rocking-chair, with an inelegant darning-basket on the table by her side. The whole effect of the room was as bare and squalid to Theron's newly informed eye as the atmosphere was offensive to his nostrils. He coughed sharply, and his wife sat up and looked at the clock. It was after eleven.

"Where on earth have you been?" she asked, with a yawn, turning up the wick of her sewing-lamp again.

"You ought never to turn down a light like that," [3] said Theron, with a complaining note in his voice. "It smells up the whole place. I never dreamed of your sitting up for me like this. You ought to have gone to bed."

"But how could I guess that you were going to be so late?" she retorted. "And you haven't told me where you were. Is this book of yours going to keep you up like this right along?"

The episode of the book was buried in the young minister's mind beneath such a mass of subsequent experiences that it required an effort for him to grasp what she was talking about. It seemed as if months had elapsed since he was in earnest about that book; and yet he had left the house full of it only a few hours before. He shook his wits together, and made answer, —

"Oh, bless you, no! Only there arose a very curious question. You have no idea, literally no conception, of the interesting and important problems which are raised by the mere fact of Abraham leaving the city of Ur. It's amazing, I assure you. I hadn't realized it myself."

"Well," remarked Alice, rising, — and with good-humor and petulance struggling sleepily in her tone, — "all I've got to say is, that if Abraham hasn't anything better to do than to keep young ministers of the gospel out, goodness knows where, till all hours of the night, I wish to gracious he'd stayed in the city of Ur [4] right straight along."

"You have no idea what a scholarly man Dr. Ledsmar is,"

[3] English ed. reads " 'If you will sew by a lamp instead of the gas, you ought never to turn it down' " for " 'You ought never to turn down a light like that.' "

[4] English ed. reads "he might better have stayed in the city of Ur' " for "I wish to gracious he'd stayed in the city of Ur.' "

Theron suddenly found himself inspired to volunteer. "He has the most marvellous collection of books, — a whole library devoted to this very subject, — and he has put them all quite freely at my disposal. Extremely kind of him, isn't it?"

"Ledsmar? Ledsmar?" queried Alice. "I don't seem to remember the name. He isn't the little man with the birthmark, who sits in the pew behind the Lovejoys, is he? I think some one said *he* was a doctor."

"Yes, a horse doctor!" said Theron, with a sniff. "No; you haven't seen this Dr. Ledsmar at all. I — I don't know that he attends *any* church regularly. I scraped his acquaintance quite by accident. He is really a character. He lives in the big house, just beyond the race-course, you know — the one with the tower at the back — "

"No, I *don't* know. How should I? I've hardly poked my nose outside of the yard since I have been here."

"Well, you shall go," said the husband, consolingly. "You *have* been cooped up here too much, poor girl. I must take you out more, really. I don't know that I could take you to the doctor's place — without an invitation, I mean. He is very [5] queer about some things. He lives there all alone, for instance, with only a Chinaman for a servant. He told me I was almost the only man he had asked under his roof for years. He isn't a practising physician at all, you know. He is a scientist; he makes experiments with lizards — and things."

"Theron," the wife said, pausing lamp in hand on her way to the bedroom, "do you be careful, now! For all you know this doctor may be a loose man, or pretty near an infidel. You've got to be mighty particular in such matters, you know, or you'll have the trustees down on you like a 'thousand of bricks.' "

"I will thank the trustees to mind their own business," said Theron, stiffly, and the subject dropped.

The bedroom window upstairs was open, and upon the fresh night air was borne in the shrill, jangling sound of a

[5] English ed. reads "a trifle" for "very."

piano, being played off somewhere in the distance, but so vehemently that the noise imposed itself upon the silence far and wide. Theron listened to this as he undressed. It proceeded from the direction of the main street, and he knew, as by instinct, that it was the Madden girl who was playing. The incongruity of the hour escaped his notice. He mused instead upon the wild and tropical tangle of moods, emotions, passions, which had grown up in that strange temperament. He found something very pathetic in that picture she had drawn of herself in forecast, roaming disconsolate through her rooms the livelong night, unable to sleep. The woful moan of insomnia seemed to make itself heard in every strain from her piano.

Alice heard it also, but being unillumined, she missed the romantic pathos. "I call it disgraceful," she muttered from her pillow, "for folks to be banging away on a piano at this time of night. There ought to be a law to prevent it."

"It may be some distressed soul," said Theron, gently, "seeking relief from the curse of sleeplessness."

The wife laughed, almost contemptuously. "Distressed fiddlesticks!" was her only other comment.

The music went on for a long time, — rising now to strident heights, now sinking off to the merest tinkling murmur, and broken ever and again by intervals of utter hush. It did not prevent Alice from at once falling sound asleep; but Theron lay awake, it seemed to him, for hours, listening tranquilly, and letting his mind wander at will through the pleasant antechambers of Sleep, where are more unreal fantasies than Dreamland itself affords.

PART II

CHAPTER XI

FOR some weeks the Rev. Theron Ware saw nothing of either the priest or the doctor, or the interesting Miss Madden.

There were, indeed, more urgent matters to think about. June had come; and every succeeding day brought closer to hand the ordeal of his first Quarterly Conference in Octavius. The waters grew distinctly[1] rougher as his pastoral bark neared this difficult passage.

He would have approached the great event with an easier mind if he could have made out just how he stood with his congregation. Unfortunately nothing in his previous experiences helped him in the least to measure or guess at the feelings of these curious Octavians. Their Methodism seemed to be sound enough, and to stick quite to the letter of the Discipline, so long as it was expressed in formulæ. It was its spirit which he felt to be complicated by all sorts of conditions wholly novel to him.

The existence of a line of street-cars in the town, for example, would not impress the casual thinker as likely to prove a rock in the path of peaceful religion. Theron, in his simplicity, had even thought, when he first saw these bobtailed cars bumping along the rails in the middle of the main street, that they must be a great convenience to people living in the outskirts, who wished to get in to church of a Sunday morning. He was imprudent enough to mention this in conversation with one of his new parishioners. Then he learned, to his considerable chagrin, that when this line was built, some years before, a bitter war of words had been fought upon the question of its being worked on the Sabbath day.

[1] English ed. reads "distinctly grew" for "grew distinctly."

The then occupant of the Methodist pulpit had so distinguished himself above the rest by the solemnity and fervor of his protests against this insolent desecration of God's day that the Methodists of Octavius still felt themselves peculiarly bound to hold this horse-car line, its management, and everything connected with it, in unbending aversion. At least once a year they were accustomed to expect a sermon denouncing it and all its impious Sunday patrons. Theron made a mental resolve that this year they should be disappointed.

Another burning problem, which he had not been called upon before to confront, he found now entangled with the mysterious line which divided a circus from a menagerie. Those itinerant tent-shows had never come his way heretofore, and he knew nothing of that fine balancing proportion between ladies in tights on horseback and cages full of deeply educational animals, which, even as the impartial rain, was designed to embrace alike the just and the unjust. There had arisen inside the Methodist society of Octavius some painful episodes, connected with members who took their children "just to see the animals," and were convicted of having also watched the Rose-Queen of the Arena, in her unequalled flying leap through eight hoops, with an ardent and unashamed eye. One of these cases still remained on the censorial docket of the church; and Theron understood that he was expected to name a committee of five to examine and try it. This he neglected to do.

He was no longer at all certain that the congregation as a whole liked his sermons. The truth was, no doubt, that he had learned enough to cease regarding the congregation as a whole. He could still rely upon carrying along with him in his discourses from the pulpit a large majority of interested and approving faces. But here, unhappily, was a case where the majority did not rule. The minority, relatively small in numbers, was prodigious in virile force.

More than twenty years had now elapsed since that minor schism in the Methodist Episcopal Church, the result of which was the independent body known as Free Methodists, had relieved the parent flock of its principal disturbing element. The rupture came fittingly at that time when all the "isms" of the argumentative fifties were hurled violently together into the melting-pot of civil war. The great Methodist Church, South, had broken bodily off on the question of State Rights. The smaller and domestic fraction of Free Methodism separated itself upon an issue which may be most readily described as one of civilization. The seceders resented growth in material prosperity; they repudiated the introduction of written sermons and organ-music; they deplored the increasing laxity in meddlesome piety, the introduction of polite manners in the pulpit and class-room, and the development of even a rudimentary desire among the younger people of the church to be like others outside in dress and speech and deportment. They did battle as long as they could, inside the fold, to restore it to the severely straight and narrow path of primitive Methodism. When the adverse odds became too strong for them, they quitted the church and set up a Bethel for themselves.

Octavius chanced to be one of the places where they were able to hold their own within the church organization. The Methodism of the town had gone along without any local secession. It still held in full fellowship the radicals who elsewhere had followed their unbridled bent into the strongest emotional vagaries, — where excited brethren worked themselves up into epileptic fits, and women whirled themselves about in weird religious ecstasies, like dervishes of the Orient, till they fell headlong in a state of trance. Octavian Methodism was spared extravagances of this sort, it is true, but it paid a price for the immunity. The people whom an open split would have taken away remained to leaven and dominate the whole lump. This small advanced section, with its men of a type all the more aggressive from its narrowness, and women who went about solemnly in plain gray garments, with tight-fitting, unadorned, mouse-colored sunbonnets, had not been able wholly to enforce its views upon the social life of the church members, but of its controlling influence upon their official and public actions there could be no doubt.

The situation had begun to unfold itself to Theron from the outset. He had recognized the episodes of the forbidden Sunday milk and of the flowers in poor Alice's bonnet as typical of much more that was to come. No week followed without bringing some new fulfilment of this foreboding. Now, at the end of two months, he knew well enough that the hitherto dominant minority was hostile to him and his ministry, and would do whatever it could against him.

Though Theron at once decided to show fight, and did not at all waver in that resolve, his courage was in the main of a despondent sort. Sometimes it would flutter up to the point of confidence, or at least hopefulness, when he met with substantial men of the church who obviously liked him, and whom he found himself mentally ranging on his side, in the struggle which was to come. But more often it was blankly apparent to him that, the moment flags were flying and drums on the roll, these amiable fair-weather friends would probably take to their heels.

Still, such as they were, his sole hope lay in their support. He must make the best of them. He set himself doggedly to the task of gathering together all those who were not his enemies into what, when the proper time came, should be known as the pastor's party. There was plenty of apostolic warrant for this. If there had not been, Theron felt that the mere elementary demands of self-defence would have justified his use of strategy.

The institution of pastoral calling, particularly that inquisitorial form of it laid down in the Discipline, had never attracted Theron. He and Alice had gone about among their previous flocks in quite a haphazard fashion, without thought of system, much less of deliberate purpose. Theron made lists now, and devoted thought and examination to the personal tastes and characteristics of the people to be cultivated.

There were some, for example, who would expect him to talk pretty much as the Discipline ordained, — that is, to ask if they had family prayer, to inquire after their souls, and generally to minister grace to his hearers, — and these in turn subdivided themselves into classes, ranging from those who would wish nothing else to those who needed only a mild spiritual flavor. There were others whom he would please much better by not talking shop at all. Although he could ill afford it, he subscribed now for a daily paper that he might have a perpetually renewed source of good conversational topics for these more worldly calls. He also bought several pounds of candy,[2] pleasing in color, but warranted to be entirely harmless, and he made a large mysterious mark on the inside of his new silk hat to remind him not to go out calling without some of this [3] in his pocket for the children.

Alice, he felt, was not helping him in this matter as effectively as he could have wished. Her attitude toward the church in Octavius might best be described by the word "sulky." Great allowance was to be made, he realized, for her humiliation over the flowers in her bonnet. That might justify her, fairly enough, in being kept away from meeting now and again by headaches, or undefined megrims. But it ought not to prevent her from going about and making friends among the kindlier parishioners who would welcome such a thing, and whom he from time to time indicated to her. She did go to some extent, it is true, but she produced, in doing so, an effect of performing a duty. He did not find traces anywhere of her having created a brilliant social impression. When they went out together, he was peculiarly conscious of having to do the work unaided.

This was not at all like the Alice of former years, of other charges. Why, she had been, beyond comparison, the most popular young woman in Tyre. What possessed her to mope like this in Octavius?

[2] English ed. reads "sweets" for "candy."
[3] English ed. reads "these" for "this."

Theron looked at her attentively nowadays, when she was unaware of his gaze, to try [4] if her face offered any answer to the riddle. It could not be suggested that she was ill. Never in her life had she been looking so well. She had thrown herself, all at once, and with what was to him an unaccountable energy, into the creation and management of a flower- garden. She was out the better part of every day, rain or shine, digging, transplanting, pruning, pottering generally about among her plants and shrubs. This work in the open air had given her an aspect of physical well-being which it was impossible to be mistaken about.

Her husband was glad, of course, that she had found some occupation which at once pleased her and so obviously conduced to health. This was so much a matter of course, in fact, that he said to himself over and over again that he *was* glad. Only — only, sometimes the thought *would* force itself upon his attention that if she did not spend so much of her time in her own garden, she would have more time to devote to winning friends for them in the Garden of the Lord, — friends whom they were going to need badly.

The young minister, in taking anxious stock of the chances for and against him, turned over often in his mind the fact that he had already won rank as a pulpit orator. His sermons had attracted almost universal attention at Tyre, and his achievement before the Conference at Tecumseh, if it did fail to receive practical reward, had admittedly distanced all the other preaching there. It was a part of the evil luck pursuing him that here in this perversely enigmatic Octavius his special gift seemed to be of no use whatever. There were times, indeed, when he was tempted to think that bad preaching was what Octavius wanted.

Somewhere he had heard of a Presbyterian minister, in charge of a big city church, who managed to keep well in with a watchfully Orthodox congregation, and at the same time establish himself in the affections of the community at

[4] English ed. reads "to see" for "to try."

large, by simply preaching two kinds of sermons. In the morning, when almost all who attended were his own communicants, he gave them very cautious and edifying doctrinal discourses, treading loyally in the path of the Westminster Confession. To the evening assemblages, made up for the larger part of outsiders, he addressed broadly liberal sermons, literary in form, and full of respectful allusions to modern science and the philosophy of the day. Thus he filled the church at both services, and put money in its treasury and his own fame before the world. There was of course the obvious danger that the pious elders who in the forenoon heard infant damnation vigorously proclaimed, would revolt when they heard after supper that there was some doubt about even adults being damned at all. But either because the same people did not attend both services, or because the minister's perfect regularity in the morning was each week regarded as a retraction of his latest vagaries of an evening, no trouble ever came.

Theron had somewhat tentatively tried this on in Octavius. It was no good. His parishioners were of the sort who would have come to church eight times a day on Sunday, instead of two, if occasion offered. The hope that even a portion of them would stop away, and that their places would be taken in the evening by less prejudiced strangers who wished for intellectual rather than theological food, fell by the wayside. The yearned-for strangers did not come; the familiar faces of the morning service all turned up in their accustomed places every evening. They were faces which confused and disheartened Theron in the daytime. Under the gaslight they seemed even harder and more unsympathetic. He timorously experimented with them for an evening or two, then abandoned the effort.

Once there had seemed the beginning of a chance. The richest banker in Octavius — a fat, sensual, hog-faced old bachelor — surprised everybody one evening by entering the church and taking a seat. Theron happened to know who he was; even if he had not known, the suppressed excitement visible in the congregation, the way the sisters turned round to look, the way the more important brethren put their heads together and exchanged furtive whispers, — would have warned him that big game was in view. He recalled afterward with something like self-disgust the eager, almost tremulous pains he himself took to please this banker. There was a part of the sermon, as it had been written out, which might easily give offence to a single man of wealth and free notions of life. With the alertness of a mental gymnast, Theron ran ahead, excised this portion, and had ready when the gap was reached some very pretty general remarks, all the more effective and eloquent, he felt, for having been extemporized. People said it was a good sermon; and after the benediction and dispersion some of the officials and principal pew-holders remained to talk over the likelihood of a capture having been effected. Theron did not get away without having this mentioned to him, and he was conscious of sharing deeply the hope of the brethren, — with the added reflection that it would be a personal triumph for himself into the bargain. He was ashamed of this feeling a little later, and of his trick with the sermon. But this chastening product of introspection was all the fruit which the incident bore. The banker never came again.

Theron returned one afternoon, a little earlier than usual, from a group of pastoral calls. Alice, who was plucking weeds in a border at the shady side of the house, heard his step, and rose from her labors. He was walking slowly, and seemed weary. He took off his high hat, as he saw her, and wiped his brow. The broiling June sun was still high overhead. Doubtless it was its insufferable heat which was accountable for the worn lines in his face and the spiritless air which the wife's eye detected. She went to the gate, and kissed him as he entered.

"I believe, if I were you," she said, "I'd carry an umbrella such scorching days as this. Nobody'd think anything of it.

I don't see why a minister shouldn't carry one as much as a woman carries a parasol."

Theron gave her a rueful, meditative sort of smile. "I suppose people really do think of us as a kind of hybrid female," he remarked. Then, holding his hat in his hand, he drew a long breath of relief at finding himself in the shade, and looked about him.

"Why, you've got more posies here, on this one side of the house alone, than mother had in her whole yard," he said, after a little. "Let's see — I know that one: that's columbine, isn't it? And that's London pride, and that's ragged robin. I don't know any of the others."

Alice recited various unfamiliar names, as she pointed out the several plants which bore them, and he listened with a kindly semblance of interest. They strolled thus to the rear of the house, where thick clumps of fragrant pinks lined both sides of the path. She picked some of these for him, and gave him more names with which to label the considerable number of other plants he saw about him.

"I had no idea we were so well provided as all this," he commented at last. "Those Van Sizers must have been tremendous hands for flowers. You were lucky in following such people."

"Van Sizers!" echoed Alice, with contempt. "All they left was old tomato cans and clamshells. Why, I've put in every blessed one of these myself, all except those peonies, there, and one brier on the side wall."

"Good for you!" exclaimed Theron, approvingly. Then it occurred to him to ask, "But where did you get them all? Around among our friends?"

"Some few," responded Alice, with a note of hesitation in her voice. "Sister Bult gave me the verbenas, there, and the white pinks were a present from Miss Stevens. But most of them Levi Gorringe was good enough to send me, — from his garden."

"I didn't know that Gorringe had a garden," said Theron.

"I thought he lived over his law-office, in the brick block, there."

"Well, I don't know that it's exactly *his*," explained Alice; "but it's a big garden somewhere outside, where he can have anything he likes." She went on with a little laugh: "I didn't like to question him too closely, for fear he'd think I was looking a gift horse in the mouth, — or else hinting for more. It was quite his own offer, you know. He picked them all out for me, and brought them here, and lent me a book telling me just what to do with each one. And in a few days, now, I am to have another big batch of plants, — dahlias and zinnias and asters and so on; I'm almost ashamed to take them. But it's such a change to find some one in this Octavius who isn't all self!"

"Yes, Gorringe is a good fellow," said Theron. "I wish he was a professing member." Then some new thought struck him. "Alice," he exclaimed, "I believe I'll go and see him this very afternoon. I don't know why it hasn't occurred to me before: he's just the man whose advice I need most. He knows these people here; he can tell me what to do."

"Aren't you too tired now?" suggested Alice, as Theron put on his hat.

"No, the sooner the better," he replied, moving now toward the gate.

"Well," she began, "if I were you, I wouldn't say too much about — that is, I — but never mind."

"What is it?" asked her husband.

"Nothing whatever," replied Alice, positively. "It was only some nonsense of mine;" and Theron, placidly accepting the feminine whim, went off down the street again.

CHAPTER XII

THE Rev. Mr. Ware found Levi Gorringe's law-office readily enough, but its owner was not in. He probably would be back again, though, in a quarter of an hour or so, the boy said, and the minister at once decided to wait.

Theron was interested in finding that this office-boy was no other than Harvey, — the lad who brought milk to the parsonage every morning. He remembered now that he had heard good things of this urchin, as to the hard work he did to help his mother, the Widow Semple, in her struggle to keep a roof over her head; and also bad things, in that he did not come regularly either to church or Sunday-school. The clergyman recalled, too, that Harvey had impressed him as a character.

"Well, sonny, are you going to be a lawyer?" he asked, as he seated himself by the window, and looked about him, first at the dusty litter of old papers, pamphlets, and tape-bound documents in bundles which crowded the stuffy chamber, and then at the boy himself.

Harvey was busy at a big box, — a rough pine dry-goods box [1] which bore the flaring label of an express company, and also of a well-known seed-firm in a Western city, and which the boy had apparently just opened. He was lifting from it, and placing on the table after he had shaken off the sawdust and moss [2] in which they were packed, small parcels of what looked in the fading light to be half-dried plants.

"Well, I don't know — I rather guess not," he made answer, as he pursued his task. "So far as I can make out, this wouldn't be the place to start in at, [3] if I *was* going to be a lawyer. A boy can learn here first-rate how to load cartridges and clean a gun, and braid trout-flies on to leaders, but I don't see much

---

[1] English ed. reads "packing case" for "dry-goods box."

[2] English ed. reads "taken off the papers and moist moss" for "shaken off the sawdust and moss."

[3] English ed. reads "start in" for "start in at."

law laying around loose. Anyway," he went on, "I couldn't afford to read law, and not be getting any wages. I have to earn money, you know."

Theron felt that he liked the boy. "Yes," he said, with a kindly tone; "I've heard that you are a good, industrious youngster. I daresay Mr. Gorringe will see to it that you get a chance to read law, and get wages too."

"Oh, I can read all there is here and welcome," the boy explained, stepping toward the window to decipher the label on a bundle of roots in his hand, "but that's no good unless there's regular practice coming into the office all the while. *That's* how you learn to be a lawyer. But Gorringe don't have what I call a practice at all. He just sees men in the other room there, with the door shut, and whatever there is to do he does it all himself."

The minister remembered a stray hint somewhere that Mr. Gorringe was a money-lender, — what was colloquially called a "note-shaver." To his rustic sense, there was something not quite nice about that occupation. It would be indecorous, he felt, to encourage further talk about it from the boy.

"What are you doing there?" he inquired, to change the subject.

"Sorting out some plants," replied Harvey. "I don't know what's got into Gorringe lately. This is the third big box he's had since I've been here, — that is, in six weeks, — besides two baskets full of rose-bushes. I don't know what he does with them. He carries them off himself somewhere. I've had kind of half a notion that he's figurin' on getting married. I can't think of anything else that would make a man spend money like water, — just for flowers and bushes. They do get foolish, you know, when they've got marriage on the brain."

Theron found himself only imperfectly following the theories of the young philosopher. It was his fact that monopolized the minister's attention.

"But as I understand it," he remarked hesitatingly, "Brother Gorringe — or rather Mr. Gorringe — gets all the plants he wants, everything he likes, from a big garden somewhere outside. I don't know that it is exactly *his;* but I remember hearing something to that effect."

The boy slapped the last sawdust off his hands, and, as he came to the window, shook his head. "These don't come from no garden outside," he declared. "They come from the dealers', and he pays solid cash for 'em. The invoice for this lot alone was thirty-one dollars and sixty cents. There it is on the table. You can see it for yourself."

Mr. Ware did not offer to look. "Very likely these are *for* the garden I was speaking of," he said. "Of course you can't go on taking plants out of a garden indefinitely without putting others in."

"I don't know anything about any garden that he takes plants *out* of," answered Harvey, and looked meditatively for a minute or two out upon the street below. Then he turned to the minister. "Your wife's doing a good deal of gardening this spring, I notice," he said casually. "You'd hardly think it was the same place, she's fixed it up so. If she wants any extra hoeing done, I can always get off Saturday afternoons."

"I will remember," said Theron. He also looked out of the window; and nothing more was said until, a few moments later, Mr. Gorringe himself came in.

The lawyer seemed both surprised and pleased at discovering the identity of his visitor, with whom he shook hands in almost an excess of cordiality. He spread a large newspaper over the pile of seedling plants on the table, pushed the packing-box under the table with his foot, and said almost peremptorily to the boy, "You can go now!" Then he turned again to Theron.

"Well, Mr. Ware, I'm glad to see you," he repeated, and drew up a chair by the window. "Things are going all right with you, I hope."

Theron noted again the waving black hair, the dark skin,

and the carefully trimmed mustache and chin-tuft which gave the lawyer's face a combined effect of romance and smartness. No; it was the eyes, cool, shrewd, dark-gray eyes, which suggested this latter quality. The recollection of having seen one of them wink, in deliberate hostility of sarcasm, when those other trustees had their backs turned, came mercifully at the moment to recall the young minister to his errand.

"I thought I would drop in and have a chat with you," he said, getting better under way as he went on. "Quarterly Conference is only a fortnight off, and I am a good deal at sea about what is going to happen."

"I'm not a church member, you know," interposed Gorringe. "That shuts me out of the Quarterly Conference."

"Alas, yes!" said Theron. "I wish it didn't. I'm afraid I'm not going to have any friends to spare there."

"What are you afraid of?" asked the lawyer, seeming now to be wholly at his ease again. "They can't eat you."

"No, they keep me too lean for that," responded Theron, with a pensive smile. "I *was* going to ask, you know, for an increase of salary, or an extra allowance. I don't see how I can go on as it is. The sum fixed by the last Quarterly Conference of the old year, and which I am getting now, is one hundred dollars less than my predecessor had. That isn't fair, and it isn't right. But so far from its looking as if I could get an increase, the prospect seems rather that they will make me pay for the gas and that sidewalk. I never recovered more than about half of my moving expenses, as you know, and — and, frankly, I don't know which way to turn. It keeps me miserable all the while."

"That's where you're wrong," said Mr. Gorringe. "If you let things like that worry you, you'll keep a sore skin all your life. You take my advice and just go ahead your own gait, and let other folks do the worrying. They *are* pretty close-fisted here, for a fact, but you can manage to rub along somehow. If you should get into any real difficulties, why, I guess —" the lawyer paused to smile in a hesitating, significant

way, — "I guess some road out can be found all right. The
main thing is, don't fret, and don't allow your wife to — to
fret either."

He stopped abruptly. Theron nodded in recognition of
his amiable tone, and then found the nod lengthening itself
out into almost a bow as the thought spread through his mind
that this had been nothing more nor less than a promise to
help him with money if worst came to worst. He looked at
Levi Gorringe, and said to himself that the intuition of
women was wonderful. Alice had picked him out as a friend
of theirs merely by seeing him pass the house.

"Yes," he said; "I am specially anxious to keep my wife
from worrying. She was surrounded in her girlhood by a good
deal of what, relatively, we should call luxury, and that makes
it all the harder for her to be a poor minister's wife. I had
quite decided to get her a hired girl, come what might, but
she thinks she'd rather get on without one. Her health is
better, I must admit, than it was when we came here. She
works out in her garden a great deal, and that seems to agree
with her." [4]

"Octavius *is* a healthy place, — that's generally admitted,"
replied the lawyer, with indifference. He seemed not to be
interested in Mrs. Ware's health, but looked intently out
through the window at the buildings opposite, and drummed
with his fingers on the arms of his chair.

Theron made haste to revert to his errand. "Of course,
your not being in the Quarterly Conference," he said, "renders [5] certain things impossible. But I didn't know but you
might have some knowledge of how matters are going, what
plans the officials of the church had; they seem to have agreed
to tell me nothing."

"Well, I *have* heard this much," responded Gorringe.
"They're figuring on getting the Soulsbys here to raise the

[4] English ed. adds the following sentence: " 'She's making a most beautiful
garden of it.' "
[5] English ed. reads "that renders" for "renders."

debt and kind o' shake things up generally. I guess that's about as good as settled. Hadn't you heard of it?"

"Not a breath!" exclaimed Theron, mournfully. "Well," he added upon reflection, "I'm sorry, downright sorry. The debt-raiser seems to me about the lowest-down thing we produce. I've heard of those Soulsbys; I saw *him* indeed [6] once at Conference, but I believe *she* is the head of the firm."

"Yes; she wears the breeches, I understand," said Gorringe, sententiously.

"I *had* hoped," the young minister began with a rueful sigh, "in fact, I felt quite confident at the outset that I could pay off this debt, and put the church generally on a new footing, by giving extra attention to my pulpit work. It is hardly for me to say it, but in other places where I have been, my preaching has been rather — rather a feature in the town itself. I have always been accustomed to attract to our services a good many non-members, and that, as you know, helps tremendously from a money point of view. But somehow that has failed here. I doubt if the average congregations are a whit larger now than they were when I came in April. I know the collections are not."

"No," commented the lawyer, slowly; "you'll never do anything in that line in Octavius. You might, of course, if you were to stay here and work hard at it for five or six years —"

"Heaven forbid!" groaned Mr. Ware.

"Quite so," put in the other. "The point is that the Methodists here are a little set by themselves. I don't know that they like one another specially, but I do know that they are not what you might call popular with people outside. Now, a new preacher at the Presbyterian church, or even the Baptist, — he might have a chance to create talk, and make a stir. But Methodist, — no! People who don't belong won't come near the Methodist church here so long as there's any other place with a roof on it to go to. Give a dog a bad name, you

[6] English ed. omits "indeed."

know. Well, the Methodists here have got a bad name; and if you could preach like Henry Ward Beecher himself you wouldn't change it, or get folks to come and hear you."

"I see what you mean," Theron responded. "I'm not particularly surprised myself that Octavius doesn't love us, or look to us for intellectual stimulation. I myself leave that pulpit more often than otherwise feeling like a wet rag, — utterly limp and discouraged. But, if you don't mind my speaking of it, *you* don't belong, and yet *you* come."

It was evident that the lawyer did not mind. He spoke freely in reply. "Oh, yes, I've got into the habit of it. I began going when I first came here, and — and so it grew to be natural for me to go. Then, of course, being the only lawyer you have, a considerable amount of my business is mixed up in one way or another with your membership; you see those are really the things which settle a man in a rut, and keep him there."

"I suppose your people were Methodists," said Theron, to fill in the pause, "and that is how you originally started with us."

Levi Gorringe shook his head. He leaned back, half closed his eyes, put his finger-tips together, and almost smiled as if something in retrospect pleased and moved him.

"No," he said; "I went to the church first to see a girl who used to go there. It was long before your time. All her family moved away years ago. You wouldn't know any of them. I was younger then, and I didn't know as much as I do now. I worshipped the very ground that girl walked on, and like a fool I never gave her so much as a hint of it. Looking back now, I can see that I might have had her if I'd asked her. But I went instead and sat around and looked at her at church and Sunday-school and prayer-meetings Thursday nights, and class-meetings after the sermon. She was devoted to religion and church work; and, thinking it would please her, I joined the church on probation. Men can fool themselves easier than they can other people. I actually believed

at the time that I had experienced religion. I felt myself full
of all sorts of awakenings of the soul and so forth. But it
was really that girl. You see I'm telling you the thing just
as it was. I was very happy. I think it was the happiest time
of my life. I remember there was a love-feast while I was on
probation; and I sat down in front, right beside her, and we
ate the little square chunks of bread and drank the water
together, and I held one corner of her hymn-book when we
stood up and sang. That was the nearest I ever got to her, or
to full membership in the church. That very next week, I
think it was, we learned that she had got engaged to the minister's son, — a young man who had just become a minister
himself. They got married, and went away — and I — somehow I never took up my membership when the six months'
probation was over. That's how it was."

"It is very interesting," remarked Theron, softly, after a
little silence, — "and very full of human nature."

"Well, now you see," said the lawyer, "what I mean when
I say that there hasn't been another minister here since, that
I should have felt like telling this story to. They wouldn't
have understood it at all. They would have thought it was
blasphemy for me to say straight out that what I took for
experiencing religion was really a girl. But you are different.
I felt that at once, the first time I saw you. In a pulpit or out
of it, what I like in a human being is that he *should* be
human."

"It pleases me beyond measure that you should like me,
then," returned the young minister, with frank gratification shining on his face. "The world is made all the sweeter
and more lovable by these — these elements of romance. I
am not one of those who would wish to see them banished or
frowned upon. I don't mind admitting to you that there is
a good deal in Methodism — I mean the strict practice of its
letter which you find here in Octavius — that is personally
distasteful to me. I read the other day of an English bishop
who said boldly, publicly, that no modern nation could prac-

tise the principles laid down in the Sermon on the Mount and survive for twenty-four hours."

"Ha, ha! That's good!" laughed the lawyer.

"I felt that it was good, too," pursued Theron. "I am getting to see a great many things differently, here in Octavius. Our Methodist Discipline is like the Beatitudes, — very helpful and beautiful if treated as spiritual suggestion, but more or less of a stumbling-block if insisted upon literally. I declare!" he added, sitting up in his chair, "I never talked like this to a living soul before in all my life. Your confidences were contagious."

The Rev. Mr. Ware rose as he spoke, and took up his hat.

"Must you be going?" asked the lawyer, also rising. "Well, I'm glad I haven't shocked you. Come in oftener when you are passing. And if you see anything I can help you in, always tell me."

The two men shook hands, with an emphatic and lingering clasp.

"*I* am glad," said Theron, "that you didn't stop coming to church just because you lost the girl."

Levi Gorringe answered the minister's pleasantry with a smile which curled his mustache upward, and expanded in little wrinkles at the ends of his eyes. "No," he said jestingly. "I'm death on collecting debts; and I reckon that the church still owes me a girl. I'll have one yet."

So, with merriment the echoes of which pleasantly accompanied Theron down the stairway, the two men parted.

CHAPTER XIII

THOUGH Time lagged in passing with a slowness which seemed born of studied insolence, there did arrive at last a day which had something definitive about it to Theron's disturbed and restless mind. It was a Thursday, and the prayer-meeting to be held that evening would be the last before the Quarterly Conference, now only four days off.

For some reason, the young minister found himself dwelling upon this fact, and investing it with importance. But yesterday the Quarterly Conference had seemed a long way ahead. To-day brought it alarmingly close to hand. He had not heretofore regarded the weekly assemblage for prayer and song as a thing calling for preparation, or for any preliminary thought. Now on this Thursday morning he went to his desk after breakfast, which was a sign that he wanted the room to himself, quite as if he had the task of a weighty sermon before him. He sat at the desk all the forenoon, doing no writing, it is true, but remembering every once in a while, when his mind turned aside from the book in his hands, that there was that prayer-meeting in the evening. Sometimes he reached the point of vaguely wondering why this strictly commonplace affair should be forcing itself thus upon his attention. Then, with a kind of mental shiver at the recollection that this was Thursday, and that the great struggle came on Monday, he would go back to his book.

There were a half-dozen volumes on the open desk before him. He had taken them out from beneath a pile of old "Sunday-School Advocates" and church magazines, where they had lain hidden from Alice's view most of the week. If there had been a locked drawer in the house, he would have used it instead to hold these books, which had come to him in a neat parcel, which also contained an amiable note from Dr. Ledsmar, recalling a pleasant evening in May, and expressing the hope that the accompanying works would be of some service. Theron had glanced at the backs of the upper-most two, and discovered that their author was Renan. Then he had hastily put the lot in the best place he could think of to escape his wife's observation.

He realized now that there had been no need for this secrecy. Of the other four books, by Sayce, Budge, Smith, and Lenormant, three indeed revealed themselves to be pub-lished under religious auspices. As for Renan, he might have known that the name would be meaningless to Alice. The feeling that he himself was not much wiser in this matter than his wife may have led him to pass over the learned text-books on Chaldean antiquity, and even the volume of Renan which appeared to be devoted to Oriental inscriptions, and take up his other book, entitled in the translation, "Recol-lections of my Youth." This he rather glanced through, at the outset, following with a certain inattention the introduc-tory sketches and essays, which dealt with an unfamiliar, and, to his notion, somewhat preposterous Breton racial type. Then, little by little, it dawned upon him that there was a connected story in all this; and suddenly he came upon it, out in the open, as it were. It was the story of how a deeply devout young man, trained from his earliest boyhood for the sacred office, and desiring passionately nothing but to be worthy of it, came to a point where, at infinite cost of pain to himself and of anguish to those dearest to him, he had to declare that he could no longer believe at all in revealed re-ligion.

Theron Ware read this all with an excited interest which no book had ever stirred in him before. Much of it he read over and over again, to make sure that he penetrated every-where the husk of French habits of thought and Catholic methods in which the kernel was wrapped. He broke off mid-way in this part of the book to go out to the kitchen to dinner, and began the meal in silence. To Alice's questions he replied briefly that he was preparing himself for the evening's prayer-meeting. She lifted her brows in such frank [1] surprise at this that he made a further and somewhat rambling explanation about having again taken up the work on his book, — the book about Abraham.

"I thought you said you'd given that up altogether," she remarked.

"Well," he said, "I *was* discouraged about it for a while. But a man never does anything big without getting discouraged over and over again while he's doing it. I don't say now that I shall write precisely *that* book, — I'm merely reading scientific works about the period, just now, — but if not that, I shall write some other book. Else how will you get that piano?" he added, with an attempt at a smile.

"I thought you had given that up, too!" she replied ruefully. Then before he could speak, she went on: "Never mind the piano; that can wait. What I've got on my mind just now isn't piano; it's potatoes. Do you know, I saw some the other day at Rasbach's, splendid potatoes, — these are some of them, — and fifteen cents a bushel cheaper than those dried-up old things Brother Barnum keeps, and so I bought two bushels. And Sister Barnum met me on the street this morning, and threw it in my face that the Discipline commands us to trade with each other. Is there any such command?"

"Yes," said the husband. "It's Section 33. Don't you remember? I looked it up in Tyre. We are to 'evidence our desire of salvation by doing good, especially to them that are of the household of faith, or groaning so to be; by employing them preferably to others; buying one of another; helping each other in business,' — and so on. Yes, it's all there."

"Well, I told her I didn't believe it was," put in Alice, "and I said that even if it was, there ought to be another section about selling potatoes to their minister for more than they're worth, — potatoes that turn all green when you boil them, too. I believe I'll read up that old Discipline myself,

[1] English ed. reads "blank" for "frank."

and see if it hasn't got some things that I can talk back with."

"The very section before that, Number 32, enjoins members against 'uncharitable or unprofitable conversation, — particularly speaking evil of magistrates or ministers.' You'd have 'em there, I think." Theron had begun cheerfully enough, but the care-worn, preoccupied look returned now to his face. "I'm sorry if we've fallen out with the Barnums," he said. "His brother-in-law, Davis, the Sunday-school superintendent, is a member of the Quarterly Conference, you know, and I've been hoping that he was on my side. I've been taking a good deal of pains to make up to him."

He ended with a sigh, the pathos of which impressed Alice. "If you think it will do any good," she volunteered, "I'll go and call on the Davises this very afternoon. I'm sure to find her at home, — she's tied hand and foot with that brood of hers, — and you'd better give me some of that candy for them."

Theron nodded his approval and thanks, and relapsed into silence. When the meal was over, he brought out the confectionery to his wife, and without a word went back to that remarkable book.

When Alice returned toward the close of day, to prepare the simple tea which was always laid a half-hour earlier on Thursdays and Sundays, she found her husband where she had left him, still busy with those new scientific works. She recounted to him some incidents of her call upon Mrs. Davis, as she took off her hat and put on the big kitchen apron, — how pleased Mrs. Davis seemed to be; how her affection for her sister-in-law, the grocer's wife, disclosed itself to be not even skin-deep; how the children leaped upon the candy as if they had never seen any before; and how, in her belief, Mr. Davis would be heart and soul on Theron's side at the Conference.

To her surprise, the young minister seemed not at all interested. He hardly looked at her during her narrative, but reclined in the easy-chair with his head thrown back, and an abstracted gaze wandering aimlessly about the ceiling. When she avowed her faith in the Sunday-school superintendent's loyal partisanship, which she did with a pardonable pride in having helped to make it secure, her husband even closed his eyes, and moved his head with a gesture which plainly bespoke indifference.

"I expected you'd be tickled to death," she remarked, with evident disappointment.

"I've a bad headache," he explained, after a minute's pause.

"No wonder!" Alice rejoined, sympathetically enough, but with a note of reproof as well. "What can you expect, staying cooped up in here all day long, poring over those books? People are all the while remarking that you study too much. I tell them, of course, that you're a great hand for reading, and always were; but I think myself it would be better if you got out more, and took more exercise, and saw people. You know lots and slathers more than *they* do now, or ever will, if you never opened another book."

Theron regarded her with an expression which she had never seen on his face before. "You don't realize what you are saying," he replied slowly. He sighed as he added, with increased gravity, "I am the most ignorant man alive!"

Alice began a little laugh of wifely incredulity, and then let it die away as she recognized that he was really troubled and sad in his mind. She bent over to kiss him lightly on the brow, and tiptoed her way out into the kitchen.

"I believe I will let you make my excuses at the prayer-meeting this evening," he said all at once, as the supper came to an end. He had eaten next to nothing during the meal, and had sat in a sort of brown-study from which Alice kindly forbore to arouse him. "I don't know — I hardly feel equal to it. They won't take it amiss — for [2] once — if you explain to them that I — I am not at all well."

"Oh, I do hope you're not coming down with anything!" Alice had risen too, and was gazing at him with a solicitude

[2] English ed. adds "the."

the tenderness of which at once comforted, and in some obscure way jarred on his nerves. "Is there anything I can do — or shall I go for a doctor? We've got mustard in the house, and senna — I think there's some senna left — and Jamaica ginger."

Theron shook his head wearily at her. "Oh, no, — no!" he expostulated. "It isn't anything that needs drugs, or doctors either. It's just mental worry and fatigue, that's all. An evening's quiet rest in the big chair, and early to bed, — that will fix me up all right."

"But you'll read; and that will make your head worse," said Alice.

"No, I won't read any more," he promised her, walking slowly into the sitting-room, and settling himself in the big chair, the while she brought out a pillow from the adjoining best bedroom, and adjusted it behind his head. "That's nice! I'll just lie quiet here, and perhaps doze a little till you come back. I feel in the mood for the rest; it will do me all sorts of good."

He closed his eyes; and Alice, regarding his upturned face anxiously, decided that already it looked more at peace than awhile ago.

"Well, I hope you'll be better when I get back," she said, as she began preparations for the evening service. These consisted in combing stiffly back the strands of light-brown hair which, during the day, had exuberantly loosened themselves over her temples into something almost like curls; in fastening down upon this rebellious hair a plain brown-straw bonnet, guiltless of all ornament save a binding ribbon of dull umber hue; and in putting on a thin dark-gray shawl and a pair of equally subdued lisle-thread gloves. Thus attired, she made a mischievous little grimace of dislike at her puritanical image in the looking-glass over the mantel, and then turned to announce her departure.

"Well, I'm off," she said. Theron opened his eyes to take in this figure of his wife dressed for prayer-meeting, and then closed them again abruptly. "All right," he murmured, and then he heard the door shut behind her.

Although he had been alone all day, there seemed to be quite a unique value and quality in this present solitude. He stretched out his legs on the opposite chair, and looked lazily about him, with the feeling that at last he had secured some leisure, and could think undisturbed to his heart's content. There were nearly two hours of unbroken quiet before him; and the mere fact of his having stepped aside from the routine of his duty to procure it marked it in his thoughts as a special occasion, which ought in the nature of things to yield more than the ordinary harvest of mental profit.

Theron's musings were broken in upon from time to time by rumbling outbursts of hymn-singing from the church next door. Surely, he said to himself, there could be no other congregation in the Conference, or in all Methodism, which sang so badly as these Octavians did. The noise, as it came to him now and again, divided itself familiarly into a main strain of hard, high, sharp, and tinny female voices, with three or four concurrent and clashing branch strains of part-singing by men who did not know how. How well he already knew these voices! Through two wooden walls he could detect the conceited and pushing note of Brother Lovejoy, who tried always to drown the rest out, and the lifeless, unmeasured weight of shrill clamor which Sister Barnum hurled into every chorus, half closing her eyes and sticking out her chin as she did so. They drawled their hymns too, these people, till Theron thought he understood that injunction in the Discipline against singing too slowly. It had puzzled him heretofore; now he felt that it must have been meant in prophecy for Octavius.

It was impossible not to recall in contrast that other church music he had heard, a month before, and the whole atmosphere of that other pastoral sitting-room, from which he had listened to it. The startled and crowded impressions of that strange evening had been lying hidden in his mind all this while, driven into a corner by the pressure of more ordinary, every-day matters. They came forth now, and passed across his brain, — no longer confusing and distorted, but in orderly and intelligible sequence. Their earlier effect had been one of frightened fascination. Now he looked them over calmly as they lifted themselves, one by one, and found himself not shrinking at all, or evading anything, but dwelling upon each in turn as a natural and welcome part of the most important experience of his life.

The young minister had arrived, all at once, at this conclusion. He did not question at all the means by which he had reached it. Nothing was clearer to his mind than the conclusion itself, — that his meeting with the priest and the doctor was the turning-point in his career. They had lifted him bodily out of the slough of ignorance, of contact with low minds and sordid, narrow things, and put him on solid ground. This book he had been reading — this gentle, tender, lovable book, which had as much true piety in it as any devotional book he had ever read, and yet, unlike all devotional books, put its foot firmly upon everything which could not be proved in human reason to be true — must be merely one of a thousand which men like Father Forbes and Dr. Ledsmar knew by heart. The very thought that he was on the way now to know them, too, made Theron tremble. The prospect wooed him, and he thrilled in response, with the wistful and delicate eagerness of a young lover.

Somehow, the fact that the priest and the doctor were not religious men, and that this book which had so impressed and stirred him was nothing more than Renan's recital of how he, too, ceased to be a religious man, did not take a form which Theron could look square in the face. It wore the shape, instead, of a vague premise that there were a great many different kinds of religions, — the past and dead races had multiplied these in their time literally into thousands, — and that each no doubt had its central support of truth somewhere for the good men who were in it, and that to call

one of these divine and condemn all the others was a part
fit only for untutored bigots. Renan had formally repudiated
Catholicism, yet could write in his old age with the deepest
filial affection of the Mother Church he had quitted. Father
Forbes could talk coolly about the "Christ-myth" without
even ceasing to be a priest, and apparently a very active and
devoted priest. Evidently there was an intellectual world, a
world of culture and grace, of lofty thoughts and the inspiring communion of real knowledge, where creeds were not
of importance, and where men asked one another, not "Is
your soul saved?" but "Is your mind well furnished?" Theron
had the sensation of having been invited to become a citizen
of this world. The thought so dazzled him that his impulses
were dragging him forward to take the new oath of allegiance
before he had had time to reflect upon what it was he was
abandoning.

The droning of the Doxology from the church outside
stirred Theron suddenly out of his revery. It had grown
quite dark, and he rose and lit the gas. "Blest be the Tie that
Binds," they were singing. He paused, with hand still in
air, to listen. That well-known phrase arrested his attention,
and gave itself a new meaning. He was bound to those people,
it was true, but he could never again harbor the delusion
that the tie between them was blessed. There was vaguely
present in his mind the consciousness that other ties were
loosening as well. Be that as it might, one thing was certain.
He had passed definitely beyond pretending to himself that
there was anything spiritually in common between him and
the Methodist Church of Octavius. The necessity of his keeping up the pretence with others rose on the instant like a
looming shadow before his mental vision. He turned away
from it, and bent his brain to think of something else.

The noise of Alice opening the front door came as a pleasant digression. A second later it became clear from the sound
of voices that she had brought some one back with her, and
Theron hastily stretched himself out again in the armchair,

with his head back in the pillow, and his feet on the other chair. He had come mighty [3] near forgetting that he was an invalid, and he protected himself the further now by assuming an air of lassitude verging upon prostration.

"Yes; there's a light burning. It's all right," he heard Alice say. She entered the room, and Theron's head was too bad to permit him to turn it, and see who her companion was.

"Theron dear," Alice began, "I knew you'd be glad to see *her,* even if you were out of sorts; and I persuaded her just to run in for a minute. Let me introduce you to Sister Soulsby. Sister Soulsby, — my husband."

The Rev. Mr. Ware sat upright with an energetic start, and fastened upon the stranger a look which conveyed anything but the satisfaction his wife had been so sure about. It was at the first blush an undisguised scowl; and only some fleeting memory of that reflection about needing now to dissemble, prevented him from still frowning as he rose to his feet, and perfunctorily held out his hand.

"Delighted, I'm sure," he mumbled. Then, looking up, he discovered that Sister Soulsby knew he was not delighted, and that she seemed not to mind in the least.

"As your good lady said, I just ran in for a moment," she remarked, shaking his limp hand with a brisk, business-like grasp, and dropping it. "I hate bothering sick people, but as we're to be thrown together a good deal this next week or so, I thought I'd like to lose no time in saying 'howdy.' I won't keep you up now. Your wife has been sweet enough to ask me to move my trunk over here in the morning, so that you'll see enough of me and to spare."

Theron looked falteringly into her face, as he strove for words which should sufficiently mask the disgust this intelligence stirred within him. A debt-raiser in the town was bad enough! A debt-raiser quartered in the very parsonage! — he ground his teeth to think of it.

Alice read his hesitation aright. "Sister Soulsby went to

[3] English ed. reads "awkwardly" for "mighty."

the hotel," she hastily put in; "and Loren Pierce was after her to come and stay at his house, and *I* ventured to tell her that I thought we could make her more comfortable here." She accompanied this by so daring a grimace and nod that her husband woke up to the fact that a point in Conference politics was involved.

He squeezed a doubtful smile upon his features. "We shall both do our best," he said. It was not easy, but he forced increasing amiability into his glance and tone. "Is Brother Soulsby here, too?" he asked.

The debt-raiser shook her head, — again the prompt, decisive movement, so like a busy man of affairs. "No," she answered. "He's doing supply down on the Hudson this week, but he'll be here in time for the Sunday morning love-feast. I always like to come on ahead, and see how the land lies. Well, good-night! Your head will be all right in the morning."

Precisely what she meant by this assurance, Theron did not attempt to guess. He received her adieu, noted the masterful manner in which she kissed his wife, and watched her pass out into the hall, with the feeling uppermost that this was a person who decidedly knew her way about. Much as he was prepared to dislike her, and much as he detested the vulgar methods her profession typified, he could not deny that she seemed a very capable sort of woman.

This mental concession did not prevent his fixing upon Alice, when she returned to the room, a glance of obvious disapproval.

"Theron," she broke forth, to anticipate his reproach, "I did it for the best. The Pierces would have got her if I hadn't cut in. I thought it would help to have her on our side. And, besides, I like her. She's the first sister I've seen since we've been in this hole that's had a kind word for me — or — or sympathized with me! And — and — if you're going to be offended — I shall cry!"

There were real tears on her lashes, ready to make good

the threat. "Oh, I guess I wouldn't," said Theron, with an approach to his old, half-playful manner. "If you like her, that's the chief thing."

Alice shook her tear-drops away. "No," she replied, with a wistful smile; "the chief thing is to have her like you. She's as smart as a steel trap, — that woman is, — and if she took the notion, I believe she could help get us a better place."

CHAPTER XIV

THE ensuing week went by with a buzz and a whirl, circling about Theron Ware's dizzy consciousness like some huge, impalpable teetotum sent spinning under Sister Soulsby's resolute hands. Whenever his vagrant memory recurred to it, in after months, he began by marvelling, and ended with a shudder of repulsion.

It was a week crowded with events, which seemed to him to shoot past so swiftly that in effect they came all of a heap. He never essayed the task, in retrospect, of arranging them in their order of sequence. They had, however, a definite and interdependent chronology which it is worth the while to trace.

Mrs. Soulsby brought her trunk round to the parsonage bright and early on Friday morning, and took up her lodgement in the best bedroom, and her headquarters in the house at large, with a cheerful and business-like manner. She desired nothing so much, she said, as that people should not put themselves out on her account, or allow her to get in their way. She appeared to mean this, too, and to have very good ideas about securing its realization.

During both Friday and the following day, indeed, Theron saw her only at the family meals. There she displayed a hearty relish for all that was set before her which quite won Mrs. Ware's heart, and though she talked rather more than Theron found himself expecting from a woman, he could not deny that her conversation was both seemly and entertaining. She had evidently been a great traveller, and referred to things she had seen in Savannah or Montreal or Los Angeles in as matter-of-fact fashion as he could have spoken of a visit to Tecumseh. Theron asked her many questions about these and other far-off cities, and her answers were all so pat and showed so keen and clear an eye that he began in spite of himself to think of her with a certain admiration.

She in turn plied him with inquiries about the principal pew-holders and members of his congregation, — their means, their disposition, and the measure of their devotion. She put these queries with such intelligence, and seemed to assimilate his replies with such an alert understanding, that the young minister was spurred to put dashes of character in his descriptions, and set forth the idiosyncrasies and distinguishing ear-marks of his flock with what he felt afterward might have been too free a tongue. But at the time her fine air of appreciation led him captive. He gossiped about his parishioners as if he enjoyed it. He made a specially happy thumbnail sketch for her of one of his trustees, Erastus Winch, the loud-mouthed, ostentatiously jovial, and really cold-hearted cheese-buyer. She was particularly interested in hearing about this man. The personality of Winch seemed to have impressed her, and she brought the talk back to him more than once, and prompted Theron to the very threshold of indiscretion in his confidences on the subject.

Save at meal-times, Sister Soulsby spent the two days out around among the Methodists of Octavius. She had little or nothing to say about what she thus saw and heard, but used it as the basis for still further inquiries. She told more than once, however, of how she had been pressed here or there to stay to dinner or supper, and how she had excused herself. "I've knocked about too much," she would explain to the Wares, "not to fight shy of random country cooking. When I find such a born cook as you are — well — I know when I'm well off." Alice flushed with pleased pride at this, and Theron himself felt that their visitor showed great good sense. By Saturday noon, the two women were calling each other by their first names. Theron learned with a certain interest that Sister Soulsby's Christian name was Candace.

It was only natural that he should give even more thought to her than to her quaint and unfamiliar old Ethiopian name. She was undoubtedly a very smart woman. To his surprise she had never introduced in her talk any of the stock religious and devotional phrases which official Methodists so universally employed in mutual converse. She might have been an insurance agent, or a school-teacher, visiting in a purely secular household, so little parade of cant was there about her.

He caught himself wondering how old she was. She seemed to have been pretty well over the whole American continent, and that must take years of time. Perhaps, however, the exertion of so much travel would tend to age one in appearance. Her eyes were still youthful, — decidedly wise eyes, but still [1] juvenile. They had sparkled with almost girlish merriment at some of his jokes. She turned them about a good deal when she spoke, making their glances fit and illustrate the things she said. He had never met any one whose eyes played so constant and prominent a part in their owner's conversation. Theron had never seen a play; but he had encountered the portraits of famous queens of the drama several times in illustrated papers or shop windows, and it occurred to him that some of the more marked contortions of Sister Soulsby's eyes — notably a trick she had of rolling them swiftly round and plunging them, so to speak, into an intent, yearning, one might almost say devouring, gaze at the speaker — were probably employed by eminent actresses like Ristori and Fanny Davenport.

The rest of Sister Soulsby was undoubtedly subordinated in interest to those eyes of hers. Sometimes her face seemed to be reviving temporarily a comeliness which had been constant in former days; then again it would look decidedly, organically, plain. It was the worn and loose-skinned face of a nervous, middle-aged woman, who had had more than her share of trouble, and drank too much tea. She wore the collar of her dress rather low; and Theron found himself wondering at this, because, though long and expansive, her neck certainly showed more cords and cavities than consorted with his vague ideal of statuesque beauty. Then he wondered at

[1] English ed. reads "yet" for "still."

himself for thinking about it, and abruptly reined up his
fancy, only to find that it was playing with speculations as
to whether her yellowish complexion was due to that tea-
drinking or came to her as a legacy of Southern blood.

He knew that she was born in the South because she said
so. From the same source he learned that her father had been
a wealthy planter, who was ruined by the war, and sank into
a premature grave under the weight of his accumulated losses.
The large dark rings around her eyes grew deeper still in
their shadows when she told about this, and her ordinarily
sharp voice took on a mellow cadence, with a soft, drawling
accent, turning u's into o's, and having no r's to speak of.
Theron had imbibed somewhere in early days the conviction
that the South was the land of romance, of cavaliers and
gallants and black eyes flashing behind mantillas and out-
spread fans, and somehow when Sister Soulsby used this
intonation she suggested all these things.

But almost all her talk was in another key, — a brisk, direct, idiomatic manner of speech, with an intonation hinting at no section in particular. It was merely that of the
city-dweller as distinguished from the rustic. She was of about
Alice's height, perhaps a shade taller. It did not escape the
attention of the Wares that she wore clothes of a more stylish
cut and a livelier arrangement of hues than any Alice had
ever dared own, even in lax-minded Tyre. The two talked
of this in their room on Friday night; and Theron explained
that congregations would tolerate things of this sort with a
stranger which would be sharply resented in the case of local
folk whom they controlled. It was on this occasion that Alice
in turn told Theron she was sure Mrs. Soulsby had false
teeth, — a confidence which she immediately regretted as
an act of treachery to her sex.

On Saturday afternoon, toward evening, Brother Soulsby
arrived, and was guided to the parsonage by his wife, who
had gone to the depot to meet him. They must have talked
over the situation pretty thoroughly on the way, for by the

time the new-comer had washed his face and hands and put on a clean collar, Sister Soulsby was ready to announce her plan of campaign in detail.

Her husband was a man of small stature and, like herself, of uncertain age. He had a gentle, if rather dry, clean-shaven face, and wore his dust-colored hair long behind. His little figure was clad in black clothes of a distinctively clerical fashion, and he had a white neck-cloth neatly tied under his collar. The Wares noted that he looked clean and amiable rather than intellectually or spiritually powerful, as he took the vacant seat between theirs, and joined them in concentrating attention upon Mrs. Soulsby.

This lady, holding herself erect and alert on the edge of the low, big easy-chair, had the air of presiding over a meeting.

"My idea is," she began, with an easy implication that no one else's idea was needed, "that your Quarterly Conference, when it meets on Monday, must be adjourned to Tuesday. We will have the people all out to-morrow morning to love-feast, and announcement can be made there, and at the morning service afterward, that a series of revival meetings are to be begun that same evening. Mr. Soulsby and I can take charge in the evening, and we'll see to it that *that* packs the house, — fills the church to overflowing Monday evening. Then we'll quietly turn the meeting into a debt-raising convention, before they know where they are, and we'll wipe off the best part of the load. Now, don't you see," she turned her eyes full upon Theron as she spoke, "you want to hold your Quarterly Conference *after* this money's been raised, not before."

"I see what you mean," Mr. Ware responded gravely. "But —"

"But what!" Sister Soulsby interjected, with vivacity.

"Well," said Theron, picking his words, "in the first place, it rests with the Presiding Elder to say whether an adjournment can be made until Tuesday, not with me."

"That's all right. Leave that to me," said the lady.

"In the second place," Theron went on, still more hesitatingly, "there seems a certain — what shall I say? — indirection in — in —"

"In getting them together for a revival, and springing a debt-raising on them?" Sister Soulsby put in. "Why, man alive, that's the best part of it. You ought to be getting some notion by this time what these Octavius folks of yours are like. I've only been here two days, but I've got their measure down to an allspice. Supposing you were to announce to-morrow that the debt was to be raised Monday. How many men with bank-accounts would turn up, do you think? You could put them all in your eye, sir, — all in your eye!"

"Very possibly you're right," faltered the young minister.

"Right? Why, of course I'm right," she said, with placid confidence. "You've got to take folks as you find them; and you've got to find them the best way you can. One place can be worked, managed, in one way, and another needs quite a different way, and both ways would be dead frosts — complete failures — in a third."

Brother Soulsby coughed softly here, and shuffled his feet for an instant on the carpet. His wife resumed her remarks with slightly abated animation, and at a slower pace.

"My experience," she said, "has shown me that the Apostle was right. To properly serve the cause, one must be all things to all men. I have known very queer things indeed turn out to be means of grace. You simply *can't* get along without some of the wisdom of the serpent. We are commanded to have it, for that matter. And now, speaking of that, do you know when the Presiding Elder arrives in town to-day, and where he is going to eat supper and sleep?"

Theron shook his head. "All I know is he isn't likely to come here," he said, and added sadly, "I'm afraid he's not an admirer of mine."

"Perhaps that's not all his fault," commented Sister Soulsby. "I'll tell you something. He came in on the same train as my husband, and that old trustee Pierce of yours was waiting for him with his buggy, and I saw like a flash what was in the wind, and the minute the train stopped I caught the Presiding Elder, and invited him in your name to come right here and stay; told him you and Alice were just set on his coming, — wouldn't take no for an answer. Of course he couldn't come, — I knew well enough he had promised old Pierce, — but we got in our invitation anyway, and it won't do you any harm. Now, that's what I call having some gumption, — wisdom of the serpent, and so on."

"I'm sure," remarked Alice, "I should have been mortified to death if he *had* come. We lost the extension-leaf to our table in moving, and four is all it'll seat decently."

Sister Soulsby smiled winningly into the wife's honest face. "Don't you see, dear," she explained patiently, "I only asked him because I knew he couldn't come. A little butter spreads a long way, if it's only intelligently warmed."

"It was certainly very ingenious of you," Theron began almost stiffly. Then he yielded to the humanities, and with a kindling smile added, "And it was as kind as kind could be. I'm afraid you're wrong about it's doing me any good, but I can see how well you meant it, and I'm grateful."

"We *could* have sneaked in the kitchen table, perhaps, while he was out in the garden, and put on the extra long tablecloth," interjected Alice, musingly.

Sister Soulsby smiled again at Sister Ware, but without any words this time; and Alice on the instant rose, with the remark that she must be going out to see about supper.

"I'm going to insist on coming out to help you," Mrs. Soulsby declared, "as soon as I've talked over one little matter with your husband. Oh, yes, you must let me this time. I insist!"

As the kitchen door closed behind Mrs. Ware, a swift and apparently significant glance shot its way across from Sister Soulsby's roving, eloquent eyes to the calmer and smaller gray orbs of her husband. He rose to his feet, made some

little explanation about being a gardener himself, and desiring to inspect more closely some rhododendrons he had
noticed in the garden, and forthwith moved decorously out
by the other door into the front hall. They heard his footsteps on the gravel beneath the window before Mrs. Soulsby
spoke again.

"You're right about the Presiding Elder, and you're wrong,"
she said. "He isn't what one might call precisely in love with
you. Oh, I know the story, — how you got into debt at Tyre,
and he stepped in and insisted on your being denied
Tecumseh and sent here instead."

"*He* was responsible for that, then, was he?" broke in
Theron, with contracted brows.

"Why, don't you make any effort to find out anything at
all?" she asked pertly enough, but with such obvious good-
nature that he could not but have pleasure in her speech.
"Why, of course he did it! Who else did you suppose?"

"Well," said the young minister, despondently, "if he's as
much against me as all that, I might as well hang up my
fiddle and go home."

Sister Soulsby gave a little involuntary groan of impatience.
She bent forward, and, lifting her eyes, rolled them at him in
a curve of downward motion which suggested to his fancy
the image of two eagles in a concerted pounce upon a lamb.

"My friend," she began, with a new note of impressiveness
in her voice, "if you'll pardon my saying it, you haven't got
the spunk of a mouse. If you're going to lay down, and let
everybody trample over you just as they please, you're right!
You *might* as well go home. But now here, this is what I
wanted to say to you: Do you just keep your hands off these
next few days, and leave this whole thing to me. I'll pull it
into shipshape for you. No — wait a minute — don't interrupt
now. I have taken a liking to you. You've got brains, and
you've got human nature in you, and heart. What you lack
is *sabe,* — common-sense. You'll get that, too, in time, and
meanwhile I'm not going to stand by and see you cut up and

fed to the dogs for want of it. I'll get you through this scrape, and put you on your feet again, right-side-up-with care, because, as I said, I like you. I like your wife, too, mind. She's a good, honest little soul, and she worships the very ground you tread on. Of course, as long as people *will* marry in their teens, the wrong people will get yoked up together. But that's neither here nor there. She's a kind, sweet little body, and she's devoted to you, and it isn't every intellectual man that gets even that much. But now it's a go, is it? You promise to keep quiet, do you, and leave the whole show absolutely to me? Shake hands on it."

Sister Soulsby had risen, and stood now holding out her hand in a frank, manly fashion. Theron looked at the hand, and made mental notes that there were a good many veins discernible on the small wrist, and that the forearm seemed to swell out more than would have been expected in a woman producing such a general effect of leanness. He caught the shine of a thin bracelet-band of gold under the sleeve. A delicate, significant odor just hinted its presence in the air about this outstretched arm, — something which was not a perfume, yet deserved as gracious a name.

He rose to his feet, and took the proffered hand with a deliberate gesture, as if he had been cautiously weighing all the possible arguments for and against this momentous compact.

"I promise," he said gravely, and the two palms squeezed themselves together in an earnest clasp.

"Right you are," exclaimed the lady, once more with cheery vivacity. "Mind, when it's all over, I'm going to give you a good, serious, downright talking to, — a regular hoeing-over. I'm not sure I sha'n't give you a sound shaking into the bargain. You need it. And now I'm going out to help Alice."

The Reverend Mr. Ware remained standing after his new friend had left the room, and his meditative face wore an even unusual air of abstraction. He strolled aimlessly over, after a time, to the desk by the window, and stood there looking out at the slight figure of Brother Soulsby, who was bending over and attentively regarding some pink blossoms on a shrub through what seemed to be a pocket magnifying-glass.

What remained uppermost in his mind was not this interesting woman's confident pledge of championship in his material difficulties. He found himself dwelling instead upon her remark about the incongruous results of early marriages. He wondered idly if the little man in the white tie, fussing out there over that rhododendron-bush, had figured in her thoughts as an example of these evils. Then he reflected that they had been mentioned in clear relation to talk about Alice.

✳   Now that he faced this question, it was as if he had been consciously ignoring and putting it aside for a long time. How was it, he asked himself now, that Alice, who had once seemed so bright and keen-witted, who had in truth started out immeasurably his superior in swiftness of apprehension and readiness in humorous quips and conceits, should have grow so dull? For she was undoubtedly slow to understand things nowadays. Her absurd lugging in of the extension-table problem, when the great strategic point of that invitation foisted upon the Presiding Elder came up, was only the latest sample of a score of these heavy-minded exhibitions that recalled themselves to him. And outsiders were apparently beginning to notice it. He knew by intuition what those phrases, "good, honest little soul" and "kind, sweet little body" signified, when another woman used them to a husband about his wife. The very employment of that word "little" was enough, considering that there was scarcely more than a hair's difference between Mrs. Soulsby and Alice, and that they were both rather tall than otherwise, as the stature of women went.

What she had said about the chronic misfortunes of intellectual men in such matters gave added point to those meaning phrases. Nobody could deny that geniuses and men of conspicuous talent had as a rule, all through history, contracted unfortunate marriages. In almost every case where their wives were remembered at all, it was on account of their abnormal stupidity, or bad temper, or something of that sort. Take Xantippe, for example, and Shakespeare's wife, and — and — well, there was Byron, and Bulwer-Lytton, and ever so many others.

Of course there was nothing to be done about it. These things happened, and one could only put the best possible face on them, and live one's appointed life as patiently and contentedly as might be. And Alice undoubtedly merited all the praise which had been so generously bestowed upon her. She *was* good and honest and kindly, and there could be no doubt whatever as to her utter devotion to him. These were tangible, solid qualities, which must always secure respect for her. It was true that she no longer seemed to be very popular among people. He questioned whether men, for instance, like Father Forbes and Dr. Ledsmar would care much about her. Visions of the wifeless and academic calm in which these men spent their lives — an existence consecrated to literature and knowledge and familiarity with all the loftiest and noblest thoughts of the past — rose and enveloped him in a cloud of depression. No such lot would be his! He must labor along among ignorant and spiteful narrow-minded people to the end of his days, pocketing their insults and fawning upon the harsh hands of jealous nonentities who happened to be his official masters, just to keep a roof over his head — or rather Alice's. He must sacrifice everything to this, — his ambitions, his passionate desires to do real good in the world on a large scale, his mental freedom, yes, even his chance of having truly elevating, intellectual friendships. For it was plain enough that the men whose friendship would be of genuine and stimulating profit to him would not like her. Now that he thought of it, she seemed latterly to make no friends at all.

Suddenly, as he watched in a blank sort of way Brother Soulsby take out a penknife, and lop an offending twig from a rose-bush against the fence, something occurred to him. There was a curious exception to that rule of Alice's isolation. She had made at least one friend. Levi Gorringe seemed to like her extremely.

As if his mind had been a camera, Theron snapped a shutter down upon this odd, unbidden idea, and turned away from the window.

The sounds of an active, almost strenuous conversation in female voices came from the kitchen. Theron opened the door noiselessly, and put in his head, conscious of something furtive in his intention.

"You must dreen every drop of water off the spinach, mind, before you put it over, or else —"

It was Sister Soulsby's sharp and penetrating tones which came to him. Theron closed the door again, and surrendered himself once more to the circling whirl of his thoughts.

CHAPTER XV

A LOVE-FEAST at nine in the morning opened the public services of a Sunday still memorable in the annals of Octavius Methodism.

This ceremony, which four times a year preceded the sessions of the Quarterly Conference, was not necessarily an event of importance. It was an occasion upon which the brethren and sisters who clung to the old-fashioned, primitive ways of the itinerant circuit-riders, let themselves go with emphasized independence, putting up more vehement prayers than usual, and adding a special fervor of noise to their "Amens!" and other interjections, — and that was all.

It was Theron's first love-feast in Octavius, and as the big class-room in the church basement began to fill up, and he noted how the men with ultra radical views and the women clad in the most ostentatious drabs and grays were crowding into the front seats, he felt his spirits sinking. He had literally to force himself from sentence to sentence, when the time came for him to rise and open the proceedings with an exhortation. He had eagerly offered this function to the Presiding Elder, the Rev. Aziel P. Larrabee, who sat in severe silence on the little platform behind him, but had been informed that that dignitary would lead off in giving testimony later on. So Theron, feeling all the while the hostile eyes of the Elder burning holes in his back, dragged himself somehow through the task. He had never known any such difficulty of speech before. The relief was almost overwhelming when he came to the customary part where all are adjured to be as brief as possible in witnessing for the Lord, because the time belongs to all the people, and the Discipline forbids the feast to last more than ninety minutes. He delivered this injunction to brevity with marked earnestness, and then sat down abruptly.

There was some rather boisterous singing, during which

the stewards, beginning with the platform, passed plates of bread cut in small cubes, and water in big plated pitchers and tumblers, about among the congregation, threading their way between the long wooden benches ordinarily occupied at this hour by the children of the Sunday-school, and helping each brother and sister in turn. They held by the old custom, here in Octavius, and all along the seats the sexes alternated, as they do at a polite dinner-table.

Theron impassively watched the familiar scene. The early nervousness had passed away. He felt now that he was not in the least afraid of these people, even with the Presiding Elder thrown in. Folks who sang with such unintelligence, and who threw themselves with such undignified fervor into this childish business of the bread and water, could not be formidable antagonists for a man of intellect. He had never realized before what a spectacle the Methodist love-feast probably presented to outsiders. What must they think of it!

He had noticed that the Soulsbys sat together, in the centre and toward the front. Next to Brother Soulsby sat Alice. He thought she looked pale and preoccupied, and set it down in passing to her innate distaste for the sombre garments she was wearing, and for the company she perforce found herself in. Another head was in the way, and for a time Theron did not observe who sat beside Alice on the other side. When at last he saw that it was Levi Gorringe, his instinct was to wonder what the lawyer must be saying to himself about these noisy and shallow enthusiasts. A recurring emotion of loyalty to the simple people among whom, after all, he had lived his whole life, prompted him to feel that it wasn't wholly nice of Gorringe to come and enjoy this revelation of their foolish side, as if it were a circus. There was some vague memory in his mind which associated Gorringe with other love-feasts, and with a cynical attitude toward them. Oh, yes! he had told how he went to one just for the sake of sitting beside the girl he admired — and was pursuing.

The stewards had completed their round, and the loud,

discordant singing came to an end. There ensued a little pause, during which Theron turned to the Presiding Elder with a gesture of invitation to take charge of the further proceedings. The Elder responded with another gesture, calling his attention to something going on in front.

Brother and Sister Soulsby, to the considerable surprise of everybody, had risen to their feet, and were standing in their places, quite motionless, and with an air of professional self-assurance dimly discernible under a large show of humility. They stood thus until complete silence had been secured. Then the woman, lifting her head, began to sing. The words were "Rock of Ages," but no one present had heard the tune to which she wedded them. Her voice was full and very sweet, and had in it tender cadences which all her hearers found touching. She knew how to sing, and she put forth the words so that each was distinctly intelligible. There came a part where Brother Soulsby, lifting his head in turn, took up a tuneful second to her air. Although the two did not, as one could hear by listening closely, sing the same words at the same time, they produced none the less most moving and delightful harmonies of sound.

The experience was so novel and charming that listeners ran ahead in their minds to fix the number of verses there were in the hymn, and to hope that none would be left out. Toward the end, when some of the intolerably self-conceited local singers, fancying they had caught the tune, started to join in, they were stopped by an indignant "sh-h!" which rose from all parts of the class-room; and the Soulsbys, with a patient and pensive kindliness written on their uplifted faces, gave that verse over again.

What followed seemed obviously restrained and modified by the effect of this unlooked-for and tranquillizing overture. The Presiding Elder was known to enjoy visits to old-fashioned congregations like that of Octavius, where he could indulge to the full his inner passion for high-pitched passionate invocations and violent spiritual demeanor, but this time he spoke temperately, almost soothingly. The most tempestuous of the local witnesses for the Lord gave in their testimony in relatively pacific tones, under the influence of the spell which good music had laid upon the gathering. There was the deepest interest as to what the two visitors would do in this way. Brother Soulsby spoke first, very briefly and in well-rounded and well-chosen, if conventional, phrases. His wife, following him, delivered in a melodious monotone some equally hackneyed remarks. The assemblage, listening in rapt attention, felt the suggestion of reserved power in every sentence she uttered, and burst forth, as she dropped into her seat, in a loud chorus of approving ejaculations. The Soulsbys had captured Octavius with their first outer skirmish line.

Everything seemed to move forward now [1] with a new zest and spontaneity. Theron had picked out for the occasion the best of those sermons which he had prepared in Tyre, at the time when he was justifying his ambition to be accounted a pulpit orator. It was orthodox enough, but had been planned as the framework for picturesque and emotional rhetoric rather than doctrinal edification. He had never dreamed of trying it on Octavius before, and only on the yesterday had quavered at his own daring in choosing it now. Nothing but the desire to show Sister Soulsby what was in him had held him to the selection.

Something of this same desire no doubt swayed and steadied him now in the pulpit. The labored slowness of his beginning seemed to him to be due to nervous timidity, until suddenly, looking down into those big eyes of Sister Soulsby's, which were bent gravely upon him from where she sat beside Alice in the minister's pew, he remembered that it was instead the studied deliberation which art had taught him. He went on, feeling more and more that the skill and histrionic power of his best days were returning to him, were as marked as ever,

[1] English ed. reads "At the service upstairs everything moved" for "Everything seemed to move forward now."

— nay, had never triumphed before as they were triumphing now. The congregation watched and listened, with open, steadfast eyes and parted lips. For the first time in all that weary quarter, their faces shone. The sustaining sparkle of their gaze lifted him to a peroration unrivalled in his own recollection of himself.

He sat down, and bent his head forward upon the open Bible, breathing hard, but suffused with a glow of satisfaction. His ears caught the music of that sighing rustle through the audience which bespeaks a profound impression. He could scarcely keep the fingers of his hands, covering his bowed face in a devotional posture as they were, from drumming a jubilant tattoo. His pulses did this in every vein, throbbing with excited exultation. The insistent whim seized him, as he still bent thus before his people, to whisper to his own heart, "At last! The dogs!"

The announcement that in the evening a series of revival meetings was to be inaugurated, had been made at the love-feast, and it was repeated now from the pulpit, with the added statement that for the once the class-meetings usually following this morning service would be suspended. Then Theron came down the steps, conscious after a fashion that the Presiding Elder had laid a propitiatory hand on his shoulder and spoken amiably about the sermon,[2] and that several groups of more or less important parishioners were waiting in the aisle and the vestibule to shake hands and tell him how much they had enjoyed the sermon. His mind perversely kept hold of the thought that all this came too late. He politely smiled his way along out, and, overtaking the Soulsbys and his wife near the parsonage gate, went in with them.

At the cold, picked-up noonday meal which was the Sunday rule of the house, Theron rather expected that his guests would talk about the sermon, or at any rate about the events of the morning. A Sabbath chill seemed to have settled upon

[2] English ed. reads "his effort" for "the sermon."

both their tongues. They ate almost in silence, and their sparse remarks touched upon topics far removed from church affairs. Alice, too, seemed strangely disinclined to conversation. The husband knew her face and its varying moods so well that he could see she was laboring under some very powerful and deep emotion. No doubt it was the sermon, the oratorical swing of which still tingled in his own blood, that had so affected her. If she had said so, it would have pleased him, but she said nothing.

After dinner, Brother Soulsby disappeared in his bedroom, with the remark that he guessed he would lie down awhile. Sister Soulsby put on her bonnet, and, explaining that she always prepared herself for an evening's work by a long solitary walk, quitted the house. Alice, after she had put the dinner things away, went upstairs, and stayed there. Left to himself, Theron spent the afternoon in the easy-chair, and, in the intervals of confused introspection, read "Recollections of my Youth" through again from cover to cover.

He went through the remarkable experiences attending the opening of the revival, when evening came, as one in a dream. Long before the hour for the service arrived, the sexton came in to tell him that the church was already nearly full, and that it was going to be impossible to preserve any distinction in the matter of pews. When the party from the parsonage went over — after another cold and mostly silent meal — it was to find the interior of the church densely packed, and people being turned away from the doors.

Theron was supposed to preside over what followed, and he did sit on the central chair in the pulpit, between the Presiding Elder and Brother Soulsby, and on the several needful occasions did rise and perfunctorily make the formal remarks required of him. The Elder preached a short, but vigorously phrased sermon. The Soulsbys sang three or four times — on each occasion with familiar hymnal words set to novel, concerted music — and then separately exhorted the assemblage. The husband's part seemed well done. If his speech lacked some of the fire of the divine girdings which older Methodists recalled, it still led straight, and with kindling fervency, up to a season of power. The wife took up the word as he sat down. She had risen from one of the side-seats; and, speaking as she walked, she moved forward till she stood within the altar-rail, immediately under the pulpit, and from this place, facing the listening throng, she delivered her harangue. Those who watched her words most intently got the least sense of meaning from them. The phrases were all familiar enough, — "Jesus a very present help," "Sprinkled by the Blood," "Comforted by the Word," "Sanctified by the Spirit," "Born into the Kingdom,"and a hundred others, — but it was as in the case of her singing: the words were old; the music was new.

What Sister Soulsby said did not matter. The way she said it — the splendid, searching sweep of her great eyes; the vibrating roll of her voice, now full of tears, now scornful, now boldly, jubilantly triumphant; the sympathetic swaying of her willowy figure under the stress of her eloquence — [3] was all wonderful. When she had finished, and stood, flushed and panting, beneath the shadow of the pulpit, she held up a hand deprecatingly as the resounding "Amens!" and "Bless the Lords!" began to well up about her.

"You have heard us sing," she said, smiling to apologize for her shortness of breath. "Now we want to hear you sing!"

Her husband had risen as she spoke, and on the instant, with a far greater volume of voice than they had hitherto disclosed, the two began "From Greenland's Icy Mountains," in the old, familiar tune. It did not need Sister Soulsby's urgent and dramatic gesture to lift people to their feet. The whole assemblage sprang up, and, under the guidance of these two powerful leading voices, thundered the hymn out as Octavius had never heard it before.

While its echoes were still alive, the woman began speaking again. "Don't sit down!" she cried. "You would stand up

[3] English ed. reads "emotions" for "eloquence."

if the President of the United States was going by, even if he was only going fishing. How much more should you stand up in honor of living souls passing forward to find their Saviour!"

The psychological moment was upon them. Groans and cries arose, and a palpable ferment stirred the throng. The exhortation to sinners to declare themselves, to come to the altar, was not only on the revivalist's lips: it seemed to quiver in the very air, to be borne on every inarticulate exclamation in the clamor of the brethren. A young woman, with a dazed and startled look in her eyes, rose in the body of the church tremblingly hesitated for a moment, and then, with bowed head and blushing cheeks, pressed her way out from the end of a crowded pew and down the aisle to the rail. A triumphant outburst of welcoming ejaculations swelled to the roof as she knelt there, and under its impetus others followed her example. With interspersed snatches of song and shouted encouragements the excitement reached its height only when twoscore people, mostly young, were tightly clustered upon their knees about the rail, and in the space opening upon the aisle. Above the confusion of penitential sobs and moans, and the hysterical murmurings of members whose conviction of entire sanctity kept them in their seats, could be heard the voices of the Presiding Elder, the Soulsbys, and the elderly deacons of the church, who moved about among the kneeling mourners, bending over them and patting their shoulders, and calling out to them: "Fasten your thoughts on Jesus!" "Oh, the Precious Blood!" "Blessed be His Name!" "Seek Him, and you shall find Him!" "Cling to Jesus, and Him Crucified!"

The Rev. Theron Ware did not, with the others, descend from the pulpit. Seated where he could not see Sister Soulsby he had failed utterly to be moved by the wave of enthusiasm she had evoked. What he heard her say disappointed him. He had expected from her more originality, more spice of her own idiomatic, individual sort. He viewed with a cold

sense of aloofness the evidence of her success when they began
to come forward and abase themselves at the altar. The instant resolve that, come what might, he would not go down
there among them, sprang up ready-made in his mind. He
saw his two companions pass him and descend the pulpit
stairs, and their action only hardened his resolution. If an
excuse were needed, he was presiding, and the place to preside in was the pulpit. But he waived in his mind the whole
question of an excuse.

After a little, he put his hand over his face, leaning the
elbow forward on the reading-desk. The scene below would
have thrilled him to the marrow six months, — yes, three
months ago. He put a finger across his eyes now, to half shut
it out. The spectacle of these silly young "mourners" — kneeling they knew not why, trembling at they could not tell what,
pledging themselves frantically to dogmas and mysteries
they knew nothing of, under the influence of a hubbub of
outcries as meaningless in their way, and inspiring in much
the same way, as the racket of a fife and drum corps, — the
spectacle saddened and humiliated him now. He was conscious of a dawning sense of shame at being even tacitly responsible for such a thing. His fancy conjured up the idea of
Dr. Ledsmar coming in and beholding this maudlin and
unseemly scene, and he felt his face grow hot at the bare
thought.

Looking through his fingers, Theron all at once saw something which caught at his breath with a sharp clutch. Alice
had risen from the minister's pew — the most conspicuous
one in the church — and was moving down the aisle toward
the rail, her uplifted face chalk-like in its whiteness, and her
eyes wide-open, looking straight ahead.

The young pastor could scarcely credit his sight. He thrust
aside his head, and bent forward, only to see his wife sink
upon her knees among the rest, and to hear this notable accession to the "mourners" hailed by a tumult of approving
shouts. Then, remembering himself, he drew back and put

up his hand, shutting out the strange scene altogether. To
see nothing at all was a relief, and under cover he closed his
eyes, and bit his teeth together.

A fresh outburst of thanksgivings, spreading noisily through
the congregation, prompted him to peer through his fingers
again. Levi Gorringe was making his way down the aisle, —
was at the moment quite in front. Theron found himself
watching this man with the stern composure of a fatalist. The
clamant brethren down below were stirred to new excitement
by the thought that the sceptical lawyer, so long with them,
yet not of them, had been humbled and won by the outpour-
ings of the Spirit. Theron's perceptions were keener. He knew
that Gorringe was coming forward to kneel beside Alice. The
knowledge left him curiously undisturbed. He saw the lawyer
advance, gently insinuate himself past the form of some kneeling mourner who was in his way, and drop on his knees
close beside the bowed figure of Alice. The two touched
shoulders as they bent forward beneath Sister Soulsby's outstretched hands, held over them as in a blessing. Theron
looked fixedly at them, and professed to himself that he was
barely interested.

A little afterward, he was standing up in his place, and
reading aloud a list of names which one of the stewards had
given him. They were the names of those who had asked
that evening to be taken into the church as members on probation. The sounds of the recent excitement were all hushed
now, save as two or three enthusiasts in a corner raised their
voices in abrupt greeting of each name in its turn, but Theron
felt somehow that this noise had been transferred to the inside of his head. A continuous buzzing went on there, so that
the sound of his voice was far-off and unfamiliar in his ears.

He read through the list — comprising some fifteen items
— and pronounced the names with great distinctness. It was
necessary to take pains with this, because the only name his
blurred eyes seemed to see anywhere on the foolscap sheet
was that of Levi Gorringe. When he had finished and was

taking his seat, some one began speaking to him from the body of the church. He saw that this was the steward, who was explaining to him that the most important name of the lot — that of Brother Gorringe — had not been read out.

Theron smiled and shook his head. Then when the Presiding Elder touched him on the arm, and assured him that he had not mentioned the name in question, he replied quite simply, and with another smile, "I thought it was the only name I did read out."

Then he sat down abruptly, and let his head fall to one side. There were hurried movements inside the pulpit, and people in the audience had begun to stand up wonderingly, when the Presiding Elder, with uplifted hands, confronted them.

"We will omit the Doxology, and depart quietly after the benediction," he said. "Brother Ware seems [4] to have been overcome by the heat."

[4] English ed. reads "appears" for "seems."

CHAPTER XVI

WHEN Theron woke next morning, Alice seemed to have dressed and left the room, — a thing which had never happened before.

This fact connected itself at once in his brain with the recollection of her having made an exhibition of herself the previous evening, — going forward before all eyes to join the unconverted and penitent sinners, as if she were some tramp or shady female, instead of an educated lady, a professing member from her girlhood, and a minister's wife. It crossed his mind that probably she had risen and got away noiselessly, for very shame at looking him in the face, after such absurd behavior.

Then he remembered more, and grasped the situation. He had fainted in church, and had been brought home and helped to bed. Dim memories of unaccustomed faces in the bedroom, of nauseous drugs and hushed voices, came to him out of the night-time. Now that he thought of it, he was a sick man. Having settled this, he went off to sleep again, a feverish and broken sleep, and remained in this state most of the time for the following twenty-four hours. In the brief though numerous intervals of waking, he found certain things clear in his mind. One was that he was annoyed with Alice, but would dissemble his feelings. Another was that it was much pleasanter to be ill than to be forced to attend and take part in those revival meetings. These two ideas came and went in a lazy, drowsy fashion, mixing themselves up with other vagrant fancies, yet always remaining on top.

In the evening the singing from the church next door filled his room. The Soulsby's part of it was worth keeping awake for. He turned over and deliberately dozed when the congregation sang.

Alice came up a number of times during the day to ask how he felt, and to bring him broth or toast-water. On several occasions, when he heard her step, the perverse inclination mastered him to shut his eyes, and pretend to be asleep, so that she might tip-toe out again. She had a depressed and thoughtful air, and spoke to him like one whose mind was on something else. Neither of them alluded to what had happened the previous evening. Toward the close of the long day, she came to ask him whether he would prefer her to remain in the house, instead of attending the meeting.

"Go, by all means," he said almost curtly.

The Presiding Elder and the Sunday-school superintendent called early Tuesday morning at the parsonage to make brotherly inquiries, and Theron was feeling so much better that he himself suggested their coming upstairs to see him. The Elder was in good spirits; he smiled approvingly, and even put in a jocose [1] word or two while the superintendent sketched for the invalid in a cheerful way the leading incidents of the previous evening.

There had been an enormous crowd, even greater than that of Sunday night, and everybody had been looking forward to another notable and exciting season of grace. These expectations were especially heightened when Sister Soulsby ascended the pulpit stairs and took charge of the proceedings. She deferred to Paul's views about women preachers on Sundays, she said; but on week-days she had just as much right to snatch brands from the burning as Paul, or Peter, or any other man. She went on like that, in a breezy, off-hand fashion which tickled the audience immensely, and led to the liveliest anticipations of what would happen when she began upon the evening's harvest of souls.

But it was something else that happened. At a signal from Sister Soulsby the stewards got up, and, in an unconcerned sort of way, went through the throng to the rear of the church, locked the doors, and put the keys in their pockets. The sister dryly explained now to the surprised congregation that there was a season for all things, and that on the

---

[1] English ed. reads "jovial" for "jocose."

present occasion they would suspend the glorious work of redeeming fallen human nature, and take up instead the equally noble task of raising some fifteen hundred dollars which the church needed in its business. The doors would only be opened again when this had been accomplished.

The brethren were much taken aback by this trick, and they permitted themselves to exchange a good many scowling and indignant glances, the while their professional visitors sang another of their delightfully novel sacred duets. Its charm of harmony for once fell upon unsympathetic ears. But then Sister Soulsby began another monologue, defending this way of collecting money, chaffing the assemblage with bright-eyed impudence on their having been trapped, and scoring, one after another, neat and jocose little personal points on local characteristics, at which everybody but the individual touched grinned broadly. She was so droll and cheeky, and withal effective in her talk, that she quite won the crowd over. She told a story about a woodchuck which fairly brought down the house.

"A man," she began, with a quizzical twinkle in her eye, "told me once about hunting a woodchuck with a pack of dogs, and they chased it so hard that it finally escaped only by climbing a butternut-tree. 'But, my friend,' I said to him, 'woodchucks can't climb trees, — butternut-trees or any other kind, — and you know it!' All he said in reply to me was: 'This woodchuck *had* to climb a tree!' And that's the way with this congregation. You think you can't raise $1,500, but you've *got* to."

So it went on. She set them all laughing; and then, with a twist of the eyes and a change of voice, lo, and behold, she had them nearly crying in the same breath. Under the pressure of these jumbled emotions, brethren began to rise up in their pews and say what they would give. The wonderful woman had something smart and apt to say about each fresh contribution, and used it to screw up the general interest a notch further toward benevolent hysteria. With songs and jokes and impromptu exhortations and prayers she kept the thing whirling, until a sort of duel of generosity began between two of the most unlikely men, — Erastus Winch and Levi Gorringe. Everybody had been surprised when Winch gave his first $50; but when he rose again, half an hour afterward, and said that, owing to the high public position of some of the new members on probation, he foresaw a great future for the church, and so felt moved to give another $25, there was general amazement. Moved by a common instinct, all eyes were turned upon Levi Gorringe, and he, without the slightest hesitation, stood up and said he would give $100. There was something in his tone which must have annoyed Brother Winch, for he shot up like a dart, and called out, "Put me down for fifty more;" and that brought Gorringe to his feet with an added $50, and then the two went on raising each other till the assemblage was agape with admiring stupefaction.

This gladiatorial combat might have been going on till now, the Sunday-school superintendent concluded, if Winch hadn't subsided. The amount of the contributions hadn't been figured up yet, for Sister Soulsby kept the list; but there had been a tremendous lot of money raised. Of that there could be no doubt.

The Presiding Elder now told Theron that the Quarterly Conference had been adjourned yesterday till to-day. He and Brother Davis were even now on their way to attend the session in the church next door. The Elder added, with an obvious kindly significance, that though Theron was too ill to attend it, he guessed his absence would do him no harm. Then the two men left the room, and Theron went to sleep again.

Another almost blank period ensued, this time lasting for forty-eight hours. The young minister was enfolded in the coils of a fever of some sort, which Brother Soulsby, who had dabbled considerably in medicine, admitted that he was puzzled about. Sometimes he thought that it was typhoid, and then again there were symptoms which looked suspiciously like brain fever. The Methodists of Octavius counted no physician among their numbers, and when, on the second day, Alice grew scared, and decided, with Brother Soulsby's assent, to call in professional advice, the only doctor's name she could recall was that of Ledsmar. She was conscious of an instinctive dislike for the vague image of him her fancy had conjured up, but the reflection that he was Theron's friend, and so probably would be more moderate in his charges, decided her.

Brother Soulsby showed a most comforting tact and swiftness of apprehension when Alice, in mentioning Dr. Ledsmar's name, disclosed by her manner a fear that his being sent for would create talk among the church people. He volunteered at once to act as messenger himself, and, with no better guide than her dim hints at direction, found the doctor and brought him back to the parsonage.

Dr. Ledsmar expressly disclaimed to Soulsby all pretence of professional skill, and made him understand that he went along solely because he liked Mr. Ware, and was interested in him, and in any case would probably be of as much use as the wisest of strange physicians, — a view which the little revivalist received with comprehending nods of tacit acquiescence. Ledsmar came, and was taken up to the sick-room. He sat on the bedside and talked with Theron awhile, and then went downstairs again. To Alice's anxious inquiries, he replied that it seemed to him merely a case of over-work and over-worry, about which there was not the slightest occasion for alarm.

"But he says the strangest things," the wife put in. "He has been quite delirious at times."

"That means only that his brain is taking a rest as well as his body," remarked Ledsmar. "That is Nature's way of securing an equilibrium of repose — of recuperation. He will come out of it with his mind all the fresher and clearer."

"I don't believe he knows shucks!" was Alice's comment

when she closed the street door upon Dr. Ledsmar. "Anybody could have come in and looked at a sick man and said, 'Leave him alone.' You expect something more from a doctor. It's his business to say what *to* do. And I suppose he'll charge two dollars for just telling me that my husband was resting!"

"No," said Brother Soulsby, "he said he never practised, and that he would come only as a friend."

"Well, it isn't my idea of a friend, — not to prescribe a single thing," protested Alice.

Yet it seemed that no prescription was needed, after all. The next morning Theron woke to find himself feeling quite restored in spirits and nerves. He sat up in bed, and after an instant of weakly giddiness, recognized that he was all right again. Greatly pleased, he got up, and proceeded to dress himself. There were little recurring hints of faintness and vertigo, while he was shaving, but he had the sense to refer these to the fact that he was very, very hungry. He went downstairs, and smiled with the pleased pride of a child at the surprise which his appearance at the door created. Alice and the Soulsbys were at breakfast. He joined them, and ate voraciously, declaring that it was worth a month's illness to have things taste so good once more.

"You still look white as a sheet," said Alice, warningly. "If I were you, I'd be careful in my diet for a spell yet."

For answer, Theron let Sister Soulsby help him again to ham and eggs. He talked exclusively to Sister Soulsby, or rather invited her by his manner to talk to him, and listened and watched her with indolent content. There was a sort of happy and purified languor in his physical and mental being, which needed and appreciated just this, — to sit next a bright and attractive woman at a good breakfast, and be ministered to by her sprightly conversation, by the flash of her informing and inspiring eyes, and the nameless sense of support and repose which her near proximity exhaled. He felt himself figuratively leaning against Sister Soulsby's buoyant personality, and resting.

Brother Soulsby, like the intelligent creature he was, ate his breakfast in peace; but Alice would interpose remarks from time to time. Theron was conscious of a certain annoyance at this, and knew that he was showing it by an exaggerated display of interest in everything Sister Soulsby said, and persisted in it. There trembled in the background of his thoughts ever and again the recollection of a grievance against his wife, — an offence which she had committed, — but he put it aside as something to be grappled and dealt with when he felt again like taking up the serious and disagreeable things of life. For the moment, he desired only to be amused by Sister Soulsby. Her casual mention of the fact that she and her husband were taking their departure that very day, appealed to him as an added reason for devoting his entire attention to her.

"You mustn't forget that famous talking-to you threatened me with, — and 'regular hoeing-over,' you know," he reminded her, when he found himself alone with her after breakfast. He smiled as he spoke, in frank enjoyment of the prospect.

Sister Soulsby nodded, and aided with a roll of her eyes the effect of mock-menace in her uplifted forefinger. "Oh, never fear," she cried. "You'll catch it hot and strong. But that'll keep till afternoon. Tell me, do you feel strong enough to go in next door and attend the trustees' meeting this forenoon? It's rather important that you should be there, if you can spur yourself up to it. By the way, you haven't asked what happened at the Quarterly Conference yesterday."

Theron sighed, and made a little grimace of repugnance. "If you knew how little I cared!" he said. "I did hope you'd forget all about mentioning that, — and everything else connected with — the next door. You talk so much more interestingly about other things."

"Here's gratitude for you!" exclaimed Sister Soulsby, with a gay simulation of despair. "Why, man alive, do you know what I've done for you? I got around on the Presiding Elder's blind side, I captured old Pierce, I wound Winch right around my little finger, I worked two or three of the class-leaders — all on your account. The result was you went through as if you'd had your ears pinned back, and been greased all over. You've got an extra hundred dollars added to your salary; do you hear? On the sixth question of the order of business the Elder ruled that the recommendation of the last conference's estimating committee could be revised (between ourselves he was wrong, but that doesn't matter), and so you're in clover. And very friendly things were said about you, too."

"It was very kind of you," said Theron. "I am really extremely grateful to you." He shook her by the hand to make up for what he realized to be a lack of fervor in his tones.

"Well, then," Sister Soulsby replied, "you pull yourself together, and take your place as chairman of the trustees' meeting, and see to it that, whatever comes up, you side with old Pierce and Winch."

"Oh, *they're* my friends now, are they?" asked Theron, with a faint play of irony about his lips.

"Yes, that's your ticket this election," she answered briskly, "and mind you vote it straight. Don't bother about reasons now. Just take it from me, as the song says, 'that things have changed since Willie died.' That's all. And then come back here, and this afternoon we'll have a good old-fashioned jaw."

The Rev. Mr. Ware, walking with ostentatious feebleness, and forcing a conventional smile upon his wan face, duly made his unexpected appearance at the trustees' meeting in one of the smaller class-rooms. He received their congratulations gravely, and shook hands with all three.[2] It required an effort to do this impartially, because, upon sight of Levi Gorringe, there rose up suddenly within him an emotion of fierce dislike and enmity. In some enigmatic way his thoughts

[2] English ed. begins a new paragraph here.

had kept themselves away from Gorringe ever since Sunday evening. Now they concentrated with furious energy and swiftness upon him. Theron seemed able in a flash of time to co-ordinate many recollections of Gorringe, — the early liking Alice had professed for him, the mystery of those purchased plants in her garden, the story of the girl he had lost in church, his offer to lend him money, the way in which he had sat beside Alice at the love-feast and followed her to the altar-rail in the evening. These raced abreast through the young minister's brain, yet with each its own image, and its relation to the others clearly defined.

He found the nerve, all the same, to take this third trustee by the hand, and to thank him for his congratulations, and even to say, with a surface smile of welcome, "It is *Brother* Gorringe, now, I remember."

The work before the meeting was chiefly of a routine kind. In most places this would have been transacted by the stewards; but in Octavius these minor officials had degenerated into mere ceremonial abstractions, who humbly ratified, or by arrangement anticipated, the will of the powerful, mortgage-owning trustees. Theron sat languidly at the head of the table while these common-place matters passed in their course, noting the intonations of Gorringe's voice as he read from his secretary's book, and finding his ear displeased by them. No issue arose upon any of these trivial affairs, and the minister, feeling faint and weary in the heat, wondered why Sister Soulsby had insisted on his coming.

All at once he sat up straight, with an instinctive warning in his mind that here was the thing. Gorringe had taken up the subject of the "debt-raising" evening, and read out its essentials as they had been embodied in a report of the stewards. The gross sum obtained, in cash and promises, was $1,560 [3]. The stewards had collected of this a trifle less than half, but hoped to get it all in during the ensuing quarter.

[3] English ed. reads "$1,860" for "$1,560."

There were, also, the bill of Mr. and Mrs. Soulsby for $150, and the increases of $100 in the pastor's salary and $25 in the apportioned contribution of the charge toward the Presiding Elder's maintenance, the two latter items of which the Quarterly Conference had sanctioned.

"I want to hear the names of the subscribers and their amounts read out," put in Brother Pierce.

When this was done, it became apparent that much more than half of the entire amount had been offered by two men. Levi Gorringe's $450 and Erastus Winch's $425 left only $690 to be divided up among some seventy or eighty other members of the congregation.

Brother Pierce speedily stopped the reading of these subordinate names. "They're of no concern whatever," he said, despite the fact that his own might have been reached in time. "Those first names are what I was getting at. Have those two first amounts, the big ones, be'n paid?"

"One has — the other not," replied Gorringe.

"*Pre*-cisely," remarked the senior trustee. "And I'm goin' to move that it needn't be paid, either. When Brother Winch, here, began hollerin' out those extra twenty-fives and fifties, that evening, it was under a complete misapprehension. He'd be'n on the cheese board that same Monday afternoon, and he'd done what he thought was a mighty big stroke of business, and he felt liberal according. I know just what that feelin' is myself. If I'd be'n makin' a mint o' money, instead o' losin' all the while, as I do, I'd 'a' done just the same. But the next day, lo, and behold, Brother Winch found that it was all a mistake, — he hadn't made a single penny."

"Fact is, I lost by the whole transaction," put in Erastus Winch, defiantly.

"Just so," Brother Pierce went on. "He lost money. You have his own word for it. Well, then, I say it would be a burning shame for us to consent to touch one penny of what he offered to give, in the fulness of his heart, while he was laborin' under that delusion. And I move he be not asked for it. We've got quite as much as we need, without it. I put my motion."

"That is, *you* don't put it," suggested Winch, correctingly. "You move it, and Brother Ware, whom we're all so glad to see able to come and preside, — he'll put it."

There was a moment's silence. "You've heard the motion," said Theron, tentatively, and then paused for possible remarks. He was not going to meddle in this thing himself, and Gorringe was the only other who might have an opinion to offer. The necessities of the situation forced him to glance at the lawyer inquiringly. He did so, and turned his eyes away again like a shot. Gorringe was looking him squarely in the face, and the look was freighted with satirical contempt.

The young minister spoke between clinched teeth. "All those in favor will say Aye."

Brothers Pierce and Winch put up a simultaneous and confident "Aye."

"No, you don't!" interposed the lawyer, with deliberate, sneering emphasis. "I decidedly protest against Winch's voting. He's directly interested, and he mustn't vote. Your chairman knows that perfectly well."

"Yes, I think Brother Winch ought not to vote," decided Theron, with great calmness. He saw now what was coming, and underneath his surface composure there were sharp flutterings.

"Very well, then," said Gorringe. "I vote No, and it's a tie. It rests with the chairman now to cast the deciding vote, and say whether this interesting arrangement shall go through or not."

"Me?" said Theron, eying the lawyer with a cool self-control which had come all at once to him. "Me? Oh, I vote Aye."

CHAPTER XVII

"Well, I did what you told me to do," Theron Ware remarked to Sister Soulsby, when at last they found themselves alone in the sitting-room after the midday meal.

It had taken not a little strategic skirmishing to secure the room to themselves, for the hospitable Alice, much touched by the thought of her new friend's departure that very evening, had gladly proposed to let all the work stand over until night, and devote herself entirely to Sister Soulsby. When, finally, Brother Soulsby conceived and deftly executed the *coup* of interesting her in the budding of roses, and then leading her off into the garden to see with her own eyes how it was done, Theron had a sense of being left alone with a co-conspirator. The notion impelled him to plunge at once into the heart of their mystery.

"I did what you told me to do," he repeated, looking up from his low easy-chair to where she sat by the desk; "and I dare say you won't be surprised when I add that I have no respect for myself for doing it."

"And yet you would go and do it right over again, eh?" the woman said, in bright, pert tones, nodding her head, and smiling at him with roguish, comprehending eyes. "Yes, that's the way we're built. We spend our lives doing that sort of thing."

"I don't know that you would precisely grasp my meaning," said the young minister, with a polite effort in his words to mask the untoward side of the suggestion. "It is a matter of conscience with me; and I am pained and shocked at myself."

Sister Soulsby drummed for an absent moment with her thin, nervous fingers on the desk-top. "I guess maybe you'd better go and lie down again," she said gently. "You're a sick man, still, and it's no good your worrying your head just now with things of this sort. You'll see them differently when you're quite yourself again."

"No, no," pleaded Theron. "Do let us have our talk out! I'm all right. My mind is clear as a bell. Truly, I've really counted on this talk with you."

"But there's something else to talk about, isn't there, besides — besides your conscience?" she asked. Her eyes bent upon him a kindly pressure as she spoke, which took all possible harshness from her meaning.

Theron answered the glance rather than her words. "I know that you are my friend," he said simply.

Sister Soulsby straightened herself, and looked down upon him with a new intentness. "Well, then," she began, "let's thrash this thing out right now, and be done with it. You say it's hurt your conscience to do just one little hundredth part of what there was to be done here. Ask yourself what you mean by that. Mind, I'm not quarrelling, and I'm not thinking about anything except just your own state of mind. You think you soiled your hands by doing what you did. That is to say, you wanted *all* the dirty work done by other people. That's it, isn't it?"

The Rev. Mr. Ware sat up, in turn, and looked doubtingly into his companion's face.

"Oh, we were going to be frank, you know," she added, with a pleasant play of mingled mirth and honest liking in her eyes.

"No," he said, picking his words, "my point would rather be that — that there ought not to have been any of what you yourself call this — this 'dirty work.' *That* is my feeling."

✳ "Now we're getting at it," said Sister Soulsby, briskly. "My dear friend, you might just as well say that potatoes are unclean and unfit to eat because manure is put into the ground they grow in. Just look at the case. Your church here was running behind every year. Your people had got into a habit of putting in nickels instead of dimes, and letting you sweat for the difference. That's a habit, like tobacco, or biting your finger-nails, or anything else. Either you were all to come to smash here, or the people had to be shaken up, stood on their heads, broken of their habit. It's my business — mine and Soulsby's — to do that sort of thing. We came here and we did it, — did it up brown, too. We not only raised all the money the church needs, and to spare, but I took a personal shine to you, and went out of my way to fix up things for you. It isn't only the extra hundred dollars, but the whole tone of the congregation is changed toward you now. You'll see that they'll be asking to have you back here, next spring. And you're solid with your Presiding Elder, too. Well, now, tell me straight, — is that worth while, or not?"

"I've told you that I am very grateful," answered the minister, "and I say it again, and I shall never be tired of repeating it. But — but it was the *means* I had in mind."

"Quite so," rejoined the sister, patiently. "If you saw the way a hotel dinner was cooked, you wouldn't be able to stomach it. Did you ever see a play? In a theatre, I mean. I supposed not. But you'll understand when I say that the performance looks one way from where the audience sit, and quite a different way when you are behind the scenes. *There* you see that the trees and houses are cloth, and the moon is tissue paper, and the flying fairy is a middle-aged woman strung up on a rope. That doesn't prove that the play, out in front, isn't beautiful and affecting, and all that. It only shows that everything in this world is produced by machinery — by organization. The trouble is that you've been let in on the stage, behind the scenes, so to speak, and you're green — if you'll pardon me — that you want to sit down and cry because the trees *are* cloth, and the moon *is* a lantern. And *I* say, Don't be such a goose!"

"I see what you mean," Theron said, with an answering smile. He added, more gravely, "All the same, the Winch business seems to me — "

"Now the Winch business is my own affair," Sister Soulsby

broke in abruptly. "I take all the responsibility for that. You need know nothing about it. You simply voted as you did on the merits of the case as he presented them, — that's all."

"But — " Theron began, and then paused. Something had occurred to him, and he knitted his brows to follow its course of expansion in his mind. Suddenly he raised his head. "Then you arranged with Winch to make those bogus offers — just to lead others on?" he demanded.

Sister Soulsby's large eyes beamed down upon him in reply, at first in open merriment, then more soberly, till their regard was almost pensive.

"Let us talk of something else," she said. "All that is past and gone. It has nothing to do with you, anyway. I've got some advice to give you about keeping up this grip you've got on your people."

The young minister had risen to his feet while she spoke. He put his hands in his pockets, and with rounded shoulders began slowly pacing the room. After a turn or two he came to the desk, and leaned against it.

"I doubt if it's worth while going into that," he said, in the solemn tone of one who feels that an irrevocable thing is being uttered. She waited to hear more, apparently. "I think I shall go away — give up the ministry," he added.

Sister Soulsby's eyes revealed no such shock of consternation as he, unconsciously, had looked for. They remained quite calm; and when she spoke, they deepened, to fit her speech, with what he read to be a gaze of affectionate melancholy, — one might say pity. She shook her head slowly.

"No — don't let any one else hear you say that," she replied. "My poor young friend, it's no good to even think it. The real wisdom is to school yourself to move along smoothly, and not fret, and get the best of what's going. I've known others who felt as you do, — of course there are times when every young man of brains and high notions feels that way, — but there's no help for it. Those who tried to get out only broke themselves. Those who stayed in, and made the best of it — well, one of them will be a bishop in another ten years."

Theron had started walking again. "But the moral deg- ✳ radation of it!" he snapped out at her, over his shoulder. "I'd rather earn the meanest living, at an honest trade, and be free from it."

"That may all be," responded Sister Soulsby. "But it isn't a question of what you'd rather do. It's what you can do. How could *you* earn a living? What trade or business do you suppose you could take up now, and get a living out of? Not one, my man, not one."

Theron stopped and stared at her. This view of his capabilities came upon him with the force and [1] effect of a blow.

"I don't discover, myself," he began stumblingly, "that I'm so conspicuously inferior to the men I see about me who do make livings, and very good ones, too."

"Of course you're not," she replied with easy promptness; "you're greatly the other way, or I shouldn't be taking this trouble with you. But you're what you are because you're where you are. The moment you try on being somewhere else, you're done for. In all this world nobody else comes to such unmerciful and universal grief as the unfrocked priest."

The phrase sent Theron's fancy roving. "I know a Catholic priest," he said irrelevantly, "who doesn't believe an atom in — in things."

"Very likely," said Sister Soulsby. "Most of us do. But you don't hear him talking about going and earning his living, I'll bet! Or if he does, he takes powerful good care not to go, all the same. They've got horse-sense, those priests. They're artists, too. They know how to allow for the machinery behind the scenes."

"But it's all so different," urged the young minister; "the same things are not expected of them. Now I sat the other night and watched those people you got up around the altar-rail, groaning and shouting and crying, and the others jump-

---

[1] English ed. omits "force and."

ing up and down with excitement, and Sister Lovejoy — did you see her? — coming out of her pew and regularly waltzing in the aisle, with her eyes shut, like a whirling dervish — I positively believe it was all that made me ill. I couldn't stand it. I can't stand it now. I won't go back to it! Nothing shall make me!"

"Oh-h, yes, you will," she rejoined soothingly. "There's nothing else to do. Just put a good face on it, and make up your mind to get through by treading on as few corns as possible, and keeping your own toes well in, and you'll be surprised how easy it'll all come to be. You were speaking of the revival business. Now that exemplifies just what I was saying, — it's a part of our machinery. Now a church is like everything else, — it's got to have a boss, a head, an authority of some sort, that people will listen to and mind. The Catholics are different, as you say. Their church is chuck-full of authority, — all the way from the Pope down to the priest, — and accordingly they do as they're told. But the Protestants, — your Methodists most of all, — they say 'No, we won't have any authority, we won't obey any boss.' Very well, what happens? We who are responsible for running the thing, and raising the money and so on, — we have to put on a spurt every once in a while, and work up a general state of excitement; and while it's going, don't you see that *that* is the authority, the motive power, whatever you like to call it, by which things are done? Other denominations don't need it. We do, and that's why we've got it."

"But the mean dishonesty of it all!" Theron broke forth. He moved about again, his bowed face drawn as with bodily suffering. "The lowborn tricks, the hypocrisies! I feel as if I could never so much as look at these people here again without disgust."

"Oh, now that's where you make your mistake," Sister Soulsby put in placidly. "These people of yours are not a whit worse than other people. They've got their good streaks and their bad streaks, just like the rest of us. Take them by and large, they're quite on a par with other folks the whole country through."

"I don't believe there's another congregation in the Conference where — where this sort of thing would have been needed, or, I might say, tolerated," insisted Theron.

"Perhaps you're right," the other assented; "but that only shows that your people here are different from the others — *not* that they're worse. You don't seem to realize: Octavius, so far as the Methodists are concerned, is twenty or thirty years behind the times. Now that has its advantages and its disadvantages. The church here is tough and coarse, and full of grit, like a grindstone; and it does ministers from other more niminy-piminy places all sorts of good to come here once in a while and rub themselves up against it. It scours the rust and mildew off from their piety, and they go back singing and shouting. But of course it's had a different effect with you. You're razor-steel instead of scythe-steel, and the grinding's been too rough and violent for you. But you see what I mean. These people here really take their primitive Methodism seriously. To them the profession of entire sanctification is truly a genuine thing. Well, don't you see, when people just *know* that they're saved, it doesn't seem to them to matter so much what they do. They feel that ordinary rules may well be bent and twisted in the interest of people so supernaturally good as they are. That's pure human nature. It's always been like that."

Theron paused in his walk to look absently at her. "That thought," he said, in a vague, slow way, "seems to be springing up in my path, whichever way I turn. It oppresses me, and yet it fascinates me, — this idea that the dead men have known more than we know, done more than we do; that there is nothing new anywhere; that — "

"Never mind the dead men," interposed Sister Soulsby.[2] "Just you come and sit down here. I hate to have you straddling about the room when I'm trying to talk to you."

[2] English ed. adds " 'They have no voice in your salary.' "

Theron obeyed, and as he sank into the low seat, Sister Soulsby drew up her chair, and put her hand on his shoulder. Her gaze rested upon his with impressive steadiness.

"And now I want to talk seriously to you, as a friend," she began. "You mustn't breathe to any living soul the shadow of a hint of this nonsense about leaving the ministry. I could see how you were feeling, — I saw the book you were reading the first time I entered this room, — and that made me like you; only I expected to find you mixing up more worldly gumption with your Renan. Well, perhaps I like you all the better for not having it — for being so delightfully fresh. At any rate, that made me sail in and straighten your affairs for you. And now, for God's sake, keep them straight. Just put all notions of anything else out of your head. Watch your chief men and women, and be friends with them. Keep your eye open for what they think you ought to do, and do it. Have your own ideas as much as you like, read what you like, say 'Damn' under your breath as much as you like, but don't let go of your job. I've knocked about too much, and I've seen too many promising young fellows cut their own throats for pure moonshine, not to have a right to say that."

Theron could not be insensible to the friendly hand on his shoulder, or to the strenuous sincerity of the voice which thus adjured him.

"Well," he said vaguely, smiling up into her earnest eyes, "if we agree that it *is* moonshine."

"See here!" she exclaimed, with renewed animation, patting his shoulder in a brisk, automatic way, to point the beginnings of her confidences: "I'll tell you something. It's about myself. I've got a religion of my own, and it's got just one plank in it, and that is that the time to separate the sheep from the goats is on Judgment Day, and that it can't be done a minute before."

The young minister took in the thought, and turned it about in his mind, and smiled upon it.

"And that brings me to what I'm going to tell you," Sister Soulsby continued. She leaned back in her chair, and crossed her knees so that one well-shaped and artistically shod foot poised itself close to Theron's hand. Her eyes dwelt upon his face with an engaging candor.

"I began life," she said, "as a girl by running away from a stupid home with a man that I knew was married already. After that, I supported myself for a good many years, — generally, at first, on the stage. I've been a front-ranker in Amazon ballets, and I've been leading lady in comic opera companies out West. I've told fortunes in one room of a mining-camp hotel where the biggest game of faro in the Territory went on in another. I've been a professional clairvoyant, and I've been a professional medium,[3] and I've been within one vote of being indicted by a grand jury, and the money that bought that vote was put up by the smartest and most famous train-gambler between Omaha and 'Frisco, a gentleman who died in his boots and took three sheriff's deputies along with him to Kingdom-Come. Now, that's *my* record."

Theron looked earnestly at her, and said nothing.

"And now take Soulsby," she went on. "Of course I take it for granted there's a good deal that he has never felt called upon to mention. He hasn't what you may call a talkative temperament. But there is also a good deal that I do know. He's been an actor, too, and to this day I'd back him against Edwin Booth himself to recite 'Clarence's Dream.' And he's been a medium, and then he was a travelling phrenologist, and for a long time he was advance agent for a British Blondes show, and when I first saw him he was lecturing on female diseases — and he had his little turn with a grand jury too. In fact, he was what you may call a regular bad old rooster."

Again Theron suffered the pause to lapse without com-

[3] English ed. reverses the order of the two preceding clauses.

ment, — save for an amorphous sort of conversation which he felt to be going on between his eyes and those of Sister Soulsby.

"Well, then," she resumed, "so much for us apart. Now about us together. We liked each other from the start.[4] We compared notes, and we found that we had both soured on living by fakes, and that we were tired of the road, and wanted to settle down and be respectable in our old age. We had a little money, — enough to see us through a year or two. Soulsby had always hungered and longed to own a garden and raise flowers, and had never been able to stay long enough in one place to see so much as a bean-pod ripen. So we took a little place in a quiet country village down on the Southern Tier, and he planted everything three deep all over the place, and I bought a roomful of cheap good books, and we started in. We took to it like ducks to water for a while, and I don't say that we couldn't have stood it out, just doing nothing, to this very day; but as luck would have it, during the first winter there was a revival at the local Methodist church, and we went every evening, — at first just to kill time, and then because we found we liked the noise and excitement and general racket of the thing. After it was all over each of us found that the other had been mighty near going up to the rail and joining the mourners. And another thing had occurred to each of us, too, — that is, what tremendous improvements there were possible in the way that amateur revivalist worked up his business. This stuck in our crops, and we figured on it all through the winter. — Well, to make a long story short, we finally went into the thing ourselves."

"Tell me one thing," interposed Theron, "I'm anxious to understand it all as we go along. Were you and he at any time sincerely converted? — that is, I mean, genuinely convicted of sin and conscious of — you know what I mean!"

"Oh, bless you, yes," responded Sister Soulsby. "Not only

---

[4] English ed. reads "from the day we met" for "from the start."

once — dozens of times — I may say every time. We couldn't
do good work if we weren't. But that's a matter of temperament — of emotions."

"Precisely. That was what I was getting at," explained
Theron.

"Well, then, hear what *I* was getting at," she went on.
"You were talking very loudly here about frauds and hypocrisies and so on, a few minutes ago. Now *I* say that Soulsby
and I do good, and that we're good fellows. Now take him,
for example. There isn't a better citizen in all Chemung
County than he is, or a kindlier neighbor, or a better or
more charitable man. I've known him to stay up a whole
winter's night in a poor Irishman's stinking and freezing
stable, trying to save his cart-horse for him, that had been
seized with some sort of fit. The man's whole livelihood, and
his family's, was in that horse; and when it died, Soulsby
bought him another, and never told even *me* about it. Now
that I call real piety, if you like."

"So do I," put in Theron, cordially.

"And this question of fraud," pursued his companion, —
"look at it in this light. You heard us sing. Well, now, I was
a singer, of course, but Soulsby hardly knew one note from
another. I taught him to sing, and he went at it patiently
and diligently, like a little man. And I invented that scheme
of finding tunes which the crowd didn't know, and so couldn't
break in on and smother. I simply took Chopin, — he is full
of sixths, you know, — and I got all sorts of melodies out of
his waltzes and mazurkas and nocturnes and so on, and I
trained Soulsby just to sing those sixths so as to make the
harmony, and there you are. He couldn't [5] sing by himself
any more than a crow, but he's got those sixths of his down
to a hair. Now that's machinery, management, organization.
We take these tunes, written by a devil-may-care Pole who
was living with George Sand openly at the time, and [6] pass

[5] English ed. reads "He still can't sing" for "he couldn't sing."
[6] English ed. adds "we."

'em off on the brethren for hymns. It's a fraud, yes; but it's a good fraud. So they are all good frauds. I say frankly that I'm glad that the change and the chance came to help Soulsby and me to be good frauds."

"And the point is that I'm to be a good fraud, too," commented the young minister.

She had risen, and he got to his feet as well. He instinctively sought for her hand, and pressed it warmly, and held it in both his, with an exuberance of gratitude and liking in his manner.

Sister Soulsby danced her eyes at him with a saucy little shake of the head.[7] "I'm afraid you'll never make a really *good* fraud," she said. "You haven't got it in you. Your intentions are all right, but your execution is hopelessly clumsy. I came up to your bedroom there twice while you were sick, just to say 'howdy,' and you kept your eyes shut, and all the while a blind horse could have told that you were wide awake."

"I must have thought it was my wife," said Theron.

[7] English ed. has new paragraph here.

PART III

———•———

CHAPTER XVIII

WHEN the lingering dusk finally settled down upon this long summer evening, the train bearing the Soulsbys homeward was already some score of miles on its way, and the Methodists of Octavius had nearly finished their weekly prayer-meeting.

After the stirring events of the revival, it was only to be expected that this routine, home-made affair should suffer from a reaction. The attendance was larger than usual, perhaps, but the proceedings were spiritless and tame. Neither the pastor nor his wife was present at the beginning, and the class-leader upon whom control devolved made but feeble headway against the spell of inertia which the hot night-air laid upon the gathering. Long pauses intervened between the perfunctory praise-offerings and supplications, and the hymns weariedly raised from time to time fell again in languor by the wayside.

Alice came in just as people were beginning to hope that some one would start the Doxology, and bring matters to a close. Her appearance apparently suggested this to the class-leader, for in a few moments the meeting had been dismissed, and some of the members, on their way out, were shaking hands with their minister's wife, and expressing the polite hope that he was better. The worried look in her face, and the obvious stains of recent tears upon her cheeks imparted an added point and fervor to these inquiries, but she replied to all in tones of studied tranquillity that, although not feeling well enough to attend prayer-meeting, Brother Ware was steadily recovering strength, and confidently expected to be in complete health by Sunday. They left her, and could hardly wait to get into the vestibule to ask one another in whispers what on earth she could have been crying about.

Meanwhile Brother Ware improved his convalescent state by pacing slowly up and down under the elms on the side of the street opposite the Catholic church. There were no houses here for a block and more; the sidewalk was broken in many places, so that passers-by avoided it; the overhanging boughs shrouded it all in obscurity; it was pre-eminently a place to be alone in.

Theron had driven to the depot with his guests an hour before, and after a period of pleasant waiting on the platform, had said good-bye to them as the train moved away. Then he turned to Alice, who had also accompanied them in the carriage, and was conscious of a certain annoyance at her having come. That long familiar talk of the afternoon had given him the feeling that he was entitled to bid farewell to Sister Soulsby — to both the Soulsbys — by himself.

"I am afraid folks will think it strange — neither of us attending the prayer-meeting," he said, with a suggestion of reproof in his tone, as they left the station-yard.

"If we get back in time, I'll run in for a minute," answered Alice, with docility.

"No — no," he broke in. "I'm not equal to walking so fast. You run on ahead, and explain matters, and I will come along slowly."

"The hack we came in is still there in the yard," the wife suggested. "We could drive home in that. I don't believe it would cost more than a quarter — and if you're feeling badly — "

"But I am *not* feeling badly," Theron replied, with frank impatience. "Only I feel — I feel that being alone with my thoughts would be good for me."

"Oh, certainly — by all means!" Alice had said, and turned sharply on her heel.

Being alone with these thoughts, Theron strolled aimlessly about, and did not think at all. The shadows gathered, and fireflies began to disclose their tiny gleams among the shrubbery in the gardens. A lamp-lighter came along, and passed him, leaving in his wake a straggling double line of lights, glowing radiantly against the black-green of the trees. This recalled to Theron that he had heard that the town council lit the street lamps by the almanac, and economized gas when moonshine was due. The idea struck him as droll, and he dwelt upon it in various aspects, smiling at some of its comic possibilities. Looking up in the middle of one of these whimsical conceits, the sportive impulse died suddenly within him. He realized that it was dark,[1] and that the massive black bulk reared against the sky on the other side of the road was the Catholic church. The other fact, that he had been there walking to and fro for some time, was borne in upon him more slowly. He turned, and resumed the pacing up and down with a still more leisurely step, musing upon the curious way in which people's minds all unconsciously follow about where instincts [2] and intuitions lead.

No doubt it was what Sister Soulsby had said about Catholics which had insensibly guided his purposeless stroll in this direction. What a woman that was! Somehow the purport of her talk — striking, and even astonishing as he had found it — did not stand out so clearly in his memory as did the image of the woman herself. She must have been extremely pretty once. For that matter she still was a most attractive-looking woman. It had been a genuine pleasure to have her in the house — to see her intelligent responsive face at the table — to have it in one's power to make drafts at will upon the fund of sympathy and appreciation, of facile mirth and ready tenderness in those big eyes of hers. He liked that phrase she had used about herself, — "a good fellow." It seemed to fit her to a "t." And Soulsby was a good fellow too. All at once it occurred to him to wonder whether they were married or not.[3]

---

[1] English ed. reads "night" for "dark."
[2] English ed. reads "impulses" for "instincts."
[3] English ed. reads "actually married" for "married or not."

But really that was no affair of his, he reflected. A citizen of the intellectual world should be above soiling his thoughts with mean curiosities of that sort, and he drove the impertinent query down again under the surface of his mind. He refused to tolerate, as well, sundry vagrant imaginings which rose to cluster about and literalize the romance of her youth which Sister Soulsby had so frankly outlined. He would think upon nothing but her as he knew her, — the kindly, quick-witted, capable and charming woman who had made such a brilliant break in the monotony of life at that dull parsonage of his. The only genuine happiness in life must consist in having bright, smart, attractive women like that always about.

The lights were visible now in the upper rooms of Father Forbes' pastorate across the way. Theron paused for a second to consider whether he wanted to go over and call on the priest. He decided that mentally he was too fagged and flat for such an undertaking. He needed another sort of companionship, — some restful, soothing human contact, which should exact nothing from him in return, but just take charge of him, with soft, wise words and pleasant plays of fancy, and jokes and — and — something of the general effect created by Sister Soulsby's eyes. The thought expanded itself, and he saw that he had never realized before, — nay, never dreamt before — what a mighty part the comradeship of talented, sweet-natured and beautiful women must play in the development of genius, the achievement of lofty aims, out in the great world of great men. To know such women — ah, that would never fall to his hapless lot.

The priest's lamps blinked at him through the trees. He remembered that priests were supposed to be even further removed from the possibilities of such contact than he was himself. His memory reverted to that horribly ugly old woman whom Father Forbes had spoken of as his housekeeper. Life under the same roof with such a hag must be even worse than — worse than —

The young minister did not finish the comparison, even in the privacy of his inner soul. He stood instead staring over at the pastorate, in a kind of stupor of arrested thought. The figure of a woman passed in view of the nearest window — a tall figure with pale summer clothes of some sort, and a broad summer hat, — a flitting effect of diaphanous shadow between him and the light which streamed from the case-ment.

Theron felt a little shiver run over him, as if the delicate coolness of the changing night-air had got into his blood. The window was open, and his strained hearing thought it caught the sound of faint laughter. He continued to gaze at the place where the vision had appeared, the while a novel and strange perception unfolded itself upon his mind.

He had come there in the hope of encountering Celia Madden.

Now that he looked this fact in the face, there was nothing remarkable about it. In truth, it was simplicity itself. He was still a sick man, weak in body and dejected in spirits. The thought of how unhappy and unstrung he was came to him now with an insistent pathos that brought tears to his eyes. He was only obeying the universal law of nature, — the law which prompts the pallid spindling sprout of the potato in the cellar to strive feebly toward the light.

From where he stood in the darkness he stretched out his hands in the direction of that open window. The gesture was his confession to the overhanging boughs, to the soft night-breeze, to the stars above, — and it bore back to him some-thing of the confessional's vague and wistful solace. He seemed already to have drawn down into his soul a taste of the refreshment it craved. He sighed deeply, and the hot moisture smarted again upon his eyelids, but this time not all in grief. With his tender compassion for himself there mingled now a flutter of buoyant prescience, of exquisite expectancy.

Fate walked abroad this summer night. The street door

of the pastorate opened, and in the flood of illumination which spread suddenly forth over the steps and sidewalk, Theron saw again the tall form, with the indefinitely light-hued flowing garments and the wide straw hat. He heard a tuneful woman's voice call out "Good-night, Maggie," and caught no response save the abrupt closing of the door, which turned everything black again with a bang. He listened acutely for another instant, and then with long, noiseless strides made his way down his deserted side of the street. He moderated his pace as he turned to cross the road at the corner, and then, still masked by the trees, halted altogether, in a momentary tumult of apprehension. No — yes — it was all right. The girl sauntered out from the total darkness into the dim starlight of the open corner.

"Why, bless me, is that you, Miss Madden?"

Celia seemed to discern readily enough, through the accents of surprise, the identity of the tall, slim man who addressed her from the shadows.

"Good-evening, Mr. Ware," she said, with prompt affability. "I'm so glad to find you out again. We heard you were ill."

"I have been very ill," responded Theron, as they shook hands and walked on together. He added, with a quaver in his voice, "I am still far from strong. I really ought not to be out at all. But — but the longing for — for — well, I *couldn't* stay in any longer. Even if it kills me, I shall be glad I came out to-night."

"Oh, we won't talk of killing," said Celia. "I don't believe in illnesses myself."

"But you believe in collapses of the nerves," put in Theron, with gentle sadness, "in moral and spiritual and mental breakdowns. I remember how I was touched by the way you told me *you* suffered from them. I had to take what you said then for granted. I had had no experience of it myself. But now I know what it is." He drew a long, pathetic sigh. "Oh, *don't* I know what it is!" he repeated gloomily.

"Come, my friend, cheer up," Celia purred at him, in soothing tones. He felt that there was a deliciously feminine and sisterly intuition in her speech, and in the helpful, nurse-like way in which she drew his arm through hers. He leaned upon this support, and was glad of it in every fibre of his being.

"Do you remember? You promised — that last time I saw you — to play for me," he reminded her. They were passing the little covered postern door at the side and rear of the church as he spoke, and he made a half halt to point the coincidence.

"Oh, there's no one to blow the organ," she said, divining his suggestion. "And I haven't the key — and, besides, the organ is too heavy and severe for an invalid. It would overwhelm you to-night.

"Not as you would know how to play it for me," urged Theron, pensively. "I feel as if good music to-night would make me well again. I am really very ill and weak — and unhappy!"

The girl seemed moved by the despairing note in his voice. She invited him by a sympathetic gesture to lean even more directly on her arm.

"Come home with me, and I'll play Chopin to you," she said, in compassionate friendliness. "He is the real medicine for bruised and wounded nerves. You shall have as much of him as you like."

The idea thus unexpectedly thrown forth spread itself like some vast and inexpressibly alluring vista before Theron's imagination. The spice of adventure in it fascinated his mind as well, but for a shrinking moment the flesh was weak.

"I'm afraid your people would — would think it strange," he faltered — and began also to recall that he had some people of his own who would be even more amazed.

"Nonsense," said Celia, in fine, bold confidence, and with a reassuring pressure on his arm. "I allow none of my people to question what I do. They never dream of such a pre-

posterous thing. Besides, you will see none of them. Mrs.
Madden is at the seaside, and my father and brother have
their own part of the house. I sha'n't listen for a minute to
your not coming. Come, I'm your doctor. I'm to make you
well again."

There was further conversation, and Theron more or less
knew that he was bearing a part in it, but his whole mind
seemed concentrated, in a sort of delicious terror, upon the
wonderful experience to which every footstep brought him
nearer. His magnetized fancy pictured a great spacious parlor,
such as a mansion like the Maddens' would of course contain,
and there would be a grand piano, and lace curtains, and
paintings in gold frames, and a chandelier, and velvet easy-
chairs, and he would sit in one of these, surrounded by all
the luxury of the rich, while Celia played to him. There
would be servants about, he presumed, and very likely they
would recognize him, and of course they would talk about it
to Tom, Dick, and Harry afterward. But he said to himself
defiantly that he didn't care.

He withdrew his arm from hers as they came upon the
well-lighted main street. He passed no one who seemed to
know him. Presently they came to the Madden place, and
Celia, without waiting for the gravelled walk, struck obliquely across the lawn. Theron, who had been lagging behind with a certain circumspection, stepped briskly to her
side now. Their progress over the soft, close-cropped turf in
the dark together, with the scent of lilies and perfumed
shrubs heavy on the night air, and the majestic bulk of the
big silent house rising among the trees before them, gave him
a thrilling sense of the glory of individual freedom.

"I feel a new man already," he declared, as they swung
along on the grass. He breathed a long sigh of content, and
drew nearer, so that their shoulders touched now and again
as they walked. In a minute more they were standing on the
doorstep, and Theron heard the significant jingle of a bunch
of keys which his companion was groping for in her elusive

pocket. He was conscious of trembling a little at the sound.

It seemed that, unlike other people, the Maddens did not have their parlor on the ground-floor, opening off the front hall. Theron stood in the complete darkness of this hall, till Celia had lit one of several candles which were in their handsticks on a sort of sideboard next the hat-rack. She beckoned him with a gesture of her head, and he followed her up a broad staircase, magnificent in its structural appointments of inlaid woods, and carpeted with what to his feet felt like down. The tiny light which his guide bore before her half revealed, as they passed in their ascent, tall lengths of tapestry, and the dull glint of armor and brazen discs in shadowed niches on the nearer wall. Over the stair-rail lay an open space of such stately dimensions, bounded by terminal lines of decoration so distant in the faint candle-flicker, that the young country minister could think of no word but "palatial" to fit it all.

At the head of the flight, Celia led the way along a wide corridor to where it ended. Here, stretched from side to side, and suspended from broad hoops of a copper-like metal, was a thick curtain, of a uniform color which Theron at first thought was green, and then decided must be blue. She pushed its heavy folds aside, and unlocked another door. He passed under the curtain behind her, and closed the door.

The room into which he had made his way was not at all after the fashion of any parlor he had ever seen. In the obscure light it was difficult to tell what it resembled. He made out what he took to be a painter's easel, standing forth independently in the centre of things. There were rows of books on rude, low shelves. Against one of the two windows was a big, flat writing-table — or was it a drawing-table? — littered with papers. Under the other window was a carpenter's bench, with a large mound of something at one end covered with a white cloth. On a table behind the easel rose a tall mechanical contrivance, the chief feature of which was a thick upright spiral screw. The floor was of bare wood stained brown. The walls of this queer room had photographs and pictures, taken apparently from illustrated papers, pinned up at random for their only ornament.

Celia had lighted three or four other candles on the mantel. She caught the dumfounded expression with which her guest was surveying his surroundings, and gave a merry little laugh.

"This is my workshop," she explained. "I keep this for the things I do badly, — things I fool with. If I want to paint, or model in clay, or bind books, or write, or draw, or turn on the lathe, or do some carpentering, here's where I do it. All the things that make a mess which has to be cleaned up — they are kept out here — because this is as far as the servants are allowed to come."

She unlocked still another door as she spoke, — a door which was also concealed behind a curtain.

"Now," she said, holding up the candle so that its reddish flare rounded with warmth the creamy fulness of her chin and throat, and glowed upon her hair in a flame of orange light — "now I will show you what is my very own."

CHAPTER XIX

THERON WARE looked about him with frankly undisguised astonishment.

The room in which he found himself was so dark at first that it yielded little to the eye, and that little seemed altogether beyond his comprehension. His gaze helplessly followed Celia and her candle about as she busied herself in the work of illumination. When she had finished, and pinched out the taper, there were seven lights in the apartment — lights beaming softly through half-opaque alternating rectangles of blue and yellow glass. They must be set in some sort of lanterns around against the wall, he thought, but the shape of these he could hardly make out.

Gradually his sight adapted itself to this subdued light, and he began to see other things. These queer lamps were placed, apparently, so as to shed a special radiance upon some statues which stood in the corners of the chamber, and upon some pictures which were embedded in the walls. Theron noted that the statues, the marble of which lost its aggressive whiteness under the tinted lights, were mostly of naked men and women; the pictures, four or five in number, were all variations of a single theme, — the Virgin Mary and the Child.

A less untutored vision than his would have caught more swiftly the scheme of color and line in which these works of art bore their share. The walls of the room were in part of flat upright wooden columns, terminating high above in simple capitals, and they were all painted in pale amber and straw and primrose hues, irregularly wavering here and there toward suggestions of white. Between these pilasters were broader panels of stamped leather, in gently varying shades of peacock blue. These contrasted colors vaguely interwove and mingled in what he could see of the shadowed ceiling far above.[1] They were repeated in the draperies and huge

---

[1] English ed. reads "high over head" for "far above."

cushions and pillows of the low, wide divan which ran about three sides of the room. Even the floor, where it revealed itself among the scattered rugs, was laid in a mosaic pattern of matched woods, which, like the rugs, gave back these same shifting blues and uncertain yellows.

The fourth side of the apartment was broken in outline at one end by the door through which they had entered, and at the other by a broad, square opening, hung with looped-back curtains of a thin silken stuff. Between the two apertures rose against the wall what Theron took at first glance to be an altar. There were pyramidal rows of tall candles here on either side, each masked with a little silken hood; below, in the centre, a shelf-like projection supported what seemed a massive, carved casket, and in the beautiful intricacies of this, and the receding canopy of delicate ornamentation which depended above it, the dominant color was white, deepening away in its shadows, by tenderly minute gradations, to the tints which ruled the rest of the room.

Celia lighted some of the high, thick tapers in these candelabra, and opened the top of the casket. Theron saw with surprise that she had uncovered the keyboard of a piano. He viewed with much greater amazement her next proceeding, — which was to put a cigarette between her lips, and, bending over one of the candles with it for an instant, turn to him with a filmy, opalescent veil of smoke above her head.

"Make yourself comfortable anywhere," she said, with a gesture which comprehended all the divans and pillows in the place. "Will you smoke?"

"I have never tried since I was a little boy," said Theron, "but I think I could. If you don't mind, I should like to see."

Lounging at his ease on the oriental couch, Theron experimented cautiously upon the unaccustomed tobacco, and looked at Celia with what he felt to be the confident quiet of a man of the world. She had thrown aside her hat, and in doing so had half released some of the heavy strands of hair coiled at the back of her head. His glance instinctively rested upon this wonderful hair of hers. There was no mistaking the sudden fascination its disorder had for his eye.

She stood before him with the cigarette poised daintily between thumb and finger of a shapely hand, and smiled comprehendingly down on her guest.

"I suffered the horrors of the damned with this hair of mine when I was a child," she said. "I daresay all children have a taste for persecuting red-heads; but it's a specialty with Irish children. They got hold somehow of an ancient national superstition, or legend, that red hair was brought into Ireland by the Danes. It's been a term of reproach with us since Brian Boru's time to call a child a Dane. I used to be pursued and baited with it every day of my life, until the one dream of my ambition was to get old enough to be a Sister of Charity, so that I might hide my hair under one of their big beastly white linen caps. I've got rather away from that ideal since, I'm afraid," she added, with a droll downward curl of her lip.

"Your hair is very beautiful," said Theron, in the calm tone of a connoisseur.

"I like it myself," Celia admitted, and blew a little smoke-ring toward him. "I've made this whole room to match it. The colors, I mean," she explained, in deference to his up-lifted brows. "Between us, we make up what Whistler would call a symphony. That reminds me — I was going to play for you. Let me finish the cigarette first."

Theron felt grateful for her reticence about the fact that he had laid his own aside. "I have never seen a room at all like this," he remarked. "You are right; it does fit you perfectly."

She nodded her sense of his appreciation. "It is what I like," she said. "It expresses *me*. I will not have anything about me — or anybody either — that I don't like. I suppose if an old Greek could see it, it would make him sick, but it represents what *I* mean by being a Greek. It is as near as an Irishman can get to it."

"I remember your puzzling me by saying that you were a Greek."

Celia laughed and tossed the cigarette-end away. "I'd puzzle you more, I'm afraid, if I tried to explain to you what I really meant by it. I divide people up into two classes, you know, — Greeks and Jews. Once you get hold of that principle, all other divisions and classifications, such as by race or language or nationality, seem pure foolishness. It is the only true division there is. It is just as true among negroes or wild Indians who never heard of Greece [2] or Jerusalem, as it is among white folks. That is the beauty of it. It works everywhere, always."

"Try it on me," urged Theron, with a twinkling eye. "Which am I?"

"Both," said the girl, with a merry nod of the head. "But now I'll play. I told you you were to hear Chopin. I prescribe him for you. He is the Greekiest of the Greeks. *There* was a nation where all the people were artists, where everybody was an intellectual aristocrat, where the Philistine was as unknown, as extinct, as the dodo. Chopin might have written his music for them."

"I am interested in Shopang," put in Theron, suddenly recalling Sister Soulsby's confidences as to the source of her tunes. "He lived with — what's his name — George something. We were speaking about him only this afternoon."

Celia looked down into her visitor's face at first inquiringly, then with a latent grin about her lips. "Yes — George something," she said, in a tone which mystified him.

The Rev. Mr. Ware was sitting up, a minute afterward, in a ferment of awakened consciousness that he had never heard the piano played before. After a little, he noiselessly rearranged the cushions, and settled himself again in a recumbent posture. It was beyond his strength to follow that first impulse, and keep his mind abreast with what his ears took in. He sighed and lay back, and surrendered his senses to the mere unthinking charm of it all.

[2] English ed. reads "Athens" for "Greece."

It was the Fourth Prelude that was singing in the air about him, — a simple, plaintive strain wandering at will over a surface of steady rhythmic movement underneath, always creeping upward through mysteries of sweetness, always sinking again in cadences of semi-tones. With only a moment's pause, there came the Seventh Waltz, — a rich, bold confusion which yet was not confused. Theron's ears dwelt with eager delight upon the chasing medley of swift, tinkling sounds, but it left his thoughts free.

From where he reclined, he turned his head to scrutinize, one by one, the statues in the corners. No doubt they were beautiful, — for this was a department in which he was all humility, — and one of them, the figure of a broad-browed, stately, though thick-waisted woman, bending slightly forward and with both arms broken off, was decently robed from the hips downward. The others were not robed at all. Theron stared at them with the erratic, rippling jangle of the waltz in his ears, and felt that he possessed a new and disturbing conception of what female emancipation meant in these later days. Roving along the wall, his glance rested again upon the largest of the Virgin pictures, — a full-length figure in sweeping draperies, its radiant, aureoled head upturned in rapt adoration, its feet resting on a crescent moon which shone forth in a bluish silver through festooned clouds of cherubs. The incongruity between the unashamed statues and this serene incarnation of holy womanhood jarred upon him for the instant. Then his mind went to the piano.

Without a break the waltz had slowed and expanded into a passage of what might be church music, an exquisitely modulated and gently solemn chant, through which a soft, lingering song roved capriciously, forcing the listener to wonder where it was coming out, even while it caressed and soothed to repose.

He looked from the Madonna to Celia. Beyond the carelessly drooping braids and coils of hair which blazed between the candles, he could see the outline of her brow and cheek, the noble contour of her lifted chin and full, modelled throat, all pink as the most delicate roseleaf is pink, against the cool lights of the altar-like wall. The sight convicted him in the court of his own soul as a prurient and mean-minded rustic. In the presence of such a face, of such music, there ceased to be any such thing as nudity, and statues no more needed clothes than did those slow, deep, magnificent chords which came now, gravely accumulating their spell upon him.

"It is all singing!" the player called out to him over her shoulder, in a minute of rest. "That is what Chopin does, — he sings!"

She began, with an effect of thinking of something else, the Sixth Nocturne, and Theron at first thought she was not playing anything in particular, so deliberately, haltingly, did the chain of charm unwind itself into sequence. Then it came closer to him than the others had done. The dreamy, wistful, meditative beauty of it all at once oppressed and inspired him. He saw Celia's shoulders sway under the impulse of the *rubato* license, — the privilege to invest each measure with the stress of the whole, to loiter, to weep, to run and laugh at will, — and the music she made spoke to him as with a human voice. There was the wooing sense of roses and moonlight, of perfumes, white skins, alluring languorous eyes, and then —

"You know this part, of course," he heard her say.

On the instant they had stepped from the dark, scented starlit garden, where the nightingale sang, into a great cathedral. A sombre and lofty anthem arose, and filled the place with the splendor of such dignified pomp of harmony and such suggestions of measureless choral power and authority that Theron sat abruptly up, then was drawn resistlessly to his feet. He stood motionless in the strange room, feeling most of all that one should kneel to hear such music.

"This you'll know too, — the funeral march from the Second Sonata," she was saying, before he realized that the end of the other had come. He sank upon the divan again, bending forward and clasping his hands tight around his knees. His heart beat furiously as he listened to the weird, mediæval processional, with its wild, clashing chords held down in the bondage of an orderly sadness. There was a pro-pelling motion in the thing — a sense of being borne bodily along — which affected him like dizziness. He breathed hard through the robust portions of stern, vigorous noise, and rocked himself to and fro when, as rosy morn [3] breaks upon a storm-swept night, the drums are silenced for the sweet, comforting strain of solitary melody. The clanging minor harmonies into which the march relapses came to their abrupt end. Theron rose once more, and moved with a hesitating step to the piano.

"I want to rest a little," he said, with his hand on her shoulder.

"Whew! so do I," exclaimed Celia, letting her hands fall with an exaggerated gesture of weariness. "The sonatas take it out of one! They are hideously difficult, you know. They are rarely played."

"I didn't know," remarked Theron. She seemed not to mind his hand upon her shoulder, and he kept it there. "I didn't know anything about music at all. What I do know now is that — that this evening is an event in my life."

She looked up at him and smiled. He read unsuspected tendernesses and tolerances of friendship in the depths of her eyes, which emboldened him to stir the fingers of that auda-cious hand in a lingering, caressing trill upon her shoulder. The movement was of the faintest, but having ventured it, he drew his hand abruptly away.

"You are getting on," she said to him. There was an enig-matic twinkle in the smile with which she continued to regard him. "We are Hellenizing you at a great rate."

A sudden thought seemed to strike her. She shifted her eyes toward vacancy with a swift, abstracted glance, reflected for a moment, then let a sparkling half-wink and the dimpling beginnings of an almost roguish smile mark her assent to the conceit, whatever it might be.

"I will be with you in a moment," he heard her say; and

[3] English ed. reads "morning" for "morn."

while the words were still in his ears she had risen and passed out of sight through the broad, open doorway to the right. The looped curtains fell together behind her. Presently a mellow light spread over their delicately translucent surface, — a creamy, undulating[4] radiance which gave the effect of moving about among the myriad folds of the silk.

Theron gazed at these curtains for a little, then straightened his shoulders with a gesture of decision, and turning on his heel, went over and examined the statues in the further corners minutely.

"If you would like some more, I will play you the Berceuse now."

Her voice came to him with a delicious shock. He wheeled round and beheld her standing at the piano, with one hand resting, palm upward, on the keys. She was facing him. Her tall form was robed now in some shapeless, clinging drapery, lustrous and creamy and exquisitely soft, like the curtains. The wonderful hair hung free and luxuriant about her neck and shoulders, and glowed with an intensity of fiery color which made all the other hues of the room pale and vague. A fillet of faint, sky-like blue drew a gracious span through the flame of red above her temples, and from this there rose the gleam of jewels. Her head inclined gently, gravely, toward him, — with the posture of that armless woman in marble he had been studying, — and her brown eyes, regarding him from the shadows, emitted light.

"It is a lullaby, — the only one he wrote," she said, as Theron, pale-faced and with tightened lips, approached her. "No — you mustn't stand there," she added, sinking into the seat before the instrument; "go back and sit where you were."

The most perfect of lullabies, with its swaying abandonment to cooing rhythm, ever and again rising in ripples to the point of insisting on something, one knows not what, and then rocking, melting away once more, passed, so to speak, over Theron's head. He leaned back upon the cush-

---

[4] English ed. reads "an undulating" for "a creamy, undulating."

ions, and watched the white, rounded forearm which the falling folds of this strange, statue-like drapery made bare.

There was more that appealed to his mood in the Third Ballade. It seemed to him that there were words going along with it, — incoherent and impulsive yet very earnest words, appealing to him in strenuous argument and persuasion. Each time he almost knew what they said, and strained after their meaning with a passionate desire, and then there would come a kind of cuckoo call, and everything would swing dancing off again into a mockery of inconsequence.

Upon the silence there fell the pure, liquid, mellifluous melody of a soft-throated woman singing to her lover.

"It is like Heine, — simply a love-poem," said the girl, over her shoulder.

Theron followed now with all his senses, as she carried the Ninth Nocturne onward. The stormy passage, which she banged finely forth, was in truth a lover's quarrel; and then the mild, placid flow of sweet harmonies into which the furore sank, dying languorously away upon a silence all alive with tender memories of sound, — was that not also a part of love?

They sat motionless through a minute, — the man on the divan, the girl at the piano, — and Theron listened for what he felt must be the audible thumping of his heart.

Then, throwing back her head, with upturned face, Celia began what she had withheld for the last, — the Sixteenth Mazurka. This strange foreign thing she played with her eyes closed, her head tilted obliquely so that Theron could see the rose-tinted, beautiful countenance, framed as if asleep in the billowing luxuriance of unloosed auburn hair. He fancied her beholding visions as she wrought the music, — visions full of barbaric color and romantic forms. As his mind swam along with the gliding, tricky phantom of a tune, it seemed as if he too could see these visions, — as if he gazed at them through her eyes.

It could not be helped. He lifted himself noiselessly to his feet, and stole with caution toward her. He would hear the rest of this weird, voluptuous fantasy standing thus, so close behind her that he could look down upon her full, uplifted face, — so close that, if she moved, that glowing nimbus of hair would touch him.

There had been some curious and awkward pauses in this last piece, which Theron, by some side cerebration, had put down to her not watching what her fingers did. There came another of these pauses now, — an odd, unaccountable halt in what seemed the middle of everything. He stared intently down upon her statuesque, dreaming face during the hush and caught his breath as he waited. There fell at last a few faltering ascending notes, making a half-finished strain, and then again there was silence.

Celia opened her eyes, and poured a direct, deep gaze into the face above hers. Its pale lips were parted in suspense, and the color had faded from its cheeks.

"That is the end," she said, and with a turn of her lithe body, stood swiftly up, even while the echoes of the broken melody seemed panting in the air about her for completion.

Theron put his hands to his face, and pressed them tightly against eyes and brow for an instant. Then, throwing them aside with an expansive downward sweep of the arms, and holding them clenched, he returned Celia's glance. It was as if he had never looked into a woman's eyes before.

"It *can't* be the end!" he heard himself saying, in a low voice charged with deep significance. He held her gaze in the grasp of his with implacable tenacity. There was a trouble about breathing, and the mosaic floor seemed to stir under his feet. He clung defiantly to the one idea of not releasing her eyes.

"How *could* it be the end?" he demanded, lifting an uncertain hand to his breast as he spoke, and spreading it there as if to control the tumultuous fluttering of his heart. "Things don't end that way!"

A sharp, blinding spasm of giddiness closed upon and shook him, while the brave words were on his lips. He blinked and tottered under it, as it passed, and then backed humbly to his divan and sat down, gasping a little, and patting his hand on his heart. There was fright written all over his whitened face.

"We — we forgot that I am a sick man," he said feebly, answering Celia's look of surprised inquiry with a forced, wan smile. "I was afraid my heart had gone wrong."

She scrutinized him for a further moment, with growing reassurance in her air. Then, piling up the pillows and cushions behind him for support, for all the world like a big sister again, she stepped into the inner room, and returned with a flagon of quaint shape and a tiny glass. She poured this latter full to the brim of a thick yellowish, aromatic liquid, and gave it him to drink.

"This Benedictine is all I happen to have," she said. "Swallow it down! It will do you good."

Theron obeyed her. It brought tears to his eyes; but, upon reflection, it was grateful and warming. He did feel better almost immediately. A great wave of comfort seemed to enfold him as he settled himself back on the divan. For that one flashing instant he had thought that he was dying. He drew a long grateful breath of relief, and smiled his content.

Celia had seated herself beside him, a little away. She sat with her head against the wall, and one foot curled under her, and almost faced him.

"I dare say we forced the pace a little," she remarked, after a pause, looking down at the floor, with the puckers of a ruminating amusement playing in the corners of her mouth. "It doesn't do for a man to get to be a Greek all of a sudden. He must work along up to it gradually."

He remembered the music. "Oh, if I only knew how to tell you," he murmured ecstatically, "what a revelation your playing has been to me! I had never imagined anything like it. I shall think of it to my dying day."

He began to remember as well the spirit that was in the air when the music ended. The details of what he had felt and said rose vaguely in his mind. Pondering them, his eye roved past Celia's white-robed figure to the broad, open doorway beyond. The curtains behind which she had disappeared were again parted and fastened back. A dim light was burning within, out of sight, and its faint illumination disclosed a room filled with white marbles, white silks, white draperies of varying sorts, which shaped themselves, as he looked, into the canopy and trappings of an extravagantly over-sized and sumptuous bed. He looked away again.

"I wish you would tell me what you really mean by that Greek idea of yours," he said with the abruptness of confusion.

Celia did not display much enthusiasm in the tone of her answer. "Oh," she said almost indifferently, "lots of things. Absolute freedom from moral bugbears, for one thing. The recognition that beauty is the only thing in life that is worth while. The courage to kick out of one's life everything that isn't worth while; and so on."

"But," said Theron, watching the mingled delicacy and power of the bared arm and the shapely grace of the hand which she had lifted to her face, "I am going to get you to teach it *all* to me." The memories began crowding in upon him now, and the baffling note upon which the mazurka had stopped short chimed like a tuning-fork in his ears. "I want to be a Greek myself, if you're one. I want to get as close to you — to your ideal, that is, as I can. You open up to me a whole world that I had not even dreamed existed. We swore our friendship long ago, you know: and now, after to-night — you and the music have decided me. I am going to put the things out of *my* life that are not worth while. Only you must help me; you must tell me how to begin."

He looked up as he spoke, to enforce the almost tender entreaty of his words. The spectacle of a yawn, only fractionally concealed behind those talented fingers, chilled his soft speech, and sent a flush over his face. He rose on the instant.

Celia was nothing abashed at his discovery. She laughed gayly in confession of her fault, and held her hand out to let him help her disentangle her foot from her draperies, and get off the divan. It seemed to be her meaning that he should continue holding her hand after she was also standing.

"You forgive me, don't you?" she urged smilingly. "Chopin always first excites me, then sends me to sleep. You see how *you* sleep to-night!"

The brown, velvety eyes rested upon him, from under their heavy lids, with a languorous kindliness. Her warm, large palm clasped his in frank liking.

"I don't want to sleep at all," Mr. Ware was impelled to say. "I want to lie awake and think about — about everything all over again."

She smiled drowsily. "And you're sure you feel strong enough to walk home?"

"Yes," he replied, with a lingering dilatory note, which deepened upon reflection into a sigh. "Oh, yes."

He followed her and her candle down the magnificent stairway again. She blew the light out in the hall, and opening the front door, stood with him for a silent moment on the threshold. Then they shook hands once more, and with a whispered good-night, parted.

Celia, returning to the blue and yellow room, lighted a cigarette and helped herself to some Benedictine in the glass which Theron had used. She looked meditatively at this little glass for a moment, turning it about in her fingers with a smile. The smile warmed itself suddenly into a joyous laugh. She tossed the glass aside, and, holding out her flowing skirts with both hands, executed a swinging pirouette in front of the gravely beautiful statue of the armless woman.

CHAPTER XX

IT was apparent to the Rev. Theron Ware, from the very first moment of waking next morning, that both he and the world had changed over night. The metamorphosis, in the harsh toils of which he had been laboring blindly so long, was accomplished. He stood forth, so to speak, in a new skin, and looked about him, with perceptions of quite an altered kind, upon what seemed in every way a fresh existence. He lacked even the impulse to turn round and inspect the cocoon from which he had emerged. Let the past bury the past. He had no vestige of interest in it.

The change was not premature. He found himself not in the least confused by it, or frightened. Before he had finished shaving, he knew himself to be easily and comfortably at home in his new state, and master of all its requirements.

It seemed as if Alice, too, recognized that he had become another man, when he went down and took his chair at the breakfast table. They had exchanged no words since their parting in the depot-yard the previous evening, — an event now faded off into remote vagueness in Theron's mind. He smiled brilliantly in answer to the furtive, half-sullen, half-curious glance she stole at him, as she brought the dishes in.

"Ah! potatoes warmed up in cream!" he said, with hearty pleasure in his tone. "What a mind-reader you are, to be sure!"

"I'm glad you're feeling so much better," she said briefly, taking her seat.

"Better?" he returned. "I'm a new being!"

She ventured to look him over more freely, upon this assurance. He perceived and catalogued, one by one, the emotions which the small brain was expressing through those shallow blue eyes of hers. She was turning over this, that, and the other hostile thought and childish grievance, — most of all she was dallying with the idea of asking him where he had been till after midnight. He smiled affably in the face of this scattering fire of peevish glances, and did not dream of resenting any phase of them all.

"I am going down to Thurston's this morning, and order that piano sent up to-day," he announced presently, in a casual way.

"Why, Theron, can we afford it?" the wife asked, regarding him with surprise.

"Oh, easily enough," he replied light-heartedly. "You know they've increased my salary."

She shook her head. "No, I didn't. How should I? You don't realize it," she went on, dolefully, "but you're getting so you don't tell me the least thing about your affairs now-adays."

Theron laughed aloud. "You ought to be grateful, — such melancholy affairs as mine have been till now," he declared, — "that is, if it weren't absurd to think such a thing." Then, more soberly, he explained: "No, my girl, it is *you* who don't realize. I am carrying big projects in my mind, — big, ambitious thoughts and plans upon which great things depend. They no doubt make me seem preoccupied and absent-minded; but it is a wife's part to understand, and make allow-ances, and not intrude trifles which may throw everything out of gear. Don't think I'm scolding, my girl. I only speak to reassure you and — and help you to comprehend. Of course I know that you wouldn't willingly embarrass my career."

"Of course not," responded Alice, dubiously; "but — but —"

"But what?" Theron felt compelled by civility to say, though on the instant he reproached himself for the weakness of it.

"Well — I hardly know how to say it," she faltered, "but it was nicer in the old days, before you bothered your head about big projects, and your career, as you call it, and were just a good, earnest, simple young servant of the Lord. Oh, Theron!" she broke forth suddenly, with tearful zeal, "I get sometimes lately almost scared lest you should turn out to be a — a *backslider!*"

The husband sat upright, and hardened his countenance. But yesterday the word would have had in it all sorts of in- herited terrors for him. This morning's dawn of a new ex- istence revealed it as merely an empty and stupid epithet.

"These are things not to be said," he admonished her, after a moment's pause, and speaking with carefully measured austerity. "Least of all are they to be said to a clergyman — by his wife."

It was on the tip of Alice's tongue to retort, "Better by his wife than by outsiders!" but she bit her lips, and kept the gibe back. A rebuke of this form and gravity was a novelty in their relations. The fear that it had been merited troubled, even while it did not convince, her mind, and the puzzled apprehension was to be read plainly enough on her face.

Theron, noting it, saw a good deal more behind. Really, it was amazing how much wiser he had grown all at once. He had been married for years, and it was only this morning that he suddenly discovered how a wife ought to be handled. He continued to look sternly away into space for a little. Then his brows relaxed slowly and under the visible influ- ence of melting considerations. He nodded his head, turned toward her abruptly, and broke the silence with labored amiability.

"Come, come — the day began so pleasantly — it was so good to feel well again — let us talk about the piano instead. That is," he added, with an obvious overture to playfulness, "if the thought of having a piano is not *too* distasteful to you."

Alice yielded almost effusively to his altered mood. They went together into the sitting-room, to measure and decide between the two available spaces which were at their disposal, and he insisted with resolute magnanimity on her settling this question entirely by herself. When at last he mentioned the fact that it was Friday, and he would look over some sermon memoranda before he went out, Alice retired to the kitchen in openly cheerful spirits.

Theron spread some old manuscript sermons before him on his desk, and took down his scribbling-book as well. But there his application flagged, and he surrendered himself instead, chin on hand, to staring out at the rhododendron in the yard. He recalled how he had seen Soulsby patiently studying this identical bush. The notion of Soulsby, not knowing at all how to sing, yet diligently learning those sixths, brought a smile to his mind; and then he seemed to hear Celia calling out over her shoulder, "That's what Chopin does, — he sings!" The spirit of that wonderful music came back to him, enfolded him in its wings. It seemed to raise itself up, — a palpable barrier between him and all that he had known and felt and done before. That was his new birth, — that marvellous night with the piano. The conceit pleased him, — not the less because there flashed along with it the thought that it was a poet that had been born. Yes; the former country lout, the narrow zealot, the untutored slave groping about in the dark after silly superstitions, cringing at the scowl of mean Pierces and Winches, was dead. There was an end of him, and good riddance. In his place there had been born a Poet, — he spelled the word out now unabashed, — a child of light, a lover of beauty and sweet sounds, a recognizable brother to Renan and Chopin — and Celia!

Out of the soothing, tenderly grateful revery, a practical suggestion suddenly took shape. He acted upon it without a moment's delay, getting out his letter-pad, and writing hurriedly, —

"DEAR MISS MADDEN, — Life will be more tolerable to me if before nightfall I can know that there is a piano under my roof. Even if it remains dumb, it will be some comfort to have it here and look at it, and imagine how a great master might make it speak.

"Would it be too much to beg you to look in at Thurston's, say at eleven this forenoon, and give me the inestimable benefit of your judgment in selecting an instrument?

"Do not trouble to answer this, for I am leaving home now, but shall call at Thurston's at eleven, and wait.

"Thanking you in anticipation,

"I am — "

Here Theron's fluency came to a sharp halt. There were adverbs enough and to spare on the point of his pen, but the right one was not easy to come at. "Gratefully," "faithfully," "sincerely," "truly," — each in turn struck a false note. He felt himself not quite any of these things. At last he decided to write just the simple word "yours," and then wavered between satisfaction at his boldness, dread lest he had been over-bold, and, worst of the lot, fear that she would not notice it one way or the other, — all the while he sealed and addressed the letter, put it carefully in an inner pocket, and got his hat.

There was a moment's hesitation as to notifying the kitchen of his departure. The interests of domestic discipline seemed to point the other way. He walked softly through the hall, and let himself out by the front door without a sound.

Down by the canal bridge he picked out an idle boy to his mind, — a lad whose aspect appeared to promise intelligence as a messenger, combined with large impartiality in sectarian matters He was to have ten cents on his return; and he might report himself to his patron at the bookstore yonder.

Theron was grateful to the old bookseller for remaining at his desk in the rear. There was a tacit compliment in the suggestion that he was not a mere customer, demanding instant attention. Besides, there was no keeping "Thurston's" out of conversations in this place.

Loitering along the shelves, the young minister's eye suddenly found itself arrested by a name on a cover. There were a dozen narrow volumes in uniform binding, huddled together under a cardboard label of "Eminent Women Series." Oddly enough, one of these bore the title "George Sand." Theron saw there must be some mistake, as he took the book down, and opened it. His glance hit by accident upon the name of Chopin. Then he read attentively until almost the stroke of eleven.

"We have to make ourselves acquainted with all sorts of queer phases of life," he explained in self-defence to the old bookseller, then counting out the money for the book from his lean purse. He smiled as he added, "There seems something almost wrong about taking advantage of the clergyman's discount for a life of George Sand."

"I don't know," answered the other, pleasantly. "Guess she wasn't so much different from the rest of 'em, — except that she didn't mind appearances. We know about her. We don't know about the others."

"I must hurry," said Theron, turning on his heel. The haste with which he strode out of the store, crossed the street, and made his way toward Thurston's, did not prevent his thinking much upon the astonishing things he had encountered in this book. Their relation to Celia forced itself more and more upon his mind. He could recall the twinkle in her eye, the sub-mockery in her tone, as she commented with that half-contemptuous "Yes — George something!" upon his blundering ignorance. His mortification at having thus exposed his dull rusticity was swallowed up in conjectures as to just what her tolerant familiarity with such things involved. He had never before met a young unmarried woman who would have confessed to him any such knowledge. But then, of course, he had never known a girl who resembled Celia in any other way. He recognized vaguely that he must provide himself with an entire new set of standards by which to measure and comprehend her. But it was for the moment more interesting to wonder what *her* standards were. Did she object to George Sand's behavior? Or did she sympathize with that sort of thing? Did those statues, and the loose-flowing diaphanous toga and unbound hair, the cigarettes, the fiery liqueur, the deliberately sensuous music, — was he to believe that they signified —?

"Good-morning, Mr. Ware. You have managed by a miracle to hit on one of my punctual days," said Celia.

She was standing on the doorstep, at the entrance to the musical department of Thurston's. He had not noticed before the fact that the sun was shining. The full glare of its strong light, enveloping her figure as she stood, and drawing the dazzled eye for relief to the bower of softened color, close beneath her parasol of creamy silk and lace, was what struck him now first of all. It was as if Celia had brought the sun with her.

Theron shook hands with her, and found joy in the perception that his own hand trembled. He put boldly into words the thought that came to him.

"It was generous of you," he said, "to wait for me out here, where all might delight in the sight of you, instead of squandering the privilege on a handful of clerks inside."

Miss Madden beamed upon him, and nodded approval.

"Alcibiades never turned a prettier compliment," she remarked. They went in together at this, and Theron made a note of the name.

During the ensuing half-hour, the young minister followed about even more humbly than the clerks in Celia's commanding wake. There were a good many pianos in the big showroom overhead, and Theron found himself almost awed by their size and brilliancy of polish, and the thought of the tremendous sum of money they represented altogether. Not so with the organist. She ordered them rolled around this way or that, as if they had been so many checkers on a draughtboard. She threw back their covers with the scant ceremony of a dispensary dentist opening paupers' mouths. She exploited their several capacities with masterful hands, not deigning to seat herself, but just slightly bending forward, and sweeping her fingers up and down their keyboards, — able, domineering fingers which pounded, tinkled, meditated, assented, condemned, all in a flash, and amid what affected the layman's ears as a hopelessly discordant hubbub.

Theron moved about in the group, nursing her parasol in his arms, and watching her. The exaggerated deference which the clerks and salesmen showed to her as the rich Miss Madden, seemed to him to be mixed with a certain assertion of the claims of good-fellowship on the score of her being a musician. There undoubtedly *was* a sense of freemasonry between them. They alluded continually in technical terms to matters of which he knew nothing, and were amused at remarks of hers which to him carried no meaning whatever. It was evident that the young men liked her, and that their liking pleased her. It thrilled him to think that she knew he liked her, too, and to recall what abundant proofs she had given that here, also, she had pleasure in the fact. He clung insistently to the memory of these evidences. They helped him to resist a disagreeable tendency to feel himself an intruder, an outsider, among these pianoforte experts.

When it was all over, Celia waved the others aside, and talked with Theron. "I suppose you want me to tell you the truth," she said. "There's nothing here really good.[1] It is always much better to buy of the makers direct."

"Do they sell on the instalment plan?" he asked. There was a wistful effect in his voice which caught her attention.

She looked away — out through the window on the street below — for a moment. Then her eyes returned to his, and regarded him with a comforting, friendly, half-motherly glance, recalling for all the world the way Sister Soulsby had looked at him at odd times.

"Oh, you want it at once — I see," she remarked softly. "Well, this Adelberger is the best value for the money."

Mr. Ware followed her finger, and beheld with dismay that it pointed toward the largest instrument in the room, — a veritable leviathan among pianos. The price of this had been mentioned as $600. He turned over the fact that this was two-thirds his yearly salary, and found the courage to shake his head.

[1] English ed. reads "really first-rate" for "really good."

"It would be too large — much too large — for the room,"
he explained. "And, besides, it is more than I like to pay —
or *can* pay, for that matter." It was pitiful to be explaining
such details, but there was no help for it.

They picked out a smaller one, which Celia said was at
least of fair quality. "Now leave all the bargaining to me,"
she adjured him. "These prices that they talk about in the
piano trade are all in the air. There are tremendous dis-
counts, if one knows how to insist upon them. All you have
to do is to tell them to send it to your house — you wanted
it to-day, you said?"

"Yes — in memory of yesterday," he murmured.

She herself gave the directions, and Thurston's people,
now all salesmen again, bowed grateful acquiescence. Then
she sailed regally across the room and down the stairs, drawing Theron in her train. The hirelings made salaams to him
as well; it would have been impossible to interpose anything
so trivial and squalid as talk about terms and dates of payment.

"I am ever so much obliged to you," he said fervently, in
the comparative solitude of the lower floor. She had paused
to look at something in the book-department.

"Of course I was entirely at your service; don't mention it,"
she replied, reaching forth her hand in an absent way for
her parasol.

He held up instead the volume he had purchased. "Guess
what that is! You never would guess in this wide world!"
His manner was sur-charged with a sense of the surreptitious.

"Well, then, there's no good trying, *is* there?" commented
Celia, her glance roving again toward the shelves.

"It is a life of George Sand," whispered Theron. "I've been
reading it this morning — all the Chopin part — while I was
waiting for you."

To his surprise, there was an apparently displeased contraction of her brows as he made this revelation. For the
instant, a dreadful fear of having offended her seized upon

and sickened him. But then her face cleared, as by magic. She smiled, and let her eyes twinkle in laughter at him, and lifted a forefinger in the most winning mockery of admonition.

"Naughty! naughty!" she murmured back, with a roguishly solemn wink.

He had no response ready for this, but mutely handed her the parasol. The situation had suddenly grown too confused for words, or even sequent thoughts. Uppermost across the hurly-burly of his mind there scudded the singular reflection that he should never hear her play on that new piano of his. Even as it flashed by out of sight, he recognized it for one of the griefs of his life; and the darkness which followed seemed nothing but a revolt against the idea of having a piano at all. He would countermand the order. He would — but she was speaking again.

They had strolled toward the door, and her voice was as placidly conventional as if the talk had never strayed from the subject of pianos. Theron with an effort pulled himself together, and laid hold of her words.

"I suppose you will be going the other way," she was saying. "I shall have to be at the church all day. We have just got a new Mass over from Vienna, and I'm head over heels in work at it. I can have Father Forbes to myself to-day, too. That bear of a doctor has got the rheumatism, and can't come out of his cave, thank Heaven!"

And then she was receding from view, up the sunlit, busy sidewalk, and Theron, standing on the doorstep, ruefully rubbed his chin. She had said he was going the other way, and, after a little pause, he made her words good, though each step he took seemed all in despite of his personal inclinations. Some of the passers-by bowed to him, and one or two paused as if to shake hands and exchange greetings. He nodded responses mechanically, but did not stop. It was as if he feared to interrupt the process of lifting his reluctant feet and propelling them forward, lest they should wheel and scuttle off in the opposite direction.

CHAPTER XXI

DELIBERATE as his progress was, the diminishing number of store-fronts along the sidewalk, and the increasing proportion of picket-fences enclosing domestic lawns, forced upon Theron's attention the fact that he was nearing home. It was a trifle past the hour for his midday meal. He was not in the least hungry; still less did he feel any desire just now to sit about in that library living-room of his. Why should he go home at all? There was no reason whatever — save that Alice would be expecting him. Upon reflection, that hardly amounted to a reason. Wives, with their limited grasp of the realities of life, were always expecting their husbands to do things which it turned out not to be feasible for them to do. The customary male animal spent a considerable part of his life in explaining to his mate why it had been necessary to disappoint or upset her little plans for his comings and goings. It was in the very nature of things that it should be so.

Sustained by these considerations, Mr. Ware slackened his steps, then halted irresolutely, and after a minute's hesitation, entered the small temperance restaurant before which, as by intuition, he had paused. The elderly woman who placed on the tiny table before him the tea and rolls he ordered, was entirely unknown to him, he felt sure, yet none the less she smiled at him, and spoke almost familiarly, —

"I suppose Mrs. Ware is at the seaside, and you are keeping bachelor's hall?"

"Not quite that," he responded stiffly, and hurried through the meagre and distasteful repast, to avoid any further conversation.

There was an idea underlying her remark, however, which recurred to him when he had paid his ten cents and got out on the street again. There was something interesting in the thought of Alice at the seaside. Neither of them had ever laid eyes on salt water, but Theron took for granted the most extravagant landsman's conception of its curative and invigorating powers. It was apparent to him that he was going to pay much greater attention to Alice's happiness and well-being in the future than he had latterly done. He had bought her, this very day, a superb new piano. He was going to simply insist on her having a hired girl. And this seaside notion, — why, that was best of all.

His fancy built up pleasant visions of her feasting her delighted eyes upon the marvel of a great ocean storm, or roaming along a beach strewn with wonderful marine shells, exhibiting an innocent joy in their beauty. The fresh sea-breeze blew through her hair, as he saw her in mind's eye, and brought the hardy flush of health back upon her rather pallid cheeks. He was prepared already hardly to know her, so robust and revivified would she have become, by the time he went down to the depot to meet her on her return.

For his imagination stopped short of seeing himself at the seaside. It sketched instead pictures of whole weeks of solitary academic calm, alone with his books and his thoughts. The facts that he had no books, and that nobody dreamed of interfering with his thoughts, subordinated themselves humbly to his mood. The prospect, as he mused fondly upon it, expanded to embrace the priest's and the doctor's libraries; the thoughts which he longed to be alone with involved close communion with their thoughts. It could not but prove a season of immense mental stimulation and ethical broadening. It would have its lofty poetic and artistic side as well; the languorous melodies of Chopin stole over his revery, as he dwelt upon these things, and soft azure and golden lights modelled forth exquisite outlines of tall marble forms.

He opened the gate leading to Dr. Ledsmar's house. His walk had brought him quite out of the town, and up, by a broad main highway which yet took on all sorts of sylvan charms, to a commanding site on the hillside. Below, in the valley, lay Octavius, at one end half-hidden in factory smoke, at the other, where narrow bands of water gleamed upon the surface of a broad plain piled symmetrically with lumber, presenting an oddly incongruous suggestion of forest odors and the simplicity of the wilderness. In the middle distance, on gradually rising ground, stretched a wide belt of dense, artificial foliage, peeping through which tiled turrets and ornamented chimneys marked the polite residences of those who, though they neither stoked the furnace fires to the west, nor sawed the lumber on the east, lived in purple and fine linen from the profits of this toil. Nearer at hand, pastures with grazing cows on the one side of the road, and the high, weather-stained board fence of the race-course on the other, completed the jumble of primitive rusticity and urban complications characterizing the whole picture.

Dr. Ledsmar's house, toward which Theron's impulses had been secretly leading him ever since Celia's parting remark about the rheumatism, was of that spacious and satisfying order of old-fashioned houses which men of leisure and means built for themselves while the early traditions of a sparse and contented homogeneous population were still strong in the Republic. There was a hospitable look about its wide veranda, its broad, low bulk, and its big, double front door, which did not fit at all with the sketch of a man-hating recluse that the doctor had drawn of himself.

Theron had prepared his mind for the effect of being admitted by a Chinaman, and was taken somewhat aback when the door was opened by the doctor himself. His reception was pleasant enough, almost cordial, but the sense of awkwardness followed him into his host's inner room and rested heavily upon his opening speech.

"I heard, quite by accident, that you were ill," he said, laying aside his hat.

"It's nothing at all," replied Ledsmar. "Merely a stiff shoulder that I wear from time to time in memory of my father. It ought to be quite gone by nightfall. It was good

of you to come, all the same. Sit down if you can find a chair.
As usual, we are littered up to our eyes here. That's it, —
throw those things on the floor."

Mr. Ware carefully deposited an armful of pamphlets on
the rug at his feet, and sat down. Litter was indeed the word
for what he saw about him. Bookcases, chairs, tables, the
corners of the floor, were all buried deep under disorderly
strata of papers, diagrams, and opened books. One could
hardly walk about without treading on them. The dust which
danced up into the bar of sunshine streaming in from the
window, as the doctor stepped across to another chair, gave
Theron new ideas about the value of Chinese servants.

"I must thank you, first of all, doctor," he began, "for
your kindness in coming when *I* was ill. 'I was sick, and ye
visited me.' "

"You mustn't think of it that way," said Ledsmar; "your
friend came for me, and of course I went; and gladly too.
There was nothing that I could do, or that anybody could do.
Very interesting man, that friend of yours. And his wife,
too, — both quite out of the common. I don't know when I've
seen two such really genuine people. I should like to have
known more of them. Are they still here?"

"They went yesterday," Theron replied. His earlier shy-
ness had worn off, and he felt comfortably at his ease. "I don't
know," he went on, "that the word 'genuine' is just what
would have occurred to me to describe the Soulsbys. They
are very interesting people, as you say, — *most* interesting, —
and there was a time, I dare say, when I should have believed
in their sincerity. But of course I saw them and their performance from the inside, — like one on the stage of a theatre,
you know, instead of in the audience, and — well, I understand things better than I used to."

The doctor looked over his spectacles at him with a suggestion of inquiry in his glance, and Theron continued: "I
had several long talks with her; she told me very frankly
the whole story of her life — and — and it was decidedly

queer, I can assure you! I may say to you — you will understand what I mean — that since my talk with you, and the
books you lent me, I see many things differently. Indeed,
when I think upon it sometimes my old state of mind seems
quite incredible to me. I can use no word for my new state
short of illumination.

Dr. Ledsmar continued to regard his guest with that calm,
interrogatory scrutiny of his. He did not seem disposed to
take up the great issue of illumination. "I suppose," he said
after a little, "no woman can come in contact with a priest
for any length of time *without* telling him the 'story of her
life,' as you call it. They all do it. The thing amounts to a
law."

The young minister's veins responded with a pleasurable
thrill to the use of the word "priest" in obvious allusion to
himself. "Perhaps in fairness I ought to explain," he said,
"that in her case it was only done in the course of a long talk
about myself. I might say that it was by way of kindly warning to me. She saw how I had become unsettled in many —
many of my former views — and she was nervous lest this
should lead me to — to —"

"To throw up the priesthood," the doctor interposed upon
his hesitation. "Yes, I know the tribe. Why, my dear sir, your
entire profession would have perished from the memory of
mankind, if it hadn't been for women. It is a very curious
subject. Lots of thinkers have dipped into it, but no one has
gone resolutely in with a search-light and exploited the whole
thing. Our boys, for instance, traverse in their younger years
all the stages of the childhood of the race. They have terrify-
ing dreams of awful monsters and giant animals of which they
have never so much as heard in their waking hours; they
pass through the lust for digging caves, building fires, sleeping out in the woods, hunting with bows and arrows, — all
remote ancestral impulses; they play games with stones,
marbles, and so on at regular stated periods of the year which
they instinctively know, just as they were played in the Bronze

Age, and heaven only knows how much earlier. But the boy
goes through all this, and leaves it behind him, — so completely that the grown man feels himself more a stranger
among boys of his own place who are thinking and doing
precisely the things he thought and did a few years before,
than he would among Kurds or Esquimaux. But the woman is
totally different. She is infinitely more precocious as a girl.
At an age when her slow brother is still stubbing along somewhere in the neolithic period, she has flown way [1] ahead to
a kind of mediæval stage, or dawn of mediævalism, which is
peculiarly her own. Having got there, she stays there; she
dies there. The boy passes her, as the tortoise did the hare.
He goes on, if he is a philosopher, and lets her remain in the
dark ages, where she belongs. If he happens to be a fool,
which is customary, he stops and hangs around in her vicinity."

Theron smiled. "We priests," he said, and paused to enjoy the words, — "I suppose I oughtn't to inquire too closely
just where we belong in the procession."

"We are considering the question impersonally," said the
doctor. "First of all, what you regard as religion is especially
calculated to attract women. They remain as superstitious to-
day, down in the marrow of their bones, as they were ten
thousand years ago. Even the cleverest of them are secretly
afraid of omens, and respect auguries. Think of the broadest
women you know. One of them will throw salt over her
shoulder if she spills it. Another drinks money from her cup
by skimming the bubbles in a spoon. Another forecasts her
future by the arrangement of tea-grounds. They make the
constituency to which an institution based on mysteries,
miracles, and the supernatural generally, would naturally
appeal. Secondly, there is the personality of the priest."

"Yes," assented Ware. There rose up before him, on the
instant, the graceful, portly figure and strong, comely face
of Father Forbes.

[1] English ed. reads "away" for "way."

"Women are not a metaphysical people. They do not easily follow abstractions. They want their dogmas and religious sentiments embodied in a man, just as they do their romantic fancies. Of course you Protestants, with your married clergy, see less of the effects of this than celibates do, but even with you there is a great deal in it. Why, the very institution of celibacy itself was forced upon the early Christian Church by the scandal of rich Roman ladies loading bishops and handsome priests with fabulous gifts, until the passion for currying favor with women of wealth, and marrying them or wheedling their fortunes from them, debauched the whole priesthood. You should read your Jerome."

"I will, — certainly," said the listener, resolving to remember the name and refer it to the old bookseller.

"Well, whatever laws one sect or another makes, the woman's attitude toward the priest survives. She desires to see him surrounded by flower-pots and candles, to have him smelling of musk. She would like to curl his hair, and weave garlands in it. Although she is not learned enough to have ever heard of such things, she intuitively feels in his presence a sort of backwash of the old pagan sensuality and lascivious mysticism which enveloped the priesthood in Greek and Roman days. Ugh! It makes one sick!"

Dr. Ledsmar rose, as he spoke, and dismissed the topic with a dry little laugh. "Come, let me show you round a bit," he said. "My shoulder is easier walking than sitting."

"Have you never written a book yourself?" asked Theron, getting to his feet.

"I have a thing on serpent-worship," the scientist replied, — "written years ago."

"I can't tell you how I should enjoy reading it," urged the other.

The doctor laughed again. "You'll have to learn German, then, I'm afraid. It is still in circulation in Germany, I believe, on its merits as a serious book. I haven't a copy of the edition in English. *That* was all exhausted by collectors who bought it for its supposed obscenity, like Burton's 'Arabian Nights.' Come this way, and I will show you my laboratory."

They moved out of the room, and through a passage, Ledsmar talking as he led the way. "I took up that subject, when I was at college, by a curious chance. I kept a young monkey in my rooms, which had been born in captivity. I brought home from a beer hall — it was in Germany — some pretzels one night, and tossed one toward the monkey. He jumped toward it, then screamed and ran back shuddering with fright. I couldn't understand it at first. Then I saw that the curled pretzel, lying there on the floor, was very like a little coiled-up snake. The monkey had never seen a snake, but it was in his blood to be afraid of one. That incident changed my whole life for me. Up to that evening, I had intended to be a lawyer."

Theron did not feel sure that he had understood the point of the anecdote. He looked now, without much interest, at some dark little tanks containing thick water, a row of small glass cases with adders and other lesser reptiles inside, and a general collection of boxes, jars, and similar receptacles connected with the doctor's pursuits. Further on was a smaller chamber, with a big empty furnace, and shelves bearing bottles and apparatus like a drug-store.

It was pleasanter in the conservatory, — a low, spacious structure with broad pathways between the plants, and an awning over the sunny side of the roof. The plants were mostly orchids, he learned. He had read of them, but never seen any before. No doubt they were curious; but he discovered nothing to justify the great fuss made about them. The heat grew oppressive inside, and he was glad to emerge into the garden. He paused under the grateful shade of a vine-clad trellis, took off his hat, and looked about him with a sigh of relief. Everything seemed old-fashioned and natural and delightfully free from pretence in the big, overgrown field of flowers and shrubs.

Theron recalled with some surprise Celia's indictment of

the doctor as a man with no poetry in his soul. "You must be extremely fond of flowers," he remarked.

Dr. Ledsmar shrugged his well shoulder. "They have their points," he said briefly. "These are all diœcious here. Over beyond are monœcious species. My work is to test the probabilities for or against Darwin's theory that hermaphroditism in plants is a late by-product of these earlier forms."

"And is his theory right?" asked Mr. Ware, with a polite show of interest.

"We may know in the course of three or four hundred years," replied Ledsmar. He looked up into his guest's face with a quizzical half-smile. "That is a very brief period for observation when such a complicated question as sex is involved," he added. "We have been studying the female of our own species for some hundreds of thousands of years, and we haven't arrived at the most elementary rules governing her actions."

They had moved along to a bed of tall plants, the more forward of which were beginning to show bloom. "Here another task will begin next month," the doctor observed. "These are salvias, pentstemons, and antirrhinums, or snapdragons, planted very thick for the purpose. Humble-bees bore holes through their base, to save the labor of climbing in and out of the flowers, and we don't quite know yet why some hive-bees discover and utilize these holes at once, while others never do. It may be merely the old-fogy conservatism of the individual, or there may be a law in it."

These seemed very paltry things for a man of such wisdom to bother his head about. Theron looked, as he was bidden, at the rows of hives shining in the hot sun on a bench along the wall, but offered no comment beyond a casual, "My mother was always going to keep bees, but somehow she never got around to it. They say it pays very well, though."

"The discovery of the reason why no bee will touch the nectar of the *Epipactis latifolia,* though it is sweet to our taste, and wasps are greedy for it, *would* pay," commented the doctor. "Not like a blue rhododendron, in mere money, but in recognition. Lots of men have achieved a half-column in the 'Encyclopedia Britannica' on a smaller basis than that."

They stood now at the end of the garden, before a small, dilapidated summer-house. On the bench inside, facing him, Theron saw a strange recumbent figure stretched at full length, apparently sound asleep, or it might be dead. Looking closer, with a startled surprise, he made out the shaven skull and outlandish garb of a Chinaman. He turned toward his guide in the expectation of a scene.

The doctor had already taken out a note-book and pencil, and was drawing his watch from his pocket. He stepped into the summer-house, and, lifting the Oriental's limp arm, took account of his pulse. Then, with head bowed low, sidewise, he listened for the heart-action. Finally, he somewhat brusquely pushed back one of the Chinaman's eyelids, and made a minute inspection of what the operation disclosed. Returning to the light, he inscribed some notes in his book, put it back in his pocket, and came out. In answer to Theron's marvelling stare, he pointed toward a pipe of odd construction lying on the floor beneath the sleeper.

"This is one of my regular afternoon duties," he explained, again with the whimsical half-smile. "I am increasing his dose monthly by regular stages, and the results promise to be rather remarkable. Heretofore, observations have been made mostly on diseased or morbidly deteriorated subjects. This fellow of mine is strong as an ox, perfectly nourished, and watched over intelligently. He can assimilate opium enough to kill you and me and every other vertebrate creature on the premises, without turning a hair, and he hasn't got even fairly under way yet."

The thing was unpleasant, and the young minister turned away. They walked together up the path toward the house. His mind was full now of the hostile things which Celia had said about the doctor. He had vaguely sympathized with her then, upon no special knowledge of his own. Now he felt that his sentiments were vehemently in accord with hers. The doctor *was* a beast.

✳ And yet — as they moved along through the garden the thought took sudden shape in his mind — it would be only justice for him to get also the doctor's opinion of Celia. Even while they offended and repelled him, he could not close his eyes to the fact that the doctor's experiments and occupations were those of a patient and exact man of science, — a philosopher. And what he had said about women, — there was certainly a great deal of acumen and shrewd observation in that. If he would only say what he really thought about Celia, and about her relations with the priest! Yes, Theron recognized now there was nothing else that he so much needed light upon as those puzzling ties between Celia and Father Forbes.

He paused, with a simulated curiosity, about one of the flower-beds. "Speaking of women and religion," — he began, in as casual a tone as he could command, — "I notice curiously enough in my own case, that as I develop in what you may call the — the other direction, my wife, who formerly was not especially devoted, is being strongly attracted by the most unthinking and hysterical side of — of our church system."

The doctor looked at him, nodded, and stooped to nip some buds from a stalk in the bed.

"And another case," Theron went on — "of course it was all so new and strange to me — but the position which Miss Madden seems to occupy about the Catholic Church here — I suppose you had her in mind when you spoke."

Ledsmar stood up. "My mind has better things to busy itself with than mad asses of that description," he replied. "She is not worth talking about, — a mere bundle of egotism, ignorance, and red-headed lewdness.[2] If she were even a type, she might be worth considering; but she is simply an abnormal sport, with a little brain addled by notions that she is

[2] English ed. reads "immodesty" for "lewdness."

like Hypatia, and a large impudence rendered intolerable by
the fact that she has money. Her father is [3] a decent man. He
ought to have her whipped."

Mr. Ware drew himself erect, as he listened to these out-
rageous words. It would be unmanly, he felt, to allow such
comments upon an absent friend to pass unrebuked. Yet
there was the courtesy due to a host to be considered. His
mind, fluttering between these two extremes, alighted
abruptly upon a compromise. He would speak so as to show
his disapproval, yet not so as to prevent his finding out what
he wanted to know. The desire to hear Ledsmar talk about
Celia and the priest seemed now to have possessed him for a
long time, to have dictated his unpremeditated visit out here,
to have been growing in intensity all the while he pretended
to be interested in orchids and bees and the drugged Chinaman. It tugged passionately at his self-control as he spoke.

"I cannot in the least assent to your characterization of the
lady," he began with rhetorical dignity.

"Bless me!" interposed the doctor, with deceptive cheer-
fulness, "that is not required of you at all. It is a strictly personal opinion, offered merely as a contribution to the general
sum of hypotheses."

"But," Theron went on, feeling his way, "of course, I
gathered that evening that you had prejudices in the matter;
but these are rather apart from the point I had in view. We
were speaking, you will remember, of the traditional attitude of women toward priests, — wanting to curl their hair
and put flowers in it, you know, — and that suggested to me
some individual illustrations, and it occurred to me to wonder just what were the relations between Miss Madden and —
and Father Forbes. She said this morning, for instance, — I
happened to meet her, quite by accident, — that she was going
to the church to practise a new piece, and that she could have
Father Forbes to herself all day. Now that would be quite
an impossible remark in our — that is, in any Protestant

[3] English ed. adds "said to be."

circles — and purely as a matter of comparison, I was curious to ask you just how much there was in it. I ask you, because going there so much you have had exceptional opportunities for —"

A sharp exclamation from his companion interrupted the clergyman's hesitating monologue. It began like a high-pitched, violent word, but dwindled suddenly into a groan of pain. The doctor's face, too, which had on the flash of Theron's turning seemed given over to unmixed anger, took on an expression of bodily suffering instead.

"My shoulder has grown all at once excessively painful," he said hastily. "I'm afraid I must ask you to excuse me, Mr. Ware."

Carrying the afflicted side with ostentatious caution, he led the way without ado round the house to the front gate on the road. He had put his left hand under his coat to press it against his aching shoulder, and his right hung palpably helpless. This rendered it impossible for him to shake hands with his guest in parting.

"You're sure there's nothing I can do," said Theron, lingering on the outer side of the gate. "I used to rub my father's shoulders and back; I'd gladly —"

"Oh, not for worlds!" groaned the doctor. His anguish was so impressive that Theron, as he walked down the road, quite missed the fact that there had been no invitation to come again.

Dr. Ledsmar stood for a minute or two, his gaze meditatively following the retreating figure. Then he went in, opening the front door with his right hand, and carrying himself once more as if there were no such thing as rheumatism in the world. He wandered on through the hall into the laboratory, and stopped in front of the row of little tanks full of water.

Some deliberation was involved in whatever his purpose might be, for he looked from one tank to another with a pondering, dilatory gaze. At last he plunged his hand into the opaque fluid and drew forth a long, slim, yellowish-green lizard, with a coiling, sinuous tail and a pointed, evil head. The reptile squirmed and doubled itself backward around his wrist, darting out and in with dizzy swiftness its tiny forked tongue.

The doctor held the thing up to the light, and, scrutinizing it through his spectacles, nodded his head in sedate approval. A grim smile curled in his beard.

"Yes, you are the type," he murmured to it, with evident enjoyment in the conceit. "Your name isn't Johnny any more. It's the Rev. Theron Ware."

CHAPTER XXII

THE annual camp-meeting of the combined Methodist districts of Octavius and Thessaly was held this year in the second half of September, a little later than usual. Of the nine days devoted to this curious survival of primitive Wesleyanism, the fifth fell upon a Saturday. On the noon of that day the Rev. Theron Ware escaped for some hours from the burden of work and incessant observation which he shared with twenty other preachers, and walked alone in the woods.

The scene upon which he turned his back was one worth looking at. A spacious, irregularly defined clearing in the forest lay level as a tennis-court, under the soft haze of autumn sunlight. In the centre was a large, roughly constructed frame building, untouched by paint, but stained and weather-beaten with time. Behind it were some lines of horse-sheds, and still further on in that direction, where the trees began, the eye caught fragmentary glimpses of low roofs and the fronts of tiny cottages, withdrawn from full view among the saplings and underbrush. At the other side of the clearing, fully fourscore tents were pitched, some gray and mended, others dazzlingly white in their newness. The more remote of these tents fell into an orderly arrangement of semi-circular form, facing that part of the engirdling woods where the trees were largest, and their canopy of overhanging foliage was lifted highest from the ground. Inside this half-ring of tents were many rounded rows of benches, which followed in narrowing lines the idea of an amphitheatre cut in two. In the centre, just under the edge of the roof of boughs, rose a wooden pagoda, in form not unlike an open-air stand for musicians. In front of this, and leading from it on the level of its floor, there projected a platform, railed round with aggressively rustic woodwork. The nearest benches came close about this platform.

At the hour when Theron started away, there were few enough signs of life about this encampment. The four or five hundred people who were in constant residence were eating their dinners in the big boarding-house, or the cottages or the tents. It was not the time of day for strangers. Even when services were in progress by daylight, the regular attendants did not make much of a show, huddled in a gray-black mass at the front of the auditorium, by comparison with the great green and blue expanses of nature about them.

The real spectacle was in the evening, when, as the shadows gathered, big clusters of kerosene torches, hung high on the trees facing the audience, were lighted. The falling darkness magnified the glow of the lights, and the size and importance of what they illumined. The preacher, bending forward over the rails of the platform, and fastening his eyes upon the abashed faces of those on the "anxious seat" beneath him, borrowed an effect of druidical mystery from the wall of blackness about him, from the flickering reflections on the branches far above, from the cool night air which stirred across the clearing. The change was in the blood of those who saw and heard him, too. The decorum and half-heartedness of their devotions by day deepened under the glare of the torches into a fervent enthusiasm, even before the services began. And if there was in the rustic pulpit a man whose prayers or exhortations could stir their pulses, they sang and groaned and bellowed out their praises with an almost barbarous license, such as befitted the wilderness.

But in the evening not all were worshippers. For a dozen miles round on the country-side, young farm-workers and their girls regarded the camp-meeting as perhaps the chief event of the year, — no more to be missed than the county fair or the circus, and offering, from many points of view, more opportunities for genuine enjoyment than either. Their behavior when they came was pretty bad, — not the less so because all the rules established by the Presiding Elders for the regulation of strangers took it for granted that they would act as viciously as they knew how. These sight-seers sometimes ventured to occupy the back benches, where the light was dim. More often they stood outside, in the circular space between the tents and the benches, and mingled cat-calls, drovers' yelps, and all sorts of mocking cries and noises with the "Amens" of the earnest congregation. Their rough horse-play on the fringe of the sanctified gathering was grievous enough; everybody knew that much worse things went on further out in the surrounding darkness. Indeed, popular report gave to these external phases of the camp-meeting an even more evil fame than attached to the later moonlight husking-bees, or the least reputable of the midwinter dances at Dave Randall's low halfway house.

Cynics said that the Methodists found consolation for this scandal in the large income they derived from their unruly visitors' gate-money. This was unfair. No doubt the money played its part, but there was something else far more important. The pious dwellers in the camp, intent upon reviving in their poor modern way the character and environment of the heroic early days, felt the need of just this hostile and scoffing mob about them to bring out the spirit they sought. Theirs was pre-eminently a fighting religion, which languished in peaceful fair weather, but flamed high in the storm. The throng of loafers and light-minded worldlings of both sexes, with their jeering interruptions and lewd levity of conduct, brought upon the scene a kind of visible personal devil, with whom the chosen could do battle face to face. The daylight services became more and more perfunctory, as the sojourn in the woods ran its course, and interest concentrated itself upon the night meetings, for the reason that *then* came the fierce wrestle with a Beelzebub of flesh and blood. And it was not so one-sided a contest, either!

No evening passed without its victors for the pulpit. Careless or mischievous young people who were pushed into the foremost ranks of the mockers, and stood grinning and grimacing under the lights, would of a sudden feel a spell clamped upon them. They would hear a strange, quavering note in the preacher's voice, catch the sense of a piercing, soul-commanding gleam in his eye, — not at all to be resisted. These occult forces would take control of them, drag them forward as in a dream to the benches under the pulpit, and abase them there like worms in the dust. And then the preacher would descend, and the elders advance, and the torch-fires would sway and dip before the wind of the mighty roar that went up in triumph from the brethren.

These combats with Satan at close quarters, if they made the week-day evenings exciting, reacted with an effect of crushing dulness upon the Sunday services. The rule was to admit no strangers to the grounds from Saturday night to Monday morning. Every year attempts were made to rescind or modify this rule, and this season at least three-fourths of the laymen in attendance had signed a petition in favor of opening the gates. The two Presiding Elders, supported by a dozen of the older preachers, resisted the change, and they had the backing of the more bigoted section of the congregation from Octavius. The controversy reached a point where Theron's Presiding Elder threatened to quit the grounds, and the leaders of the open-Sunday movement spoke freely of the ridiculous figure which its cranks and fanatics made poor Methodism cut in the eyes of modern go-ahead American civilization. Then Theron Ware saw his opportunity, and preached an impromptu sermon upon the sanctity of the Sabbath, which ended all discussion. Sometimes its arguments seemed to be on one side, sometimes on the other, but always they were clothed with so serene a beauty of imagery, and moved in such a lofty and rarefied atmosphere of spiritual exaltation, that it was impossible to link them to so sordid a thing as this question of gate-money. When he had finished, nobody wanted the gates opened. The two factions found that the difference between them had melted out of existence. They sat entranced by the charm of the sermon; then, glancing around at the empty benches, glaringly numerous in the afternoon sunlight, they whispered regrets that ten thousand people had not been there to hear that marvellous discourse. Theron's conquest was of exceptional dimensions. The majority, whose project he had defeated, were strangers who appreciated and admired his effort most. The little minority of his own flock,[1] though less susceptible to the influence of graceful diction and delicately balanced rhetoric, were proud of the distinction he had reflected upon them, and delighted with him for having won their fight. The Presiding Elders wrung his hand with a significant grip. The extremists of his own charge beamed friendship upon him for the first time. He was the veritable hero of the week.

The prestige of this achievement made it the easier for Theron to get away by himself next day, and walk in the woods. A man of such power had a right to solitude. Those who noted his departure from the camp remembered with pleasure that he was to preach again on the morrow. He was going to commune with God in the depths of the forest, that the Message next day might be clearer and more luminous still.

Theron strolled for a little, with an air of aimlessness, until he was well outside the more or less frequented neighborhood of the camp. Then he looked at the sun and the lay of the land with that informing scrutiny of which the farm-bred boy never loses the trick, turned, and strode at a rattling pace down the hillside. He knew nothing personally of this piece of woodland, — a spur of the great Adirondack wilderness thrust southward into the region of homesteads and dairies and hop-fields, — but he had prepared himself by a study of the map, and he knew where he wanted to go. Very soon he hit upon the path he had counted upon finding, and at this he quickened his gait.

Three months of the new life had wrought changes in Theron. He bore himself more erectly, for one thing; his

---

[1] English ed. reads "His own flock, who led the minority" for "The little minority of his own flock."

shoulders were thrown back, and seemed thicker. The alteration was even more obvious in his face. The effect of lank,
wistful, sallow juvenility had vanished. It was the countenance
of a mature, well-fed, and confident man, firmer and more
rounded in its outlines, and with a glow of health on its
whole surface. Under the chin were the suggestions of fulness
which bespeak an easy mind. His clothes were new; the frock-
coat fitted him, and the thin, dark-colored autumn overcoat,
with its silk lining exposed at the breast, gave a masculine
bulk and shape to his figure. He wore a shining tall hat, and,
in haste though he was, took pains not to knock it against low-
hanging branches.

All had gone well — more than well — with him. The second Quarterly Conference had passed without a ripple. Both
the attendance and the collections at his church were larger
than ever before, and the tone of the congregation toward
him was altered distinctly for the better. As for himself, he
viewed with astonished delight the progress he had made in
his own estimation. He had taken Sister Soulsby's advice,
and the results were already wonderful. He had put aside,
once and for all, the thousand foolish trifles and childish per-
plexities which formerly had racked his brain, and worried
him out of sleep and strength. He borrowed all sorts of
books boldly now from the Octavius public library, and
could swim with a calm mastery and enjoyment upon the
deep waters into which Draper and Lecky and Laing and the
rest had hurled him. He dallied pleasurably, a little languorously, with a dozen aspects of the case against revealed
religion, ranging from the mild heterodoxy of Andover's
qualms to the rude Ingersoll's rollicking negation of God
himself, as a woman of coquetry might play with as many
would-be lovers. They amused him; they were all before him
to choose; and he was free to postpone indefinitely the act of
selection. There was a sense of the luxurious in this position
which softened bodily as well as mental fibres. He ceased to
grow indignant at things below or outside his standards, and

he bought a small book which treated of the care of the hand and fingernails.

Alice had accepted with deference his explanation that shapely hands played so important a part in pulpit oratory. For that matter, she now accepted whatever he said or did with admirable docility. It was months since he could remember her venturing upon a critical attitude toward him. She had not wished to leave home, for the seaside or any other resort, during the summer, but had worked outside in her garden more than usual. This was inexpensive, and it seemed to do her as much good as a holiday could have done. Her new devotional zeal was now quite an old thing; it had not slackened at all from the revival pitch. At the outset she had tried several times to talk with her husband upon this subject. He had discouraged conversation about her soul and its welfare, at first obliquely, then, under compulsion, with some directness. His thoughts were absorbed, he said, by the contemplation of vast, abstract schemes of creation and the government of the universe, and it only diverted and embarrassed his mind to try to fasten it upon the details of personal salvation. Thereafter the topic was not broached between them.

She bestowed a good deal of attention, too, upon her piano. The knack of a girlish nimbleness of touch had returned to her after a few weeks, and she made music which Theron supposed was very good, — for her. It pleased him, at all events, when he sat and listened to it; but he had a far greater pleasure, as he listened, in dwelling upon the memories of the yellow and blue room which the sounds always brought up. Although three months had passed, Thurston's had never asked for the first payment on the piano, or even sent in a bill. The impressed him as being peculiarly graceful behavior on his[2] part, and he recognized its delicacy by not going near Thurston's at all.

An hour's sharp walk, occasionally broken by short cuts

[2] English ed. reads "their" for "his."

across open pastures, but for the most part on forest paths, brought Theron to the brow of a small knoll, free from underbrush, and covered sparsely with beech-trees. The ground was soft with moss and the powdered remains of last year's foliage; the leaves above him were showing the first yellow stains of autumn. A sweet smell of ripening nuts was thick upon the air, and busy rustlings and chirpings through the stillness told how the chipmunks and squirrels were attending to their harvest.

Theron had no ears for these noises of the woodland. He had halted, and was searching through the little vistas offered between the stout gray trunks of the beeches for some sign of a more sophisticated sort. Yes! there were certainly voices to be heard, down in the hollow. And now, beyond all possibility of mistake, there came up to him the low, rhythmic throb of music. It was the merest faint murmur of music, made up almost wholly of groaning bass notes, but it was enough. He moved down the slope, swiftly at first, then with increasing caution. The sounds grew louder as he advanced, until he could hear the harmony of the other strings in its place beside the uproar of the big fiddles, and distinguish from both the measured noise of many feet moving as one.

He reached a place from which, himself unobserved, he could overlook much of what he had come to see.

The bottom of the glade below him lay out in the full sunshine, as flat and as velvety in its fresh greenness as a garden lawn. Its open expanse was big enough to accommodate several distinct crowds, and here the crowds were, — one massed about an enclosure in which young men were playing at football, another gathered further off in a horseshoe curve at the end of a baseball diamond, and a third thronging at a point where the shade of overhanging woods began, focussed upon a centre of interest which Theron could not make out.[3] Closer at hand, where a shallow stream rippled along over its black-slate bed, some little boys, with legs

[3] English ed. reads "identify" for "make out."

bared to the thighs, were paddling about, under the charge
of two men clad in long black gowns. There were others of
these frocked monitors scattered here and there upon the
scene, — pallid, close-shaven, monkish figures, who none the
less wore modern hats, and superintended with knowledge
the games of the period. Theron remembered that these
were the Christian Brothers, the semi-monastic teachers of
the Catholic school.

And this was the picnic of the Catholics of Octavius. He
gazed in mingled amazement and exhilaration upon the
spectacle. There seemed to be literally thousands of people
on the open fields before him, and apparently there were still
other thousands in the fringes of the woods round about.
The noises which arose from this multitude — the shouts of
the lads in the water, the playful squeals of the girls in the
swings, the fused uproar of the more distant [4] crowds, and
above all the diligent, ordered strains of the dance-music
proceeding from some invisible distance in the greenwood —
charmed his ears with their suggestion of universal merriment. He drew a long breath — half pleasure, half wistful
regret — as he remembered that other gathering in the forest
which he had left behind.

At any rate, it should be well behind him to-day, whatever
the morrow might bring! Evidently he was on the wrong side
of the circle for the headquarters of the festivities. He turned
and walked to the right through the beeches, making a détour,
under cover, of the crowds at play. At last he rounded the
long oval of the clearing, and found himself at the very edge
of that largest throng of all, which had been too far away
for comprehension at the beginning. There was no mystery
now. A rough, narrow shed, fully fifty feet in length, imposed
itself in an arbitrary line across the face of this crowd, divid-
ing it into two compact halves. Inside this shed, protected
all round by a waist-high barrier of boards, on top of which
ran a flat, table-like covering, were twenty men in their shirt-

[4] English ed. reads "remoter" for "more distant."

sleeves, toiling ceaselessly to keep abreast of the crowd's thirst for beer. The actions of these bar-tenders greatly impressed Theron. They moved like so many machines, using one hand, apparently, to take money and give change, and with the other incessantly sweeping off rows of empty glasses, and tossing forward in their place fresh, foaming glasses five at a time. Hundreds of arms and hands were continually stretched out, on both sides of the shed, toward this streaming bar, and through the babel of eager cries rose without pause the racket of mallets tapping new kegs.

Theron had never seen any considerable number of his fellow-citizens engaged in drinking lager beer before. His surprise at the facility of those behind the bar began to yield, upon observation, to a profound amazement at the thirst of those before it. The same people seemed to be always in front, emptying the glasses faster than the busy men inside could replenish them, and clamoring tirelessly for more. New-comers had to force their way to the bar by violent efforts, and once there they stayed until pushed bodily aside. There were actually women to be seen here and there in the throng, elbowing and shoving like the rest for a place at the front. Some of the more gallant young men fought their way outward, from time to time, carrying for safety above their heads glasses of beer which they gave to young and pretty girls, standing on the fringe of the crowd, among the trees.

Everywhere a remarkable good-humor prevailed. Once a sharp fight broke out, just at the end of the bar nearest Theron, and one young man was knocked down. A rush of onlookers confused everything before the minister's eyes for a minute, and then he saw the aggrieved combatant up on his legs again, consenting under the kindly pressure of the crowd to shake hands with his antagonist, and join him in more beer. The incident caught his fancy. There was something very pleasingly human, he thought, in this primitive readiness to resort to fisticuffs, and this frank and genial reconciliation.

Perhaps there was something contagious in this whole-sale display of thirst, for the Rev. Mr. Ware became conscious of a notion that he should like to try a glass of beer. He recalled having heard that lager was really a most harmless beverage. Of course it was out of the question that he should show himself at the bar. Perhaps some one would bring him out a glass, as if he were a pretty girl. He looked about for a possible messenger. Turning, he found himself face to face with two smiling people, into whose eyes he stared for an instant in dumfounded blankness. Then his countenance flashed with joy, and he held out both hands in greeting. It was Father Forbes and Celia.

"We stole down upon you unawares," said the priest, in his cheeriest manner. He wore a brown straw hat, and loose clothes hardly at all clerical in form, and had Miss Madden's arm drawn lightly within his own. "We could barely believe our eyes, — that it could be you whom we saw, here among the sinners!"

"I am in love with your sinners," responded Theron, as he shook hands with Celia, and trusted himself to look fully into her eyes. "I've had five days of the saints, over in another part of the woods, and they've bored the head off me."

CHAPTER XXIII

At the command of Father Forbes, a lad who was loitering near them went down through the throng to the bar, and returned with three glasses of beer. It pleased the Rev. Mr. Ware that the priest should have taken it for granted that he would do as the others did. He knocked his glass against theirs in compliance with a custom strange to him, but which they seemed to understand very well. The beer itself was not so agreeable to the taste as he had expected, but it was cold and refreshing.

When the boy had returned with the glasses, the three stood for a moment in silence, meditatively watching the curious scene spread below them. Beyond the bar, Theron could catch now through the trees regularly recurring glimpses of four or five swings in motion. These were nearest him, and clearest to the vision as well, at the instant when they reached their highest forward point. The seats were filled with girls, some of them quite grown young women, and their curving upward sweep through the air was disclosing at its climax a remarkable profusion of white skirts and black stockings. The sight struck him as indecorous in the extreme, and he turned his eyes away. They met Celia's; and there was something latent in their brown depths which prompted him, after a brief dalliance of interchanging glances, to look again at the swings.

"That old maid Curran is really too ridiculous, with those white stockings of hers," remarked Celia; "some friend ought to tell her to dye them."

"Or pad them," suggested Father Forbes, with a gay little chuckle. "I daresay the question of swings and ladies' stockings hardly arises with you, over at the camp-meeting, Mr. Ware?"

Theron laughed aloud at the conceit. "I should say not!" he replied.

"I'm just dying to see a camp-meeting!" said Celia. "You hear such racy accounts of what goes on at them."

"Don't go, I beg of you!" urged Theron, with doleful emphasis. "Don't let's even talk about them. I should like to feel this afternoon as if there was no such thing within a thousand miles of me as a camp-meeting. Do you know, all this interests me enormously. It is a revelation to me to see these thousands of good, decent, ordinary people, just frankly enjoying themselves like human beings. I suppose that in this whole huge crowd there isn't a single person who will mention the subject of his soul to any other person all day long."

"I should think the assumption was a safe one," said the priest, smilingly, "unless," he added on after-thought, "it be by way of a genial profanity. There used to be some old Clare men who said 'Hell to my soul!' when they missed at quoits, but I haven't heard it for a long time. I daresay they're all dead."

"I shall never forget that death-bed — where I saw you first," remarked Theron, musingly. "I date from that experience a whole new life. I have been greatly struck lately, in reading our 'Northern Christian Advocate' to see in the obituary notices of prominent Methodists how over and over again it is recorded that they got religion in their youth through being frightened by some illness of their own, or some epidemic about them. The cholera year of 1832 seems to have made Methodists hand over fist. Even to this day our most successful revivalists, those who work conversions whole-sale wherever they go, do it more by frightful pictures of hell-fire surrounding the sinner's death-bed than anything else. You could hear the same thing at our camp-meeting to-night, if you were there."

"There isn't so much difference as you think," said Father Forbes, dispassionately. "Your people keep examining their souls, just as children keep pulling up the bulbs they have planted to see are there any roots yet. Our people are more satisfied to leave their souls alone, once they have been planted, so to speak, by baptism. But fear of hell governs them both, pretty much alike. As I remember saying to you once before, there is really nothing new under the sun. Even the saying isn't new.[1] Though there seem to have been the most tremendous changes in races and civilizations and religions, stretching over many thousands of years, yet nothing is in fact altered very much. Where religions are [2] concerned, the human race are still very like savages in a dangerous wood in the dark, telling one another ghost stories around a campfire. They have always been like that."

"What nonsense!" cried Celia. "I have no patience with such gloomy rubbish. The Greeks had a religion full of beauty and happiness and light-heartedness, and they weren't frightened of death at all. They made the image of death a beautiful boy, with a torch turned down. Their greatest philosophers openly preached and practised the doctrine of suicide when one was tired of life. Our own early Church was full of these broad and beautiful Greek ideas. You know that yourself! And it was only when your miserable Jeromes and Augustines and Cyrils brought in the abominable meannesses and cruelties of the Jewish Old Testament, and stamped out the sane, and lovely Greek elements in the Church, that Christians became the poor, whining, cowardly egotists they are, troubling about their [3] little tin-pot souls, and scaring themselves in their churches by skulls and crossbones."

"My dear Celia," interposed the priest, patting her shoulder gently, "we will have no Greek debate to-day. Mr. Ware has been permitted to taboo camp-meetings, and I claim the privilege to cry off on Greeks. Look at those fellows down there, trampling over one another to get more beer. What have they to do with Athens, or Athens with them? I take it, Mr. Ware," he went on, with a grave face but a twinkling

---

[1] English ed. reads "is not quite original" for "isn't new."
[2] English ed. reads "theology is" for "religions are."
[3] English ed. adds "own."

eye, "that what we are observing here in front of us is symbolical of a great ethical and theological revolution, which
in time will modify and control the destiny of the entire
American people. You see those young Irishmen there, struggling like pigs at a trough to get their fill of German beer.
That signifies a conquest of Teuton over Kelt more important
and far-reaching in its results than the landing of Hengist
and Horsa. The Kelt has come to grief heretofore — or at
least been forced to play second fiddle to other races — because he lacked the right sort of a drink. He has in his blood
an excess of impulsive, imaginative, even fantastic qualities.
It is much easier for him to make a fool of himself, to begin
with, than it is for people of slower wits and more sluggish
temperaments. When you add whiskey to that, or that essence
of melancholia which in Ireland they call 'porther,' you get
the Kelt at his very weakest and worst. These young men
down there are changing all that. They have discovered
lager. Already many of them can outdrink the Germans at
their own beverage. The lager-drinking Irishman in a few
generations will be a new type of humanity, — the Kelt at
his best. He will dominate America. He will be *the* American.
And his church — with the Italian element thrown clean out
of it, and its Pope living, say, in Baltimore or Georgetown —
will be the Church of America."

"Let us have some more lager at once," put in Celia. "This
revolution can't be hurried forward too rapidly."

Theron could not feel sure how much of the priest's discourse was in jest, how much in earnest. "It seems to me,"
he said, "that as things are going, it doesn't look much as if
the America of the future will trouble itself about any kind
of a church. The march of science must very soon produce
a universal scepticism. It is in the nature of human progress.
What all intelligent men recognize to-day, the masses must
surely come to see in time."

Father Forbes laughed outright this time. "My dear Mr.
Ware," he said, as they touched glasses again, and sipped

the fresh beer that had been brought them, "of all our fictions there is none so utterly baseless and empty as this idea that humanity progresses. The savage's natural impression is that the world he sees about him was made for him, and that the rest of the universe is subordinated to him and his world, and that all the spirits and demons and gods occupy themselves exclusively with him and his affairs. That idea was the basis of every pagan religion, and it is the basis of the Christian religion, simply because it is the foundation of human nature. That foundation is just as firm and unshaken to-day as it was in the Stone Age. It will always remain, and upon it will always be built some kind of a religious superstructure. 'Intelligent men,' as you call them, really have very little influence, even when they all pull one way. The people as a whole soon get tired of them. They give too much trouble. The most powerful forces in human nature are self-protection and inertia. The middle-aged man has found out that the chief wisdom in life is to bend to the pressures about him, to shut up and do as others do. Even when he thinks he has rid his own mind of superstitions, he sees that he will best enjoy a peaceful life by leaving other peoples' superstitions alone. That is always the ultimate view of the crowd."

"But I don't see," observed Theron, "granting that all this is true, how you think the Catholic Church will come out on top. I could understand it of Unitarianism, or Universalism, or the Episcopal Church, where nobody seems to have to believe particularly in anything except the beauty of its burial service, but I should think the very rigidity of the Catholic creed would make it impossible. There everything is hard and fast; nothing is elastic; there is no room for compromise."

"The Church is always compromising," explained the priest, "only it does it so slowly that no one man lives long enough to quite catch it at the trick. No; the great secret of the Catholic Church is that it doesn't debate with sceptics. No matter what points you make against it, it is never betrayed into answering back. It simply says these things are sacred mysteries, which you are quite free to accept and be saved, or reject and be damned. There is something intelligible and fine about an attitude like that. When people have grown tired of their absurd and fruitless wrangling over texts and creeds which, humanly speaking, are all barbaric nonsense, they will come back to repose pleasantly under the Catholic roof, in that restful house where things are taken for granted. There the manners are charming, the service excellent, the decoration and upholstery most acceptable to the eye, and the music" — he made a little mock bow here to Celia — "the music at least is divine. There you have nothing to do but be agreeable, and avoid scandal, and observe the convenances. You are no more expected to express doubts about the Immaculate Conception than you are to ask the lady whom you take down to dinner how old she is. Now that is, as I have said, an intelligent and rational church for people to have. As the Irish civilize themselves, — you observe them diligently engaged in the process down below there, — and the social roughness of their church becomes softened and ameliorated, Americans will inevitably be attracted toward it. In the end, it will embrace them all, and be modified by them, and in turn influence their development, till you will have a new nation and a new national church, each representative of the other."

"And all this is to be done by lager beer!" Theron ventured to comment, jokingly. He was conscious of a novel perspiration around the bridge of his nose, which was obviously another effect of the drink.

The priest passed the pleasantry by. "No," he said seriously; "what you must see is that there must always be a church. If one did not exist, it would be necessary to invent it. It is needed, first and foremost, as a police force. It is needed, secondly, so to speak, as a fire insurance. It provides the most even temperature and pure atmosphere for the growth of young children. It furnishes the best obtainable social machinery for marrying off one's daughters, getting to know the right people, patching up quarrels, and so on. The priesthood earn their salaries as the agents for these valuable social arrangements. Their theology is thrown in as a sort of intellectual diversion, like the ritual of a benevolent organization. There are some who get excited about this part of it, just as one hears of Free-Masons who believe that the sun rises and sets to exemplify their ceremonies. Others take their duties more quietly, and, understanding just what it all amounts to, make the best of it, like you and me."

Theron assented to the philosophy and the compliment by a grave bow. "Yes, that is the idea, — to make the best of it," he said, and fastened his regard boldly this time upon the swings.

"We were both ordained by our bishops," continued the priest, "at an age when those worthy old gentlemen would not have trusted our combined wisdom to buy a horse for them."

"And I was married," broke in Theron, with an eagerness almost vehement, "when I had only just been ordained! At the worst, *you* had only the Church fastened upon your back, before you were old enough to know what you wanted. It is easy enough to make the best of *that*; but it is different with me."

A marked silence followed this outburst. The Rev. Mr. Ware had never spoken of his marriage to either of these friends before; and something in their manner seemed to suggest that they did not find the subject inviting, now that it had been broached. He himself was filled with a desire to say more about it. He had never clearly realized before what a genuine grievance it was. The moisture at the top of his nose merged itself into tears in the corners of his eyes, as the cruel enormity of the sacrifice he had made in his youth rose before him. His whole life had been fettered and darkened by it. He turned his gaze from the swings toward Celia, to claim the sympathy he knew she would feel for him.

But Celia was otherwise engaged. A young man had come

up to her, — a tall and extremely thin young man, soberly dressed, and with a long, gaunt, hollow-eyed face, the skin of which seemed at once florid and pale. He had sandy hair and the rough hands of a workman; but he was speaking to Miss Madden in the confidential tones of an equal.

"I can do nothing at all with him," this newcomer said to her. "He'll not be said by me. Perhaps he'd listen to you!"

"It's likely I'll go down there!" said Celia. "He may do what he likes for all me! Take my advice, Michael, and just go your way, and leave him to himself. There was a time when I would have taken out my eyes for him, but it was love wasted and thrown away. After the warnings he's had, if he *will* bring trouble on himself, let us make it no affair of ours."

Theron had found himself exchanging glances of inquiry with this young man. "Mr. Ware," said Celia, here, "let me introduce you to my brother Michael, — my full brother."

Mr. Ware remembered him now, and began, in response to the other's formal bow, to say something about their having met in the dark, inside the church. But Celia held up her hand. "I'm afraid, Mr. Ware," she said hurriedly, "that you are in for a glimpse [4] of the family skeleton. I will apologize for the infliction in advance."

Wonderingly, Theron followed her look, and saw another young man who had come up the path from the crowd below, and was close upon them. The minister recognized in him a figure which had seemed to be the centre of almost every group about the bar that he had studied in detail. He was a small, dapper, elegantly attired youth, with dark hair, and the handsome, regularly carved face of an actor. He advanced with a smiling countenance and unsteady step, — his silk hat thrust back upon his head, his frock-coat and vest unbuttoned, and his neckwear disarranged, — and saluted the company with amiability.

"I saw you up here, Father Forbes," he said, with a thickened and erratic utterance. "Whyn't you come down and

[4] English ed. reads "an exhibition" for "a glimpse."

join us? I'm setting 'em up for everybody. You got to take care of the boys, you know. I'll blow in the last cent I've got in the world for the boys, every time, and they know it. They're solider for me than they ever were for anybody. That's how it is. If you stand by the boys, the boys'll stand by you. I'm going to the Assembly for this district, and they ain't nobody can stop me. The boys are just red hot for me. Wish you'd come down, Father Forbes, and address a few words to the meeting, — just mention that I'm a candidate and say I'm bound to win, hands down. That'll make you solid with the boys, and we'll be all good fellows together. Come on down!"

The priest affably disengaged his arm from the clutch which the speaker had laid upon it, and shook his head in gentle deprecation. "No, no; you must excuse me, Theodore," he said. "We mustn't meddle in politics, you know."

"Politics be damned!" urged Theodore, grabbing the priest's other arm, and tugging at it stoutly to pull him down the path. "I say, boys!" he shouted to those below, "here's Father Forbes, and he's going to come down and address the meeting. Come on, Father! Come down, and have a drink with the boys!"

It was Celia who sharply pulled his hand away from the priest's arm this time. "Go away with you!" she snapped in low, angry tones at the intruder. "You should be ashamed of yourself! If you can't keep sober yourself, you can at least keep your hands off the priest. I should think you'd have more decency, when you're in such a state as this, than to come where I am. If you've no respect for yourself, you might have that much respect for me! And before strangers, too!"

"Oh, I mustn't come where *you* are, eh?" remarked the peccant Theodore, straightening himself with an elaborate effort. "You've bought these woods, have you? I've got a hundred friends here, all the same, for every one you'll ever have in your life, Red-head, and don't you forget it."

"Go and spend your money with them, then, and don't come insulting decent people," said Celia.

"Before strangers, too!" the young man called out, with beery sarcasm. "Oh, we'll take care of the strangers all right." He had not seemed to be aware of Theron's presence, much less his identity before; but he turned to him now with a knowing grin. "I'm running for the Assembly, Mr. Ware," he said, speaking loudly and with deliberate effort to avoid the drunken elisions and comminglings to which his speech tended, "and I want you to fix up the Methodists solid for me. I'm going to drive over to the camp-meeting to-night, me and some of the boys in a barouche, and I'll put a twenty-dollar bill on their plate. Here it is now, if you want to see it."

As the young man began fumbling in a vest-pocket, Theron gathered his wits together. "You'd better not go this evening," he said, as convincingly as he knew how; "because the gates will be closed very early, and the Saturday-evening services are of a particularly special nature, quite reserved for those living on the grounds."

"Rats!" said Theodore, raising his head, and abandoning the search for the bill. "Why don't you speak out like a man, and say you think I'm too drunk?"

"I don't think that is a question which need arise between us, Mr. Madden," murmured Theron, confusedly.

"Oh, don't you make any mistake! A hell of a lot of questions arise between us, Mr. Ware," cried Theodore, with a sudden accession of vigor in tone and mien. "And one of 'em is — go away from me, Michael! — one of 'em is, I say, why don't you leave our girls alone? They've got their own priests to make fools of themselves over, without any sneak of a Protestant parson coming meddling round them. You're a married man into the bargain; and you've got in your house this minute a piano that my sister bought and paid for. Oh, I've seen the entry in Thurston's books! You have the cheek to talk to me about being drunk — why —"

These remarks were never concluded, for Father Forbes

here clapped a hand abruptly over the offending mouth, and flung his free arm in a tight grip around the young man's waist. "Come with me, Michael!" he said, and the two men led the reluctant and resisting Theodore at a sharp pace off into the woods.

Theron and Celia stood and watched them disappear among the undergrowth. "It's the dirty Foley blood that's in him," he heard her say, as if between clenched teeth.

The girl's big brown eyes, when Theron looked into them again, were still fixed upon the screen of foliage, and dilated like those of a Medusa mask. The blood had gone away, and left the fair face and neck as white, it seemed to him, as marble. Even her lips, fiercely bitten together, appeared colorless. The picture of consuming and powerless rage which she presented, and the shuddering tremor which ran over her form, as visible as the quivering track of a gust of wind across a pond, awed and frightened him.

Tenderness toward her helpless state came too, and uppermost. He drew her arm into his, and turned their backs upon the picnic scene.

"Let us walk a little up the path into the woods," he said, "and get away from all this."

"The further away the better," she answered bitterly, and he felt the shiver run through her again as she spoke.

The methodical waltz-music from the unseen dancing platform rose again above all other sounds. They moved up the woodland path, their steps insensibly falling into the rhythm of its strains, and vanished from sight among the trees.

CHAPTER XXIV

THERON and Celia walked in silence for some minutes, until the noises of the throng they had left behind were lost. The path they followed had grown indefinite among the grass and creepers of the forest carpet; now it seemed to end altogether in a little copse of young birches, the delicately graceful stems of which were clustered about a parent stump, long since decayed and overgrown with lichens and layers of thick moss.

As the two paused, the girl suddenly sank upon her knees, then threw herself face forward upon the soft green bank which had formed itself above the roots of the ancient mother-tree. Her companion looked down in pained amazement at what he saw. Her body shook with the violence of recurring sobs, or rather gasps of wrath and grief. Her hands, with stiffened, claw-like fingers, dug into the moss and tangle of tiny vines, and tore them by the roots. The half-stifled sounds of weeping that arose from where her face grovelled in the leaves were terrible to his ears. He knew not what to say or do, but gazed in resourceless suspense at the strange figure she made. It seemed a cruelly long time that she lay there, almost at his feet, struggling fiercely with the fury that was in her.

All at once the paroxysms passed away, the sounds of wild weeping ceased. Celia sat up, and with her handkerchief wiped the tears and leafy fragments from her face. She re-arranged her hat and the braids of her hair with swift, instinctive touches, brushed the woodland débris from her front, and sprang to her feet.

"I'm all right now," she said briskly. There was palpable effort in her light tone, and in the stormy sort of smile which she forced upon her blotched and perturbed countenance, but they were only too welcome to Theron's anxious mood.

"Thank God!" he blurted out, all radiant with relief. "I feared you were going to have a fit — or something."

Celia laughed, a little artificially at first, then with a genuine surrender to the comic side of his visible fright. The mirth came back into the brown depths of her eyes again,[1] and her face cleared itself of tear-stains and the marks of agitation. "I *am* a nice quiet party for a Methodist minister to go walking in the woods with, am I not?" she cried, shaking her skirts and smiling at him.

"I am not a Methodist minister — please!" answered Theron, — "at least not to-day, — and here — with you! I am just a man, — nothing more, — a man who has escaped from lifelong imprisonment, and feels for the first time what it is to be free!"

"Ah, my friend," Celia said, shaking her head slowly, "I'm afraid you deceive yourself. You are not by any means free. You are only looking out of the window of your prison, as you call it. The doors are locked, just the same."

"I will smash them!" he declared, with confidence. "Or for that matter, I *have* smashed them, — battered them to pieces. You don't realize what progress I have made, what changes there have been in me since that night, — you remember that wonderful night! I am quite another being, I assure you! And really it dates from way beyond that, — why, from the very first evening, when I came to you in the church. The window in Father Forbes' room was open, and I stood by it listening to the music next door, and I could just faintly see on the dark window across the alley-way a stained-glass picture of a woman. I suppose it was the Virgin Mary. She had hair like yours, and your face, too; and that is why I went into the church and found you. Yes, that is why."

Celia regarded him with gravity. "You will get yourself into great trouble, my friend," she said.

"That's where you're wrong," put in Theron. "Not that I'd mind any trouble in this wide world, so long as you called me 'my friend,' but I'm not going to get into any at all. I know a trick worth two of that. I've learned to be a showman.

---

[1] English ed. omits "again."

I can preach now far better than I used to, and I can get through my work in half the time, and keep on the right side of my people, and get along with perfect smoothness. I was too green before. I took the thing seriously, and I let every mean-fisted curmudgeon and crazy fanatic worry me, and keep me on pins and needles. I don't do that any more. I've taken a new measure of life. I see now what life is really worth, and I'm going to have my share of it. Why should I deliberately deny myself all possible happiness for the rest of my days, simply because I made a fool of myself when I was in my teens? Other men are not eternally punished like that, for what they did as boys, and I won't submit to it either. I will be as free to enjoy myself as — as Father Forbes."

Celia smiled softly, and shook her head again. "Poor man, to call *him* free!" she said: "why, he is bound hand and foot. You don't in the least realize how he is hedged about, the work he has to do, the thousand suspicious eyes that watch his every movement, eager to bring the Bishop down upon him. And then think of his sacrifice, — the great [2] sacrifice of all, — to never know what love means, to forswear his manhood, to live a forlorn, celibate life — you have no idea how sadly that appeals to a woman."

"Let us sit down here for a little," said Theron; "we seem at the end of the path." She seated herself on the root-based mound, and he reclined at her side, with an arm carelessly extended behind her on the moss.

"I can see what you mean," he went on, after a pause. "But to me, do you know, there is an enormous fascination in celibacy. You forget that I know the reverse of the medal. I know how the mind can be cramped, the nerves harassed, the ambitions spoiled and rotted, the whole existence darkened and belittled, by — by the other thing. I have never talked to you before about my marriage."

"I don't think we'd better talk about it now," observed Celia. "There must be many more amusing topics."

[2] English ed. reads "greatest" for "great."

He missed the spirit of her remark. "You are right," he said slowly. "It *is* too sad a thing to talk about. But there! it is my load, and I bear it, and there's nothing more to be said."

Theron drew a heavy sigh, and let his fingers toy abstractedly with a ribbon on the outer edge of Celia's penumbra of apparel.

"No," she said. "We mustn't snivel, and we mustn't sulk. When I get into a rage it makes me ill, and I storm my way through it and tear things, but it doesn't last long, and I come out of it feeling all the better. I don't know that I've ever seen your wife. I suppose *she* hasn't got red hair?"

"I think it's a kind of light brown," answered Theron, with an effect of exerting his memory.

"It seems that you only take notice of hair in stained-glass windows," was Celia's comment.

"Oh-h!" he murmured reproachfully, "as if — as if — but I won't say what I was going to."

"That's not fair!" she said. The little touch of whimsical mockery which she gave to the serious declaration was delicious to him. "You have me at such a disadvantage! Here am I rattling out whatever comes into my head, exposing all my lightest emotions, and laying bare my very heart in candor, and you meditate, you turn things over cautiously in your mind, like a second Machiavelli. I grow afraid of you; you are so subtle and mysterious in your reserves."

Theron gave a tug at the ribbon, to show the joy he had in her delicate chaff. "No, it is you who are secretive," he said. "You never told me about — about the piano."

The word was out! A minute before it had seemed incredible to him that he should ever have the courage to utter it — but here it was. He laid firm hold upon the ribbon, which it appeared hung from her waist, and drew himself a trifle nearer to her. "I could never have consented to take it. I'm afraid," he went on in a low voice, "if I had known. And even as it is, I fear it won't be possible."

"What are you afraid of?" asked Celia. "Why shouldn't you take it? People in your profession never do get anything unless it's given to them, do they? I've always understood it was like that. I've often read of donation parties — that's what they're called, isn't it? — where everybody is supposed to bring some gift to the minister. Very well, then, I've simply had a donation party of my own, that's all. Unless you mean that my being a Catholic makes a difference. I had supposed you were quite free from that kind of prejudice."

"So I am! Believe me, I am!" urged Theron. "When I'm with you, it seems impossible to realize that there are people so narrow and contracted in their natures as to take account of such things. It is another atmosphere that I breathe near you. How could you imagine that such a thought — about our difference of creed — would enter my head? In fact," he concluded with a nervous half-laugh, "there isn't any such difference. Whatever your religion is, it's mine too. You remember — you adopted me as a Greek."

"Did I?" she rejoined. "Well, if that's the case, it leaves you without a leg to stand on. I challenge you to find any instance where a Greek made any difficulties about accepting a piano from a friend. But seriously — while we are talking about it — you introduced the subject: I didn't — I might as well explain to you that I had no such intention, when I picked the instrument out. It was later, when I was talking to Thurston's people about the price, that the whim seized me. Now it is the one fixed rule of my life to obey my whims. Whatever occurs to me as a possibly pleasant thing to do, straight like a flash, I go and do it. It is the only way that a person with means, with plenty of money, can preserve any freshness of character. If they stop to think what it would be prudent to do, they get crusted over immediately. That is the curse of rich people, — they teach themselves to distrust and restrain every impulse toward unusual actions. They get to feel that it is more necessary for them to be cautious and conventional than it is for others. I would rather work at a

wash-tub than occupy that attitude toward my bank account.
I fight against any sign of it that I detect rising in my mind.
The instant a wish occurs to me, I rush to gratify it. That
is my theory of life. That accounts for the piano; and I don't
see that you've anything to say about it at all."

It seemed very convincing, this theory of life. Somehow,
the thought of Miss Madden's riches had never before assumed prominence in Theron's mind. Of course her father
was very wealthy, but it had not occurred to him that the
daughter's emancipation might run to the length of a personal fortune. He knew so little of rich people and their ways!

He lifted his head, and looked up at Celia with an awakened humility and awe in his glance. The glamour of a
separate banking-account shone upon her. Where the soft
woodland light played in among the strands of her disordered
hair, he saw the veritable gleam of gold. A mysterious new
suggestion of power blended itself with the beauty of her
face, was exhaled in the faint perfume of her garments.
He maintained a timorous hold upon the ribbon, wondering
at his hardihood in touching it, or being near her at all.

"What surprises me," he heard himself saying, "is that
you are contented to stay in Octavius. I should think that you
would travel — go abroad — see the beautiful things of the
world, surround yourself with the luxuries of big cities, —
and that sort of thing."

Celia regarded the forest prospect straight in front of her
with a pensive gaze. "Sometime — no doubt I will sometime,"
she said abstractedly.

"One reads so much nowadays," he went on, "of American
heiresses going to Europe and marrying dukes and noblemen.
I suppose you will do that too. Princes would fight one
another for *you*."

The least touch of a smile softened for an instant the impassivity of her countenance. Then she stared harder than
ever at the vague, leafy distance. "That is the old-fashioned
idea," she said, in a musing tone, "that women must belong

to somebody, as if they were curios, or statues, or race-horses. You don't understand, my friend, that I have a different view. I am myself, and I belong to myself, exactly as much as any man. The notion that any other human being could conceivably obtain the slightest property rights in me is as preposterous, as ridiculous, as — what shall I say? — as the notion of your being taken out with a chain on your neck and sold by auction as a slave, down on the canal bridge. I should be ashamed to be alive for another day, if any other thought were possible to me."

"That is not the generally accepted view, I should think," faltered Theron.

"No more is it the accepted view that young married Methodist ministers should sit out alone in the woods with red-headed Irish girls. No, my friend, let us find what the generally accepted views are, and as fast as we find them set our heels on them. There is no other way to live like real human beings. What on earth is it to me that other women crawl about on all-fours, and fawn like dogs on any hand that will buckle a collar onto them, and toss them the leavings of the table? I am not related to them. I have nothing to do with them. They cannot make any rules for me. If pride and dignity and independence are dead in them, why, so much the worse for them! It is no affair of mine. Certainly it is no reason why I should get down and grovel also. No; I at least stand erect on my legs."

Mr. Ware sat up, and stared confusedly, with round eyes and parted lips, at his companion. Instinctively his brain dragged forth to the surface those epithets which the doctor had hurled in bitter contempt at her, — and "mad ass, a mere bundle of egotism, ignorance, and red-headed lewdness." The words rose in their order on his memory, hard and sharp-edged, like arrow-heads. But to sit there, quite at her side; to breathe the same air, and behold the calm loveliness of her profile; to touch the ribbon of her dress, — and all the while to hold these poisoned darts of abuse levelled in thought at her breast, — it was monstrous. He could have killed the doctor at that moment. With an effort, he drove the foul things from his mind, — scattered them back into the darkness. He felt that he had grown pale, and wondered if she had heard the groan that seemed to have been forced from him in the struggle. Or was the groan imaginary?

Celia continued to sit unmoved, composedly looking upon vacancy. Theron's eyes searched her face in vain for any sign of consciousness that she had astounded and bewildered him. She did not seem to be thinking of him at all. The proud calm of her thoughtful countenance suggested instead occupation with lofty and remote abstractions and noble ideals. Contemplating her, he suddenly perceived that what she had been saying was great, wonderful, magnificent. An involuntary thrill ran through his veins at recollection of her words. His fancy likened it to the sensation he used to feel as a youth, when the Fourth of July reader bawled forth that opening clause: "When, in the course of human events, it becomes necessary," etc. It was nothing less than another Declaration of Independence he had been listening to.

He sank again recumbent at her side, and stretched the arm behind her, nearer than before. "Apparently, then, you will never marry." His voice trembled a little.

"Most certainly not!" said Celia.

"You spoke so feelingly a little while ago," he ventured along, with hesitation, "about how sadly the notion of a priest's sacrificing himself — never knowing what love meant — appealed to a woman. I should think that the idea of sacrificing herself would seem to her even sadder still."

"I don't remember that we mentioned *that*," she replied. "How do you mean, — sacrificing herself?"

Theron gathered some of the outlying folds of her dress in his hand, and boldly patted and caressed them. "You, so beautiful and so free, with such fine talents and abilities," he murmured; "you, who could have the whole world at your feet, — are you, too, never going to know what love means?

Do you call that no sacrifice? To me it is the most terrible
that my imagination can conceive."

Celia laughed, — a gentle, amused little laugh, in which
Theron's ears traced elements of tenderness. "You must regu-
late that imagination of yours," she said playfully. "It con-
ceives the thing that is not. Pray, when" — and here, turning
her head, she bent down upon his face a gaze of arch mock-
seriousness — "pray, when did I describe myself in these
terms? When did I say that I should never know what love
meant?"

For answer Theron laid his head down upon his arm,
and closed his eyes, and held his face against the draperies
encircling her. "I cannot think!" he groaned.

The thing that came uppermost in his mind, as it swayed
and rocked in the tempest of emotion, was the strange remi-
niscence of early childhood in it all. It was like being a little
boy again, nestling in an innocent, unthinking transport of
affection against his mother's skirts. The tears he felt scald-
ing his eyes were the spontaneous, unashamed tears of a child;
the tremulous and exquisite joy which spread, wave-like,
over him, at once reposeful and yearning, was full of infantile
purity and sweetness. He had not comprehended at all before
what wellsprings of spiritual beauty, what limpid depths of
idealism, his nature contained.

"We were speaking of our respective religions," he heard
Celia say, as imperturbably as if there had been no digression
worth mentioning.

"Yes," he assented, and moved his head so that he looked
up at her back hair, and the leaves high above, mottled
against the sky. The wish to lie there, where now he could
just catch the rose-leaf line of her under-chin as well, was
very strong upon him. "Yes?" he repeated.

"I cannot talk to you like that," she said; and he sat up
again shamefacedly.

"Yes — I think we were speaking of religions — some time
ago," he faltered, to relieve the situation. The dreadful
thought that she might be annoyed began to oppress him.

"Well, you said whatever my religion was, it was yours too. That entitles you at least to be told what the religion is. Now, I am a Catholic."

Theron, much mystified, nodded his head. Could it be possible, — was there coming a deliberate suggestion that he should become a convert? "Yes — I know," he murmured.

"But I should explain that I am only a Catholic in the sense that its symbolism is pleasant to me. You remember what Schopenhauer said, — you cannot have the water by itself: you must also have the jug that it is in. Very well; the Catholic religion is my jug. I put into it the things I like. They were all there long ago, thousands of years ago. The Jews threw them out; we will put them back again. We will restore art and poetry and the love of beauty, and the gentle, spiritual, soulful life. The Greeks had it; and Christianity would have had it too, if it hadn't been for those brutes they call the Fathers. They loved ugliness and dirt and the thought of hell-fire. They hated women. In all the earlier stages of the Church, women were very prominent in it. Jesus himself appreciated women, and delighted to have them about him, and talk with them and listen to them. That was the very essence of the Greek spirit; and it breathed into Christianity at its birth a sweetness and a grace which twenty generations of cranks and savages like Paul and Jerome and Tertullian weren't able to extinguish. But the very man, Cyril, who killed Hypatia, and thus began the dark ages, unwittingly did another thing which makes one almost forgive him. To please the Egyptians, he secured the Church's acceptance of the adoration of the Virgin. It is that idea which has kept the Greek spirit alive, and grown and grown, till at last it will rule the world. It was only epileptic Jews who could imagine a religion without sex in it."

"I remember the pictures of the Virgin in your room," said Theron, feeling more himself again. "I wondered if they quite went with the statues."

The remark won a smile from Celia's lips.

"They get along together better than you suppose," she

answered. "Besides, they are not all pictures of Mary. One of them, standing on the moon, is of Isis with the infant Horus in her arms. Another might as well be Mahamie, bearing the miraculously born Buddha, or Olympias with her child Alexander, or even Perictione holding her babe Plato, — all these were similar cases, you know. Almost every religion had its Immaculate Conception. What does it all come to, except to show us that man turns naturally toward the worship of the maternal idea? That is the deepest of all our instincts, — love of woman, who is at once daughter and wife and mother. It is that that makes the world go round."

Brave thoughts shaped themselves in Theron's mind, and shone forth in a confident yet wistful smile on his face.

"It is a pity you cannot change estates with me for one minute," he said, in steady, low tones. "Then you would realize the tremendous truth of what you have been saying. It is only your intellect that has reached out and grasped the idea. If you were in my place, you would discover that your heart was bursting with it as well."

Celia turned and looked at him.

"I myself," he went on, "would not have known, half an hour ago, what you meant by the worship of the maternal idea. I am much older than you. I am a strong, mature man. But when I lay down there, and shut my eyes, — because the charm and marvel of this whole experience had for the moment overcome me, — the strangest sensation seized upon me. It was absolutely as if I were a boy again, a good, pure-minded, fond little child, and you were the mother that I idolized."

Celia had not taken her eyes from his face. "I find myself liking you better at this moment," she said, with gravity, "than I have ever liked you before."

Then, as by a sudden impulse, she sprang to her feet. "Come!" she cried, her voice and manner all vivacity once more, "we have been here long enough."

Upon the instant, as Theron was more laboriously getting up, it became apparent to them both that perhaps they had been there too long.

A boy with a gun under his arm, and two gray squirrels tied by the tails slung across his shoulder, stood at the entrance to the glade, some dozen paces away, regarding them with undisguised interest. Upon the discovery that he was in turn observed, he resumed his interrupted progress through the woods, whistling softly as he went, and vanished among the trees.

"Heavens above!" groaned Theron, shudderingly.

"Know him?" he went on, in answer to the glance of inquiry on his companion's face. "I should think I did! He spades my — my wife's garden for her. He used to bring our milk. He works in the law office of one of my trustees, — the one who isn't friendly to me, but is very friendly indeed with my — with Mrs. Ware. Oh, what shall I do? It may easily mean my ruin!"

Celia looked at him attentively. The color had gone out of his face, and with it the effect of earnestness and mental elevation which, a minute before, had caught her fancy. "Somehow, I fear that I do not like you quite so much just now, my friend," she remarked.

"In God's name, don't say that!" urged Theron. He raised his voice in agitated entreaty. "You don't know what these people are, — how they would leap at the barest hint of a scandal about me. In my position I am a thousand times more defenceless than any woman. Just a single whisper, and I am done for!"

"Let me point out to you, Mr. Ware," said Celia, slowly, "that to be seen sitting and talking with me, whatever doubts it may raise as to a gentleman's intellectual condition, need not necessarily blast his social reputation beyond all hope whatever."

Theron stared at her, as if he had not grasped her meaning. Then he winced visibly under it, and put out his hand to implore her. "Forgive me! Forgive me!" he pleaded. "I was beside myself for the moment with the fright of the thing. Oh, say you do forgive me, Celia!" He made haste to support this daring use of her name. "I have been so happy to-day

— so deeply, so vastly happy — like the little child I spoke of — and that is so new in my lonely life — that — the suddenness of the thing — it just for the instant unstrung me. Don't be too hard on me for it! And I had hoped, too — I had had such genuine heartfelt pleasure in the thought, — that, an hour or two ago, when *you* were unhappy, perhaps it had been some sort of consolation to you that I was with you."

Celia was looking away. When he took her hand she did not withdraw it, but turned and nodded in musing general assent to what he had said. "Yes, we have both been unstrung, as you call it, to-day," she said, "decidedly out of pitch. Let each forgive the other, and say no more about it."

She took his arm, and they retraced their steps along the path, again in silence. The labored noise of the orchestra, as it were, returned to meet them. They halted at an intersecting footpath.

"I go back to my slavery, — my double bondage," said Theron, letting his voice sink to a sigh. "But even if I am put on the rack for it, I shall have had one day of glory."

"I think you may kiss me, in memory of that one day — or of a few minutes in that day," said Celia.

Their lips brushed each other in a swift, almost perfunctory caress.

Theron went his way at a hurried pace, the sobered tones of her "good-bye" beating upon his brain with every measure of the droning waltz-music.

PART IV

CHAPTER XXV

THE memory of the kiss abode with Theron. Like Aaron's rod, it swallowed up one by one all competing thoughts and recollections, and made his brain its slave.

Even as he strode back through the woods to the camp-meeting, it was the kiss that kept his feet in motion, and guided their automatic course. All along the watches of the restless night, it was the kiss that bore him sweet company, and wandered with him from one broken dream of bliss to another. Next day, it was the kiss that made of life for him a sort of sunlit wonderland. He preached his sermon in the morning, and took his appointed part in the other services of afternoon and evening, apparently to everybody's satisfaction: to him it was all a vision.

When the beautiful moon rose, this Sunday evening,[1] and glorified the clearing and the forest with its mellow harvest radiance, he could have groaned with the burden of his joy. He went out alone into the light, and bared his head to it, and stood motionless for a long time. In all his life, he had never been impelled as [2] powerfully toward earnest and soulful thanksgiving. The impulse to kneel, there in the pure, tender moonlight, and lift up offerings of praise to God, kept uppermost in his mind. Some formless reservation restrained him from the act itself, but the spirit of it hallowed his mood. He gazed up at the broad luminous face of the satellite. "You are our God," he murmured. "Hers and mine! You are the most beautiful of heavenly creatures, as she is of the angels on earth. I am speechless with reverence for you both."

[1] English ed. reads "night" for "evening."
[2] English ed. reads "so" for "as."

It was not until the camp-meeting broke up, four days later, and Theron with the rest returned to town, that the material aspects of what had happened, and might be expected to happen, forced themselves upon his mind. The kiss was a child of the forest. So long as Theron remained in the camp, the image of the kiss, which was enshrined in his heart and ministered to by all his thoughts, continued enveloped in a haze of sylvan mystery, like a dryad. Suggestions of its beauty and holiness came to him in the odors of the woodland, at the sight of wild flowers and water-lilies. When he walked alone in unfamiliar parts of the forest, he carried about with him the half-conscious idea of somewhere coming upon a strange, hidden pool which mortal eye had not seen before, — a deep, sequestered mere of spring-fed waters, walled in by rich, tangled growths of verdure, and bearing upon its virgin bosom only the shadows of the primeval wilderness, and the light of the eternal skies. His fancy dwelt upon some such nook as the enchanted home of the fairy that possessed his soul. The place, though he never found it, became real to him. As he pictured it, there rose sometimes from among the lily-pads, stirring the translucent depths and fluttering over the water's surface drops like gems,[3] the wonderful form of a woman, with pale leaves wreathed in her luxuriant red hair, and a skin which gave forth light.

With the home-coming to Octavius, his dreams began to take more account of realities. In a day or two he was wide awake, and thinking hard. The kiss was as much as ever the ceaseless companion of his hours, but it no longer insisted upon shrouding itself in vines and woodland creepers, or outlining itself in phosphorescent vagueness against mystic backgrounds of nymph-haunted glades. It advanced out into the noonday, and assumed tangible dimensions and substance. He saw that it was related to the facts of his daily life, and had, in turn, altered his own relations to all these facts.

---

[3] English ed. reads "fluttering the water's surface with drops like gems" for "fluttering over the water's surface drops like gems."

What ought he to do? What *could* he do? Apparently, nothing but wait. He waited for a week, — then for another week. The conclusion that the initiative had been left to him began to take shape in his mind. From this it seemed but a step to the passionate resolve to act at once.

Turning the situation over and over in his anxious thoughts, two things stood out in special prominence. One was that Celia loved him. The other was that the boy in Gorringe's law office, and possibly Gorringe, and heaven only knew how many others besides, had reasons for suspecting this to be true.[4]

And what about Celia? Side by side with the moving rapture of thinking about her as a woman, there rose the substantial satisfaction of contemplating her as Miss Madden. She had kissed him, and she was very rich. The things gradually linked themselves before his eyes. He tried a thousand varying guesses at what she proposed to do, and each time reined up his imagination by the reminder that she was confessedly a creature of whims, who proposed to do nothing, but was capable of all things.

And as to the boy. If he had blabbed what he saw, it was incredible that somebody should not take the subject up, and impart a scandalous twist to it, and send it rolling like a snowball to gather up exaggeration and foul innuendo till it was big enough to overwhelm him. What would happen to him if a formal charge were preferred against him? He looked it up in the Discipline. Of course, if his accusers magnified their mean suspicions and calumnious imaginings to the point of formulating a charge, it would be one of immorality. They could prove nothing; there was nothing to prove. At the worst, it was an indiscretion, which would involve his being admonished by his Presiding Elder. Or if these narrow bigots confused slanders with proofs, and showed that they intended to convict him, then it would be open to him to withdraw from the ministry, in advance of his condemnation.

[4] English ed. reads "the case" for "true."

His relation to the church would be the same as if he had
been expelled, but to the other world it would be different.
And supposing he did withdraw from the ministry?

Yes; this was the important point. What if he did abandon
this mistaken profession of his? On its mental side the relief
would be prodigious, unthinkable. But on the practical side,
the bread-and-butter side? For some days Theron paused with
a shudder when he reached this question. The thought of the
plunge into unknown material responsibilities gave him a
sinking heart. He tried to imagine himself lecturing, canvassing for books or insurance policies, writing for newspapers — and remained frightened. But suddenly one day it
occurred to him that these qualms and forebodings were
sheer folly. Was not Celia rich? Would she not with light-
ning swiftness draw forth that check-book, like the flashing
sword of a champion from its scabbard, and run to his relief?
Why, of course. It was absurd not to have thought of that
before.

He recalled her momentary anger with him, that afternoon
in the woods, when he had cried out that discovery would
mean ruin to him. He saw clearly enough now that she had
been grieved at his want of faith in her protection. In his
flurry of fright, he had lost sight of the fact that, if exposure
and trouble came to him, she would naturally feel that she
had been the cause of his martyrdom. It was plain enough
now. If he got into hot water, it would be solely on account
of his having been seen with her. He had walked into the
woods with her, — "the further the better" had been her own
words, — out of pure kindliness, and the desire to lead her
away from the scene of her brother's and her own humiliation. But why amplify arguments? Her own warm heart
would tell her, on the instant, how he had been sacrificed for
her sake, and would bring her, eager and devoted, to his
succor.

That was all right, then. Slowly, from this point, suggestions expanded themselves. The future could be, if he willed
it, one long serene triumph of love, and lofty intellectual

companionship, and existence softened and enriched at every point by all that wealth could command, and the most exquisite tastes suggest. Should he will it! Ah! the question answered itself. But he could not enter upon this beckoning heaven of a future until he had freed himself. When Celia said to him, "Come!" he must not be in the position to reply, "I should like to, but unfortunately I am tied by the leg." He should have to leave Octavius, leave the ministry, leave everything. He could not begin too soon to face these contingencies.

Very likely Celia had not thought it out as far as this. With her, it was a mere vague "sometime I may." But the harder masculine sense, Theron felt, existed for the very purpose of correcting and giving point to these loose feminine notions of time and space. It was for him to clear away the obstacles, and map the plans out with definite decision.

One warm afternoon, as he lolled in his easy-chair under the open window of his study, musing upon the ever-shifting phases of this vast, complicated, urgent problem, some chance words from the sidewalk in front came to his ears, and, coming, remained to clarify his thoughts.

Two ladies whose voices were strange to him had stopped — as so many people almost daily stopped — to admire the garden of the parsonage. One of them expressed her pleasure in general terms. Said the other, —

"My husband declares those dahlias alone couldn't be matched for fifty [5] dollars, and that some of those gladiolus must have cost three or four dollars apiece. I know we've spent simply oceans of money on our garden, and it doesn't begin to compare with this."

"It seems like a sinful waste to me," said her companion.

"No-o," the other hesitated. "No, I don't think quite that — if you can afford it just as well as not. But it does seem to me that I'd rather live in a little better house, and not spend it *all* on flowers. Just *look* at that cactus!"

The voices died away. Theron sat up, with a look of

[5] English ed. reads "thirty" for "fifty."

arrested thought upon his face, then sprang to his feet and moved hurriedly through the parlor to an open front window. Peering out with caution he saw that the two women receding from view were fashionably dressed and evidently came from homes of means. He stared after them in a blank way until they turned a corner.

He went into the hall then, put on his frock-coat and hat, and stepped out into the garden. He was conscious of having rather avoided it heretofore, — not altogether without reasons of his own, lying unexamined somewhere in the recesses of his mind. Now he walked slowly about, and examined the flowers with great attentiveness. The season was advancing, and he saw that many plants had gone out of bloom. But what a magnificent plentitude of blossoms still remained!

Fifty dollars' worth of dahlias, — that was what the stranger had said. Theron hardly brought himself to credit the statement; but all the same it was apparent to even his uninformed eye that these huge, imbricated, flowering masses, with their extraordinary half-colors, must be unusual. He remembered that the boy in Gorringe's office had spoken of just one lot of plants costing thirty-one dollars and sixty cents, and there had been two other lots as well. The figures remained surprisingly distinct in his memory. It was no good deceiving himself any longer: of course these were the plants that Gorringe had spent his money upon, here all about him.

As he surveyed them with a sour regard, a cool breeze stirred across the garden. The tall, overladen flower-spikes of gladioli bent and nodded at him; the hollyhocks and flaming alvias, the clustered blossoms on the standard roses, the delicately painted lilies on their stilt-like stems, fluttered in the wind, and seemed all bowing satirically to him. "Yes, Levi Gorringe paid for us!" He almost heard their mocking declaration.

Out in the back-yard, where a longer day of sunshine dwelt, there were many other flowers, and notably a bed of geraniums which literally made the eye ache. Standing at this rear corner of the house, he caught the droning sound of Alice's voice, humming a hymn to herself as she went about her kitchen work.[6] He saw her through the open window. She was sweeping, and had a sort of cap on her head which did not add to the graces of her appearance. He looked at her with a hard glance, recalling as a fresh grievance the ten days of intolerable boredom he had spent cooped up in a ridiculous little tent with her, at the camp-meeting. She must have realized at the time how odious the enforced companionship was to him. Yes, beyond doubt she did. It came back to him now that they had spoken but rarely to each other. She had not even praised his sermon upon the Sabbath-question, which every one else had been in raptures over. For that matter she no longer praised anything he did, and took obvious pains to preserve toward him a distant demeanor. So much the better, he felt himself thinking, If she chose to behave in that offish and unwifely fashion, she could blame no one but herself for its results.

She had seen him, and came now to the window, watering-pot and broom in hand. She put her head out, to breathe a breath of dustless air, and began as if she would smile on him. Then her face chilled and stiffened, as she caught his look.

"Shall you be home for supper?" she asked, in her iciest tone.

He had not thought of going out before. The question, and the manner of it, gave immediate urgency to the idea of going somewhere. "I may or I may not," he replied. "It is quite impossible for me to say." He turned on his heel with this, and walked briskly out of the yard and down the street.

It was the most natural thing that presently he should be strolling past the Madden house, and letting a covert glance stray over its front and the grounds about it, as he loitered along. Every day since his return from the woods he had given the fates this chance of bringing Celia to meet him, without avail. He had hung about in the vicinity of the Catholic

[6] English ed. begins new paragraph here.

church on several evenings as well, but to no purpose. The organ inside was dumb, and he could detect no signs of Celia's presence on the curtains of the pastorate next door. This day, too, there was no one visible at the home of the Maddens, and he walked on, a little sadly. It was weary work waiting for the signal that never came.

But there were compensations. His mind reverted doggedly to the flowers in his garden, and to Alice's behavior toward him. They insisted upon connecting themselves in his thoughts. Why should Levi Gorringe, a money-lender, and therefore the last man in the world to incur reckless expenditure, go and buy perhaps a hundred dollars' worth of flowers for his wife's garden? It was time — high time — to face this question. And his experiencing religion afterward, just when Alice did, and marching down to the rail to kneel beside her, — that was a thing to be thought of, too.

Meditation, it is true, hardly threw fresh light upon the matter. It was incredible, of course, that there should be anything wrong. To even shape a thought of Alice in connection with gallantry would be wholly impossible. Nor could it be said that Gorringe, in his new capacity as a professing church-member, had disclosed any sign of ulterior motives, or of insincerity. Yet there the facts were. While Theron pondered them, their mystery, if they involved a mystery, baffled him altogether. But when he had finished, he found himself all the same convinced that neither Alice nor Gorringe would be free to blame him for anything he might do. He had grounds for complaint against them. If he did not himself know just what these grounds were, it was certain enough that *they* knew. Very well, then, let them take the responsibility for what happened.

It was indeed awkward that at the moment, as Theron chanced to emerge temporarily from his brown-study, his eyes fell upon the spare, well-knit form of Levi Gorringe himself, standing only a few feet away, in the staircase entrance to his law office. His lean face, browned by the summer's exposure, had a more Arabian aspect than ever. His hands were in his pockets, and he held an unlighted cigar between his teeth. He looked the Rev. Mr. Ware over calmly, and nodded recognition.

Theron had halted instinctively. On the instant he would have given a great deal not to have stopped at all. It was stupid of him to have paused, but it would not do now to go on without words of some sort. He moved over to the doorway, and made a half-hearted pretence of looking at the photographs in one of the show-cases at its side. As Mr. Gorringe did not take his hands from his pockets, there was no occasion for any formal greeting.

"I had no idea that they took such good pictures in Octavius," Theron remarked after a minute's silence, still bending in examination of the photographs.

"They ought to; they charge New York prices," observed the lawyer, sententiously.

Theron found in the words confirmation of his feeling that Gorringe was not naturally a lavish or extravagant man. Rather was he a careful and calculating man, who spent money only for a purpose. Though the minister continued gazing at the stiff presentments of local beauties and swains, his eye seemed to see salmon-hued hollyhocks and spotted lilies instead. Suddenly a resolve came to him. He stood erect, and faced his trustee.

"Speaking of the price of things," he said, with an effort of arrogance in his measured tone, "I have never had an opportunity before of mentioning the subject of the flowers you have so kindly furnished for my — for *my* garden."

"Why mention it now?" queried Gorringe, with nonchalance. He turned his cigar about with a movement of his lips, and worked it into the corner of his mouth. He did not find it necessary to look at Theron at all.

"Because," began Mr. Ware, and then hesitated — "because — well, it raises a question of my being under obligation, which I —"

"Oh, no, sir," said the lawyer; "put that out of your mind. You are no more under obligation to me than I am to you. Oh, no, make yourself easy about that. Neither of us owes the other anything."

"Not even good-will, — I take that to be your meaning," retorted Theron, with some heat.

"The words are yours, sir," responded Gorringe, coolly. "I do not object to them."

"As you like," put in the other. "If it be so, why, then all the more reason why I should, under the circumstances —"

"Under what circumstances?" interposed the lawyer. "Let us be clear about this thing as we go along. To what circumstances do you refer?"

He had turned his eyes now, and looked Theron in the face. A slight protrusion of his lower jaw had given the cigar an upward tilt under the black mustache.

"The circumstances are that you have brought or sent to my garden a great many very expensive flower-plants and bushes and so on."

"And you object? I had not supposed that clergymen in general — and you in particular — were so sensitive. Have donation parties, then, gone out of date?"

"I understand your sneer well enough," retorted Theron, "but that can pass. The main point is, that you did me the honor to send these plants, — or to smuggle them in, — but never once designed to hint to me that you had done so. No one told me. Except by mere accident, I should not have known to this day where they came from."

Mr. Gorringe twisted the cigar at another angle, with lines of grim amusement about the corner of his mouth. "I should have thought," he said with dry deliberation, "that possibly this fact might have raised in your mind the conceivable hypothesis that the plants might not be intended for you at all."

"That is precisely it, sir," said Theron. There were people passing, and he was forced to keep his voice down. It would have been a relief, he felt, to shout. "That is it, — they were *not* intended for me."

"Well, then, what are you talking about?" The lawyer's speech had become abrupt almost to incivility.

"I think my remarks have been perfectly clear," said the minister, with dignity. It was a new experience to be addressed in that fashion. It occurred to him to add, "Please remember that I am not in the witness-box, to be bullied or insulted by a professional."

Gorringe studied Theron's face attentively with a cold, searching scrutiny. "You may thank your stars you're not!" he said, with significance.

What on earth could he mean? The words and the menacing tone greatly impressed Theron. Indeed, upon reflection, he found that they frightened him. The disposition to adopt a high tone with the lawyer was melting away.

"I do not see," he began, and then deliberately allowed his voice to take on an injured and plaintive inflection, — "I do not see why you should adopt this tone toward me — Brother Gorringe."

The lawyer scowled, and bit sharply into the cigar, but said nothing.

"If I have unconsciously offended you in any way," Theron went on, "I beg you to tell me how. I liked you from the beginning of my pastorate here, and the thought that latterly we seemed to be drifting apart has given me much pain. But now it is still more distressing to find you actually disposed to quarrel with me. Surely, Brother Gorringe, between a pastor and a probationer who —"

"No," Gorringe broke in; "quarrel isn't the word for it. There isn't any quarrel, Mr. Ware." He stepped down from the door-stone to the sidewalk as he spoke, and stood face to face with Theron. Working-men with dinner-pails, and factory girls, were passing close to them, and he lowered his voice to a sharp, incisive half-whisper as he added, "It wouldn't be worth any grown man's while to quarrel with so poor a creature as you are."

Theron stood confounded, with an empty stare of bewilderment on his face. It rose in his mind that the right thing to feel was rage, righteous indignation, fury; but for the life of him, he could not muster any manly anger. The character of the insult stupefied him.

"I do not know that I have anything to say to you in reply," he remarked, after what seemed to him a silence of minutes. His lips framed the words automatically, but they expressed well enough the blank vacancy of his mind. The suggestion that anybody deemed him a "poor creature" grew more astounding, incomprehensible, as it swelled in his brain.

"No, I suppose not," snapped Gorringe. "You're not the sort to stand up to men; your form is to go round the corner and take it out of somebody weaker than yourself, — a defenceless woman, for instance."

"Oh — ho!" said Theron. The exclamation had uttered itself. The sound of it seemed to clarify his muddled thoughts; and as they ranged themselves in order, he began to understand.[7] "Oh — ho!" he said again, and nodded his head in token of comprehension.

The lawyer, chewing his cigar with increased activity, glared at him. "What do you mean?" he demanded peremptorily.

"Mean?" said the minister. "Oh, nothing that I feel called upon to explain to you."

It was passing strange, but his self-possession had all at once returned to him. As it became more apparent that the lawyer was losing his temper, Theron found the courage to turn up the corners of his lips in show of a bitter little smile of confidence. He looked into the other's dusky face, and flaunted this smile at it in contemptuous defiance. "It is not a subject that I can discuss with propriety — at this stage," he added.

"Damn you! Are you talking about those flowers?"

"Oh, I am not talking about anything in particular," returned Theron, "not even the curious choice of language which my latest probationer seems to prefer."

[7] English ed. adds "his new advantage."

"Go and strike my name off the list!" said Gorringe, with rising passion. "I was a fool to ever have it there. To think of being a probationer of *yours* — my God!"

"That will be a pity — from one point of view," remarked Theron, still with the ironical smile on his lips. "You seemed to enter upon the new life with such deliberation and fixity of purpose, too! I can imagine the regrets your withdrawal will cause, in certain quarters. I only hope that it will not discourage those who accompanied you to the altar, and shared your enthusiasm at the time." He had spoken throughout with studied slowness and an insolent nicety of utterance.

"You had better go away!" broke forth Gorringe. "If you don't, I shall forget myself."

"For the first time?" asked Theron. Then, warned by the flash in the lawyer's eye, he turned on his heel and sauntered, with a painstaking assumption of a mind quite at ease, up the street.

Gorringe's own face twitched and his veins tingled as he looked after him. He spat the shapeless cigar out of his mouth into the gutter, and, drawing forth another from his pocket, clenched it between his teeth, his gaze following the tall form of the Methodist minister till it was merged in the crowd.

"Well, I'm damned!" he said aloud to himself.

The photographer had come down to take in his show-cases for the night. He looked up from his task at the exclamation, and grinned inquiringly.

"I've just been talking to a man," said the lawyer, "who's so much meaner than any other man I ever heard of that it takes my breath away. He's got a wife that's as pure and good as gold, and he knows it, and she worships the ground he walks on, and he knows that too. And yet the scoundrel is around trying to sniff out some shadow of a pretext for misusing her worse than he's already done. Yes, sir; he'd be actually tickled to death if he could nose up some hint of a scandal about her, — something that he could pretend to believe, and work for his own advantage, to levy blackmail, or get rid of her, or whatever suited his book. I didn't think there was such an out-and-out cur on this whole footstool. I almost wish, by God, I'd thrown him into the canal!"

"Yes, you lawyers must run against some pretty snide specimens," remarked the photographer, lifting one of the cases from its sockets.

CHAPTER XXVI

THERON spent half an hour in aimless strolling about the streets. From earliest boyhood his mind had always worked most clearly when he walked alone. Every mental process which had left a mark upon his memory and his career, — the day-dreams of future academic greatness and fame which had fashioned themselves in his brain as a farm lad; the meditations, raptures, and high resolves of his student period at the seminary; the more notable sermons and powerful discourses by which he had revealed the genius that was in him to astonished and delighted assemblages, — all were associated in his retrospective thoughts with solitary rambles.

He had a very direct and vivid consciousness now that it was good to be on his legs, and alone. He had never in his life been more sensible of the charm of his own companionship. The encounter with Gorringe seemed to have cleared all the clouds out of his brain, and restored lightness to his heart. After such an object lesson, the impossibility of his continuing to sacrifice himself to a notion of duty to these low-minded and coarse-natured villagers was beyond all argument. There could no longer be any doubt about his moral right to turn his back upon them, to wash his hands of the miserable combination of hypocrisy and hysterics which they called their spiritual life.

And the question of Gorringe and Alice, that too stood precisely where he wanted it. Even in his own thoughts, he preferred to pursue it no further. Between them somewhere an offence of concealment, it might be of conspiracy, had been committed against him. It was no business of his to say more, or to think more. He rested his case simply on the fact, which could not be denied, and which he was not in the least interested to have explained, one way or the other. The recollection of Gorringe's obvious disturbance of mind was especially pleasant to him. He himself had been magnanimous almost to the point of weakness. He had gone out of his way to call the man "brother," and to give him an opportunity of behaving like a gentleman; but his kindly forbearance had been wasted. Gorringe was not the man to understand generous feelings, much less rise to their level. He had merely shown that he would be vicious if he knew how. It was more important and satisfactory to recall that he had also shown a complete comprehension of the injured husband's grievance. The fact that he had recognized it was enough, — was, in fact, everything.

In the background of his thoughts Theron had carried along a notion of going and dining with Father Forbes when the time for the evening meal should arrive. The idea in itself attracted him, as a fitting capstone to his resolve not to go home to supper. It gave just the right kind of character to his domestic revolt. But when at last he stood on the door-step of the pastorate, waiting for an answer to the tinkle of the electric bell he had heard ring inside, his mind contained only the single thought that now he should hear something about Celia. Perhaps he might even find her there; but he put that suggestion aside as slightly unpleasant.

The hag-faced housekeeper led him, as before, into the dining-room. It was still daylight, and he saw on the glance that the priest was alone at the table, with a book beside him to read from as he ate.

Father Forbes rose and came forward, greeting his visitor with profuse urbanity and smiles. If there was a perfunctory note in the invitation to sit down and share the meal, Theron did not catch it. He frankly displayed his pleasure as he laid aside his hat, and took the chair opposite his host.

"It is really only a few months since I was here, in this room, before," he remarked, as the priest closed his book and tossed it to one side, and the housekeeper came in to lay another place. "Yet it might have been years, many long years, so tremendous is the difference that the lapse of time has wrought in me."

"I am afraid we have nothing to tempt you very much, Mr. Ware," remarked Father Forbes, with a gesture of his plump white hand which embraced the dishes in the centre of the table. "May I send you a bit of this boiled mutton? I have very homely tastes when I am by myself."

"I was saying," Theron observed, after some moments had passed in silence, "that I date such a tremendous revolution in my thoughts, my beliefs, my whole mind and character, from my first meeting with you, my first coming here. I don't know how to describe to you the enormous change that has come over me; and I owe it all to you."

"I can only hope, then, that it is entirely of a satisfactory nature," said the priest, politely smiling.

"Oh, it is so splendidly satisfactory!" said Theron, with fervor. "I look back at myself now with wonder and pity. It seems incredible that, such a little while ago, I should have been such an ignorant and unimaginative clod of earth, content with such petty ambitions and actually proud of my limitations."

"And you have larger ambitions now?" asked the other. "Pray let me help you to some potatoes.[1] I am afraid that ambitions only get in our way and trip us up. We clergymen are like street-car horses. The more steadily we jog along between the rails, the better it is for us."

"Oh, I don't intend to remain in the ministry," declared Theron. The statement seemed to him a little bald, now that he had made it; and as his companion lifted his brows in surprise, he added stumblingly: "That is, as I feel now, it seems to me impossible that I should remain much longer. With you, of course, it is different. You have a thousand things to interest and pleasantly occupy you in your work and its ceremonies, so that mere belief or non-belief in the dogma hardly matters. But in our church dogma is everything. If you take that away, or cease to have its support, the rest is intolerable, hideous."

[1] English ed. reads "turnips."

Father Forbes cut another slice of mutton for himself. "It is a pretty serious business to make such a change at your time of life. I take it for granted you will think it all over carefully before you commit yourself." He said this with an almost indifferent air, which rather chilled his listener's enthusiasm.

"Oh, yes," Theron made answer; "I shall do nothing rash. But I have a good many plans for the future."

Father Forbes did not ask what these were, and a brief further period of silence fell upon the table.

"I hope everything went off smoothly at the picnic," Theron ventured, at last. "I have not seen any of you since then."

The priest shook his head and sighed. "No," he said. "It is a bad business. I have had a great deal of unhappiness out of it this past fortnight. That young man who was rude to you — of course it was mere drunken, irresponsible nonsense on his part — has got himself into a serious scrape, I'm afraid. It is being kept quite within the family, and we hope to manage so that it will remain there, but it has terribly upset his father and his sister. But that, after all, is not so hard to bear as the other affliction that has come upon the Maddens. You remember Michael, the other brother? He seems to have taken cold that evening, or perhaps over-excited himself. He has been seized with quick consumption. He will hardly last till snow flies."

"Oh, I *am* grieved to hear that!" Theron spoke with tremulous earnestness. It seemed to him as if Michael were in some way related to him.

"It is very hard upon them all," the priest went on. "Michael is as sweet and holy a character as it is possible for any one to think of. He is the apple of his father's eye. They were inseparable, those two. Do you know the father, Mr. Madden?"

Theron shook his head. "I think I have seen him," he said. "A small man, with gray whiskers."

"A peasant," said Father Forbes, "but with a heart of gold.

Poor man! he has had little enough out of his riches. Ah, the West Coast people, what tragedies I have seen among them over here! They have rudimentary lung organizations, like a frog's, to fit the mild, wet soft air they live in. The sharp air here kills them off like flies in a frost. Whole families go. I should think there are a dozen of old Jeremiah's children in the cemetery. If Michael could have passed his twenty-eighth year, there would have been hope for him, at least till his thirty-fifth. These pulmonary things seem to go by sevens, you know."

"I didn't know," said Theron. "It is very strange — and very sad." His startled mind was busy, all at once, with conjectures as to Celia's age.

"The sister — Miss Madden — seems extremely strong," he remarked tentatively.

"Celia may escape the general doom," said the priest. His guest noted that he clenched his shapely white hand on the table as he spoke, and that his gentle, carefully modulated voice had a gritty hardness in its tone. "*That* would be too dreadful to think of," he added.

Theron shuddered in silence, and strove to shut his mind against the thought.

"She has taken Michael's illness so deeply to heart," the priest proceeded, "and devoted herself to him so untiringly that I get a little nervous about her. I have been urging her to go away and get a change of air and scene, if only for a few days. She does not sleep well, and that is always a bad thing."

"I think I remember her telling me once that sometimes she had sleepless spells," said Theron. "She said that then she banged on her piano at all hours, or dragged the cushions about from room to room, like a wild woman. A very interesting young lady, don't you find her so?"

Father Forbes let a wan smile play on his lips. "What, our Celia?" he said. "Interesting! Why, Mr. Ware, there is no one like her in the world. She is as unique as — what shall I say? — as the Irish are among races. Her father and mother were both born in mud-cabins, and she — she might be the daughter of a hundred kings, except that they seem mostly rather under-witted than otherwise. She always impresses me as a sort of atavistic idealization of the old Kelt at his finest and best. There in Ireland you got a strange mixture of elementary early peoples, walled off from the outer world by the four seas, and free to work out their own racial amalgam on their own lines. They brought with them at the outset a great inheritance of Eastern mysticism. Others lost it, but the Irish, all alone on their island, kept it alive and brooded on it, and rooted their whole spiritual side in it. Their religion is full of it; their blood is full of it; our Celia is fuller of it than anybody else. The Ireland of two thousand years ago is incarnated in her. They are the merriest people and the saddest, the most turbulent and the most docile, the most talented and the most unproductive, the most practical and the most visionary, the most devout and the most pagan. These impossible contradictions war ceaselessly in their blood. When I look at Celia, I seem to see in my mind's eye the fair young ancestral mother of them all."

Theron gazed at the speaker with open admiration. "I love to hear you talk," he said simply.

An unbidden memory flitted upward in his mind. Those were the very words that Alice had so often on her lips in their old courtship days. How curious it was! He looked at the priest, and had a quaint sensation of feeling as a romantic woman must feel in the presence of a specially impressive masculine personality. It was indeed strange that this soft-voiced, portly creature in a gown, with his white, fat hands and his feline suavity of manner, should produce such a commanding and unique effect of virility. No doubt this was a part of the great sex mystery which historically surrounded the figure of the celibate priest as with an atmosphere. Women had always been prostrating themselves before it. Theron, watching his companion's full, pallid face in the lamp-light, tried to fancy himself in the priest's place, looking down upon these worshipping female forms. He wondered what the celibate's attitude really was. The enigma fascinated him.

Father Forbes, after his rhetorical outburst, had been eating. He pushed aside his cheese-plate. "I grow enthusiastic on the subject of my race sometimes," he remarked, with the suggestion of an apology. "But I make up for it other times — most of the time — by scolding them. If it were not such a noble thing to be an Irishman, it would be ridiculous."

"Ah," said Theron, deprecatingly, "who would not be enthusiastic in talking of Miss Madden? What you said about her was perfect. As you spoke, I was thinking how proud and thankful we ought to be for the privilege of knowing her — we who do know her well — although of course your friendship with her is vastly more intimate than mine — than mine could ever hope to be."

The priest offered no comment, and Theron went on: "I hardly know how to describe the remarkable impression she makes upon me. I can't imagine to myself any other young woman so brilliant or broad in her views, or so courageous. Of course, her being so rich makes it easier for her to do just what she wants to do, but her bravery is astonishing all the same. We had a long and very sympathetic talk in the woods, that day of the picnic, after we left you. I don't know whether she spoke to you about it?"

Father Forbes made a movement of the head and eyes which seemed to negative the suggestion.

"Her talk," continued Theron, "gave me quite new ideas of the range and capacity of the female mind. I wonder that everybody in Octavius isn't full of praise and admiration for her talents and exceptional character. In such a small town as this, you would think she would be the centre of attention, — the pride of the place."

"I think she has as much praise as is good for her," remarked the priest, quietly.

"And here's a thing that puzzles me," pursued Mr. Ware.

"I was immensely surprised to find that Dr. Ledsmar doesn't even think she is smart, — or at least he professes the utmost intellectual contempt for her, and says he dislikes her into the bargain. But of course she dislikes him, too, so that's only natural. But I can't understand his denying her great ability."

The priest smiled in a dubious way. "Don't borrow unnecessary alarm about that, Mr. Ware," he said, with studied smoothness of modulated tones. "These two good friends of mine have much enjoyment out of the idea that they are fighting for the mastery over my poor unstable character. It has grown to be a habit with them, and a hobby as well, and they pursue it with tireless zest. There are not many intellectual diversions open to us here, and they make the most of this one. It amuses them, and it is not without its charms for me, in my capacity as an interested observer. It is a part of the game that they should pretend to themselves that they detest each other. In reality I fancy they like each other very much. At any rate, there is nothing to be disturbed about."

His mellifluous tones had somehow the effect of suggesting to Theron that he was an outsider and would better mind his own business. Ah, if this purring pussy-cat of a priest only knew how little of an outsider he really was! The thought gave him an easy self-control.

"Of course," he said, "our warm mutual friendship makes the observation of these little individual vagaries merely a part of a delightful whole. I should not dream of discussing Miss Madden's confidences to me, or the doctor's either, outside our own little group."

Father Forbes reached behind him and took from a chair his black three-cornered cap with the tassel. "Unfortunately I have a sick call waiting me," he said, gathering up his gown and slowly rising.

"Yes, I saw the man sitting in the hall," remarked Theron, getting to his feet.

"I would ask you to go upstairs and wait," the priest went on, "but my return, unhappily, is quite uncertain. Another evening I may be more fortunate. I am leaving town to-morrow for some days,[2] but when I get back —"

The polite sentence did not complete itself. Father Forbes had come out into the hall, giving a cool nod to the working-man, who rose from the bench as they passed, and shook hands with his guest on the doorstep.

When the door had closed upon Mr. Ware, the priest turned to the man. "You have come about those frames," he said. "If you will come upstairs, I will show you the prints, and you can give me a notion of what can be done with them. I rather fancy the idea of a triptych in carved old English, if you can manage it."

After the workman had gone away, Father Forbes put on slippers and an old loose soutane, lighted a cigar, and push-ing an easy-chair over to the reading lamp, sat down with a book. Then something occurred to him, and he touched the house-bell at his elbow.

"Maggie," he said gently, when the housekeeper appeared at the door, "I will have the coffee and *fine* champagne up here, if it is no trouble. And — oh, Maggie — I was compelled this evening to turn the blameless visit of the framemaker into a venial sin, and that[3] involves a needless wear and tear of conscience. I think that — hereafter — you understand? — I am not invariably at home when the Rev. Mr. Ware does me the honor to call."

[2] English ed. reads "I am going to New York tomorrow evening" for "I am leaving town to-morrow for some days."

[3] English ed. reads "such things involve" for "that involves."

CHAPTER XXVII

THAT night brought the first frost of the season worth counting. In the morning, when Theron came downstairs, his casual glance through the window caught a desolate picture of blackened dahlia stalks and shrivelled blooms. The gayety and color of the garden were gone, and in their place was shabby and dishevelled ruin. He flung the sash up and leaned out. The nipping autumn air was good to breathe. He looked about him, surveying the havoc the frost had wrought among the flowers, and smiled.

At breakfast he smiled again, — a mirthless and calculated smile. "I see that Brother Gorringe's flowers have come to grief over night," he remarked.

Alice looked at him before she spoke, and saw on his face a confirmation of the hostile hint in his voice. She nodded in a constrained way, and said nothing.

"Or rather, I should say," Theron went on, with deliberate words, "the late Brother Gorringe's flowers."

"How do you mean — *late*?" asked his wife, swiftly.

"Oh, calm yourself!" replied the husband. "He is not dead. He has only intimated to me his desire to sever his connection. I may add that he did so in a highly offensive manner."

"I am very sorry," said Alice, in a low tone, and with her eyes on her plate.

"I took it for granted you would be grieved at his backsliding," remarked Theron, making his phrases as pointed as he could. "He was such a promising probationer, and you took such a keen interest in his spiritual awakening. But the frost has nipped his zeal, — along with the hundred or more dollars' worth of flowers by which he testified his faith. I find something interesting in their having been blasted simultaneously."

Alice dropped all pretence of interest in her breakfast. With a flushed face and lips tightly compressed, she made a movement as if to rise from her chair. Then, changing her mind, she sat bolt upright and faced her husband.

"I think we had better have this out right now," she said, in a voice which Theron hardly recognized. "You have been hinting round the subject long enough, — too long. There are *some* things nobody is obliged to put up with, and this is one of them. You will oblige me by saying out in so many words what it is you are driving at."

The outburst astounded Theron. He laid down his knife and fork, and gazed at his wife in frank surprise. She had so accustomed him, of late, to a demeanor almost abject in its depressed docility that he had quite forgotten the Alice of the old days, when she had spirit and courage enough for two, and a notable tongue of her own. The flash in her eyes and the lines of resolution about her mouth and chin for a moment daunted him. Then he observed by a flutter of the frill at her wrist that she was trembling.

"I am sure I have nothing to 'say out in so many words,' as you put it," he replied, forcing his voice into cool, impassive tones. "I merely commented upon a coincidence, that was all. If, for any reason under the sun, the subject chances to be unpleasant to you, I have no earthly desire to pursue it."

"But I insist upon having it pursued!" returned Alice. "I've had just all I can stand of your insinuations and innuendoes, and it's high time we had some plain talk. Ever since the revival, you have been dropping sly, underhand hints about Mr. Gorringe and — and me. Now I ask you what you mean by it."

Yes, there was a shake in her voice, and he could see how her bosom heaved in a tremor of nervousness. It was easy for him to be very calm.

"It is you who introduce these astonishing suggestions, not I," he replied coldly. "It is you who couple your name with his, — somewhat to my surprise, I admit, — but let me suggest that we drop the subject. You are excited just now, and you might say things that you would prefer to leave unsaid. It would surely be better for all concerned to say no more about it."

Alice, staring across the table at him with knitted brows, emitted a sharp little snort of indignation. "Well, I never! Theron, I wouldn't have thought it of you!"

"There are so many things you wouldn't have thought, on such a variety of subjects," he observed, with a show of resuming his breakfast. "But why continue? We are only angering each other."

"Never mind that," she replied, with more control over her speech. "I guess things have come to a pass where a little anger won't do any harm. I have a right to insist on knowing what you mean by your insinuations."

Theron sighed. "Why will you keep harping on the thing?" he asked wearily. "I have displayed no curiosity. I don't ask for any explanations. I think I mentioned that the man had behaved insultingly to me, — but that doesn't matter. I don't bring it up as a grievance. I am very well able to take care of myself. I have no wish to recur to the incident in any way. So far as I am concerned, the topic is dismissed."

"Listen to me!" broke in Alice, with eager gravity. She hesitated, as he looked up with a nod of attention, and reflected as well as she was able among her thoughts for a minute or two. "This is what I want to say to you. Ever since we came to this hateful Octavius, you and I have been drifting apart, — or no, that doesn't express it, — simply rushing away from each other. It only began last spring, and now the space between us is so wide that we are worse than complete strangers. For strangers at least don't hate each other, and I've had a good many occasions lately to see that you positively do hate me —"

"What grotesque absurdity!" interposed Theron, impatiently.

"No, it isn't absurdity; it's gospel truth," retorted Alice. "And — don't interrupt me — there have been times, too, when I have had to ask myself if I wasn't getting almost to hate you in return. I tell you this frankly."

"Yes, you are undoubtedly frank," commented the husband, toying with his teaspoon. "A hypercritical person might consider, almost too frank."

Alice scanned his face closely while he spoke, and held her breath as if in expectant suspense. Her countenance clouded once more. "You don't realize, Theron," she said gravely; "your voice when you speak to me, your look, your manner, they have all changed. You are like another man, — some man who never loved me, and doesn't even know me, much less like me. I want to know what the end of it is to be. Up to the time of your sickness last summer, until after the Soulsbys went away, I didn't let myself get down-right discouraged. It seemed too monstrous for belief that you should go away out of my life like that. It didn't seem possible that God could allow such a thing. It came to me that I had been lax in my Christian life, especially in my position as a minister's wife, and that this was my punishment. I went to the altar, to intercede with Him, and to try to loose my burden at His feet. But nothing has come of it. I got no help from you."

"Really, Alice," broke in Theron, "I explained over and over again to you how preoccupied I was — with the book — and affairs generally."

"I got no assistance from Heaven either," she went on declining the diversion he offered. "I don't want to talk impiously, but if there is a God, he has forgotten me, his poor heart-broken hand-maiden."

"You *are* talking impiously, Alice," observed her husband. "And you are doing me cruel injustice, into the bargain."

"I only wish I were!" she replied; "I only wish to God I were!"

"Well, then, accept my complete assurance that you are, — that your whole conception of me, and of what you are pleased to describe as my change toward you, is an entire and utter mistake. Of course, the married state is no more exempt from the universal law of growth, development, alteration, than any other human institution. On its spiritual side, of course, viewed either as a sacrament, or as —"

"Don't let us go into that," interposed Alice, abruptly. "In fact, there is no good in talking any more at all. It is as if we didn't speak the same language. You don't understand what I say; it makes no impression upon your mind."

"Quite to the contrary," he assured her; "I have been deeply interested and concerned in all you have said. I think you are laboring under a great delusion, and I have tried my best to convince you of it; but I have never heard you speak more intelligibly or, I might say, effectively."

A little gleam of softness stole over Alice's face. "If you only gave me a little more credit for intelligence," she said, "you would find that I am not such a blockhead as you think I am."

"Come, come!" he said, with a smiling show of impatience. "You really mustn't impute things to me wholesale, like that."

She was glad to answer the smile in kind. "No; but truly," she pleaded, "you don't realize it, but you have grown into a way of treating me as if I had absolutely no mind at all."

"You have a very admirable mind," he responded, and took up his teaspoon again. She reached for his cup, and poured out hot coffee for him. An almost cheerful spirit had suddenly descended upon the breakfast table.

"And now let me say the thing I have been aching to say for months," she began, in a less burdened voice.

He lifted his brows. "Haven't things been discussed pretty fully already?" he asked.

The doubtful, harassed expression clouded upon her face at his words, and she paused. "No," she said resolutely, after an instant's reflection; "it is my duty to discuss this, too. It is a misunderstanding all round. You remember that I told you Mr. Gorringe had given me some plants, which he got from some garden or other?"

"If you really wish to go on with the subject — yes — I have a recollection of that particular falsehood of his."

"He did it with the kindest and friendliest motives in the world!" protested Alice. "He saw how down-in-the-mouth and moping I was here, among these strangers, — and I really was getting quite peaked and run-down, — and he said I stayed indoors too much, and it would do me all sorts of good to work in the garden, and he would send me some plants. The next I knew, here they were, with a book about mixing soils and planting, and so on. When I saw him next, and thanked him, I suppose I showed some apprehension about his having laid out money on them, and he, just to ease my mind, invented the story about his getting them for nothing. When I found out the truth — I got it out of that boy, Harvey Semple — he admitted it quite frankly, — said he was wrong to deceive me."

"This was in the fine first fervor of his term of probation, I suppose," put in Theron. He made no effort to dissemble the sneer in his voice.

"Well," answered Alice, with a touch of acerbity, "I have told you now, and it is off my mind. There never would have been the slightest concealment about it, if you hadn't begun by keeping me at arm's length, and making it next door to impossible to speak to you at all, and if —"

"And if he hadn't lied." Theron, as he finished her sentence for her, rose from the table. Dallying [1] for a brief moment by his chair, there seemed the magnetic premonition in the air of some further and kindlier word. Then he turned and walked sedately into the next room, and closed the door behind him. The talk was finished; and Alice, left alone, passed the knuckle of her thumb over one swimming eye and then the other, and bit her lips and swallowed down the sob that rose in her throat.

[1] English ed. reads "He dallied" for "Dallying."

CHAPTER XXVIII

It was early afternoon when Theron walked out of his yard, bestowing no glance upon the withered and tarnished show of the garden, and started with a definite step down the street. The tendency to ruminative loitering, which those who saw him abroad always associated with his tall, spare [1] figure, was not suggested to-day. He moved forward like a man with a purpose.

All the forenoon in the seclusion of the sitting-room, with a book opened before him, he had been thinking hard. It was not the talk with Alice that occupied his thoughts. That rose in his mind from time to time, only as a disagreeable blur, and he refused to dwell upon it. It was nothing to him, he said to himself, what Gorringe's motives in lying had been. As for Alice, he hardened his heart against her. Just now it was her mood to try and make up to him. But it had been something different yesterday, and who could say what it would be to-morrow? He really had passed the limit of patience with her shifting emotional vagaries, now lurching in this direction, now in that. She had had her chance to maintain a hold upon his interest and imagination, and had let it slip. These were the accidents of life, the inevitable harsh happenings in the great tragedy of Nature. They could not be helped, and there was nothing more to be said.

He had bestowed much more attention upon what the priest had said the previous evening. He passed in review all the glowing tributes Father Forbes had paid to Celia. They warmed his senses as he recalled them, but they also, in a curious, indefinite way, caused him uneasiness. There had been a personal fervor about them which was something more than priestly. He remembered how the priest had

---

[1] English ed. omits "spare."

turned pale and faltered when the question whether Celia would escape the general doom of her family came up. It was not a merely pastoral agitation that, he felt sure.

A hundred obscure hints, doubts, stray little suspicions, crowded upward together in his thoughts. It became apparent to him now that from the outset he had been conscious of something queer, — yes, from that very first day when he saw the priest and Celia together, and noted their glance of recognition inside the house of death. He realized now, upon reflection, that the tone of other people, his own parishioners and his casual acquaintances in Octavius alike, had always had a certain note of reservation in it when it touched upon Miss Madden. Her running in and out of the pastorate at all hours, the way the priest patted her on the shoulder before others, the obvious dislike the priest's ugly old housekeeper bore her, the astonishing freedom of their talk with each other, — these dark memories loomed forth out of a mass of sinister conjecture.

He could bear the uncertainty no longer. Was it indeed not entirely his own fault that it had existed thus long? No man with the spirit of a mouse would have shilly-shallied in this preposterous fashion, week after week, with the fever of a beautiful woman's kiss in his blood, and the woman herself living only round the corner. The whole world had been as good as offered to him, — a bewildering world of wealth and beauty and spiritual exaltation and love, — and he, like a weak fool, had waited for it to be brought to him on a salver, as it were, and actually forced upon his acceptance! "That is my failing," he reflected; "these miserable ecclesiastical bandages of mine have dwarfed my manly side. The meanest of Thurston's clerks would have shown a more adventurous spirit and a bolder nerve. If I do not act at once, with courage and resolution, everything will be lost. Already she must think me unworthy of the honor it was in her sweet will to bestow." Then he remembered that she was now always at home. "Not another hour of foolish indecision!" he whispered to himself. " I will put my destiny to the test. I will see her to-day!"

A middle-aged, plain-faced servant answered his ring at the door-bell of the Madden mansion. She was palpably Irish, and looked at him with a saddened preoccupation in her gray eyes, holding the door only a little ajar.

Theron had got out one of his cards. "I wish to make inquiry about young Mr. Madden, — Mr. Michael Madden," he said, holding the card forth tentatively: "I have only just heard of his illness, and it has been a great grief to me."

"He is no better," answered the woman, briefly.

"I am the Rev. Mr. Ware," he went on, "and you may say that, if he is well enough, I should be glad to see him."

The servant peered out at him with a suddenly altered expression, then shook her head. "I don't think he would be wishing to see *you*," she replied. It was evident from her tone that she suspected the visitor's intentions.

Theron smiled in spite of himself. "I have not come as a clergyman," he explained, "but as a friend of the family. If you will tell Miss Madden that I am here, it will do just as well. Yes, we won't bother him. If you will kindly hand my card to his sister."

When the domestic turned at this and went in, Theron felt like throwing his hat in the air, there where he stood. The woman's churlish sectarian prejudices had played ideally into his hands. In no other imaginable way could he have asked for Celia so naturally. He wondered a little that a servant at such a grand house as this should leave callers standing on the doorstep. Still more he wondered what he should say to the lady of his dreams when he came into her presence.

"Will you please to walk this way?" The woman had returned. She closed the door noiselessly behind him, and led the way, not up the sumptuous staircase, as Theron had expected, but along through the broad hall, past several large doors, to a small curtained archway at the end. She pushed aside this curtain,[2] and Theron found himself in a sort of conservatory, full of the hot, vague light of sunshine falling through ground-glass. The air was moist and close, and heavy with the smell of verdure and wet earth. A tall bank of palms, with ferns sprawling at their base, reared itself directly in front of him. The floor was of mosaic, and he saw now that there were rugs upon it, and that there were chairs and sofas, and other signs of habitation. It was, indeed, only half a greenhouse, for the lower part of it was in rosewood panels, with floral paintings on them, like a room.

Moving to one side of the barrier of palms, he discovered, to his great surprise, the figure of Michael, sitting propped up with pillows in a huge easy-chair. The sick man was looking at him with big, gravely intent eyes. His face did not show as much change as Theron had in fancy pictured. It had seemed almost as bony and cadaverous on the day of the picnic. The hands spread out on the chair-arms were very white and thin, though, and the gaze in the blue eyes had a spectral quality which disturbed him.

Michael raised his right hand, and Theron, stepping forward, took it limply in his for an instant. Then he laid it down again. The touch of people about to die had always been repugnant to him. He could feel on his own warm palm the very damp of the grave.

"I only heard from Father Forbes last evening of your — your ill-health," he said, somewhat hesitatingly. He seated himself on a bench beneath the palms, facing the invalid, but still holding his hat. "I hope very sincerely that you will soon be all right again."

"My sister is lying down in her room," answered Michael. He had not taken his sombre and embarrassing gaze from the other's face. The voice in which he uttered this uncalled-for remark was thin in fibre, cold and impassive. It fell upon Theron's ears with a suggestion of hidden meaning. He looked uneasily into Michael's eyes, and then away again. They

[2] English ed. reads "portière" for "curtain."

seemed to be looking straight through him, and there was no shirking the sensation that they saw and comprehended things with an unnatural prescience.

"I hope she is feeling better," Theron found himself saying. "Father Forbes mentioned that she was a little under the weather. I dined with him last night."

"I am glad that you came," said Michael, after a little pause. His earnest, unblinking eyes seemed to supplement his tongue with speech of their own. "I do be thinking a great deal about you. I have matters to speak of to you, now that you are here."

Theron bowed his head gently, in token of grateful attention. He tried the experiment of looking away from Michael, but his glance went back again irresistibly, and fastened itself upon the sick man's gaze, and clung there.

"I am next door to a dead man," he went on, paying no heed to the other's deprecatory gesture. "It is not years or months with me, but weeks. Then I go away to stand up for judgment on my sins, and [3] if it is His merciful will, I shall see God. So I say my good-byes now, and so you will let me speak plainly, and not think ill of what I say. You are much changed, Mr. Ware, since you came to Octavius, and it is not a change for the good."

Theron lifted his brows in unaffected surprise, and put inquiry into his glance.

"I don't know if Protestants will be saved, in God's good time, or not," continued Michael. "I find there are different opinions among the clergy about that, and of course it is not for me, only a plain mechanic, to be sure where learned and pious scholars are in doubt. But I am sure about one thing. Those Protestants, and others too, mind you, who profess and preach good deeds, and themselves do bad deeds, — they will never be saved. They will have no chance at all to escape hell-fire."

"I think we are all agreed upon that, Mr. Madden," said Theron, with surface suavity.

[3] English ed. adds "some time."

"Then I say to you, Mr. Ware, you are yourself in a bad path. Take the warning of a dying man, sir, and turn from it!"

The impulse to smile tugged at Theron's facial muscles. This was really too droll. He looked up at the ceiling, the while he forced his countenance into a polite composure, then turned again to Michael, with some conciliatory commonplace ready for utterance. But he said nothing, and all suggestion of levity left his mind, under the searching inspection bent upon him by the young man's hollow eyes. What did Michael suspect? What did he know? What was he hinting at, in this strange talk of his?

"I saw you often on the street when first you came here," continued Michael. "I knew the man who was here before you, — that is, by sight, — and he was not a good man. But your face, when you came, pleased me. I liked to look at you. I was tormented just then, do you see, that so many decent, kindly people, old school-mates and friends and neighbors of mine, — and, for that matter, others all over the country — must lose their souls because they were Protestants. All my boyhood and young manhood, that thought took the joy out of me. Sometimes I usen't to sleep a whole night long, for thinking that some lad I had been playing with, perhaps in his own house, that very day, would be taken when he died, and his mother too, when she died, and thrown into the flames of hell for all eternity. It made me so unhappy that finally I wouldn't go to any Protestant boy's house, and have his mother be nice to me, and give me cake and apples, — and me thinking all the while that they were bound to be damned, no matter how good they were to me."

The primitive humanity of this touched Theron, and he nodded approbation with a tender smile in his eyes, forgetting for a moment that a personal application of the monologue had been hinted at.

"But then later, as I grew up," the sick man went on, "I learned that it was not altogether certain. Some of the authorities, I found, maintained that it was doubtful, and some said openly that there must be salvation possible for good people who lived in ignorance of the truth through no fault of their own. Then I had hope one day, and no hope the next, and as I did my work I thought it over, and in the evenings my father and I talked it over, and we settled nothing of it at all. Of course, how could we?"

"Did you ever discuss the question with your sister?" it occurred suddenly to Theron to interpose. He was conscious of some daring in doing so, and he fancied that Michael's drawn face clouded a little at his words.

"My sister is no theologian," he answered briefly. "Women have no call to meddle with such matters. But I was saying — it was in the middle of these doubtings of mine that you came here to Octavius, and I noticed you on the streets, and once in the evening — I made no secret of it to my people — I sat in the back of your church and heard you preach. As I say, I liked you. It was your face, and what I thought it showed of the man underneath it, that helped settle my mind more than anything else. I said to myself: 'Here is a young man, only about my own age, and he has education and talents, and he does not seek to make money for himself, or a great name, but he is content to live humbly on the salary of a book-keeper, and devote all his time to prayer and the meditation of his religion, and preaching, and visiting the sick and the poor, and comforting them. His very face is a pleasure and a help for those in suffering and trouble to look at. The very sight of it makes one believe in pure thoughts and merciful deeds. I will not credit it that God intends damning such a man as that, or any like him!'"

Theron bowed, with a slow, hesitating gravity of manner, and deep, not wholly complacent, attention on his face. Evidently all this was by way of preparation for something unpleasant.

"That was only last spring," said Michael. His tired voice sank for a sentence or two into a meditative half-whisper. "And it was *my* last spring of all. I shall not be growing weak any more, or drawing hard breaths, when the first warm weather comes. It will be one season to me hereafter, always the same." He lifted his voice with perceptible effort. "I am talking too much. The rest I can say in a word. Only half a year has gone by, and you have another face on you entirely. I had noticed the small changes before, one by one. I saw the great change, all of a sudden, the day of the picnic. I see it a hundred times more now, as you sit there. If it seemed to me like the face of a saint before, it is more like the face of a bar-keeper now!"

This was quite too much. Theron rose, flushed to the temples, and scowled down at the helpless man in the chair. He swallowed the sharp words which came uppermost, and bit and moistened his lips as he forced himself to remember that this was a dying man, and Celia's brother, to whom she was devoted, and whom he himself felt he wanted to be very fond of. He got the shadow of a smile on to his countenance.

"I fear you have tired yourself unduly," he said, in as non-contentious a tone as he could manage. He even contrived a little deprecatory laugh. "I am afraid your real quarrel is with the air of Octavius. It agrees with me so wonderfully, — I am getting as fat as a seal. But I do hope I am not paying for it by such a wholesale deterioration inside. If my own opinion could be of any value, I should assure you that I feel myself an infinitely better and broader and stronger man than I was when I came here."

Michael shook his head dogmatically. "That is the greatest pity of all," he said, with renewed earnestness. "You are entirely deceived about yourself. You do not at all realize how you have altered your direction, or where you are going. It was a great misfortune for you, sir, that you did not keep among your own people. That poor half-brother of mine, though the drink was in him when he said that same to you, never spoke a truer word. Keep among your own people, Mr. Ware! When you go among others — you know what I mean [4] — you have no proper understanding of what their sayings and doings really mean. You do not realize that they are held up by the power of the true Church, as a little child

[4] English ed. reads "refer to" for "mean."

learning to walk is held up with a belt by its nurse. They can say and do things, and no harm at all come to them, which would mean destruction to you, because they have help, and you are walking alone. And so be said by me, Mr. Ware! Go back to the way you were brought up in, and leave alone the people whose ways are different from yours. You are a married man, and you are the preacher of a religion, such as it is. There can be nothing better for you than to go and strive to be a good husband, and to set a good example to the people of your Church, who look up to you — and mix yourself up no more with outside people and outside notions that only do you mischief. And that is what I wanted to say to you."

Theron took up his hat. "I take in all kindness what you have felt it your duty to say to me, Mr. Madden," he said. "I am not sure that I have altogther followed you, but I am very sure you mean it well."

"I mean well by you," replied Michael, wearily moving his head on the pillow, and speaking in an undertone of languor and pain, "and I mean well by others, that are nearer to me, and that I have a right to care more about. When a man lies by the side of his open grave, he does not be meaning ill to any human soul."

"Yes — thanks — quite so!" faltered Theron. He dallied for an instant with the temptation to seek some further explanation, but the sight of Michael's half-closed eyes and worn-out expression decided him against it. It did not seem to be expected, either, that he should shake hands, and with a few perfunctory words of hope for the invalid's recovery, which fell with a jarring note of falsehood upon his own ears, he turned and left the room. As he did so, Michael touched a bell on the table beside him.

Theron drew a long breath in the hall, as the curtain fell behind him. It was an immense relief to escape from the oppressive humidity and heat of the flower-room, and from that ridiculous bore of a Michael as well.

The middle-aged, grave-faced servant, warned by the bell, stood waiting to conduct him to the door.

"I am sorry to have missed Miss Madden," he said to her. "She must be quite worn out. Perhaps later in the day —"

"She will not be seeing anybody to-day," [5] returned the woman. "She is going to New York this evening, and she is taking some rest against the journey."

"Will she be away long?" he asked mechanically. The servant's answer, "I have no idea," hardly penetrated his consciousness at all.

He moved down the steps, and along the gravel to the street, in a maze of mental confusion. When he reached the sidewalk, under the familiar elms, he paused, and made a definite effort to pull his thoughts together, and take stock of what had happened, of what was going to happen; but the thing baffled him. It was as if some drug had stupefied his faculties.

He began to walk, and gradually saw that what he was thinking about [6] was the fact of Celia's departure for New York that evening. He stared at this fact, at first in its nakedness, then clothed with reassuring suggestions that this was no doubt a trip she very often made. There was a blind sense of comfort in this idea, and he rested himself upon it. Yes, of course, she travelled a great deal. New York must be as familiar to her as Octavius was to him. Her going there now was quite a matter of course, — the most natural thing in the world.

Then there burst suddenly uppermost in his mind the other fact, — that Father Forbes was also going to New York that evening. The two things spindled upward, side by side, yet separately, in his mental vision; then they twisted and twined themselves together. He followed their convolutions miserably, walking as if his eyes were shut.

In slow fashion matters defined and arranged themselves

---

[5] English ed. reads "the day" for "to-day."

[6] English ed. reads "his mind stumbled at" for "he was thinking about."

before him. The process of tracing their sequence was all torture, but there was no possibility, no notion, of shirking any detail of the pain. The priest had spoken of his efforts to persuade Celia to go away for a few days, for rest and change of air and scene. He must have known only too well that she was going, but of that he had been careful to drop no hint. The possibility of accident was too slight to be worth considering. People on such intimate terms as Celia and the priest — people with such facilities for seeing each other whenever they desired — did not find themselves on the same train of cars, with the same long journey in view, by mere chance.

Theron walked until dusk began to close in upon the autumn day. It grew colder, as he turned his face homeward. He wondered if it would freeze again over-night, and then remembered the shrivelled flowers in his wife's garden. For a moment they shaped themselves in a picture before his mind's eye; he saw their blackened foliage, their sicklied, drooping stalks, and wilted blooms, and as he looked, they restored themselves to the vigor and grace and richness of color of summer-time, as vividly as if they had been painted on a canvas. Or no, the picture he stared at was not on canvas, but on the glossy, varnished panel of a luxurious sleeping-car. He shook his head angrily and blinked his eyes again and again, to prevent their seeing, seated together in the open window above this panel, the two people he knew were there, gloved and habited for the night's journey, waiting for the train to start.

.   .   .   .   .

"Very much to my surprise," he found himself saying to Alice, watching her nervously as she laid the supper-table, "I find I must go to Albany to-night. That is, it isn't absolutely necessary, for that matter, but I think it may easily turn out to be greatly to my advantage to go. Something has arisen — I can't speak about it as yet — but the sooner I see the Bishop about it the better. Things like that occur in a man's life, where boldly striking out a line of action, and following it up without an instant's delay, may make all the difference in the world to him. To-morrow it might be too late; and, besides, I can be home the sooner again."

Alice's face showed surprise, but no trace of suspicion. She spoke with studied amiability during the meal, and deferred with such unexpected tact to his implied desire not to be questioned as to the mysterious motives of the journey, that his mood instinctively softened and warmed toward her, as they finished supper.

He smiled a little. "I do hope I sha'n't have to go on to-morrow to New York; but these Bishops of ours are such gad-abouts one never knows where to catch them. As like as not Sanderson may be down in New York, on Book-Concern business or something; and if he is, I shall have to chase him up. But, after all, perhaps the trip will do me good, — the change of air and scene, you know."

"I'm sure I hope so," said Alice, honestly enough. "If you do go on to New York, I suppose you'll go by the river-boat. Everybody talks so much of that beautiful sail down the Hudson."

"That's an idea!" exclaimed Theron, welcoming it with enthusiasm. "It hadn't occurred to me. If I do have to go, and it is as lovely as they make out, the next time I promise I won't go without you, my girl. I *have* been rather out of sorts lately," he continued. "When I come back, I daresay I shall be feeling better, more like my old self. Then I'm going to try, Alice, to be nicer to you than I have been of late. I'm afraid there was only too much truth in what you said this morning."

"Never mind what I said this morning — or any other time," broke in Alice, softly. "Don't ever remember it again, Theron, if only — only —"

He rose as she spoke, moved round the table to where she sat, and, bending over her, stopped the faltering sentence with a kiss. When was it, he wondered, that he had last kissed her? It seemed years, ages, ago.

An hour later, with hat and overcoat on, and his valise in his hand, he stood on the doorstep of the parsonage, and kissed her once more before he turned and descended into the darkness. He felt like whistling as his feet sounded firmly on the plank sidewalk beyond the gate. It seemed as if he had never been in such capital good spirits before in his life.

CHAPTER XXIX

THE train was at a standstill somewhere, and the dull, ashen beginnings of daylight had made a first feeble start toward effacing the lamps in the car-roof, when the new day opened for Theron. A man who had just come in stopped at the seat upon which he had been stretched through the night, and, tapping him brusquely on the knee, said, "I'm afraid I must trouble you, sir." After a moment of sleep-burdened confusion, he sat up, and the man took the other half of the seat and opened a newspaper, still damp from the press. It was morning, then.

Theron rubbed a clear space upon the clouded window with his thumb, and looked out. There was nothing to be seen but a broad stretch of tracks, and beyond this the shadowed outlines of wagons and machinery in a yard, with a background of factory buildings.

The atmosphere in the car was vile beyond belief. He thought of opening the window, but feared that the peremptory-looking man with the paper, who had wakened him and made him sit up, might object. They were the only people in the car who were sitting up. Backwards and forwards, on either side of the narrow aisle, the dim light disclosed recumbent forms, curled uncomfortably into corners, or sprawling at difficult angles which involved the least interference with one another. Here and there an upturned face gave a livid patch of surface for the mingled play of the gray dawn and the yellow lamp-light. A ceaseless noise of snoring was in the air.

He got up and walked to the tank of ice-water at the end of the aisle, and took a drink from the most inaccessible portion of the common tin-cup's rim. The happy idea of going out on the platform struck him, and he acted upon it. The morning air was deliciously cool and fresh by contrast, and he filled his lungs with it again and again. Standing here, he could discern beyond the buildings to the right the faint purplish outlines of great rounded hills. Some workmen, one of them bearing a torch, were crouching along under the side of the train, pounding upon the resonant wheels with small hammers. He recalled having heard the same sound in the watches of the night, during a prolonged halt. Some one had said it was Albany. He smiled in spite of himself at the thought that Bishop Sanderson would never know about the visit he had missed.

Swinging himself to the ground, he bent sidewise and looked forward down the long train. There were five, six, perhaps more, sleeping-cars on in front. Which one of them, he wondered — and then there came the sharp "All aboard!" from the other side, and he bundled up the steps again, and entered the car as the train slowly resumed its progress.

He was wide-awake now, and quite at his ease. He took his seat, and diverted himself by winking gravely at a little child facing him on the next seat but one. There were four other children in the family party, encamped about the tired and still sleeping mother whose back was turned to Theron. He recalled now having noticed this poor woman last night, in the first stage of his journey, — how she fed her brood from one of the numerous baskets piled under their feet, and brought water in a tin dish of her own from the tank to use in washing their faces with a rag, and loosened their clothes to dispose them for the night's sleep. The face of the woman, her manner and slatternly aspect, and the general effect of her belongings, bespoke squalid ignorance and poverty. Watching her, Theron had felt curiously interested in the performance. In one sense, it was scarcely more human than the spectacle of a cat licking her kittens, or a cow giving suck to her calf. Yet, in another, was there anything more human?

The child who had wakened before the rest regarded him with placidity, declining to be amused by his winkings, but exhibiting no other emotion. She had been playing by herself with a couple of buttons tied on a string, and after giving a civil amount of attention to Theron's grimaces, she turned again to the superior attractions of this toy. Her self-possession, her capacity for self-entertainment, the care she took not to arouse the others, all impressed him very much. He felt in his pocket for a small coin, and, reaching forward, offered it to her. She took it calmly, bestowed a tranquil gaze upon him for a moment, and went back to the buttons. Her indifference produced an unpleasant sensation upon him somehow, and he rubbed the steaming window clear again, and stared out of it.

The wide river lay before him, flanked by a precipitous wall of cliffs which he knew instantly must be the Palisades. There was an advertisement painted on them which he tried in vain to read. He was surprised to find they interested him so slightly. He had heard all his life of the Hudson, and especially of it just at this point. The reality seemed to him almost commonplace. His failure to be thrilled depressed him for the moment.

"I suppose those *are* the Palisades?" he asked his neighbor.

The man glanced up from his paper, nodded, and made as if to resume his reading. But his eye had caught something in the prospect through the window which arrested his attention. "By George!" he exclaimed, and lifted himself to get a clearer view.

"What is it?" asked Theron, peering forth as well.

"Nothing; only Barclay Wendover's yacht is still there. There's been a hitch of some sort. They were to have left yesterday."

"Is that it, — that long black thing?" queried Theron. "That can't be a yacht, can it?"

"What do you think it is?" answered the other. They were looking at a slim, narrow hull, lying at anchor, silent and motionless on the drab expanse of water. "If that ain't a yacht, they haven't begun building any yet. They're taking her over to the Mediterranean for a cruise, you know, — around India and Japan for the winter, and home by the

South Sea Islands. Friend o' mine's in the party. Wouldn't mind the trip myself."

"But do you mean to say," asked Theron, "that that little shell of a thing can sail across the ocean? Why, how many people would she hold?"

The man laughed. "Well," he said, "there's room for two sets of quadrilles in the chief saloon, if the rest keep their legs well up on the sofas. But there's only ten or a dozen in the party this time. More than that rather get in one another's way, especially with so many ladies on board."

Theron asked no more questions, but bent his head to see the last of this wonderful craft. The sight of it, and what he had heard about it, suddenly gave point and focus to his thoughts. He knew at last what it was that had lurked, formless and undesignated, these many days in the background of his dreams. The picture rose in his mind now of Celia as the mistress of a yacht. He could see her reclining in a low easy-chair upon the polished deck, with the big white sails billowing behind her, and the sun shining upon the deep blue waves, and glistening through the splash of spray in the air, and weaving a halo of glowing gold about her fair head. Ah, how the tender visions crowded now upon him! Eternal summer basked round this enchanted yacht of his fancy, — summer sought now in Scottish firths or Norwegian fiords, now in quaint old Southern harbors, ablaze with the hues of strange costumes and half-tropical flowers and fruits, now in far away Oriental bays and lagoons, or among the coral reefs and palm-trees of the luxurious Pacific. He dwelt upon these new imaginings with the fervent [1] longing of an inland-born boy. Every vague yearning he had ever felt toward salt-water stirred again in his blood at the thought of the sea — with Celia.

Why not? She had never visited any foreign land. "Some-time," she had said, "sometime, no doubt I will." He could hear again the wistful, musing tone of her voice. The thought

[1] English ed. reads "fervid" for "fervent."

had fascinations for her, it was clear. How irresistibly would it not appeal to her, presented with the added charm of a roving, vagrant independence on the high seas, free to speed in her snow-winged chariot wherever she willed over the deep, loitering in this place, or up-helm-and-away to another, with no more care or weight of responsibility than the gulls tossing through the air in her wake!

Theron felt, rather than phrased to himself, that there would not be "ten or a dozen in the party" on that yacht. Without defining anything in his mind, he breathed in fancy the same bold ocean breeze which filled the sails, and toyed with Celia's hair; he looked with her as she sat by the rail, and saw the same waves racing past, the same vast dome of cloud and ether that were mirrored in her brown eyes, and there was no one else anywhere near them. Even the men in sailors' clothes, who would be pulling at ropes, or climbing up tarred ladders, kept themselves considerably outside the picture. Only Celia sat there, and at her feet, gazing up again into her face as in the forest, the man whose whole being had been consecrated to her service, her worship, by the kiss.

"You've passed it now. I was trying to point out the Jumel house to you, — where Aaron Burr lived, you know."

Theron roused himself from his day-dream, and nodded with a confused smile at his neighbor. "Thanks," he faltered; "I didn't hear you. The train makes such a noise, and I must have been dozing."

He looked about him. The night aspect, as of a tramps' lodging-house, had quite disappeared from the car. Everybody was sitting up; and the more impatient were beginning to collect their bundles and hand-bags from the racks and floor. An expressman came through, jangling a huge bunch of brass checks on leathern thongs over his arm, and held parley with passengers along the aisle. Outside, citified streets, with stores and factories, were alternating in the moving panorama with open fields; and, even as he looked, these vacant spaces ceased altogether, and successive regular lines of pavement, between two tall rows of houses all alike, began to stretch out, wheel to the right, and swing off out of view, for all the world like the avenues of hop-poles he remembered as a boy. Then [2] was a long tunnel, its darkness broken at stated intervals by brief bursts of daylight from overhead, and out of this all at once the train drew up its full length in some vast, vaguely lighted enclosure, and stopped.

"Yes, this is New York," said the man, folding up his paper, and springing to his feet. The narrow aisle was filled with many others who had been prompter still; and Theron stood, bag in hand, waiting till this energetic throng should have pushed itself bodily past him forth from the car. Then he himself made his way out, drifting with a sense of helplessness in their resolute wake. There rose in his mind the sudden conviction that he would be too late. All the passengers in the forward sleepers would be gone before he could get there. Yet even this terror gave him no new power to get ahead of anybody else in the tightly packed throng.

Once on the broad platform, the others started off briskly; they all seemed to know just where they wanted to go, and to feel that no instant of time was to be lost in getting there. Theron himself caught some of this urgent spirit, and hurled himself along in the throng with reckless haste, knocking his bag against peoples' legs, but never pausing for apology or comment until he found himself abreast of the locomotive at the head of the train. He drew aside from the main current here, and began searching the platform, far and near, for those he had travelled so far to find.

The platform emptied itself. Theron lingered on in puzzled hesitation, and looked about him. In the whole immense station, with its acres of tracks and footways, and its incessantly shifting processions of people, there was visible nobody else who seemed also in doubt, or who appeared cap-

[2] English ed. reads "there" for "then."

able of sympathizing with indecision in any form. Another train came in, some way over to the right, and before it had fairly stopped, swarms of eager men began boiling out of each end of each car, literally precipitating themselves over one another, it seemed to Theron, in their excited dash down the steps. As they caught their footing below, they started racing pell-mell down the platform to its end; there he saw them, looking more than ever like clustered bees in the distance, struggling vehemently in a dense mass up a staircase in the remote corner of the building.

"What are those folks running for? Is there a fire?" he asked an amiable-faced young mulatto, in the uniform of the sleeping car-service, who passed him with some light hand-bags.

"No; they's Harlem people, I guess — jes' catchin' the Elevated — that's all, sir," he answered obligingly.

At the moment some passengers emerged slowly from one of the sleeping-cars, and came loitering [3] toward him.

"Why, are there people still in these cars?" he asked eagerly. "Haven't they all gone?"

"Some has; some ain't," the porter replied. "They most generally take their time about it. They ain't no hurry, so long's they get out 'fore we're drawn round to the drill-yard."

There was still hope, then. Theron took up his bag and walked forward, intent upon finding some place from which he could watch unobserved the belated stragglers issuing from the sleeping-cars. He started back all at once, confronted by a semi-circle of violent men with whips and badges, who stunned his hearing by a sudden vociferous outburst of shouts and yells. They made furious gestures at him with their whips and fists, to enforce the incoherent babel of their voices; and in these gestures, as in their faces and cries, there seemed a great deal of menace and very little invitation. There was a big policeman sauntering near by, and Theron got the idea that it was his presence alone which

[3] English ed. reads "walked in a leisurely way" for "came loitering."

protected him from open violence at the hands of these savage hack-men. He tightened his clutch on his valise, and, turning his back on them and their uproar, tried to brave it out and stand where he was. But the policeman came lounging slowly toward him, with such authority in his swaying gait, and such urban omniscience written all over his broad, sandy face, that he lost heart, and beat an abrupt retreat off to the right, where there were a number of doorways, near which other people had ventured to put down baggage on the floor.

Here, somewhat screened from observation, he stood for a long time, watching at odd moments the ceaselessly varying phases of the strange scene about him, but always keeping an eye on the train he had himself arrived in. It was slow and dispiriting work. A dozen times his heart failed him, and he said to himself mournfully that he had had his journey for nothing. Then some new figure would appear, alighting from the steps of a sleeper, and hope revived in his breast.

At last, when over half an hour of expectancy had been marked off by the big clock overhead, his suspense came to an end. He saw Father Forbes' erect and substantial form, standing on the car platform nearest of all, balancing himself with his white hands on the rails, waiting for something. Then after a little he came down, followed by a black porter, whose arms were burdened by numerous bags and parcels. The two stood a minute or so more in hesitation at the side of the steps. Then Celia descended, and the three advanced.

The importance of not being discovered was uppermost in Theron's mind, now that he saw them actually coming toward him. He had avoided this the previous evening, in the Octavius depot, with some skill, he flattered himself. It gave him a pleasurable sense of being a man of affairs, almost a detective, to be confronted by the necessity now of baffling observation once again. He was still rather without plans for keeping them in view, once they left the station. He had supposed that he would be able to hear what hotel they directed their driver to take them to, and, failing that, he had fostered a notion, based upon a story he had read when a boy, of throwing himself into another carriage, and bidding his driver to pursue them in hot haste, and on his life not fail to track them down. These devices seemed somewhat empty, now that the urgent moment was at hand; and as he drew back behind some other loiterers, out of view, he sharply racked his wits for some way of coping with this most pressing problem.

It turned out, however, that there was no difficulty at all. Father Forbes and Celia seemed to have no use for the hackman, but moved straight forward toward the street, through the doorway next to that in which Theron cowered. He stole round, and followed them at a safe distance, making Celia's hat, and the portmanteau perched on the shoulder of the porter behind her, his guides. To his surprise, they still kept on their course when they had reached the sidewalk, and went over the pavement across an open square which spread itself directly in front of the station. Hanging as far behind as he dared, he saw them pass to the other sidewalk diagonally opposite, proceed for a block or so along this, and then separate at a corner. Celia and the negro lad went down a side street, and entered the door of a vast, tall red-brick building which occupied the whole block. The priest, turning on his heel, came back again and went boldly up the broad steps of the front entrance to this same structure, which Theron now discovered to be the Murray Hill Hotel.

Fortune had indeed favored him. He not only knew where they were, but he had been himself a witness to the furtive way in which they entered the house by different doors. Nothing in his own limited experience of hotels helped him to comprehend the notion of a separate entrance for ladies and their luggage. He did not feel quite sure about the significance of what he had observed, in his own mind.[4] But it was apparent to him that there was something under-handed about it.

After lingering awhile on the steps of the hotel, and satis-fying himself by peeps through the glass doors that the coast was clear, he ventured inside. The great corridor con-tained many people, coming, going, or standing about, but none of them paid any attention to him. At last he made up his mind, and beckoned a colored boy to him from a group gathered in the shadows of the big central staircase. Explain-ing that he did not at that moment wish a room, but de-sired to leave his bag, the boy took him to a cloak-room, and got him a check for the thing. With this in his pocket he felt himself more at ease, and turned to walk away. Then sud-denly he wheeled, and, bending his body over the counter of the cloak-room, astonished the attendant inside by the eagerness with which he scrutinized the piled rows of port-manteaus, trunks, overcoats, and bundles in the little en-closure.

"What is it you want? Here's your bag, if you're looking for that," this man said to him.

"No, thanks; it's nothing," replied Theron, straightening himself again. He had had a narrow escape. Father Forbes and Celia, walking side by side, had come down the small passage in which he stood, and had passed him so closely that he had felt her dress brush against him. Fortunately he had seen them in time, and by throwing himself half into the cloak-room, had rendered recognition impossible.

He walked now in the direction they had taken, till he came to the polite colored man at an open door on the left, who was bowing people into the breakfast room. Standing in the doorway, he looked about him till his eye lighted upon his two friends, seated at a small table by a distant

---

[4] English ed. reads "in his own mind about the significance of what he had observed." for "about the significance of what he had observed, in his own mind."

window, with a black waiter, card in hand, bending over in consultation with them.

Returning to the corridor, he made bold now to march up to the desk and examine the register. The priest's name was not there. He found only the brief entry, "Miss Madden, Octavius," written, not by her, but by Father Forbes. On the line were two numbers in pencil, with an "and" between them. An indirect question to one of the clerks helped him to an explanation of this. When there were two numbers, it meant that the guest in question had a parlor as well as a bedroom.

Here he drew a long, satisfied breath, and turned away. The first half of his quest stood completed, — and that much more fully and easily than he had dared to hope. He could not but feel a certain new respect for himself as a man of resource and energy. He had demonstrated that people could not fool with him with impunity.

It remained to decide what he would do with his discovery, now that it had been so satisfactorily made. As yet, he had given this hardly a thought. Even now, it did not thrust itself forward as a thing demanding instant attention. It was much more important, first of all, to get a good breakfast. He had learned that there was another and less formal eating-place, downstairs in the basement by the bar, with an entrance from the street. He walked down by the inner stairway instead, feeling himself already at home in the big hotel. He ordered an ample breakfast, and came out while it was being served to wash and have his boots blacked, and he gave the man a quarter of a dollar. His pockets were filled with silver quarters, half-dollars, and dollars almost to a burdensome point, and in his valise was a bag full of smaller change, including many rolls of copper cents which Alice always counted and packed up on Mondays. In the hurry of leaving he had brought with him the church collections for the past two weeks. It occurred to him that he must keep a strict account of his expenditure. Meanwhile he gave ten cents to another man in a silk-sleeved cardigan jacket, who had merely stood by and looked at him while his boots were being polished. There was a sense of metropolitan affluence in the very atmosphere.

The little table in the adjoining room, on which Theron found his meal in waiting for him, seemed a vision of delicate napery and refined appointments in his eyes. He was wolfishly hungry, and the dishes he looked upon gave him back assurances by sight and smell that he was very happy as well. The servant in attendance had an extremely white apron and a kindly black face. He bowed when Theron looked at him, with the air of a lifelong admirer and humble friend.

"I suppose you'll have claret with your breakfast, sir?" he remarked, as if it were a matter of course.

"Why, certainly," answered Theron, stretching his legs contentedly under the table, and tucking the corner of his napkin in his neckband. — "certainly, my good man."

CHAPTER XXX

At ten o'clock Theron, loitering near the bookstall in the corridor, saw Father Forbes come downstairs, pass out through the big front doors, get into a carriage, and drive away.

This relieved him of a certain sense of responsibility, and he retired to a corner sofa and sat down. The detective side of him being off duty, so to speak, there was leisure at last for reflection upon the other aspects of his mission. Yes; it was high time for him to consider what he should do next.

It was easier to recognize this fact, however, than to act upon it. His mind was full of tricksy devices for eluding this task of serious thought which he sought to impose upon it. It seemed so much pleasanter not to think at all — but just to drift. He found himself watching with envy the men who, as they came out from their breakfast, walked over to the bookstall, and bought cigars from the row of boxes nestling there among the newspaper piles. They had such evident delight in the work of selection; they took off the ends of the cigars so carefully, and lighted them with such meditative attention, — he could see that he was wofully handicapped by not knowing how to smoke. He had had the most wonderful breakfast of his life, but even in the consciousness of comfortable repletion which pervaded his being, there was an obstinate sense of something lacking. No doubt a good cigar was the thing needed to round out the perfection of such a breakfast. He half rose once, fired by a sudden resolution to go over and get one. But of course that was nonsense; it would only make him sick. He sat down, and determinedly set himself to thinking.

The effort finally brought fruit — and of a kind which gave him a very unhappy quarter of an hour. The lover part of him was uppermost now, insistently exposing all its raw surfaces to the stings and scalds of jealousy. Up to this moment, his brain had always evaded the direct question of how he and the priest relatively stood in Celia's estimation. It forced itself remorselessly upon him now; and his thoughts, so far from shirking the subject, seemed to rise up to meet it. It was extremely unpleasant, all this.

But then a calmer view asserted itself. Why go out of his way to invent anguish for himself? The relations between Celia and the priest, whatever they might be, were certainly of old standing. They had begun before his time. His own romance was a more recent affair, and must take its place, of course, subject to existing conditions. It was all right for him to come to New York, and satisfy his legitimate curiosity as to the exact character and scope of these conditions. But it was foolish to pretend to be amazed or dismayed at the discovery of their existence. They were a part of the situation which he, with his eyes wide open, had accepted. It was his function to triumph over them, to supplant them, to rear the edifice of his own victorious passion upon their ruins. It was to this that Celia's kiss had invited him. It was for this that he had come to New York. To let his purpose be hampered or thwarted now by childish doubts and jealousies would be ridiculous.

He rose, and holding himself very erect, walked with measured deliberation across the corridor and up the broad staircase. There was an elevator near at hand, he had noticed, but he preferred the stairs. One or two of the colored boys clustered about the foot of the stairs looked at him, and he had a moment of dreadful apprehension lest they should stop his progress. Nothing was said, and he went on. The numbers on the first floor were not what he wanted, and after some wandering about he ascended to the next, and then to the third. Every now and then he encountered attendants, but intuitively he bore himself with an air of knowing what he was about which protected him from inquiry.

Finally he came upon the hall-way he sought. Passing along, he found the doors bearing the numbers he had memorized so well. They were quite close together, and there was nothing to help him guess which belonged to the parlor. He hesitated, gazing wistfully from one to the other. In the instant of indecision, even while his alert ear caught the sound of feet coming along toward the passage in which he stood, a thought came to quicken his resolve. It became apparent to him that his discovery gave him a certain measure of freedom with Celia, a sort of right to take things more for granted than heretofore. He chose a door at random, and rapped distinctly on the panel.

"Come!"

The voice he knew for Celia's. The single word, however, recalled the usage of Father Forbes, which he had noted more than once at the pastorate, when Maggie had knocked.

He straightened his shoulders, took his hat off, and pushed open the door. It *was* the parlor, — a room of sofas, pianos, big easy-chairs, and luxurious bric-à-brac. A tall woman was walking up and down in it, with bowed head. Her back was at the moment toward him; and he looked at her, saying to himself that this was the lady of his dreams, the enchantress of the kiss, the woman who loved him — but somehow it did not seem to his senses to be Celia.

She turned, and moved a step or two in his direction before she mechanically lifted her eyes, and saw who was standing in her doorway. She stopped short, and regarded him. Her face was in the shadow, and he could make out nothing of its expression, save that there was a general effect of gravity about it.

"I cannot receive you," she said. "You must go away. You have no business to come like this without sending up your card."

Theron smiled at her. The notion of taking in earnest her inhospitable words did not at all occur to him. He could see now that her face had vexed and saddened lines upon it, and the sharpness of her tone remained in his ears. But he smiled again gently, to reassure her.

"I ought to have sent up my name, I know," he said,

"but I couldn't bear to wait. I just saw your name on the register, and — you *will* forgive me, won't you? — I ran to you at once. I know you won't have the heart to send me away!"

She stood where she had halted, her arms behind her, looking him fixedly in the face. He had made a movement to advance, and offer his hand in greeting, but her posture checked the impulse. His courage began to falter under her inspection.

"Must I really go down again?" he pleaded. "It's a crushing penalty to suffer for such a little indiscretion. I was so excited to find you here — I never stopped to think. Don't send me away; please don't!"

Celia raised her head. "Well, shut the door, then," she said, "since you are so anxious to stay. You would have done much better, though, very much better indeed, to have taken the hint and gone away."

"Will you shake hands with me, Celia?" he asked softly, as he came near her.

"Sit there, please!" she made answer, indicating a chair in the middle of the room. He obeyed her, but to his surprise, instead of seating herself as well, she began walking up and down the length of the floor again. After a turn or two she stopped in front of him, and looked him full in the eye. The light from the windows was on her countenance now, and its revelations vaguely troubled him. It was a Celia he had never seen before who confronted him.

"I am much occupied by other matters," she said, speaking with cold impassivity, "but still I find myself curious to know just what limits you set to your dishonesty."

Theron stared up at her. His lips quivered, but no speech came to them. If this was all merely fond playfulness, it was being [1] carried to a heart-aching point.

"I saw you hiding about in the depot at home last evening," she went on. "You come up here, pretending to have

---

[1] English ed. reads "might be" for "was being."

discovered me by accident, but I saw you following me from the Grand Central this morning."

"Yes, I did both these things," said Theron, boldly. A fine bravery tingled in his veins all at once. He looked into her face and found the spirit to disregard its frowning aspect. "Yes, I did them," he repeated defiantly. "That is not the hundredth part, or the thousandth part, of what I would do for your sake. I have got way beyond caring for any consequences. Position, reputation, the good opinion of fools, — what are they? Life itself, — what does it amount to? Nothing at all — with you in the balance!"

"Yes — but I am not in the balance," observed Celia, quietly. "That is where you have made your mistake."

Theron laid aside his hat. Women were curious creatures, he reflected. Some were susceptible to one line of treatment, some to another. His own reading of Celia had always been that she liked opposition, of a smart, rattling, almost cheeky, sort. One got on best with her by saying bright things. He searched his brain now for some clever quip that would strike sparks from the adamantine mood which for the moment it was her whim to assume. To cover the process, he smiled a little. Then her beauty, as she stood before him, her queenly form clad in a more stiffly fashionable dress than he had seen her wearing before, appealed afresh and overwhelmingly to him. He rose to his feet.

"Have you forgotten our talk in the woods?" he murmured with a wooing note. "Have you forgotten the kiss?"

She shook her head calmly. "I have forgotten nothing."

"Then why play with me so cruelly now?" he went on, in a voice of tender deprecation. "I know you don't mean it, but all the same it bruises my heart a little. I build myself so wholly upon you, I have made existence itself depend so completely upon your smile, upon a soft glance in your eyes, that when they are not there, why, I suffer, I don't know how to live at all. So be kinder to me, Celia!"

"I was kinder, as you call it, when you came in," she replied. "I told you to go away. That was pure kindness, — more kindness than you deserved."

Theron looked at his hat, where it stood on the carpet by his feet. He felt tears coming into his eyes. "You tell me that you remember," he said, in depressed tones, "and yet you treat me like this! Perhaps I am wrong. No doubt it is my own fault. I suppose I ought not to have come down here at all."

Celia nodded her head in assent to his view.

"But I swear that I was helpless in the matter," he burst forth. "I *had* to come! It would have been literally impossible for me to have stayed at home, knowing that you were here, and knowing also that — that —"

"Go on!" said Celia, thrusting forth her underlip a trifle, and hardening still further the gleam in her eye, as he stumbled over his sentence and left it unfinished. "What was the other thing that you were 'knowing'?"

"Knowing, — " he took up the word hesitatingly, — "knowing that life would be insupportable to me if I could not be near you."

She curled her lip at him. "You skated over the thin spot very well," she commented. "It was on the tip of your tongue to mention the fact that Father Forbes came with me. Oh, I can read you through and through, Mr. Ware."

In a misty way Theron felt things slipping from his grasp. The rising moisture blurred his eyes as their gaze clung to Celia.

"Then if you do read me," he protested, "you must know how utterly my heart and brain are filled with you. No other man in all the world can yield himself so absolutely to the woman he worships as I can. You have taken possession of me so wholly, I am not in the least master of myself any more. I don't know what I say or what I do. I am not worthy of you, I know. No man alive could be that. But no one else will idolize and reverence you as I do. Believe me when I say that, Celia! And how can you blame me, in your heart, for following you? Whither thou goest, I will go, and where thou lodgest I will lodge; thy people shall be my people, and thy God my God; where thou diest, will I die, and there will I be buried. The Lord do so to me, and more also, if aught but death part thee and me!"

Celia shrugged her shoulders, and moved a few steps away from him. Something like despair seized upon him.

"Surely," he urged with passion, — "surely I have a right to remind you of the kiss!"

She turned. "The kiss," she said meditatively. "Yes, you have a right to remind me of it. Oh, yes, an undoubted right. You have another right too, — the right to have the kiss explained to you. It was of the good-bye order. It signified that we weren't to meet again, and that just for one little moment I permitted myself to be sorry for you. That was all."

He held himself erect under the incredible words, and gazed blankly at her. The magnitude of what he confronted bewildered him; his mind was incapable of taking it in. "You mean —" he started to say, and then stopped, help- lessly staring into her face, with a dropped jaw. It was too much to try to think what she meant.

A little side-thought sprouted in the confusion of his brain. It grew until it spread a bitter smile over his pale face. "I know so little about kisses," he said; "I am such a greenhorn at that sort of thing. You should have had pity on my inexperience and told me just what brand of kiss it was I was getting. Probably I ought to have been able to distinguish, but you see I was brought up in the country — on a farm. They don't have kisses in assorted varieties there."

She bowed her head slightly. "Yes, you are entitled to say that," she assented. "I was to blame, and it is quite fair that you should tell me so. You spoke of your inexperience, your innocence. That was why I kissed you in saying good- bye. It was in memory of that innocence of yours, to which you yourself had been busy saying good-bye ever since I first saw you. The idea seemed to me to mean something at the moment. I see now that it was too subtle. I do not usually err on that side."

Theron kept his hold upon her gaze, as if it afforded him bodily support. He felt that he ought to stoop and take up his hat, but he dared not look away from her. "Do you not err now, on the side of cruelty?" he asked her piteously.

It seemed for the instant as if she were wavering, and he swiftly thrust forth other pleas. "I admit that I did wrong to follow you to New York. I see that now. But it was an offence committed in entire good faith. Think of it, Celia! I have never seen you since that day, — that day in the woods. I have waited — and waited — with no sign from you, no chance of seeing you at all. Think what that meant to me! Everything in the world had been altered for me, torn up by the roots. I was a new being, plunged into a new existence. The kiss had done that. But until I saw you again, I could not tell whether this vast change in me and my life was for good or for bad, — whether the kiss had come to me as a blessing or a curse. The suspense was killing me, Celia! That is why, when I learned that you were coming here, I threw everything to the winds and followed you. You blame me for it, and I bow my head and accept the blame. But are you justified in punishing me so terribly, — in going on after I have confessed my error, and cutting my heart into little strips, putting me to death by torture?"

"Sit down," said Celia, with a softened weariness in her voice. She seated herself in front of him as he sank into his chair again. "I don't want to give you unnecessary pain, but you have insisted on forcing yourself into a position where there isn't anything else but pain. I warned you to go away, but you wouldn't. No matter how gently I may try to explain things to you, you are bound to get nothing but suffering out of the explanation. Now shall I still go on?"

He inclined his head in token of assent, and did not lift it again, but raised toward her a disconsolate gaze from a pallid, drooping face.

"It is all in a single word, Mr. Ware," she proceeded, in low tones. "I speak for others as well as myself, mind you, — we find that you are a bore."

Theron's stiffened countenance remained immovable. He continued to stare unblinkingly up into her eyes.

"We were disposed to like you very much when we first knew you," Celia went on. "You impressed us as an innocent, simple, genuine young character, full of mother's milk. It was like the smell of early spring in the country to come in contact with you. Your honesty of nature, your sincerity in that absurd religion of yours, your general *naïveté* of mental and spiritual get-up, all pleased us a great deal. We thought you were going to be a real acquisition."

"Just a moment — whom do you mean by 'we'?" He asked the question calmly enough, but in a voice with an effect of distance in it.

"It may not be necessary to enter into that," she replied. "Let me go on. But then it became apparent, little by little, that we had misjudged you. We liked you, as I have said, because you were unsophisticated and delightfully fresh and natural. Somehow we took it for granted you would stay so. But that is just what you didn't do, — just what you hadn't the sense to try to do. Instead, we found you inflating yourself with all sorts of egotisms and vanities. We found you presuming upon the friendships which had been mistakenly extended to you. Do you want instances? You went to Dr. Ledsmar's house that very day after I had been with you to get a piano at Thurston's, and tried to inveigle him into talking scandal about me. You came to me with tales about him. You went to Father Forbes, and sought to get him to gossip about us both. Neither of those men will ever ask you inside his house again. But that is only one part of it. Your whole mind became an unpleasant thing to contemplate. You thought it would amuse and impress us to hear you ridiculing and reviling the people of your church, whose money supports you, and making a mock of the things they believe in, and which you for your life wouldn't dare let them know you didn't believe in. You talked to us slightingly about your wife. What were you thinking of, not to comprehend that that would disgust us? You showed me once — do you remember? — a life of George Sand that you had just bought, — bought because you had just discovered that she had an unclean side to her life. You chuckled as you spoke to me about it, and you were for all the world like a little nasty boy, giggling over something dirty that older people had learned not to notice. These are merely random incidents. They are just samples, picked hap-hazard, of the things in you which have been opening our eyes, little by little, to our mistake. I can understand that all the while you really fancied that you were expanding, growing, in all directions. What you took to be improvement was degeneration. When you thought that you were impressing us most by your smart sayings and doings, you were reminding us most of the fable about the donkey trying to play lapdog. And it wasn't even an honest, straightforward donkey at that!"

She uttered these last words sorrowfully, her hands clasped in her lap, and her eyes sinking to the floor. A silence ensued. Then Theron reached a groping hand out for his hat, and, rising, walked with a lifeless, automatic step to the door.

He had it half open, when the impossibility of leaving in this way towered suddenly in his path and overwhelmed him. He slammed the door to, and turned as if he had been whirled round by some mighty wind. He came toward her, with something almost menacing in the vigor of his movements, and in the wild look upon his white, set face. Halting before her, he covered the tailor-clad figure, the coiled red hair, the upturned face with its simulated calm, the big brown eyes, the rings upon the clasped fingers, with a sweeping, comprehensive glare of passion.

"This is what you have done to me, then!"

His voice was unrecognizable in his own ears, — hoarse and broken, but with a fright-compelling something in it which stimulated his rage. The horrible notion of killing her, there where she sat, spread over the chaos of his mind with an effect of unearthly light, — red and abnormally evil. It was like that first devilish radiance ushering in Creation, of which the first-fruit was Cain. Why should he not kill her? In all ages, women had been slain for less. Yes, — and men had been hanged. Something rose and stuck in his dry throat; and as he swallowed it down, the sinister flare of murderous fascination died suddenly away into darkness. The world was all black again, — plunged in the Egyptian night which lay upon the face of the deep while the earth was yet without form and void. He was alone on it, — alone among awful, planetary solitudes which crushed him.

The sight of Celia, sitting motionless only a pace in front of him, was plain enough to his eyes. It was an illusion. She was really a star, many millions of miles away. These things were hard to understand; but they were true, none the less. People seemed to be about him, but in fact he was alone. He recalled that even the little child in the car, playing with those two buttons on a string, would have nothing to do with him. Take his money, yes; take all he would give her — but not smile at him, not come within reach of him! Men closed the doors of their houses against him. The universe held him at arm's length as a nuisance.

He was standing with one knee upon a sofa. Unconsciously he had moved round to the side of Celia; and as he caught the effect of her face now in profile, memory-pictures began all at once building themselves in his brain, — pictures of her standing in the darkened room of the cottage of death, declaiming the *Confiteor*; of her seated at the piano, under the pure, mellowed candle-light; of her leaning her chin on her hands, and gazing meditatively at the leafy background of the woods they were in; of her lying back, indolently content, in the deck-chair on the yacht of his fancy,

— that yacht which a few hours before had seemed so brilliantly and bewitchingly real to him, and now — now — !

He sank in a heap upon the couch, and, burying his face among its cushions, wept and groaned aloud. His collapse was absolute. He sobbed with the abandonment of one who, in the veritable presence of death, lets go all sense of relation to life.

Presently some one was touching him on the shoulder, — an incisive, pointed touch, — and he checked himself, and lifted his face.

"You will have to get up, and present some sort of an appearance, and go away at once," Celia said to him in low, rapid tones. "Some gentlemen are at the door, whom I have been waiting for."

As he stupidly sat up and tried to collect his faculties, Celia had opened the door and admitted two visitors. The foremost was Father Forbes; and he, with some whispered, smiling words, presented to her his companion, a tall, robust, florid man of middle-age, with a frock-coat and a gray mustache, sharply waxed. The three spoke for a moment together. Then the priest's wandering eye suddenly lighted upon the figure on the sofa. He stared, knitted his brows, and then lifted them in inquiry as he turned to Celia.

"Poor man!" she said readily, in tones loud enough to reach Theron. "It is our neighbor, Father, the Rev. Mr. Ware. He hit upon my name in the register quite unexpectedly, and I had him come up. He is in sore distress, — a great and sudden bereavement. He is going now. Won't you speak to him in the hall, — a few words, Father? It would please him. He is terribly depressed."

The words had drawn Theron to his feet, as by some mechanical process. He took up his hat and moved dumbly to the door. It seemed to him that Celia intended offering to shake hands; but he went past her with only some confused exchange of glances and a murmured word or two. The tall stranger, who drew aside to let him pass, had acted as if he expected to be introduced. Theron, emerging into the hall, leaned against the wall and looked dreamily at the priest, who had stepped out with him.

"I am very sorry to learn that you are in trouble, Mr. Ware," Father Forbes said, gently enough, but in hurried tones. "Miss Madden is also in trouble.[2] I mentioned to you that her brother had got into a serious scrape.[3] I have brought my old friend, General Brady, to consult with her about the matter. He knows all the parties concerned, and he can set things right if anybody can."

"It's a mistake about me, — I'm not in any trouble at all," said Theron. "I just dropped in to make a friendly call."

The priest glanced sharply at him, noting with a swift, informed scrutiny how he sprawled against the wall, and what vacuity his eyes and loosened lips expressed.

"Then you have a talent for the inopportune amounting to positive genius," said Father Forbes, with a stormy smile.

"Tell me this, Father Forbes," the other demanded, with impulsive suddenness, "is it true that you don't want me in your house again? Is that the truth or not?"

"The truth is always relative, Mr. Ware," replied the priest, turning away, and closing the door of the parlor behind him with a decisive sound.

Left alone, Theron started to make his way downstairs. He found his legs wavering under him and making zigzag movements of their own, in a bewildering fashion. He referred this at first, in an outburst of fresh despair, to the effects of his great grief. Then, as he held tight to the banister and governed his descent step by step, it occurred to him that it must be the wine he had had for breakfast. Upon examination, he was not so unhappy, after all.

[2] English ed. adds "I think."
[3] English ed. adds "It might easily be made unpleasant for him and his family, but there is a hope it might be hushed up."

CHAPTER XXXI

AT the second peal of the door-bell, Brother Soulsby sat up in bed. It was still pitch-dark, and the memory of the first ringing fluttered musically in his awakening consciousness as a part of some dream he had been having.

"Who the deuce can that be?" he mused aloud, in querulous resentment at the interruption.

"Put your head out of the window, and ask," suggested his wife, drowsily.

The bell-pull scraped violently in its socket, and a third outburst of shrill reverberations clamored through the silent house.

"Whatever you do, I'd do it before he yanked the whole thing to pieces," added the wife, with more decision.

Brother Soulsby was wide awake now. He sprang to the floor, and, groping about in the obscurity, began drawing on some of his clothes. He rapped on the window during the process, to show that the house was astir, and a minute afterward made his way out of the room and down the stairs, the boards creaking under his stockinged feet as he went.

Nearly a quarter of an hour passed before he returned. Sister Soulsby, lying in sleepy quiescence, heard vague sounds of voices at the front door, and did not feel interested enough to lift her head and listen. A noise of footsteps on the sidewalk followed, first receding from the door, then turning toward it, this second time marking the presence of more than one person. There seemed in this the implication of a guest, and she shook off the dozing impulses which enveloped her faculties, and waited to hear more. There came up, after further muttering of male voices, the undeniable chink of coins striking against one another. Then more footsteps, the resonant slam of a carriage door out in the street, the grinding of wheels turning on the frosty road, and the racket of a vehicle and horses going off at a smart pace into the night. Somebody had come, then. She yawned at the thought, but remained well awake, tracing idly in her mind, as various slight sounds rose from the lower floor, the different things Soulsby was probably doing. Their spare room was down there, directly underneath, but curiously enough no one seemed to enter it. The faint murmur of conversation which from time to time reached her came from the parlor instead. At last she heard her husband's soft tread coming up the staircase, and still there had been no hint of employing the guest-chamber. What could he be about? she wondered.

Brother Soulsby came in, bearing a small lamp in his hand, the reddish light of which, flaring upward, revealed an unlooked-for display of amusement on his thin, beardless face. He advanced to the bedside, shading the glare from her blinking eyes with his palm, and grinned.

"A thousand guesses, old lady," he said, with a dry chuckle, "and you wouldn't have a ghost of a chance. You might guess till Hades froze over seven feet thick, and still you wouldn't hit it."

She sat up in turn. "Good gracious, man," she began, "you don't mean —" Here the cheerful gleam in his small eyes reassured her, and she sighed relief, then smiled confusedly. "I half thought, just for the minute," she explained, "it might be some bounder who'd come East to try and blackmail me. But no, who is it — and what on earth have you done with him?"

Brother Soulsby cackled in merriment. "It's Brother Ware of Octavius, out on a little bat, all by himself. He says he's been on the loose only two days; but it looks more like a fortnight."

"*Our* Brother Ware?" she regarded him with open-eyed surprise.

"Well, yes, I suppose he's *our* Brother Ware, — some," returned Soulsby, genially. "He seems to think so, anyway."

"But tell me about it!" she urged eagerly. "What's the matter with him? How does he explain it?"

"Well, he explains it pretty badly, if you ask me," said Soulsby, with a droll, joking eye and a mock-serious voice. He seated himself on the side of the bed, facing her, and still considerately shielding her from the light of the lamp he held.[1] "But don't think I suggested any explanations. I've been a mother myself. He's merely filled himself up to the neck with rum, in the simple, ordinary, good old-fashioned way. That's all. What is there to explain about that?"

She looked meditatively at him for a time, shaking her head. "No, Soulsby," she said gravely, at last. "This isn't any laughing matter. You may be sure something bad has happened, to set him off like that. I'm going to get up and dress right now. What time is it?"

"Now don't you do anything of the sort," he urged persuasively. "It isn't five o'clock; it'll be dark for nearly an hour yet. Just you turn over, and have another nap. He's all right. I put him on the sofa, with the buffalo robe round him. You'll find him there, safe and sound, when it's time for white folks to get up. You know how it breaks you up all day, not to get your full sleep."

"I don't care if it makes me look as old as the everlasting hills," she said. "Can't you understand, Soulsby? The thing worries me, — gets on my nerves. I couldn't close an eye, if I tried. I took a great fancy to that young man. I told you so at the time."

Soulsby nodded, and turned down the wick of his lamp a trifle. "Yes, I know you did," he remarked in placidly non-contentious tones. "I can't say I saw much in him myself, but I daresay you're right." There followed a moment's silence, during which he experimented in turning the wick up again. "But, anyway," he went on, "there isn't anything

---

[1] English ed. reads "brightness of the lamp" for "light of the lamp he held."

you can do. He'll sleep it off, and the longer he's left alone the better. It isn't as if we had a hired girl, who'd come down and find him there, and give the whole thing away. He's fixed up there perfectly comfortable; and when he's had his sleep out, and wakes up on his own account, he'll be feeling a heap better."

The argument might have carried conviction, but on the instant the sound of footsteps came to them from the room below. The subdued noise rose regularly, as of one pacing to and fro.

"No, Soulsby, *you* come back to bed, and get *your* sleep out. I'm going downstairs. It's no good talking; I'm going."

Brother Soulsby offered no further opposition, either by talk or demeanor, but returned contentedly to bed, pulling the comforter over his ears, and falling into the slow, measured respiration of tranquil slumber before his wife was ready to leave the room.

The dim, cold gray of twilight was sifting furtively through the lace curtains of the front windows when Mrs. Soulsby, lamp in hand, entered the parlor. She confronted a figure she would have hardly recognized. The man seemed to have been submerged in a bath of disgrace. From the crown of his head to the soles of his feet, everything about him was altered, distorted, smeared with an intangible effect of shame. In the vague gloom of the middle distance, between lamp and window, she noticed that his shoulders were crouched, like those of some shambling tramp. The frowsy shadows of a stubble beard lay on his jaw and throat. His clothes were crumpled and hung awry; his boots were stained with mud. The silk hat on the piano told its battered story with dumb eloquence.

Lifting the lamp, she moved forward a step, and threw its light upon his face. A little groan sounded involuntarily upon her lips. Out of a mask of unpleasant features, swollen with drink and weighted by the physical craving for rest and sleep, there stared at her two bloodshot eyes, shining with the wild light of hysteria. The effect of dishevelled hair, relaxed muscles, and rough, half-bearded lower face lent to these eyes, as she caught their first glance, an unnatural glare. The lamp shook in her hand for an instant. Then, ashamed of herself, she held out her other hand fearlessly to him.

"Tell me all about it, Theron," she said calmly, and with a soothing, motherly intonation in her voice.

He did not take the hand she offered, but suddenly, with a wailing moan, cast himself on his knees at her feet. He was so tall a man that the movement could have no grace. He abased his head awkwardly, to bury it among the folds of the skirts at her ankles. She stood still for a moment, looking down upon him. Then, blowing out the light, she reached over and set the smoking lamp on the piano near by. The daylight made things distinguishable in a wan, uncertain way, throughout the room.

"I have come out of hell, for the sake of hearing some human being speak to me like that!"

The thick utterance proceeded in a muffled fashion from where his face grovelled against her dress. Its despairing accents appealed to her, but even more was she touched by the ungainly figure he made, sprawling on the carpet.

"Well, since you are out, stay out," she answered, as reassuringly as she could. "But get up and take a seat here beside me, like a sensible man, and tell me all about it. Come! I insist!"

In obedience to her tone, and the sharp tug at his shoulder with which she emphasized it, he got slowly to his feet, and listlessly seated himself on the sofa to which she pointed. He hung his head, and began catching his breath with a periodical gasp, half hiccough, half sob.

"First of all," she said, in her brisk, matter-of-fact manner, "don't you want to lie down there [2] again, and have me

---

[2] English ed. reads "here" for "there."

tuck you up snug with the buffalo robe, and go to sleep? That would be the [3] best thing you could do."

He shook his head disconsolately, from side to side. "I can't" he groaned, with a swifter recurrence of the sob-like convulsions. "I'm dying for sleep, but I'm too — too frightened!"

"Come, I'll sit beside you till you drop off," she said, with masterful decision. He suffered himself to be pushed into recumbency on the couch, and put his head with docility on the pillow she brought from the spare room. When she had spread the fur over him, and pushed her chair close to the sofa, she stood by it for a little, looking down in meditation at his demoralized face. Under the painful surface-blur of wretchedness and fatigued debauchery, she traced reflectively the lineaments of the younger and cleanlier countenance she had seen a few months before. Nothing essential had been taken away. There was only this pestiferous overlaying of shame and cowardice to be removed. The face underneath was still all right.

With a soft, maternal touch, she smoothed the hair from his forehead into order. Then she seated herself, and, when he got his hand out from under the robe and thrust it forth timidly, she took it in hers and held it in a warm, sympathetic grasp. He closed his eyes at this, and gradually the paroxysmal catch in his breathing lapsed. The daylight strengthened, until at last tiny flecks of sunshine twinkled in the meshes of the further curtains at the window. She fancied him asleep, and gently sought to disengage her hand, but his fingers clutched at it with vehemence, and his eyes were wide open.

"I can't sleep at all," he murmured. "I want to talk."

"There's nothing in the world to hinder you," she commented smilingly.

"I tell you the solemn truth," he said, lifting his voice in dogged assertion: "the best sermon I ever preached in my

[3] English ed. adds "very."

life, I preached only three weeks ago, at the camp-meeting. It was admitted by everybody to be far and away my finest effort! They will tell you the same!"

"It's quite likely," assented Sister Soulsby. "I quite believe it."

"Then how can anybody say that I've degenerated, that I've become a fool?" he demanded.

"I haven't heard anybody hint at such a thing," she answered quietly.

"No, of course, *you* haven't heard them!" he cried. "*I* heard them, though!" Then, forcing himself to a sitting posture, against the restraint of her hand, he flung back the covering. "I'm burning hot already! Yes, those were the identical words: I haven't improved; I've degenerated. People hate me; they won't have me in their houses. They say I'm a nuisance and a bore. I'm like a little nasty boy. That's what they say. Even a young man who was dying — lying right on the edge of his open grave — told me solemnly that I reminded him of a saint once, but I was only fit for a barkeeper now. They say I really don't know anything at all. And I'm not only a fool, they say, I'm a dishonest fool into the bargain!"

"But who says such twaddle as that?" she returned consolingly. The violence of his emotion disturbed her. "You musn't imagine such things. You are among friends here. Other people are your friends, too. They have the very highest opinion of you."

"I haven't a friend on earth but you!" he declared solemnly. His eyes glowed fiercely, and his voice sank into a grave intensity of tone. "I was going to kill myself. I went on to the big bridge to throw myself off, and a policeman saw me trying to climb over the railing, and he grabbed me and marched me away. Then he threw me out at the entrance, and said he would club my head off if I came there again. And then I went and stood and let the cable-cars pass close by me, and twenty times I thought I had the nerve to throw myself under the next one, and then I waited for the next

— and — I was afraid! And then I was in a crowd somewhere, and the warning came to me that I was going to die. The fool needn't go kill himself: God would take care of that. It was my heart, you know. I've had that terrible fluttering once before. It seized me this time, and I fell down in the crowd, and some people walked over me, but some one else helped me up, and let me sit down in a big lighted hallway, the entrance to some theatre, and some one brought me some brandy, but somebody else said I was drunk, and they took it away again, and put me out. They could see I was a fool, that I hadn't a friend on earth. And when I went out, there was a big picture of a woman in tights, and the word 'Amazons' overhead — and then I remembered you. I knew *you* were my friend, — the only one I have on earth."

"It is very flattering, — to be remembered like that," said Sister Soulsby, gently. The disposition to laugh was smothered by a pained perception of the suffering he was undergoing. His face had grown drawn and haggard under the burden of his memories as he rambled on.

"So I came straight to you," he began again. "I had just money enough left to pay my fare. The rest is in my valise at the hotel, — the Murray Hill Hotel. It belongs to the church. I stole it from the church. When I am dead they can get it back again!"

Sister Soulsby forced a smile to her lips. "What nonsense you talk — about dying!" she exclaimed. "Why, man alive, you'll sleep this all off like a top, if you'll only lie down and give yourself a chance. Come, now, you must do as you're told."

With a resolute hand, she made him lie down again, and once more covered him with the fur. He submitted, and did not even offer to put out his arm this time, but looked in piteous dumbness at her for a long time.[4] While she sat thus in silence, the sound of Brother Soulsby moving about upstairs became audible.

Theron heard it, and the importance of hurrying on some

---

[4] **English ed. reads "space" for "time."**

further disclosure seemed to suggest itself. "I can see you think I'm just drunk," he said, in low, sombre tones. "Of course that's what *he* thought. The hackman thought so, and so did the conductor, and everybody. But I hoped you would know better. I was sure you would see that it was something worse than that. See here, I'll tell you. Then you'll understand. I've been drinking for two days and one whole night, on my feet all the while, wandering alone in that big strange New York, going through places where they murdered men for ten cents, mixing myself up with the worst people in low bar-rooms and dance-houses, and they saw I had money in my pocket, too — and yet nobody touched me or offered to lay a finger on me. Do you know why? They understood that I wanted to get drunk, and couldn't. The Indians won't harm an idiot, or lunatic, you know. Well, it was the same with these vilest of the vile. They saw that I was a fool whom God had taken hold of, to break his heart first, and then to craze his brain, and then to fling him on a dunghill to die like a dog. They believe in God, those people. They're the only ones who do, it seems to me. And they wouldn't interfere when they saw what He was doing to me. But I tell you I wasn't drunk. I haven't been drunk. I'm only heart-broken, and crushed out of shape and life, — that's all. And I've crawled here just to have a friend by me when — when I come to the end."

"You're not talking very sensibly, or very bravely either, Theron Ware," [5] remarked his companion. "It's cowardly to give way to notions like that."

"Oh, I'm not afraid to die; don't think that," he remonstrated wearily. "If there is a Judgment, it has hit me as hard as it can already. There can't be any hell worse than that I've gone through. Here I am talking about hell," he continued, with a pained contraction of the muscles about his mouth, — a still-born, malformed smile, — "as if I be-

[5] English ed. omits "Ware."

lieved in one! I've got way through all my beliefs, you know.
I tell you that frankly."

"It's none of my business," she reassured him. "I'm not
your Bishop, or your confessor. I'm just your friend, your
pal, that's all."

"Look here!" he broke in, with some animation and a new
intensity of glance and voice. "If I was going to live, I'd
have some funny things to tell. Six months ago I was a good
man. I not only seemed to be good, to others and to myself,
but I *was* good. I had a soul; I had a conscience. I was going
along doing my duty, and I was happy in it. We were poor,
Alice and I, and people behaved rather hard toward us, and
sometimes we were a little down in the mouth about it; but
that was all. We really were happy; and I, — I really was a
good man. Here's the kind of joke God plays! You see me
here six months after. Look at me! I haven't got an honest
hair in my head. I'm a bad man through and through, that's
what I am. I look all around at myself, and there isn't an
atom left anywhere of the good man I used to be. And,
mind you, I never lifted a finger to prevent the change. I
didn't resist once; I didn't make any fight. I just walked
deliberately down-hill, with my eyes wide open. I told myself all the while that I was climbing up-hill instead, but I
knew in my heart that it was a lie. Everything about me was
a lie. I wouldn't be telling the truth, even now, if — if I
hadn't come to the end of my rope. Now, how do you explain that? How *can* it be explained? Was I really rotten to
the core all the time, years ago, when I seemed to everybody,
myself and the rest, to be good and straight and sincere?
Was it all a sham, or does God take a good man and turn
him into an out-and-out bad one, in just a few months, —
in the time that it takes an ear of corn to form and ripen
and go off with the mildew? Or isn't there any God at all, —
but only men who live and die like animals? And that would
explain my case, wouldn't it? I got bitten and went vicious

and crazy, and they've had to chase me out and hunt me to my death like a mad dog! Yes, that makes it all very simple. It isn't worth while to discuss me at all as if I had a soul, is it? I'm just one more mongrel cur that's gone mad, and must be put out of the way. That's all."

"See here," said Sister Soulsby, alertly, "I half believe that a good cuffing is what you really stand in need of. Now you stop all this nonsense, and lie quiet and keep still! Do you hear me?"

The jocose sternness which she assumed, in words and manner, seemed to soothe him. He almost smiled up at her in a melancholy way, and sighed profoundly.

"I've told you my religion before," she went on with gentleness. "The sheep and the goats are to be separated on Judgment Day, but not a minute sooner. In other words, as long as human life lasts, good, bad, indifferent are all braided up together in every man's nature, and every woman's too. You weren't altogether good a year ago, any more than you're altogether bad now. You were some of both then; you're some of both now. If you've been making an extra sort of fool of yourself lately, why, now that you recognize it, the only thing to do is to slow steam, pull up, and back engine in the other direction. In that way you'll find things will even themselves up. It's a see-saw with all of us, Theron Ware, — sometimes up; sometimes down. But nobody is rotten clear to the core."

He closed his eyes, and lay in silence for a time.

"This is what day of the week?" he asked, at last.

"Friday, the nineteenth."

"Wednesday, — that would be the seventeenth. That was the day ordained for my slaughter. On that morning, I was the happiest man in the world. No king could have been so proud and confident as I was. A wonderful romance had come to me. The most beautiful young woman in the world, the most talented too, was waiting for me. An express train was carrying me to her, and it couldn't go fast enough to keep up with my eagerness. She was very rich, and she loved me, and we were to live in eternal summer, wherever we liked, on a big, beautiful yacht. No one else had such a life before him as that. It seemed almost too good for me, but I thought I had grown and developed so much that perhaps I would be worthy of it. Oh, how happy I was! I tell you this because — because *you* are not like the others. You will understand."

"Yes, I understand," she said patiently. "Well — you were being so happy."

"That was in the morning, — Wednesday the seventeenth, — early in the morning. There was a little girl in the car, playing with some buttons, and when I tried to make friends with her, she looked at me, and she saw, right at a glance, that I was a fool. 'Out of the mouths of babes and sucklings,' you know. She was the first to find it out. It began like that, early in the morning. But then after that everybody knew it. They had only to look at me and they said: 'Why, this is a fool, — like a little nasty boy; we won't let him into our houses; [6] we find him a bore.' That is what they said."

"Did *she* say it?" Sister Soulsby permitted herself to ask.

For answer Theron bit his lips, and drew his chin under the fur, and pushed his scowling face into the pillow. The spasmodic, sob-like gasps began to shake him again. She laid a compassionate hand upon his hot brow.

"That is why I made my way here to you," he groaned piteously. "I knew you would sympathize; I could tell it all to you. And it was so awful, to die there alone in the strange city — I couldn't do it — with nobody near me who liked me, or thought well of me. Alice would hate me. There was no one but you. I wanted to be with you — at the last."

His quavering voice broke off in a gust of weeping, and his face frankly surrendered itself to the distortions of a crying child's countenance, wide-mouthed and tragically grotesque in its abandonment of control.

---

[6] English ed. reads "house" for "houses."

Sister Soulsby, as her husband's boots were heard descending the stairs, rose, and drew the robe up to half cover his agonized visage. She patted the sufferer softly on the head, and then went to the stair-door.

"I think he'll go to sleep now," she said, lifting her voice to the new-comer, and with a backward nod toward the couch. "Come out into the kitchen while I get breakfast, or into the sitting-room, or somewhere, so as not to disturb him. He's promised me to lie perfectly quiet, and try to sleep."

When they had passed together out of the room, she turned. "Soulsby," she said with half-playful asperity, "I'm disappointed in you. For a man who's knocked about as much as you have, I must say you've picked up an astonishingly small outfit of gumption. That poor creature in there is no more drunk than I am. He's been drinking, — yes, drinking like a fish; but it wasn't able to make him drunk. He's past being drunk; he's grief-crazy. It's a case of 'woman.' Some girl has made a fool of him, and decoyed him up in a balloon, and let him drop. He's been hurt bad, too."

"We have all been hurt in our day and generation," responded Brother Soulsby, genially. "Don't you worry; he'll sleep that off, too. It takes longer than drink, and it doesn't begin to be so pleasant, but it can be slept off. Take my word for it, he'll be a different man by noon."

When noon came, however, Brother Soulsby was on his way to summon one of the village doctors. Toward nightfall, he went out again to telegraph for Alice.

CHAPTER XXXII

SPRING fell early upon the pleasant southern slopes of the Susquehanna county. The snow went off as by magic. The trees budded and leaved before their time. The birds came and set up their chorus in the elms, while winter seemed still a thing of yesterday.

Alice, clad gravely in black, stood again upon a kitchen-stoop, and looked across an intervening space of back-yards and fences to where the tall boughs, fresh in their new verdure, were silhouetted against the pure blue sky. The prospect recalled to her irresistibly another sunlit morning, a year ago, when she had stood in the doorway of her own kitchen, and surveyed a scene not unlike this; it might have been with the same carolling robins, the same trees, the same azure segment of the tranquil, speckless dome. Then she was looking out upon surroundings novel and strange to her, among which she must make herself at home as best she could. But at least the ground was secure under her feet; at least she had a home, and a word from her lips could summon her husband out, to stand beside her with his arm about her, and share her buoyant, hopeful joy in the promises of spring.

To think that that was only one little year ago, — the mere revolution of four brief seasons! And now!

Sister Soulsby, wiping her hands on her apron, came briskly out upon the stoop. Some cheerful commonplace was on her tongue, but a glance at Alice's wistful face kept it back. She passed an arm around her waist instead, and stood in silence, looking at the elms.

"It brings back memories to me, — all this," said Alice, nodding her head, and not seeking to dissemble the tears which sprang to her eyes.

"The men will be down in a minute, dear," the other reminded her. "They'd nearly finished packing before I put the biscuits in the oven. We mustn't wear long faces before folks, you know."

"Yes, I know," murmured Alice. Then, with a sudden impulse, she turned to her companion. "Candace," she said fervently, "we're alone here for the moment; I must tell you that if I don't talk gratitude to you, it's simply and solely because I don't know where to begin, or what to say. I'm just dumfounded at your goodness. It takes my speech away. I only know this, Candace: God will be very good to you."

"Tut! tut!" replied Sister Soulsby, "that's all right, you dear thing. I know just how you feel. Don't dream of being under obligation to explain it to me, or to thank us at all. We've had all sorts of comfort out of the thing, — Soulsby and I. We used to get downright lonesome, here all by ourselves, and we've simply had a winter of pleasant company instead, that's all. Besides, there's solid satisfaction in knowing that at last, for once in our lives, we've had a chance to be of some real use to somebody who truly needed it. You can't imagine how stuck up that makes us in our own conceit. We feel as if we were George Peabody and Lady Burdett-Coutts, and several other philanthropists thrown in. No, seriously, don't think of it again. We're glad to have been able to do it all; and if you only go ahead now, and prosper and be happy, why, that will be the only reward we want."

"I hope we shall do well," said Alice. "Only tell me this, Candace. You do think I was right, don't you, in insisting on Theron's leaving the ministry altogether? He seems convinced enough now that it was the right thing to do; but I grow nervous sometimes lest he should find it harder than he thought to get along in business, and regret the change — and blame me."

"I think you may rest easy in your mind about that," the other responded. "Whatever else he does, he will never want to come within gunshot of a pulpit again. It came too near murdering him for that."

Alice looked at her doubtfully. "Something came near murdering him, I know. But it doesn't seem to me that I would say it was the ministry. And I guess you know pretty well yourself what it was. Of course, I've never asked any questions, and I've hushed up everybody at Octavius who tried to quiz me about it, — his disappearance and my packing up and leaving, and all that — and I've never discussed the question with you — but —"

"No, and there's no good going into it now," put in Sister Soulsby, with amiable decisiveness. "It's all past and gone. In fact, I hardly remember much about it now myself. He simply got into deep water, poor soul, and we've floated [1] him out again, safe and sound. That's all. But all the same, I was right in what I said. He was a mistake in the ministry."

"But if you'd known him in previous years," urged Alice, plaintively, "before we were sent to that awful Octavius. He was the very ideal of all a young minister should be. People used to simply worship him, he was such a perfect preacher, and so pure-minded and friendly with everybody, and threw himself into his work so. It was all that miserable, contemptible Octavius that did the mischief."

Sister Soulsby slowly shook her head. "If there hadn't been a screw loose somewhere," she said gently, "Octavius wouldn't have hurt him. No, take my word for it, he never was the right man for the place. He seemed to be, no doubt, but he wasn't. When pressure was put on him, it found out his weak spot like a shot, and pushed on it, and — well, it came near smashing him, that's all."

"And do you think he'll always be a — a back-slider," mourned Alice.

"For mercy's sake, don't ever try to have him pretend to be anything else!" exclaimed the other. "The last state of that man would be worse than the first. You must make up your mind to that. And you mustn't show that you're nervous about it. You mustn't get nervous! You mustn't be afraid of things. Just you keep a stiff upper lip, and say you *will*

[1] English ed. reads "fished" for "floated."

get along, you *will* be happy. That's your only chance, Alice. He isn't going to be an angel of light, or a saint, or anything of that sort, and it's no good expecting it. But he'll be just an average kind of man, — a little sore about some things, a little wiser than he was about some others. You can get along perfectly with him, if you only keep your courage up, and don't show the white feather."

"Yes, I know; but I've had it pretty well taken out of me," commented Alice. "It used to come easy to me to be cheerful and resolute and all that; but it's different now."

Sister Soulsby stole a swift glance at the unsuspecting face of her companion which was not all admiration, but her voice remained patiently affectionate. "Oh, that'll all come back to you, right enough. You'll have your hands full, you know, finding a house, and unpacking all your old furniture, and buying new things, and getting your home settled. It'll keep you so busy you won't have time to feel strange or lonesome, one bit. You'll see how it'll tone you up. In a year's time you won't know yourself in the looking-glass."

"Oh, my health is good enough," said Alice; "but I can't help thinking, suppose Theron should be taken sick again, away out there among strangers. You know he's never appeared to me to have quite got his strength back. These long illnesses, you know, they always leave a mark on a man."

"Nonsense! He's strong as an ox," insisted Sister Soulsby. "You mark my word, he'll thrive in Seattle like a green bay-tree."

"Seattle!" echoed Alice, meditatively. "It *sounds* like the other end of the world, doesn't it?"

The noise of feet in the house broke upon the colloquy, and the women went indoors, to join the breakfast party. During the meal, it was Brother Soulsby who bore the burden of the conversation. He was full of the future of Seattle and the magnificent impending development of that Pacific [2] section. He had been out there, years ago, when it was next door

[2] English ed. reads "whole" for "Pacific."

to uninhabited. He had visited the district twice since, and the changes discoverable each new time were more wonderful than anything Aladdin's lamp ever wrought. He had secured for Theron, through some of his friends in Portland, the superintendency of a land and real estate company, which had its headquarters in Seattle, but ambitiously linked its affairs with the future of all Washington Territory. In an hour's time the hack would come to take the Wares and their baggage to the depot, the first stage in their long journey across the continent to their new home. Brother Soulsby amiably filled the interval with reminiscences of the Oregon of twenty years back, with instructive dissertations upon the soil, climate, and seasons of Puget Sound and the Columbia valley, and, above all, with helpful characterizations of the social life which had begun to take form in this remotest West. He had nothing but confidence, to all appearances, in the success of his young friend, now embarking on this new career. He seemed so sanguine about it that the whole atmosphere of the breakfast room lightened up, and the parting meal, surrounded by so many temptations to distraught broodings and silences as it was, became almost jovial in its spirit.

At last, it was time to look for the carriage. The trunks and hand-bags were ready in the hall, and Sister Soulsby was tying up a package of sandwiches for Alice to keep by her in the train.

Theron, with hat in hand, and overcoat on arm, loitered restlessly into the kitchen, and watched this proceeding for a moment. Then he sauntered out upon the stoop, and lifting his head and drawing as long a breath as he could, looked over at the elms.

Perhaps the face was older and graver; it was hard to tell. The long winter's illness, with its recurring crises and sustained confinement, had bleached his skin and reduced his figure to gauntness, but there was none the less an air of restored and secure good health about him. Only in the eyes themselves, as they rested briefly upon the prospect, did a substantial change suggest itself. They did not dwell fondly upon the picture of the lofty, spreading boughs, with their waves of sap-green leafage stirring against the blue. They did not soften and glow this time, at the thought of how wholly one felt sure of God's goodness in these wonderful new mornings of spring. Can't believe this anymore

They looked instead straight through the fairest and most moving spectacle in nature's processional, and saw afar off, in conjectural vision, a formless sort of place which was Seattle. They surveyed its impalpable outlines, its undefined dimensions, with a certain cool glitter of hard-and-fast resolve. There rose before his fancy, out of the chaos of these shapeless imaginings, some faces of men, then more behind them, then a great concourse of uplifted countenances, crowded close together as far as the eye could reach. They were attentive faces all, rapt, eager, credulous to a degree. Their eyes were admiringly bent upon a common object of excited interest. They were looking at *him;* they strained their ears to miss no cadence of his voice. Involuntarily he straightened himself, stretched forth his hand with the pale, thin fingers gracefully disposed, and passed it slowly before him from side to side, in a comprehensive, stately gesture. The audience rose at him, as he dropped his hand, and filled his daydream with a mighty roar of applause, in volume like an ocean tempest, yet pitched for his hearing alone.

He smiled, shook himself with a little delighted tremor, and turned on the stoop to the open door.

"What Soulsby said about politics out there interested me enormously," he remarked to the two women. "I shouldn't be surprised if I found myself doing something in that line. I can speak, you know, if I can't do anything else. Talk is what tells, these days. Who knows? I may turn up in Washington a full-blown senator before I'm forty. Stranger things have happened than that, out West!"

"We'll come down and visit you then, Soulsby and I,"

said Sister Soulsby, cheerfully. "You shall take us to the White House, Alice, and introduce us."

"Oh, it isn't likely *I* would come East," said Alice, pensively. "Most probably I'd be left to amuse myself in Seattle. But there — I think that's the carriage driving up to the door."

THE END.

Failed in East and is now going West like so many others

BIBLIOGRAPHY

Atherton, Gertrude, "Harold Frederic," *The Bookman* (London), 15:37 (November 1898).

Conrad, Joseph, Introduction to *Stephen Crane,* by Thomas Beer (New York: A. A. Knopf, 1923).

Crane, Stephen, "Harold Frederic," *The Chap-Book,* 8:358–359 (March 15, 1898).

"The Damnation of Theron Ware," *The Critic,* 28:309–310 (May 2, 1896).

Danby, Frank, "Mr. Harold Frederic's New Novel," *The Saturday Review* (London), 81:295–296 (March 21, 1896).

Frederic, Harold, "How to Write a Short Story," *The Bookman,* 5:44–45 (March 1897).

Guiney, Louise Imogen, "Harold Frederic: A Half-Length Sketch from the Life," *The Book Buyer,* 17:600–604 (January 1899).

Haines, Paul, "Harold Frederic," Unpublished Doctoral dissertation, New York University, 1945.

"Harold Frederic," *The Book Buyer,* 8:151–152 (May 1891).

Harris, Frank, "Harold Frederic *Ad Memoriam,*" *The Saturday Review* (London) 86:526–528 (October 22, 1898).

"*Illumination* and Its Author," *The Bookman* (London), 10:136–138 (August 1896).

Lovett, Robert Morss, Introduction to *The Damnation of Theron Ware* (New York: Albert and Charles Boni, 1924).

McWilliams, Carey, "Harold Frederic: 'A Country Boy of Genius,'" *University of California Chronicle,* 35:21–34 (1933).

"Mr. Frederic's *The Damnation of Theron Ware,*" *Atlantic Monthly,* 78:270–272 (August 1896).

Quinn, Arthur H., *American Fiction* (New York: D. Appleton-Century, 1936).

Raleigh, John H., "*The Damnation of Theron Ware,*" *American Literature* 30:210–227 (1958–1959).

"Recent Fiction," *The Dial,* 20:336 (June 1, 1896).

"Some Recollections of Harold Frederic," *The Saturday Review* (London), 86:571–572 (October 29, 1898).

Walcutt, C. C., "Harold Frederic and American Naturalism," *American Literature,* 11:11–22 (March 1939).

Walcutt, C. C., *American Literary Naturalism, A Divided Stream* (Minneapolis: University of Minnesota Press, 1956).

THE JOHN HARVARD LIBRARY

*The intent of
Waldron Phoenix Belknap, Jr.,
as expressed in an early will, was for
Harvard College to use the income from a
permanent trust fund he set up, for "editing and
publishing rare, inaccessible, or hitherto unpublished
source material of interest in connection with the
history, literature, art (including minor and useful
art), commerce, customs, and manners or way of
life of the Colonial and Federal Periods of the United
States . . . In all cases the emphasis shall be on the
presentation of the basic material." A later testament
broadened, this statement, but Mr. Belknap's interests remained constant until his death.*

*In linking the name of the first benefactor of
Harvard College with the purpose of this later,
generous-minded believer in American culture the
John Harvard Library seeks to emphasize the importance of Mr. Belknap's purpose. The John Harvard
Library of the Belknap Press of Harvard University
Press exists to make books and documents
about the American past more readily
available to scholars and the
general reader.*